Oil

Oil *Jonathan Black*

Hart-Davis, MacGibbon   London

Granada Publishing Limited
First published in Great Britain 1975
by Hart-Davis, MacGibbon Ltd
Frogmore, St Albans, Hertfordshire AL2 2NF and
3 Upper James Street, London W1R 4BP

ISBN 0 246 10888 6

Printed in Great Britain by
Fletcher & Son Ltd,
Norwich

To Hill with thanks

Author's Note

Although this is a novel, a work of fiction, I have relied heavily on historical fact to provide a true picture of how the world's petroleum industry actually operates.

The accounts I have given of international intrigue and rivalry over Middle Eastern oil concessions are accurate. For example, there are cited acid, undiplomatic messages exchanged by President Franklin D. Roosevelt and British Prime Minister Winston Churchill at the height of World War Two. These are authentic and a matter of public record – albeit one must search through such arcane publications as the State Department's *Foreign Relations of the United States* to find them.

I would also like to say that many of the strategies and tactics employed by my wholly imaginary major oil companies have their close parallels in history, or in the headlines, as the world has so recently and painfully learned.

Oil is wealth and power.

It can mean peace – or war.

Above all, oil and oilmen are a law unto themselves.

JONATHAN BLACK

Venice, Italy
1974

BOOK ONE

1

James L. Northcutt settled his big frame into a lounge chair aboard his private Boeing 727/100. Although there were other passengers, he had indicated that he wanted to be alone for a while and, since they were all his employees, they deferred to his wishes.

Northcutt's rough-hewn features, permanently weathered to a mahogany hue by sun and wind, reflected an inner elation. He grinned with satisfaction as he looked out through the window next to him. A large number of Chinese Government dignitaries had come to the Peking airport to see him off and to once again emphasize the magnitude of the success that had been achieved.

'Would you care for anything, Mr Northcutt?' asked one of the four stewardesses who served as cabin attendants aboard the Boeing.

'The usual,' he replied.

'A double Jack Daniel's?'

'Yep.'

The stewardess beamed a smile, but hesitated.

'Mr Northcutt.'

'Yes?' A thick eyebrow rose.

'I – that is, may I offer my congratulations?'

'You may – and I thank you for them.'

Northcutt's grey eyes followed the girl as she went off towards the well-stocked bar at the forward end of the plane's lounge compartment. She returned with his drink, placed it on the table in front of him.

The Boeing's Rolls-Royce engines were whining into life.

Jim Northcutt ignored the drink for a moment. Instead, he reached into his watch pocket and took out a gold chain he carried there. A charm dangled from it, a tiny gold oil derrick with black onyx set in a plume shape above the crown block to represent a gusher. He had been given it for luck long ago, and as he fingered the charm pensively, his eyes glowed with satisfaction.

What he had achieved in Peking would be the capstone of his spectacular career in the oil industry. He held the charm between large, strong fingers and relished his sense of accomplishment. He had successfully concluded the last difficult round of negotiations with Chinese Government officials. He was carrying off a prize that represented an eight-billion-dollar potential for his company. Now he was eager to return home and impatient to implement the vast, sweeping projects he had undertaken.

The plane had begun to taxi.

Northcutt replaced the chain and gusher charm in his watch pocket. I can't remember when I felt better, he mused. He reached for his glass of whisky and drank it slowly. When the plane was airborne, he pulled a sack of Bull Durham from the breast pocket of his jacket and, still ebullient, rolled a cigarette and lit it.

The Boeing 727 with the words *Northcutt International Petroleum Company* emblazoned in blue on its white fuselage touched down at Orly Airport outside Paris a little before 1 P.M. local time. It remained on the ground only long enough to disembark the specialists and technicians who had accompanied James Northcutt to Peking. Northcutt shook hands with each of them and once again expressed his appreciation for their contributions to the final success of his dealings with the Chinese. The plane received runway priority, taxied to the head of a long queue of commercial airliners and took off for Nice, where it landed less than three-quarters of an hour later.

At Nice, James Northcutt transferred directly to a waiting – and also private – Alouette helicopter. He ignored immigration and customs formalities. Many years before, he had given ailing French shipyards a $55 million transfusion in contracts for tanker construction. A grateful President Charles de Gaulle rewarded the expatriate American oil billionaire by appointing him an Officer of the Légion d'Honneur. De Gaulle also ordered that he be permanently accorded Freedom of the Port at all French ports of entry.

Northcutt was especially glad for the privilege this day. If his presence at the Nice airport became generally known, he was certain to be mobbed by members of the French press. Despite his pride and jubilation over what he had achieved in China, Northcutt preferred to avoid journalists. For more than two months, the world had been sliding deeper into what the media labelled 'The Second Global Energy Crisis', a situation worsened by another oil embargo imposed on Western nations by the Arab oil-producing countries.

The reporters would not be content to ask about the outcome of the already highly publicized venture in China. They would bombard him with questions regarding the energy crisis and Arab embargo. Northcutt had no desire to make public statements on those matters. Appropriately handcrafted answers could be given out later in his name by vice-presidents or public relations men on his payrolls.

'Let's get on our way home – *toute de suite*,' Northcutt told the helicopter pilot, his deep baritone voice easily carrying above the sound of the idling engines and clack of the slowly revolving blades. He hoisted himself aboard with remarkable agility and insisted on occupying the co-pilot's seat.

The 'copter lifted off and headed south-west along the Côte d'Azur. The trip was short. Very soon, the Alouette was settling down on the helipad at Bonheur, James Northcutt's huge estate near Cap d'Antibes, his favourite among the homes he owned in both hemispheres.

The main structure, a seventy-four-room mansion, was elegantly splendid in its Mediterranean-villa style and surrounded by lesser buildings, all designed and sited to maintain aesthetic harmony. One of these buildings contained offices for a corps of aides and secretaries. Bonheur was more than a residence for its owner. It was the headquarters from which James L. Northcutt exercised final authority and control over his worldwide network of business enterprises.

Medding, the English butler, was genuinely pleased to see his employer. He, too, extended enthusiastic congratulations for the results Northcutt had achieved in Peking.

'Thank you, Medding,' Northcutt said, openly proud. 'Things did work out remarkably well.' He cocked an inquisitive eyebrow. 'Where is Miss Wallace?'

'Shopping in Paris, sir. She's expected this afternoon.'

Funny, James Northcutt reflected. Not so very long ago, the absence of one of his women when he returned from an extended journey would have irritated, even angered, him. Now his reaction was casual, almost indifferent.

'Mr Schlechter arrived shortly after noon,' Medding announced. 'He was given his usual suite in the west wing.'

'Where is he now?'

'In your study, sir. Shall I tell him you've arrived?'

'No, I'll join him there.'

Northcutt turned and, still greatly exhilarated, walked with jaunty, long-legged strides down a corridor that led off to the right. Bowls of fresh-cut flowers from the gardens of the estate stood on tables. Paintings from his superb collection of Impressionists and post-Impressionists hung on the walls. A Seurat, a Manet, two Redons, a Cézanne.

James Northcutt's study was spacious and high-ceilinged. Large windows looked out over acres of gardens and lawn that sloped gently down to a broad, white-sanded beach beyond which lay the Mediterranean. Inside the study, recessed bookshelves flanked a great fireplace. Several Fauvist paintings were on the walls. Northcutt seemed to draw strength from their explosive colours when he worked, and he thought their formalized distortions somehow reflected his personal view of life and the world around him. Furniture in the room achieved an ideal balance between utilitarian efficiency and luxurious comfort.

Samuel Schlechter sat in an armchair, reading a book. When Northcutt entered, he rose to his feet and advanced a step. The two men shook hands, smiling at each other. Their manner of greeting gave evidence of long intimacy and complete mutual trust and confidence.

Their physical appearances were in sharp contrast. Tall, wide-shouldered and still hard-muscled, Northcutt towered over Samuel Schlechter, who was several inches shorter, no more than five-nine in height. Lithe and dapper, Schlechter's features were smooth and more than slightly saturnine in their cast.

Officially, Samuel Schlechter was James L. Northcutt's attorney. In operative fact, he was the oil billionaire's American-based alter ego. Northcutt had lived in France for many years. But the Northcutt International Petroleum Company – NIPCO – and its principal subsidiaries were US corporations. Their home offices were in New York City, where Schlechter resided, had his law firm and served as James Northcutt's first deputy and right arm.

Northcutt formulated the grand strategies. Sam Schlechter strained the concepts through legal sieves, transmuted them into viable plans, saw to their execution and held the reins on Board members and six-figure-salaried executives. Together, Northcutt and Schlechter had built an empire. Together, they were continuing to expand it.

'You didn't tell me much on the phone, Sam,' Northcutt said when they were seated. Schlechter had called him in Peking and stated only that he was coming to Bonheur to discuss urgent matters.

'Any idea how many eavesdroppers there must be on a New York-to-Peking hookup?' Schlechter grimaced.

Northcutt's grey eyes expressed curiosity. 'So you're here. Should I be glad to see you?'

'Hardly. My news isn't good, Jim.'

'Mine is.' The oilman evidently chose to ignore Schlechter's reply, for he was bursting with enthusiasm. 'It's the best. I got everything wrapped up – but of course, you've heard. All sorts of announcements and communiqués were given out to correspondents. We've taken a giant step, Sam.'

It had been the biggest coup of his career. Red China, technologically limited in ability to exploit its enormous oil reserves and faced with perennial agricultural crises, had renounced sacred Maoist dogmas and put out feelers for aid from Western free enterprise. The major oil companies had responded by making tentative inquiries through traditional channels. James Northcutt and his independent company followed the entrepreneurial examples set by Occidental Petroleum's Armand Hammer in his dealings with the Soviet Union.

Northcutt made several trips to Peking, conducted negotiations on a personal level, conferring with Chinese Cabinet ministers and finally with Premier Chou En-lai himself. During this last two-week stay in the People's Republic of China, he had reached agreement with the Chinese on specific projects and contract terms. NIPCO was to receive oil exploration and drilling concessions in vast areas of China, with the American company to have a considerable share of all the oil produced.

In addition, NIPCO was to build – and for ten years operate – a number of refineries, pipelines, petrochemical and fertilizer plants in China. Experts estimated the agreements represented a staggering trade potential of over eight billion dollars for the United States – and for NIPCO.

Naturally, US Government approval would be needed before the agreements became effective. However, considering the new fuel shortage and energy crisis in America, Northcutt was certain the necessary approvals would be granted very quickly.

'Yep, we've taken a real giant step,' Northcutt repeated, rubbing his large, powerful hands.

'That's the trouble, Jim,' Samuel Schlechter said dourly. 'You and NIPCO have taken too many big steps.'

'Now wait a minute. I thought everybody was cheering.' Northcutt's brow seamed and his jawline hardened.

'*Almost* everybody,' Schlechter said. 'The media are calling you "the one-man answer to the fuel shortage" and "the oil tycoon who'll close the trade-deficit gap singlehanded". Read the papers and news magazines and listen to the television commentators – and you're practically a national hero.'

'Then who's making waves all of a sudden?' Northcutt demanded.

'Who? The Majors, of course. NIPCO has always broken every rule of their club. Now it's about to shut the club members out of China. That, my friend, has them in one hell of an uproar.'

James Northcutt's frown deepened.

Northcutt International Petroleum was an independent company that had frequently defied and opposed the 'Majors', the handful of supercorporations that shared a monopoly of over 80 per cent of the Western world's oil reserves and refining and distribution facilities. Ostensibly in competition with each other, major oil companies worked in close concert to maintain their supremacy. They had many grievances against NIPCO, which was the largest of the independents and had never been their docile collaborator.

NIPCO joined in no price-fixing agreements. Its NIPpy brand gasoline sold for two to four cents less per gallon than Major brands. Worse, NIPCO played no part in the manipulations that created largely artificial global 'energy crises' out of basically manageable shortages of crude oil. During the entire previous 'oil famine', NIPCO had delivered normal allocations of all fuels to its dealers and distributors. This did grave damage to the public image of the giants who pleaded acute scarcity and slashed their allocations of gasoline, fuel and heating oils by as much as half.

Northcutt International even managed to avoid being af-

16

fected by either the first or the most recent Arab oil embargo. Its fields in Qantara, a Persian Gulf island-emirate, continued to produce at full capacity.

Now, NIPCO seemed on the verge of success in its negotiations with Peking.

'China's the last great underdeveloped source of oil on earth,' Schlechter continued. 'No limits to the possibilities – or the profits – there. The Majors want the Chinese concessions and plant construction and operation contracts for themselves. Three of them have already joined up to prevent NIPCO from getting them – and to break you *and* NIPCO in the process.'

'God damn it, Sam!' Northcutt flared. 'They farted around appointing special study committees and flitting in and out of the State Department. I didn't. I started out by going to Peking and talking hard facts and figures. They could have done the same.'

'But they didn't. Now their Boards of Directors are demanding to know why, and herds of overpaid executives are having cardiac arrests. Jobs and reputations and corporate images can only be saved by bloodletting. Your blood. Ours. NIPCO's.'

The oilman said, 'Three company presidents didn't suddenly decide to concentrate on screwing NIPCO and me. Who's behind it?'

'Jersey Crest.'

Northcutt's big hands clenched. He and his companies had been fighting a running battle with the Jersey Crest Oil Company for decades. Successive Jersey Crest managements had inherited their corporation's animosity towards NIPCO. Now Northcutt had to contend with the man who hated him most, Powell Pierce, Jersey Crest's president for many years and currently its Board Chairman.

Jim Northcutt frowned.

'You forget, Sam. NIPCO isn't a corner candy store. We have over three billion in consolidated assets, more than thirty thousand employees.'

Schlechter remained glum.

'NIPCO's still not a member of the Majors' club. Take Exxon, for example. It has roughly eight times NIPCO's assets, nets almost two and a half billion annually. Jersey Crest alone is much bigger than NIPCO. It's lined up with Richland Consolidated and Western Impex. Together, they have greater resources than even Exxon.' He was silent for a moment, lips tight and turned down at the corners.

'You're the last person I need to remind that busting independents is the Majors' favourite sport,' he went on. 'The three-way combo Jersey Crest has formed could destroy NIPCO.'

Oil was a law unto itself, unchanging in its anarchy, Jim reflected. In the old days, big companies and lease hounds bribed county clerks to forge property records or make them vanish. Small operators were run off their leases, their rigs dynamited, their drilling crews beaten, even murdered, by hired goons. The shoestring wildcatter survived only by sufferance – or by fighting back savagely, using the same gutter tactics that were employed against him.

Had anything really changed?

'All right, counsellor,' Northcutt said. 'What options do we have?'

'Not many,' Schlechter replied. 'One, NIPCO could start by raising retail prices to the same levels as the Majors. At the same time we could cut back on production to help them maintain their phoney fuel shortage.'

'No.'

The attorney indulged in a small smile. 'Two, offer the Jersey Crest combine a share of the Chinese deal.'

'I'll offer them nothing!' Northcutt snapped.

Schlechter's smile deepened. 'Third —'

'We'll take the bastards on,' Jim interrupted.

Sam Schlechter gazed evenly at his friend. Northcutt remained the tough, scrappy maverick he had always been.

'There's something you ought to take into consideration,' Schlechter said. 'News that three Majors are out to break NIPCO will spread fast. We'll have swarms of sharpshooters trying to knock off what they can while we're busy with Powell Pierce.'

'Naturally.' Northcutt laughed. 'The oil business has always been overrun with scavengers. You swat 'em like flies.'

'If you spot them in time. It's when they come up from behind ...'

Schlechter didn't finish the sentence, for the study door opened and Barbara Wallace entered. She was blonde, statuesque, radiating the mixture of sensuality and surface charm that so many rich and powerful men demand in their mistresses. And she's 100 per cent, practised bitch, Schlechter told himself.

'Darling!' Barbara Wallace exclaimed and rushed to North-cutt's chair. She leaned down, flung her arms around him and kissed him. She quickly straightened up, flashed Schlechter a smile, then turned back to Jim.

'I've missed you,' she murmured. 'It feels as though you've been gone for months.' She gave him a sly and provocative look. 'Do you feel the same way – or did your hosts supply delicate maidens in blue pyjamas to amuse you?' She tickled the back of his neck.

'No maidens – and damned little amusement,' Jim grinned. 'Until you've seen a six-hour-long opera-ballet called *The Victory of the People*, you'll never know how dead the lively arts can be.'

'Poor darling!' Barbara said. Then her face brightened. 'I bought some lovely things in Paris,' she said. 'Would you like to see them, Jim?'

He hesitated for a moment, then got to his feet.

'We'll talk later, Sam,' he said.

Schlechter nodded and watched Northcutt and Barbara leave the study. He had often wondered whether James Northcutt's sexual drive was a manifestation, or even the source, of his strength or if it was his outstanding weakness. He once again pondered the question that had no answer.

2

25 June

James Northcutt had come up the hard way, from the oil fields. He had been a roustabout, tool dresser, driller. Then he had gone on his own as a shoestring wildcatting operator and gradually built NIPCO, over which he had absolute control, owning 61 per cent of the company's stock.

Powell Pierce, Board Chairman of the Jersey Crest Oil Company, was an entirely different breed of oilman. A New England Brahmin and Harvard Business School graduate, Pierce joined Jersey Crest in the early 1930s. He had risen steadily in the organization, becoming a vice-president, then president and finally Chairman of the Board.

Jersey Crest Oil had thousands of stockholders, not one of whom owned more than the 9 per cent bloc held by Powell Pierce. Yet, his power in Jersey Crest was hardly less absolute than that which James Northcutt wielded over NIPCO. Pierce had a stately suite of offices on the top floor of the Jersey Crest Tower on Manhattan's Madison Avenue. White-haired, sedate, he sat behind an antique rosewood desk. He looked as though he might have been the dean emeritus of a small but exclusive New England college rather than the chief executive officer of a major oil company.

Guy Bannister was seated across the desk. A one-time CIA agent, Bannister radiated the air of efficiency and reliability that was mandatory in his profession. He headed Federpol, a private organization that specialized in what the firm's letterhead described as 'Industrial Security'. Top corporate executives were aware the term was highly elastic. Any man they retained to stretch it had to be entirely trustworthy.

'May I assume the NIPCO-oriented projects are under control?' Pierce said.

'They are,' Guy Bannister replied. 'Care for progress reports?'

'Only to the extent it's advisable for me to know.'

'Of course.'

Bannister was frequently called upon to perform unorthodox services. 'Organic jobs' was how he classified them in his mind. For these assignments, clients paid large sums. But they wished to hear only the fewest necessary details about how they were performed.

'My Middle Eastern sub-contractor should be delivering any day,' Guy Bannister said. 'Then I've closed with a group that will take care of the retailing aspect. I expect quick results from them.' He paused, glanced at his Rolex: 10.06. 'I'll be back at my office in fifteen minutes and double-check on both.'

'And Washington?' Pierce inquired.

'I'm sending a man down there later today,' Bannister replied. 'That particular item should be wrapped up by late afternoon.'

Powell Pierce leaned back in his chair. He was satisfied. All the major surgery would be performed by expert hands.

Federpol operated internationally, but had its headquarters in a Radio City skyscraper. Bannister returned there.

Once inside his private soundproofed office, he placed an overseas telephone call.

According to his trilingual business cards – English, French, Turkish – Gerhard Hohenberg was a commodities broker with offices on the Istiklal Caddesi in Istanbul.

Hohenberg's telephone rang. He answered and was told there was a call coming through from New York City. He waited, cursing silently, while the Turkish operator bumbled as Turkish operators invariably do and the line crackled with static. At last, he could hear.

'There's been no word from you in three days, Hohenberg.'

'So?' Gerhard Hohenberg had respect for Guy Bannister's money, but none whatsoever for Bannister himself. Indeed, he had no respect for any human being but Gerhard Hohenberg. 'When there is anything to tell you, you will hear from me.'

'But you've pushed the buttons?'

The expression irritated Hohenberg. It was typically American.

'I am unable to hear you,' he said. That will make the pig shout, he thought and relished the idea of the former CIA man's discomfiture at having to strain his lungs. He smiled as he held the receiver away from his ear.

'Did you push the buttons – start the machinery?' Bannister must have been bellowing at the other end of the line.

Gerhard Hohenberg tired of the game.

'The crews were sent out by air,' he said. 'They arrived at their destination. I should have reports soon. When I do, I shall notify you. *Auf wiedersehen.*' He hung up. The man was an impatient fool. But most Americans were, Hohenberg reflected. Even when they were shady operators working for immensely wealthy clients. Perhaps even more so. They believed that assignments on a scale as large as the one Bannister had given him could be carried out overnight.

Hohenberg shrugged. If the men in his 'crews' didn't carry out their assignments that day, they would another, whenever they believed it safest to do so. It made no difference. The results would be the same. Guy Bannister, the impatient intermediary, would receive full value for the money he had paid to Gerhard Hohenberg on behalf of his client.

Bannister's next telephone call was local. To the Italo-American Fidelity Realtors on Third Avenue. He spoke with Charles Farrier, head of the firm.

'What's the latest?' Bannister asked.

'Our appraisers will be surveying the first property tonight,' Charles Farrier – neé Carlo Maniscalco – told him.

'The survey has to be thorough. Top to bottom.'

'It'll be done right.'

'And the other properties, down south and in New England?'

'We'll get to them,' Charles Farrier said. 'You can't rush these things any faster than we already are.'

Hanging up, Bannister sent for Russell Peterson, a key aide to whom he paid a $65,000-a-year salary, but privately viewed with contempt. Peterson was intelligent and dependable, but Bannister considered him nothing more than a high-level errand boy.

Thirtyish, with the freshly scrubbed-and-shaven look of the programmed young executive extolled in management manuals, Russell Peterson sensed his employer's contempt and resented it. He knew the importance of his position in the Federpol operational scheme and realized that many of Bannister's successes were largely due to his work as emissary and go-between.

However, Peterson was intimidated by Bannister and straitjacketed by the salary he received. There had been some unpleasantness about his taking kickbacks while holding a middle-management job with his previous employer, an electronics firm. He could not hope to work in conventional fields and earn as much. He needed the high pay. He and his wife Mae were perpetually extended beyond their means.

'You look happy this morning,' Peterson said.

'I am.' Bannister smiled. 'The big client's satisfied and so far all the news is good.' His smile deepened. 'Some parts of this NIPCO project may turn out to be a cinch. Northcutt's people will never know what hit them. Neither will Northcutt.'

Peterson wet his lips.

'Guy . . .'

'Don't pee in your pants, Russ. You're not involved in any of the organic angles. You might watch the newspapers closely from here on in, though. You'll begin to get an education in how this business really operates.'

22

Bannister's mood changed. He became serious and peremptory.

'Clear on how to handle your end?' he demanded.

'You briefed me pretty thoroughly yesterday,' Peterson said. 'I have everything squared away.'

'When is your appointment with Gerlach?'

'At three-thirty.'

'Okay, then,' Bannister nodded. 'You can make a one o'clock flight for Washington from La Guardia. I'll see you tomorrow.'

Arthur Gerlach was the new US President's most trusted aide and his chief advisor. Ever since the Inaugural six months before, Gerlach had reigned as straw boss of the White House staff and as guardian of the Oval Office.

Outwardly bluff and hearty in the manner of a goal-oriented physical education instructor, Arthur Gerlach was a shrewd, icily realistic politician. He was also highly accessible, particularly to anyone representing a heavy contributor to the President's election campaign funds.

Russell Peterson worked for Federpol.

Federpol had been retained by Jersey Crest Oil.

Jersey Crest Oil and its Board Chairman, Powell Pierce, had funnelled several hundred thousand dollars into the President's campaign in laundered cash.

Thus, Arthur Gerlach had every reason to provide a gracious welcome to Russell Peterson when he appeared in his White House office. The presidential advisor offered the appropriate preliminary phrases, then settled back to learn what was wanted of him and the Administration.

Russell Peterson began cautiously, travelling in wide verbal circles before edging in on the vital subjects to be discussed. Gerlach listened to all the preambles with only half an ear.

'... oil-industry leaders are gravely concerned over recent developments in American–Chinese trade relations,' Peterson was saying. 'They're afraid the United States may be placed in an embarrassing situation by irresponsible firms and individuals.'

Russell Peterson cleared his throat.

'Several top-level petroleum industry executives have been sufficiently disturbed by the developments to confer and give them serious study. They have reached an opinion consensus.'

Gerlach hid his amusement at Peterson's stilted circumlocutions. Hell, he thought, the 'top-level executives' were Powell Pierce, his associates in Jersey Crest and their counterparts in Western Impex and Richland Consolidated.

'They believe the federal government should look closely at the negotiations Northcutt International Petroleum has been conducting in Peking,' Peterson went on. 'NIPCO may not have the capability to fulfil the agreements under discussion. If it failed, China's faith in the strength of US industry would vanish. Peking would very likely turn to other countries – West Germany, France or even Japan.'

Gerlach read the message between the lines. Jersey Crest and its corporate allies were Majors, high on the list of the nation's largest corporations. They were also proven friends of the Administration. They did not want NIPCO to conclude the agreements with China. They had paid well in advance to have their requests given consideration, he reflected. No doubt they would pay much more to have them granted. Being on his own White House home grounds, Presidential Advisor Arthur Gerlach could afford to be blunt and candid.

'I understand fully,' he said. 'What you really mean is that Powell Pierce wants the Administration to give NIPCO a hard time. We're to set up policy obstacles, create bureaucratic delays and otherwise hamper and harass.'

Russell Peterson brushed non-existent lint from a trouser leg.

'Mr Pierce made no such suggestions. His interest in the matter is first as a citizen, second as a member of the business community —'

'For God's sake, save the horseshit,' Arthur Gerlach interrupted. 'Pierce and his group will have Executive branch cooperation. It can be arranged for NIPCO's deal to get so far bogged down it sinks without trace – and it'll be made to look normal and natural.'

Peterson brushed more imaginary lint.

'Of course, it would be unfortunate if the United States lost out completely,' he said. 'Perhaps . . .'

Gerlach's rough features mirrored cynical amusement. 'Perhaps Peking can be convinced it's wiser and safer to deal with a consortium of Majors. Jersey Crest, Richland Consolidated and Western Impex, for example.'

'Certainly the Chinese would have no worries about performance.' Peterson nodded. 'No question about those companies fulfilling.'

Time to twist the screw a bit, Arthur Gerlach decided.

'Maybe not. But I have to worry about the home-front press and public. The Majors haven't been doing so well on fulfilling, Peterson. They promised more fuel and lower prices. Instead, they delivered a worse fuel shortage than the last, and prices are shooting up. Only NIPCO kept its production high and prices low. If we take from NIPCO and give to the three Majors, this Administration is liable to catch hell from the media and that poor limping character, the man in the street.'

'I'm not an oilman,' Peterson countered. 'But I know the present oil shortage was brought about by unforeseeable factors.'

'That's a lot of crap. But in any case, we might be able to help' – Gerlach gave Peterson a sly look – 'provided you can get the idea past Engelhardt.'

That's it, Peterson thought. He had been briefed about the possible mention of Rowan Engelhardt. He was the Secretary of the National Energy Resources Department, a recently created Cabinet post. Engelhardt and Gerlach worked closely together amassing private fortunes by selling – or simply leasing – their considerable influence within the young Administration.

'Mr Pierce will follow any of Secretary Engelhardt's suggestions to the letter,' Peterson said.

Gerlach studied his visitor and sensed more was wanted.

'What else can we do for you?' he asked.

Peterson leaned forward in his chair.

'It's hardly necessary to mention that the petroleum industry requires stability and cohesion,' he said. 'James Northcutt and his company are disruptive factors...'

Gerlach tuned out, reflecting on what he knew about Northcutt and NIPCO. In wealth, James Northcutt was on a par with H. L. Hunt and J. Paul Getty. *Fortune* Magazine had recently estimated Northcutt's personal net worth at $1·75 billion. He owned clear-cut numerical stock control of NIPCO, the nation's – and probably the world's – largest independent oil company. NIPCO was a wholly integrated and self-sufficient operation. It engaged in oil exploration and production, transportation and refining and marketing. NIPpy – 'The Power-Packed Wildcat' – was a trademark familiar to consumers of all petroleum products on both the East and West coasts.

None the less, the colossus was vulnerable, Gerlach mused, open to Executive branch attack from numerous federal departments and bureaux and regulatory agencies. Northcutt could be gelded if sufficient power and effort were used against him. Gerlach tuned back in on Russell Peterson's monologue.

'... companies plan an all-out competitive campaign against NIPCO. With an assist from your quarter, the disruptive factors will be neutralized or eliminated and needed stability achieved in the oil industry.'

Powell Pierce wants to destroy NIPCO and leave James Northcutt bleeding under the rubble, Presidential Advisor Arthur Gerlach translated silently. He gave a mental shrug. That was how major oil companies had always operated, how they'd become Majors in the first place. They either swallowed troublesome independents whole or destroyed them. It was how they were able to maintain their price-fixing cartels, create fuel shortages, make enormous profits, continue to win their monopoly games.

Historically, the major oil companies were untouchable. No presidential administration since that of Theodore Roosevelt had dared oppose them. Harding, Coolidge, Hoover and Johnson had truckled to the Majors. Even FDR, Truman, Eisenhower, Kennedy and Nixon treated them with deferential respect. *This* Administration's not going to break that precedent, Gerlach assured himself. Nothing could be gained and much would be lost by busking the tide. On the other hand, riding it would surely be highly profitable.

'I'm on the wave length, Peterson,' he said. He formed a nutcracker with his hands. 'Pierce's combine squeezes from one side. He'd like to have me start the Uncle Sam machinery moving to squeeze from another.

'A big order,' he continued. 'Northcutt has some powerful friends up on Capitol Hill. Then, as I mentioned before, he has a lot of public and media sympathy and support.' Now let's get it across that the price tag at this end will be high. 'I hope Mr Pierce realizes that breaking NIPCO will be a tough proposition – neither easy nor cheap.'

Russell Peterson recognized the cue.

'One million,' he said, dropping his voice.

That was the amount Powell Pierce was ready to offer for

across-the-board co-operation from Gerlach and National Energy Resources Secretary Rowan Engelhardt.

Gerlach's expression didn't change, but he whistled inwardly.

'You won't even have to see Engelhardt,' he said. 'I'll talk to him myself. I guarantee we'll work things out to Pierce's satisfaction.'

3

26 June

Jim Northcutt had been married once. The marriage ended in divorce. He and his wife Pamela had one child – a daughter, Katherine. To Northcutt, she was always Kathy or Kath, and while his marriage lasted, he doted on the child. After the divorce, and although Pamela was granted custody, father and daughter kept in close touch, saw each other frequently and developed a relationship that was unusual for the depth of their mutual respect and understanding.

Kathy Northcutt inherited traits and qualities from both her parents. She had her mother's coppery red hair and exquisitely moulded features and her father's grey eyes. That combination was no less striking than the mix of ingredients making up her nature and personality.

Her quick, perceptive mind could have come from either parent. Maternal genes endowed her with natural grace and charm. But her fiercely independent spirit, tendency to be outspoken and her sense of direct, elemental justice were all pure James Northcutt. Like her father, she was difficult to control, impossible to dominate. She went her own way, arrived at her own decisions, feared nothing and blamed no one but herself for whatever mistakes she made.

At twenty-nine, Kathy Northcutt was tall, with a slender figure that, like a delicate but exotic perfume, suggested an exciting sensual femininity. Her facial planes and features blended into a lovely image that gave an impression of aristocracy with a vague, elusive hint of the Oriental.

Kathy had never shown any desire to marry. She frankly admitted and just as frankly satisfied her preference for serially monogamous relationships with men of whom she was fond. When a man began to bore her, Kathy usually managed to end the affair in a civilized manner and remain on friendly terms with her former lover.

Edward McVey gave off all the warning signals of being an exception. The problem was that McVey insisted he was deeply in love with Kathy and became increasingly possessive during the six months their affair had lasted. He persisted in asking her to marry him. Her intuition told her he was sincere, but only to a point. She sensed that while Edward McVey earned an excellent income from investments, he was intrigued by the prospect of marrying the only child of James Northcutt, one of the world's wealthiest men.

Kathy repeatedly told herself it would be an easy matter for her to end the affair if – damn it! – Ed McVey wasn't such a delightful companion and particularly such a magnificent lover.

Kathy and McVey had attended a dinner party the night before, then returned to her luxurious Upper East Side apartment and gone to bed, making love for hours. They had slept, awakening a little after dawn to make love again.

She found it odd that the doubts and ambivalent thoughts about McVey formed in her mind as she felt the beginning tremors, the third time – or was it the fourth? – she had experienced them since awakening.

Then all conscious thoughts were blocked out by sensations of pure pleasure as he increased the tempo of his thrusts, carrying her to a peak and holding her there. She cried out, gripped him more tightly with her arms and legs and strained her body against his. The waves of sensation finally subsided. Kathy's muscles relaxed and she knew that he, too, had achieved orgasm. They lay in each other's arms, temporarily sated. Then Edward McVey kissed her and eased himself to the edge of the bed.

'Cigarette?' he asked.

'Uh-uh.'

He took a Marlboro from a pack on the bedside table, lit it with his Cartier lighter.

'Kathy —'

'Don't talk, Ed,' Kathy murmured. 'I'm savouring.'

He turned his head, gazed at her, smiled. Kathy heard an alarm bell ring deep in the back of her brain. The smile. It was just a shade – a barely perceptible shade – too loving and affectionate. You're overdoing it, friend, she said silently, now very much alert and wary.

He held his cigarette in one hand, reached to caress her with the other. Kathy moved slightly, just beyond his easy reach. His eyes narrowed.

'Hey, what's the matter?'

'Nothing.' The hell it's nothing. You're great in the sack and you really do want to marry me, but I'm not about to marry you or anyone else. What's more, I'll be damned if I let myself be owned or even have someone think he owns me!

'You're awfully serious, Kathy.'

'Am I? Umm. Guess I am. I'm planning a trip.' She was. She had been for the last several seconds.

'You're planning a *what*?'

'A trip. To France. To see my father. I always visit him every few months.' She did. 'I haven't since you and I got involved.'

Ed McVey's face went out of control for a split second, long enough for Kathy to read full, final confirmation of what she'd intuitively sensed even though the expression of indignation faded almost immediately.

Good-bye, Ed, Kathy said silently and waited for his next words.

'When are you planning to leave, honey?' he asked.

'I'll be flying tonight,' she replied.

He stared at her, his face registering frustration and disbelief.

'Tonight? But what about your apartment here?'

'The housekeeper and maid can close it up.'

Kathy smiled inwardly. Now that she had made her decision, she felt free. And, she looked forward eagerly to seeing her father. They were not merely father and daughter but close friends. She adored him.

Russell Peterson and his wife lived in an over-mortgaged house in Westchester. It was one of Guy Bannister's affectations to be at work in the Federpol offices by nine o'clock every morning, and he demanded the same of all who were in his employ. This meant Peterson had to get up early so that he could commute into New York on time. Since he drove in daily, he did not have the train commuter's chance to read the morning paper while travelling, and so he scanned *The New*

York Times while having breakfast.

Peterson had forgotten Guy Bannister's injunction to 'watch the newspapers closely'. His mind was preoccupied with the successful meeting he had had with Arthur Gerlach in Washington the day before. He sipped coffee and gave the front page of the *Times* a cursory glance. The headlines dealt mainly with stories related to what had already been labelled 'The Second World Energy Crisis'.

PRESIDENT PLANS FRESH INITIATIVES
IN EFFORTS TO END ARAB OIL EMBARGO

CRITICS CHARGE OIL COMPANIES
MANIPULATE PRODUCTION FIGURES

DWINDLING FUEL SUPPLIES FORCE
500,000 MORE LAYOFFS IN WEEK

He turned the page.

'Russ,' his wife said.

'What is it, Mae?' He didn't look up from the paper.

'We got one of those notices from Diners yesterday,' Mae Peterson said. 'You know. No cheque, and they suspend our credit card.'

'Send them a cheque for two hundred.' He turned another page. 'That'll satisfy their computer for a month.'

'If I do, we'll be short – the maid's salary –'

'I'll raise some cash today.' Once he told Bannister about the results he had obtained with Gerlach, he could improvise some innocuous excuse for a several-hundred-dollar salary advance.

He turned yet another page, and his eyes grew wide as he suddenly remembered Bannister's words. The item was only two or three paragraphs long, but he needed to read only the first:

Two persons died last night in Brooklyn when a Northcutt International Petroleum Company service station's underground gasoline storage tanks exploded and caused a fire that burned for hours. Police and Fire Department officials say the cause of the explosion is not known, but that investigations are underway. The dead have not yet been identified. Their bodies were charred beyond recognition...'

Peterson thrust the newspaper aside.

'Anything the matter?' his wife asked. She sounded worried.

'Huh? Oh. No. Nothing. Why?'

'You – well, you suddenly turned pale and bit your lip.'

'Did I?' A forced smile. 'The stock market went down again yesterday. That's all.'

The Petersons' maid appeared from the kitchen carrying a small silver tray covered by a napkin.

'Like some more fresh toast, Mr Peterson?' the maid asked, whisking off the napkin and holding the tray in front of him.

Peterson could not help but look. There were several slices of toast piled on the tray. The topmost slice was scorched black at the edges. He flung down his napkin and left the table hurriedly.

4

27 June

It was a warm, clear day. James Northcutt swam several lengths of the large sweetwater pool at Bonheur with surprisingly powerful strokes, then clambered up on the edge of the pool. He sat there and grinned at Samuel Schlechter, who occupied an umbrella-shaded deck chair.

'You should take more exercise, Sam,' Northcutt said.

'Lots of things I should do,' Schlechter retorted. 'Like take myself back to New York. With the trouble we've got —'

'Not yet. We've got to do a little more talking and thinking.'

'You pay the bills, Jim,' Schlechter said with a resigned shrug.

Barbara Wallace, blonde hair up, bathing cap in one hand and Junoesque body barely supported by a micro-bikini, emerged from the main house.

'Morning,' Northcutt said to her absently. He stood up on the poolside deck. 'Sam and I are going back to work.'

'But darling. I thought you and I could go for a swim.'

'Sorry. I've been out here over an hour.' A mildly reproving smile. 'Maybe you should get up earlier.'

Northcutt and Schlechter disappeared into the nearby bathhouse to shower and change out of their swimming trunks.

Barbara glared after them, crumpling, then flinging her bathing cap on the deck.

A secretary intercepted Northcutt as he and Sam Schlechter were about to enter the study.

'This Telex just came in,' she said, giving Northcutt a sheet of paper. 'It seems to have been delayed for some reason, but it looks important enough for you to see personally.'

'Thanks, Marie.'

Northcutt sat down behind his study desk, read the Telex and frowned.

'How often do service station storage tanks blow up, Sam?' he asked.

Schlechter blinked at the unexpected question.

'Damned seldom. They're mostly underground, protected by all sorts of safety devices. However, actuarial figures might show that such things occasionally do happen. Why?'

'Seems we have a dealer-leased station in Brooklyn – or we had, until last night. The underground tanks blew, killing two people. Damage runs about a half-million.'

'That doesn't sound right, Jim.'

'Depends on how you look at it,' Northcutt muttered.

'What?'

'Using dynamite on the competition was a favourite stunt in the old days. Could be that history repeats.' His face hardened. 'Those tanks didn't blow. They were blown.'

'I'm inclined to be doubtful,' Schlechter said. 'What's to be gained by destroying —'

'For Christ's sake! Suppose three, six or even more NIPCO stations blow up. Then our contracted dealers get anonymous tips. They either stop handling NIPCO products – or else. Then they get another hint. Maybe for insurance, they ought to switch over and sell some other company's gas and oil —'

'Jim, this isn't the Harry Sinclair and Edward Doheny era in the oil business.'

'Who says it isn't?' Northcutt snorted. 'The *Oil and Gas Journal*? The Harvard Business School hypocrites the Majors hire as executives but use as pimps? The oil business is what it's always been. Dog eat dog.'

He stared at the Telex again.

'You said it yourself. Underground tanks just don't explode.'

'The dealer himself could have enemies. Maybe he was in the hands of loan sharks —'

'Too much of a coincidence in light of what you already told me. When I was a wildcatter, I developed a sixth sense. Right between my shoulder blades.'

Samuel Schlechter inclined his head to one side, listened. Jim Northcutt was certainly not paranoid. His intuition in regard to the petroleum industry was uncanny.

'Right now, I'm thinking the way Powell Pierce and his people think,' Northcutt continued. 'NIPCO's always been a thorn, now it's a harpoon, in their sidos. They're out to get NIPCO and me. They're also out to make money. Those are the base reference points.'

The oilman grinned sourly.

'Pierce has two other Majors hooked up with Jersey Crest, Richland Consolidated and Western Impex. All three are in direct competition with us wherever we market. If our independent dealers cancel their contracts with NIPCO, one of two things happens. Either those dealers go out of business, which means that much less competition, or they contract with one of the three companies. That means they'll have more outlets. However it works out, it will add a couple of billion more to their sales.'

Jim Northcutt's eyes had grown dark.

'Sam, you're a good judge of character. Who's the best all-around young executive we have on NIPCO's payrolls?'

The attorney was silent for several seconds.

'Jack Anders is good,' he suggested.

'But he has a desk-bound mentality.'

'There's Ralph Pettingill in Tulsa. He runs the whole mid-continent operation. Ralph spent several years in the field.'

Northcutt registered brief interest, then shook his head.

'Pettingill hasn't the hard edge I'm looking for. I want a man who knows this business inside out. He's got to be loyal enough to take orders without question and trusted to carry 'em out. On the other hand, he's got to have the guts to talk back – to you or me or anybody else – if he thinks he's right. And he should have a streak of hard-nosed bastard in him.'

Schlechter smiled. 'You're looking for someone to be in direct charge of the defensive —'

'Defensive, my ass! Counteroffensive. I want a man who'll lead the charges while we two older farts play field-marshal.'

'Mark Radford,' Schlechter said without hesitation.

Northcutt grinned. 'He's the one I had in mind all along. I only wanted a cross-reading.'

Mark Radford was thirty-five, and the resident manager of NIPCO's Middle Eastern operations on the Persian Gulf island of Qantara. No Ivy League product, Radford had attended the Colorado School of Mines on a scholarship, working nights, weekends and during vacations to pay for his room, board, extras and hell raising. During summer vacations, he had worked as an oil fields roustabout.

Radford had gained his experience and promotions with NIPCO via an even tougher route, out on the company's far-flung drilling sites. Although they were separated by age and background, Northcutt felt that Mark Radford was basically cut from his own breed. Rugged, independent, able to innovate and improvise, Radford possessed the qualities that made wildcatters of an earlier generation what they were.

'I'll send for Mark immediately,' Northcutt declared. 'Even allowing for connecting-flight layovers, he should be here tomorrow.'

Lunch was served on an awninged outdoor terrace. There were only three at the table. Jim Northcutt and Samuel Schlechter hardly spoke. Barbara Wallace chattered, seeking to attract and hold Northcutt's attention.

'... Rainier and Grace are having a gala next month and I know that' – Barbara almost said 'we', hastily caught herself – 'that you received an invitation, Jim.'

Northcutt idly watched a servant clearing the dishes on which the avocado vinaigrette had been served.

'Wasn't aware that I had, and I couldn't care less.' He seemed bored.

Medding stepped on to the terrace, smiling broadly.

'Beg your pardon, Mr Northcutt, but Miss Katherine arrived only a moment ago.'

'Kathy?' Jim Northcutt rose from his chair. 'Where is she?'

'Right here, Dad.'

Kathy hurried across the terrace, hugged and kissed her father.

'Hello, Sam.' Kathy kissed Schlechter on one cheek and patted the other. 'How's my favourite godfather?' She had known Schlechter most of her life. When Kathy had reached twenty-

34

one, she had asked him to be her attorney.

'Fine,' Sam smiled. 'I don't have to ask you if you're feeling as good as you look.'

Damned if she isn't more beautiful than the last time I saw her, Jim Northcutt thought, with paternal pride.

Kathy and Barbara exchanged greetings that seemed genuine enough to anyone who observed them, but carried their own subliminal messages.

'Medding, a place for my daughter.'

'Of course, Mr Northcutt.'

'Hungry, Kathy?'

'Famished.' She took an empty chair.

Barbara gave her a bright look.

'Any truth to the rumours I've heard about your being engaged, Kathy?' Barbara inquired, going for what she believed to be a vulnerable point. After all, Kathy Northcutt was twenty-nine and still single.

Northcutt looked startled. He had heard no such rumours.

'They're perennial,' Kathy replied airily. 'I have enormous appeal. Every man I meet wants to marry me.' She nodded towards her father. 'And why not? Who wouldn't want to marry a billionaire's daughter? They all think it's the next best thing to marrying the billionaire himself.' And up yours, *Miss* Wallace.

'How come you didn't let me know you were coming, Kath?' Jim Northcutt asked. His daughter usually phoned several days before her trips to Bonheur, and he delighted in making special arrangements for her entertainment. 'I'd have invited people, given a party...'

'I was moved by a sudden impulse at dawn,' Kathy said, cheerfully starting on the avocado vinaigrette Medding had brought for her. 'I hate to tell you, but you were the handiest excuse I could find at that moment.'

'Excuse for what?'

Kathy sipped the chilled Pouilly-Fuissé Medding poured into her glass.

'To get out from under.' Literally and figuratively, she mused.

'Anyone I know?' her father inquired.

Kathy shook her head. Soft red hair glowed and shimmered. 'He would have loved nothing better than to know you, though. As his father-in-law. It all became too depressingly obvious.'

Conversation ceased temporarily as tiny, delicately fried Mediterranean shrimps were served.

'I hope you'll be staying a while,' Northcutt said to his daughter.

'Two weeks, maybe more, Dad. It depends.'

Jim Northcutt knew better than to ask Kathy on what her decision depended. She had her own mind. It was one of the countless reasons he was so very fond of her. Still, he could not help but regret that Katherine wasn't his son instead of his daughter.

He stared moodily at his plate. He thought of the battle that lay ahead to save NIPCO. I'll fight it, he told himself, but even if I win, there's no one to take over after me.

'Hey, why the blues?' Kathy demanded.

'Some people read tea leaves,' Jim Northcutt said. 'I read fried shrimp.'

'Fascinating. What do you see, guru?'

'That our excellent chef has one less grey hair than he had before he started,' Northcutt replied.

Medding, hovering nearby, sprang forward and whisked the plate away.

5

27 June

One of the most widely held beliefs in the petroleum industry is that there are 'natural' oilmen, individuals who have an innate affinity for oil, almost as if they had high-gravity crude rather than blood flowing through their veins. James Northcutt was said to be one of the foremost among the 'naturals'. Throughout his career – as hired-hand driller, shoestring wildcatter and progressively wealthier oil magnate, he had demonstrated a remarkable instinct for sensing the presence of oil, even on properties geologists and geophysicists had pronounced worthless.

Nothing had proven this skill graphically (or more profitably to NIPCO) than his acquisition – in 1957 – of the exclusive exploration and drilling concession for Qantara. An arid, two-thousand-square-mile emirate on the east coast of the Arabian Peninsula, Qantara had been surveyed by several other oil companies. All declared the country to be as dry of oil as it was of fresh water. The emirate seemed to have nothing to offer. Its poverty-ridden population of some 175,000 led nomadic existences or lived in miserable mud-hut villages. About 15,000 of them inhabited Ayat, a ghastly slum that served as Qantara's capital.

Northcutt ignored the verdicts passed by others. He made his own 'survey', low-level overflights of Qantara in a Beechcraft Bonanza. He then entered into concession negotiations with Emir Maktoum ben Khalifah, the hereditary ruler of Qantara. NIPCO brought in its first producing wells in 1960. During the ensuing years, oil wrought barely credible transformations in the emirate. By 1973, oil royalties provided Qantara with an annual per capita income of $2,200, not much below that of Kuwait.

Ayat grew to a city of fifty thousand. It had wide, paved streets. These were lined with concrete-and-steel office buildings, apartment houses and private residences, all of which were air-conditioned and had tinted, heat-resistant glass in their windows. Even lesser sheikhs boasted Cadillacs, Lincoln Continentals and Mercedes Benzes.

The Emir Maktoum ben Khalifah's vast new palace was an Arabian Nights nightmare. The gaudy monstrosity had been created by a firm of American architects who plagiarized at random from Saarinen, Breuer, Gropius and Wright. The Emir was delighted. His palace gave him much *sharaf* – honour – and *ilham'dilla*, how the royalties continued to mount!

Qantara did not join other Arab countries in either the first or the current oil embargo. The Emir Maktoum ben Khalifah refused to participate in the global blackmail for a variety of reasons that had nothing to do with ethical considerations. They were purely personal. In the days before NIPCO discovered oil on the island, he had been treated as a poor and rather pathetic relation by other Arab rulers, and the memory rankled. For another, Sheikh Maktoum was concerned with politics only as they pertained directly to his own domains. The Pan-Arab mystique aroused no fervour in his princely – but parochial – bosom. And, above all, he was determined that oil revenues should continue flowing into his treasury.

37

Qantara production gave NIPCO the edge that permitted deliveries of normal fuel and petroleum-product allocations to its dealers and distributors. Crude taken from Qantara fields accounted for almost one-quarter of all the company's production in both hemispheres.

Like all American oil companies operating in the Middle East, Northcutt International Petroleum provided its American employees with facilities for a lifestyle equal to US middle-class standards. NIPCO had built a large housing compound outside Ayat. It was a transplanted, self-contained slice of American suburbia.

There were neat white bungalows and two-storey apartment blocks. Other structures housed a school for employees' children, the company commissary, a clubhouse, a theatre where motion pictures were shown and Little Theatre Groups presented plays, a hospital and other facilities and amenities. All that expatriated Americans could desire – from Libby's canned pineapple juice to tennis courts and even a nine-hole golf course – were provided.

Out on the exploration and drilling sites scattered widely over sun-seared desert land, there were fewer frills and luxuries. But the men who did the actual work of finding and producing oil lived comfortably. They were able to make frequent trips to Ayat and were given liberal leaves with pay for visits to Lebanon, Turkey, Europe or even back home to the United States.

NIPCO's Qantara administrative offices were located in a gleaming five-storey building on Ayat's Souk el Najaf, now a broad avenue. A decade earlier, it had been an alley of decrepit, vermin-ridden shops. It was in this building that Mark Radford, the NIPCO resident manager, held conferences and did his paper work. Such work had to be sandwiched in between tasks he considered more important. These were inspection and supervisory visits to exploration and drilling sites, producing wells and other company installations on the island.

Mark Radford was a big, muscular man whose sandy hair had been bleached a pale straw colour and skin burned almost chocolate brown by exposure to the Middle Eastern sun. He chafed whenever it was necessary for him to remain behind his desk. He disliked dictating reports, answering home-office inquiries, going through the endless rituals of haggling with avaricious – and invariably long-winded – Qantari officials. But Mark performed these chores as he did those he enjoyed more: capably and efficiently.

On this June afternoon, Mark Radford was at his desk, fuming over weekly crude-production reports that somehow didn't balance as they should.

'Mark.' It was his secretary. 'This bounced in a minute ago.' She handed him a cablegram. Radford grunted, scanned the message, cursed silently. Now what the hell, he thought.

RADFORD NIPCO AYAT QANTARA

PROCEED BONHEUR IMMEDIATELY REPEAT IMMEDIATELY STOP HAND OVER TO UNGAR ON TEMPORARY BASIS STOP EXPECT YOU TOMORROW

JAMES L. NORTHCUTT

Orders are orders, Mark grumbled. Luckily, Chuck Ungar, the deputy resident manager, was also in his office. Radford sent for him.

Ungar was a grizzled oil fields veteran. No one could remember ever having seen him without a lifeless cigar clamped between his teeth.

'What's up?' Ungar asked.

'You tell me,' Radford shrugged, tossing him the cable. 'Maybe the Old Man wants to let me sun myself on the Riviera a while.'

'Fat chance,' Ungar snorted. 'I been working for him thirty years. He's got some loaded see-gar to hand you.' He gnawed at his own cigar stump. 'My guess is he's going to dump more work in our laps. Wants to break the news personally.' He squinted at Mark. 'When you leaving?'

'Soon's I get out to the compound and pack.'

'Yeah,' Chuck Ungar nodded approvingly. 'His fuse gets awful damned short if you keep him waiting.' He shifted the cigar stub. 'Anything special you want me to take care of?'

'It's all yours, Chuck. And since you're in charge as of right now, have somebody crank up a company Pilatus. I'll fly to Kuwait, take the first west-bound commercial flight from there.'

Despite its oil wealth, Qantara was served by no major international commercial airline. NIPCO maintained its own fleet of Porter Pilatus STOL aircraft for use within the emirate and also to ferry company personnel back and forth to the nearest large commercial airport, which was in Kuwait.

'Oh, something else,' Mark said, knowing that Ungar's hatred of paper work was even greater than his own. 'Sweat over these reports and try to make some sense out of 'em. I can't.'

'You bastard!' The older man grinned as he took the reports. He shook Radford's hand, wished him happy landings.

An hour and a half later, Mark Radford boarded one of NIPCO's Pilatus turboprop aircraft. He buckled himself into a seat. The pilot gunned the engine, and moments later the plane was airborne and headed for Kuwait City.

Chuck Ungar called it a day at seven and left the NIPCO administrative headquarters.

Unlike other NIPCO American employees, Ungar did not live in the company's housing compound. Since he was directly responsible for the NIPCO tank farm and refinery complex at the company-built port of Batir, five miles north of Ayat, he had his house there. Ungar and his wife Edna occupied a comfortable, six-room bungalow provided for them by the company.

The Batir complex covered an area of nearly six hundred acres. Pipelines brought crude from the producing fields to the giant storage tanks. A small fraction of the crude was refined into gasoline and other products for NIPCO's own use and for local consumption. Most of the crude oil was pumped aboard NIPCO supertankers for shipment to NIPCO refineries in the United States and Europe.

Ungar found that his wife had arrived home only a short time before he did.

'I was playing bridge at the compound,' Edna Ungar explained. 'But dinner's ready.' The cook who was one of their three Arab servants had prepared the meal.

'Great,' Ungar said. 'I'm hungry.'

While they ate, Ungar told her about the cable from James Northcutt and Mark Radford's departure.

'That leaves me responsible for the whole shebang,' he complained.

After dinner, they each had a Scotch highball, listened to the radio for a while and then bathed and went to bed. They were asleep by eleven.

*   *   *

40

Shortly after midnight, a large and powerful motorboat, its engines idling, eased against one of the NIPCO docks at Batir. Once the boat was secured, nine men clambered up on the dock. One remained at the controls.

An Arab watchman making his rounds saw the shadowy figures. He sauntered over to them without any particular interest. Many NIPCO employees went night fishing in the Persian Gulf. He assumed it was such a fishing party coming back in, but he wanted to demonstrate that he was doing his job.

'*Alla massik bilkhair, shû bitâmir*,' he punctiliously addressed the nearest figure. 'Good evening. What is your command?'

There were two finger-snap sounds as a silenced revolver cut the watchman down. One bullet punched into his stomach, the other ripped through his skull. He was dead before he struck the concrete pavement and lay still, sprawled in a welter of blood and brain matter.

'Finished. We do the rest now.' The man who had fired spoke in English but with a heavy German accent.

The nine men moved quickly and purposefully along the dock. All were armed. Six carried heavy haversacks slung over their shoulders. When they reached the edge of the refinery complex area, they split into three groups and went separate ways. One group headed towards the refinery itself. The second angled off in the direction of the tank farm. The third kept to the shadows, carefully avoiding floodlighted areas and the occasional bored watchman making his rounds. These three men found their way easily to Chuck Ungar's bungalow.

Halting, they observed that there was no one in sight, no sign of movement. The house was dark. The man who had shot the watchman grunted. He was clearly the leader of the trio. He went to the front door of the bungalow, his companions following directly behind him. He pushed the button set into the door frame. A buzzer could be heard inside. The man waited only a moment, then pressed the button again.

Chuck Ungar stirred, muttered, awoke. He switched on the bedside lamp. It was 12.36 A.M. Who in the name of Christ could be at the door at this hour of the night, he wondered fuzzily. The light awakened his wife, and the door buzzer sounded again.

'What is it, Chuck?' Edna Ungar asked. Her voice was a sleepy mumble.

'Beats me, but I'll find out.' The servants slept in separate quarters located twenty yards behind the house. He would have to answer the door himself.

Ungar swung out of bed, pulled on his faded cotton robe, swore under his breath and went to the front door to open it. When he did, his jaw dropped in astonishment and sudden terror. A man had stepped forward, thrust a gun muzzle into Ungar's belly. Two others stood behind the first, also with guns, also pointing them.

It was impossible, Ungar thought. Insane.

'Back inside!' The order was emphasized by a gesture with the gun. 'Go quick – now!'

The accent was Kraut, Chuck Ungar told himself. That made everything even more insane. But a gun muzzle was being driven hard into his stomach, and he stepped back, the men crowding after him. When they were all inside, one of the group closed the door.

'Your bedroom,' the leader rasped. 'Where is it?' He was the burliest of the trio, Ungar noted. The second man was tall and thin, the third of medium build.

'Please. My wife's in there. Whatever you want, leave her out of it.' What could they possibly want? He didn't keep much cash around the house. Perhaps a hundred dollars' worth of Qantari piasters. Edna's jewellery? She had never liked jewellery and owned very little.

'The bedroom.' The gun muzzle gouged painfully into Ungar's belly. He glanced down. My God, he thought. A ·38 with a silencer attached. The other two men's weapons were also equipped with silencers. 'Show us!'

Ungar turned. Now the ·38 reamed into his spine. He went towards the bedroom.

'Chuck!' Edna Ungar sat bolt upright in bed and screamed. She tried to leap out of bed and go to him.

'Stay there!' the burly man ordered.

The tall, thin one glanced at him, received a nod. He put his revolver away in a shoulder holster, produced an axe handle from his hip pocket and moved to the side of the bed nearest Edna Ungar. The short member of the trio remained in the bedroom doorway.

The horror came a split second later.

Chuck Ungar felt the first stabbing pain, connected it in his mind with the finger-snap noise he heard. But he didn't feel the other two bullets that drilled into him or hear the other faint reports of the silenced revolver held against his back. He felt or heard or knew nothing more as he pitched forward.

Edna Ungar saw her husband die. She opened her mouth to cry out, but she was not given time to make a sound. The man standing next to the bed swung the axe handle like a club, smashed it into her face, crushing bone and pulping flesh. She fell back, her face a hideous concave wound.

The man leaned down and stripped off the bedsheet that covered Edna Ungar. In a minute he had finished. There was a lot of blood.

'Good,' the leader of the trio grunted. When the bodies were found and it became known how the woman had died, every American female on Qantara would clamour to leave. Many male employees who had wives and daughters with them would also panic. NIPCO would be left shorthanded at a time when it would need workers most.

The three men turned off the lights as they left the house. They returned directly to the boat. They were joined several minutes later by the two other parties. The men in them no longer carried haversacks.

It was 1.08 A.M. when the man who had remained at the controls started the engines. The motorboat eased quietly away from the dock, made a wide, sweeping turn and headed out into the Persian Gulf. It was two miles offshore before the throttles were opened to Full. The engines roared. The boat leaped forward, its prow rising high as it streaked through the water.

Less than half an hour passed.

Then the demolition charges that had been planted in the tank farm and refinery went off. Their loud explosions were lost as they merged with the earth-shaking blasts that followed. Two million gallons of gasoline and thousands of barrels of crude oil burst into sheets of flame that flared high into the sky and turned the night into a red, thundering hell.

6

28 June

Samuel Schlechter had obtained the information about the Jersey Crest consortium and its intentions from his own sources. He'd said nothing to NIPCO's New York home-office executives about the development, going straight to James Northcutt.

Thus, NIPCO President Peter Keely and his subordinate platoons of vice-presidents had remained euphoric over the excellent progress that had been made by Northcutt in Peking. They were totally unprepared for the reports that suddenly began coming into their offices in the fifty-seven-storey NIPCO Building on Fifth Avenue.

First, there had been the explosion and fire that destroyed a NIPCO dealer's service station in Brooklyn and killed two people. Then, on the very next night, two more NIPCO stations had burned – luckily without loss of life. One was in Worcester, Massachusetts, the other in Atlanta, Georgia.

Bad as these incidents were, they shrank in significance as Telexes started to pour in from Qantara. Tersely worded, they told of a catastrophe on a huge scale.

'Batir complex raided. Attacked by unknown saboteurs. Deputy Resident Manager Ungar, wife, three refinery workers, one watchman killed. Refinery, tank farm blasted, apparently by high-explosive charges. Refinery damage serious. Three tanks afire. Loading facilities also seriously damaged, unusable.'

'Resident Manager Radford absent. En route France conference with JLN.'

'Available firefighting equipment, ours and Qantari, inadequate. Impossible extinguish tank fires. These must burn selves out.'

'Identity, numbers, origins saboteurs unknown.'

The Telexes came sporadically. They were signed by George Needham, next in line of authority to Chuck Ungar. They were sent from Qantara commencing at 2.30 A.M., local time, reaching New York when it was 6.30 A.M. there.

Peter Keeley, president of NIPCO, was notified at his home. He summoned several key executives, held a crash meeting in the NIPCO Building. All this took several hours. It was almost 11 P.M., New York time, when Keeley placed a trans-atlantic call to Bonheur and had James Northcutt awakened.

Keeley relayed the news and was surprised by Northcutt's immediate reaction. Northcutt showed no initial concern over the damage in Qantara.

'Are you sure about Ungar and his wife?' Northcutt demanded.

'Yes, J.L.,' Keeley replied. 'Needham confirmed the list of dead twice. But we have the tank farm and refinery problem —'

'The hell with that!' Northcutt rasped. Chuck Ungar had worked for him over thirty years. Ungar was – had been – a friend. He swallowed hard. 'All right, Pete,' he said after a moment, his voice uneven. 'Send out whatever is needed. Never mind expense or any other God-damned thing!'

'J.L., according to Needham, Mark Radford's on his way to see you.'

'He is. I ordered him to come here.'

'Might be a good idea to turn him around and send him back.'

'No, I'll need Radford here more than ever now,' Northcutt said. Peter Keeley thought the statement puzzling, but he didn't question it.

'George Needham is a good man,' Northcutt continued. 'He can handle whatever needs to be handled.'

When the conversation was finished, Jim Northcutt showered and dressed hurriedly. He went to the guest suite Samuel Schlechter occupied in the west wing, woke the attorney and told him of the call from Peter Keeley.

Ten minutes later, the two men sat in Northcutt's study. The servants were already up and about, but the secretarial staff had not yet arrived to start the day's work.

Northcutt rang for his butler.

'Coffee – strong, Medding,' he said. 'We'll have it here.'

'When the ladies come down for breakfast and ask for you, sir?'

'Tell them we're tied up. No one is to disturb us.'

A few minutes later, Medding brought an enormous Georgian silver pot filled with coffee, served the two men and then left.

James Northcutt's features were craggy, but generally mobile. They froze only when he was filled with rage, and they solidified now.

'It's going to be worse than we thought,' he said to Schlechter.

'You were right,' Sam muttered. 'We are still in the Harry Sinclair and Edward Doheny era.' Stunned, he could offer nothing constructive for the moment.

Jim Northcutt poured himself another cup of coffee.

'We'll be in a hell of a shape if the Qantara operation is knocked out and we can't ship crude.'

'That's unarguable.' Schlechter rubbed at his temples as though it would help erase his feelings of deep depression. Any interruption in crude shipments from Qantara meant a 23 per cent shortfall in the company's refining needs. Fuel and other petroleum-product allocations to dealers and distributors would have to be slashed accordingly. The effect on NIPCO's entire marketing structure would be disastrous.

'We can't even hope to buy spot crude and close the gap,' Northcutt growled. 'The Majors have every drop under control for this new God-damned phoney shortage!'

Normally, companies engaged exclusively in oil production had some excess stocks of crude they would immediately sell to refiners or pipeline companies on the spot market. All such supplies had evaporated – or been made to evaporate – as the 'Second World Energy Crisis' deepened with astonishing speed.

Jim Northcutt lapsed into silence, his mind working. Nearly two minutes passed before he looked up, fixing Schlechter with grey eyes that were suddenly alive and glowing with determination.

'What I said before still goes,' he declared. 'We'll battle the bastards all the way. In every way. Now let's do a little of our own scheming!'

Mark Radford arrived at Bonheur half an hour before lunch was to be served. The news media had not yet received the story of the Qantara sabotage. He was completely ignorant of what had happened since his departure from Ayat. 'Don't tell Radford – or Kathy or Barbara – anything until after we've eaten,' Northcutt had warned Schlechter.

46

Lunch was again served on the terrace. Mark Radford had been to Bonheur often. Northcutt liked receiving first-hand reports from his managers in the field. These gave him clear insights into company operations, and he delighted in hearing the anecdotes of field men, with whom his wildcatter's nature identified. Radford had met Barbara Wallace on two of his previous visits. His reactions on both occasions were negative. They were again. She had lasted almost a year as Jim Northcutt's mistress, and Mark could not quite understand how or why.

He recognized Barbara as a brittle opportunist. Tits, twat and tinsel, Mark reflected, and Northcutt keeps falling for the combination. But then, every man's sex life is his own business, and James Northcutt has a right to his own, no matter what it costs him.

Mark had not met Katherine Northcutt before. A beauty, yes, he thought, watching her across the table. However, if she's as much like her father as everyone claims, a far more formidable handful than any rational man would want to go after.

'Your family with you in Qantara, Mr Radford?' Kathy asked.

Despite his preoccupation, James Northcutt heard the question.

'Nope, Mark doesn't have a family in Qantara,' he replied before Redford could speak. 'He's like me. A one-time loser and single, courtesy of the courts.'

'Oh? I didn't know you were married and divorced,' Barbara chimed in.

Mark shrugged. 'Got my final papers four, five years ago.' And one marital straitjacket was enough, thanks.

He looked out over the Mediterranean. 'Done any fishing lately, J.L.?' James Northcutt had spasmodic urges to go deep-sea fishing, but seldom if ever managed to catch anything when he went.

'Not recently,' Northcutt said and seemed once more to retire into private thought.

Strange, Radford mused. Something must be really bugging the Old Man. Usually any mention of fishing would cause Northcutt to laugh and recount his latest dismal tale of failure as an angler. Mark glanced at Sam Schlechter. The attorney had a thin, fixed smile on his face. It was patently bogus. He's out of it, too, Radford thought. He and Northcutt have something heavy on their minds.

'I forgot to ask, Mark,' Barbara spoke up again. 'Did you have a good flight?'

Not that you really give a shit, Mark thought, but if you want to make conversation, I'll go along.

'Flights,' he said. 'Plural. Qantara to Kuwait, Kuwait to Beirut. Next Beirut to Paris via Rome. Finally Paris to Nice. All in all, a drag.'

'You must be exhausted,' Kathy said, then smiled. 'Only you certainly don't look it.'

'My retarded development. I climb aboard an aeroplane, and I sleep like a baby, Miss Northcutt.'

'The name is Kathy, Mark.' She cocked an eyebrow in a replica of her father's mannerism. 'Did the stewardesses tuck you in?'

Barbara Wallace became aware that no one was paying any attention to her.

'Mark mentioned fishing a few minutes ago, Jim,' she said, smiling directly at Northcutt. 'Shall we go out and try our luck this afternoon?'

The oilman stared at her, the question not registering for a moment. Then he frowned, shook his head.

'I'll be busy,' he growled.

'Maybe Mark —'

'He'll be busy, too. With Sam and me.'

'What, no post-prandial nap for Mark?' Kathy laughed. 'After all, Dad, he's had a long, rough trip.'

'Why, Kathy,' Barbara interjected. 'Your maternal instinct is showing.'

James Northcutt wasn't listening.

'Gentlemen, if you've finished lunch, we'll excuse ourselves and have coffee in my study.'

7

28 June (Afternoon)

'Better hear the latest from Qantara, Mark,' Northcutt began when they were seated in his study.

'The latest?' Radford said. 'I only left yesterday. Everything is under control – except for routine headaches and standard chaos.'

'Brace yourself, son.' The oilman rubbed a hand against his jaw and took a deep breath. 'Things sometimes change fast.' He quickly related the details he'd received about the Qantara sabotage.

Mark listened, stunned, barely able to believe what he heard. Chuck Ungar, his wife and others had been murdered. The Batir installations had been blasted and were burning. Shock, horror and anger boiled inside him. Anger – at James Northcutt – manifested itself first.

'You waited this long to tell me?' he demanded, raising his large frame out of his chair. 'For Christ's sake! We all sat around outside having lunch like it was a quiet Sunday in Grosse Pointe!'

'Sit down, Mark,' Northcutt ordered.

'Like hell I will. I've got to get back to Qantara.'

'I said sit down.' There was authority – and something more – in the oilman's tone. A faint pleading note? No, Mark thought. Not from James L. Northcutt. He hesitated a moment, then obeyed.

'George Needham's taken charge in Qantara,' Northcutt said. 'He'll have to run the operation for a while.'

'My job —'

'Mark, right now your job is to keep quiet and listen. When Sam and I tell you what we know, you'll see that Qantara is only a sideshow. Then it'll be your decision.'

'Decision? About what?'

'Whether or not you want to ride through the worst storm of your life – or mine.'

Radford frowned, his apprehensions increasing.

'Go ahead, Sam,' Northcutt said. 'You start.'

Schlechter spoke for about fifteen minutes. Then Northcutt picked up where he left off, talking for another ten minutes. Together, they gave Radford the full story of the concerted efforts being made to put NIPCO out of business.

'Your turn, Mark,' Northcutt said. 'Ask questions.'

Radford could not understand why Northcutt had taken him so far into his confidence, and said as much.

'Simple,' the oil magnate replied. 'NIPCO's in trouble, being hit from all sides. We're going to hit back. Sam and I can boil up ideas, pull strings and manipulate switches and levers. But we need somebody to take charge of the actual infighting.'

Radford blinked. 'There are a hundred men senior to me on the payroll.'

Northcutt stood up, started to pace the floor.

'Seniority doesn't count a damn in this mess,' he said. 'Sam and I considered all the possibles. We narrowed down to you.' He stopped, facing Mark. 'You'll be taking on a hell of a load. There'll be plenty of risks, even personal danger. This isn't going to be a boardroom battle. It'll be gutter fighting.'

Mark Radford's blue eyes narrowed. He realized he owed much to James Northcutt. The oilman had hired him personally when he graduated from college and had treated him – well, hell, almost like a son – even while rawhiding him mercilessly, making him work to the limit for every promotion and word of praise.

All the same, Mark thought, even with that I've just been told I don't know what the hell I'm really getting myself into. Sure, I'm tempted to side with the Old Man, tell him I'm ready to go for broke. The crusty, nonconformist old bastard built NIPCO out of nothing, and he's still a wildcatter at heart. Damn it, he's one of the few men I've ever met whose hand-shake is worth more than any signed-and-sealed contract.

Radford suddenly began to appreciate his own sense of loyalty to Jim Northcutt. None the less . . .

'I'm not sold – not yet, J.L.,' he said. 'You tell me I'm supposed to straw-boss the "infighting". That's not much to go on.'

'Afraid there's no applicable job description in the personnel manual,' Northcutt retorted drily. 'You'll run a guerrilla operation, Mark. You won't be alone, though.'

'Sorry. It's still hazy.'

'Is it?' Northcutt said. 'We're up against power. Three

Majors. They're safe and snug. They work through layers of middlemen so nothing can be proved against them. In the meantime, people are murdered, our retailers are firebombed and Qantara is wrecked.' A scowl darkened his face. 'And the storm's barely brewed yet. What can I tell you, son? I intend to try and save my company. If you stick, we'll all be fighting for our lives – it could be literally.'

Mark Radford felt a surge of excitement. It's getting to me, he realized – and why shouldn't it? A hell of a lot of my sweat's gone into NIPCO, too. The Qantara operation's been my baby for three years. Chuck Ungar and his wife were my friends – and it could have been me instead of Chuck who got killed. Sure, NIPCO was up against power. Enormous power. And that would make it all the more satisfying to fight and win and accomplish the impossible. Now the picture came into sharper focus. Intimidation and terror could only be countered in kind.

'Suppose we have to draw blood ourselves?' he asked.

'Suppose we do?' Northcutt said, his face impassive.

Radford was silent a moment.

'If I say yes, who'll be looking over my shoulder?'

'Nobody,' Northcutt replied. 'You'll report to Sam and me. Otherwise, you'll be your own boss.'

'I might not want even you asking me too much.'

'You won't be asked, Mark. You'll be given all possible backing, without reservations.'

I'd need plenty of support, Mark reflected, all you could supply, and probably more.

The odds against NIPCO appeared overwhelming. If I got in as deep as Northcutt wants me to and NIPCO loses, I'd never have another decent job with any oil company. Provided I was even still alive.

Mark bit his lip and shrugged. Suddenly, none of the dangers and imponderables seemed to matter. If the Old Man and Sam Schlechter were willing to stake everything and take on the odds . . .

'When do we get down to hard-facts planning?' Radford demanded abruptly.

Jim Northcutt's right eyebrow veered upward.

'You're in?' he asked.

'We may all wind up sorry,' Radford replied. 'But I'm in.'

James Northcutt's face relaxed and he grinned. I can still

pick the men from the boys, he thought. He saw his own younger self reflected in Mark Radford. The wildcatter breed may be thinning out, but thank God it hasn't vanished, Northcutt mused.

How many times did I stake everything on all-out gambles, he reflected. Who could count? His entire career had been a series of battles, all uphill, many that had seemed suicidal. The trick lay in outmanoeuvring the opposition – and when that couldn't be done, in playing rougher and dirtier.

'I learned early,' Northcutt muttered.

'Sorry, Jim, I didn't hear you,' Schlechter said.

'I was thinking out loud,' Northcutt told him. He paused and when he spoke again, the timbre of his deep baritone voice was charged with fresh vitality.

'Mark wants to know when we can start making concrete plans.' He looked at Radford. 'We've already made some, Mark.' He turned back to Schlechter. 'Give Mark a rundown on what you and I have discussed so far.'

Northcutt didn't listen as Schlechter leaned forward, focused his attention on Radford and began to speak. He was lost in his own thoughts. It's been a long climb to the top, he mused, and it could be one hell of a long and fast fall. But I did learn my lessons early.

His mind travelled back in time to another, remote day in June, and his eyes grew distant as memory images began unreeling.

1

It was 13 June 1921, and James L. Northcutt – four months past his twenty-first birthday – stared moodily through the windshield of his Model T Ford roadster.

The car's headlights cast yellow patches on the rutted dirt road that led from Stainesville to Logan, traversing one of the richest oil-producing areas in Oklahoma. The night air was warm and reeked with the pervasive odour of unrefined petroleum . . .

Oil, Jim Northcutt thought with a sense of elation.

Oil!

The demand for oil was soaring, exceeding supply. Crude brought three dollars and more at the wellhead for each and every barrel that gushed or flowed or was pumped to the surface.

No matter how I may miscalculate in other ways, my timing is right, Northcutt assured himself. Even so, he was tense, fully aware that he was literally driving out of one life and into another. His existence as a free-floating, top-wage-earning oil well driller was over. Before him were all the countless risks and uncertainties that beset the small-scale independent operator. From now on, he would be a shoestring wildcatter. A hunch-playing gambler boring blindly into the earth and hoping to hit pay sand. Provided the predators and scavengers didn't destroy him and his hopes.

It was the second time in Jim Northcutt's life that he had made a break of such magnitude. The first had been at sixteen, and Jim never regretted what he'd done . . .

James Northcutt's father was a Cape Girardeau, Missouri, feed-and-grain merchant who committed suicide after being ruined in the 1907 panic. Jim's mother died a year later of pneumonia. The boy was 'taken in' by Webster Northcutt, a paternal uncle, and his wife Emily. They were pious hypocrites who told Jim that God rewarded those who worked and saved and punished those who did not.

Webster Northcutt made his living as a general trader. Such

men were familiar and largely parasitical figures in rural areas. General traders bought and sold land, livestock, crops, anything and everything. They had but one guiding rule: to buy at minimum lows (almost always from farmers in desperate need of cash) and sell at maximum highs. Between the principles – or lack of them – implied by these two extremes, general traders recognized few if any ethical considerations. Yet, like Jim's uncle, they were usually the staunchest of community pillars, the most ardent church-goers.

Jim Northcutt lived with his uncle and aunt for almost eight years. From the beginning he was required to work hard for Webster Northcutt. There were chores to be done before school, much heavier work in Webster's warehouse after school, on Saturdays and during vacations. Instead of being paid, Jim was repeatedly told of his good fortune at having an uncle and aunt willing to show Christian charity to an orphan.

Some wild gene in the boy's make-up enabled him to see through the hypocrisies. He rebelled inwardly, refused to submerge his personality and become the psalm-singing cipher his uncle and aunt sought to make of him.

When he reached sixteen, Jim's nature turned inner rebellion into open revolt. He left with one change of clothing in a decrepit valise, less than two dollars in his pockets and a fierce determination in his heart. From then on, he would live by his own code, shape his own future. He had no clear idea of where he was going or what he would do when he got there. But he was aware of a new oil boom in Kansas and heard there was always work in the oil fields.

Jim hopped freight cars to reach Kansas. As he was frequently thrown off trains by brakemen or railroad police, the trip to Wichita took more than three days. From there, he hitched rides aboard mule-drawn freight wagons carrying supplies to the El Dorado fields north-east of the town.

The boy reached the oil fields broke and hungry but not dismayed. Suddenly, he found himself in his natural element. The countryside was studded with gaunt wooden derricks. The air reeked with the stench of crude oil. An oil rush was in full swing. The rate at which new wells were being drilled was governed only by the availability of equipment and labour.

Big for his age and eager to work, Jim made his way to the nearest drilling site. He approached the foreman and asked for a job.

'You look like you got a strong back, son,' the foreman said. 'But the only job I can give you'll probably bust it in half.'

'Bullshit!' Jim retorted. 'My ass won't even drag!'

The foreman laughed and hired the boy to do heavy labour on a twelve-hour shift for three – later four – dollars a day. At first, Jim spent all he earned on pursuits that taught him about sex, the difference between good liquor and bad and how to recognize a marked deck or a pair of loaded dice.

Then, gradually, he began to change. He saw with increasing fascination that fortunes were being made – and lost – overnight in the oil fields. He boomed around, working in Louisiana, Texas and finally Oklahoma. From each of his jobs, he learned something about drilling for oil. Intelligent, capable, conscientious, he was made a tool dresser. Then, shortly before he reached twenty-one, he qualified as a full-fledged driller.

With that, Northcutt started to save some of his pay – as a driller, he earned fourteen dollars a day – and more of what he won playing poker or dice. He was by then determined to prospect for oil on his own. In the spring of 1921, Jim took a job as a driller with the McMan Oil Company in the recently discovered Osage County, Oklahoma, oil fields. At that time, according to his most optimistic calculations, he still needed two more years to save up sufficient capital to start wildcatting. But that had been before he met Verna Fletcher and, through her, Abraham Schlechter...

The Model T jounced along noisily. Familiar with the route he was following, Jim Northcutt recognized the western outskirts of Logan. He slowed the car. The Cedar Creek quarter was just ahead. It was where the oil boomtown's worst booze joints, gambling dives and cribs were located. At one-thirty in the morning there were likely to be dozens of oil field workers staggering around on the road or lying drunk in the middle of it.

Jim worked his lips, moistening them. He could have used a drink himself, he thought. He wouldn't have to wait long. Another fifteen minutes or so and he'd be with Verna Fletcher. The whisky they would have together would help relax him. Their lovemaking afterwards would relax him even more, provide full outlet for all his inner tensions. He smiled in anticipation, watching the road ahead. Suddenly he slammed his booted foot against the brake and gear pedals.

'Jesus Christ!' he exclaimed as the Ford shuddered to a stop.

His headlights illuminated the scene clearly. A terror-stricken Indian had run out into the road pursued by a white man brandishing a long-bladed knife. Jim's reactions were automatic, yet there was nothing he could do to prevent what was happening. The white man caught the Indian by the shoulder, spun him around and then slashed his belly open with one swift, vicious stroke of the knife. The Indian screamed – once – and crumpled to the ground, his entrails spilling from the great gash in his stomach.

Jim scooped up the heavy, metal tyre tool that lay on the floorboard and vaulted from the Model T. The Indian was writhing on the ground. The white man leaned over his victim, stabbed him in the chest and, straightening up, drove a steel-shod boot heel into his face.

'Fucking bastard!' the white man cursed, then heard Jim Northcutt running towards him and whirled around. He stood, feet braced, bloodstained knife ready in his hand.

Jim was big – six-two and hard-muscled – but the man was bigger. Two inches taller, outweighing him by at least thirty pounds. He was obviously an oil field worker. Probably a black-smith or tool dresser from the look of his massive shoulder and arm muscles. And he was drunk, but not so drunk that he didn't know what he was doing.

'Stay back or I'll geld you like a damn hog!' he roared.

Aware he was starkly outlined by his car's headlights, Jim hesitated. The huge figure hurtled towards him, the blood-slicked knife gleaming. The man's size was his worst liability. He wasn't quite fast enough on his feet. Jim gauged his on-rushing approach to the inch, waited until the last split second, sidestepped and swung the tyre tool as he would a cleaver, chopping the narrow edge down on the hand holding the knife. Metal smashed bone and the knife dropped.

'You son of a bitch!' The man bellowed with pain, but he hadn't been stopped. His uninjured hand went for Jim's throat, the fingers gouging into flesh. His knee drove for Northcutt's groin.

Jim had no choice but to swing the tyre tool again, this time hacking at the base of the man's skull. Once more, bone splintered under the impact of steel. The giant gave a long,

56

soughing cry as life went out of him, and his hand raked along Jim's body as he fell.

Northcutt found himself soaked with sweat, his heart pounding inside his rib cage. For a long moment he stared down at the motionless bulk of the man he had killed. Then he walked slowly to where the Indian lay, the blood that had poured out of him forming a large pool and soaking into the hard-packed earth.

'A kid – sixteen, maybe seventeen,' Jim muttered without realizing he spoke aloud. He glanced to his right and left. There were shadowy figures visible on both sides of the road. They were people who had been attracted by the screams and shouts. They had come scuttling out of the scabrous Cedar Creek shanties, none of them desiring or daring to interfere, all of them eager to watch. Doubtless they had enjoyed what they had seen. Murder and mayhem were everyday occurrences in Logan, as they were in all oil boomtowns. But even so, it wasn't often that Cedar Creek scum could observe so much violence and bloodshed conveniently illuminated by automobile headlights. Already, some men were coming closer, avid to obtain better views of the two bodies.

'Shag your butts and get Donovan!' Jim barked at a group of the nearest onlookers. His voice, deep and resonant, carried authority. The men delayed only a moment, then hurried off to find Jack Donovan, Logan's first – and only very recently appointed – police chief.

Jack Donovan and a deputy arrived some twenty minutes later in a Dodge touring car. Donovan was tough and efficient. He had earned the nickname 'Fighting Jack' honestly in a dozen shoot-outs. Jim knew him only by sight and reputation.

'Who're you? Where do you work?' Donovan demanded of Jim.

'James L. Northcutt. I'm a driller for McMan Oil. Until last night, that is.'

'Got yourself fired?'

'I quit.'

'Wait a minute.' Donovan frowned. 'You the Northcutt who lives with Verna Fletcher?'

'Yes.' Jim fished a Bull Durham sack from his denim shirt pocket and rolled a cigarette. 'Seems you got everybody in town tabbed.'

'More or less have to,' Donovan said. He peered at Jim closely. 'What happened?' His manner showed he had already sized up the situation and was accustomed to far worse. This was hardly surprising, for Logan averaged two homicides a night. Jim related everything in a few sentences.

'That's it, then.' Jack Donovan stifled a yawn. 'The big bastard killed the Indian, and you killed him in self-defence. There's no identification on him. I don't suppose you know who he was?'

'No. Never saw him around before.' Jim took a last drag on his cigarette, and flipped it away. He gestured towards the crowd of oil field workers, cardsharps, pimps, whores and assorted Cedar Creek riffraff. 'Maybe some of these people know.'

'Think any of 'em would tell me?' Donovan snorted.

'I guess not. Want me to hang around longer?'

'Hell, no,' Donovan said. 'Ain't nobody gives a shit about an Indian kid and some drunken bum. Won't even need an inquest. You can head on.'

Jim pushed his way through the crowd. No one paid the least attention to him. Several people were speculating over why the white man might have killed the Indian youth.

'... musta caught him trying to steal his dough ...'

'... could be he just hated Indians ...'

'... sure had to be pissed off to cut the kid like he did ...'

Northcutt returned to his Model T. It had a self starter, and he kicked the engine into life and drove away. The incident had left a deep impression, one wholly alien to his nature. Jim was anything but superstitious. He placed no stock in portents or auguries.

Still, this was the first day of his new life, his career as a wildcatter. It had opened with him seeing a murder and having to kill a man to prevent being killed. Despite himself, Jim Northcutt could not help but wonder if this wasn't somehow an omen for the future.

He passed through the Cedar Creek quarter and started up the long, steep slope of Cedar Hill Avenue. He was impatient and eager to reach Verna Fletcher's place. By then, it was three o'clock in the morning – which was just as well, too, he reflected. Things would be quiet and Verna would be waiting for him. And, at that moment, he wanted Verna more than he wanted anything else.

58

2

Verna Fletcher appeared to be anything but the proprietress of an oil boomtown parlourhouse. Honey-hued hair framed a winsome, oval face. Her great, long-lashed blue eyes were serene. Freckles sprinkled over the bridge of her nose enhanced the impression that she was younger than her not-quite – fully lived – twenty-four years. Her seeming naïveté was all the more surprising because the Philadelphia bookkeeper's daughter had previously been the mistress of a succession of well-to-do men. She had cannily saved the brushoff money she received from each until she had enough to come to Oklahoma and open her own bordello.

As Jim had anticipated, all was quiet at Verna Fletcher's establishment. The last quick-trick customers had departed. Those spending the night had gone to rooms with the girls they had chosen. Verna was awake, fully dressed and waiting in the parlour for him. Jim drank a large whisky and told her what had happened. She listened and felt a sense of grateful relief that he was unhurt.

Most of Verna Fletcher's previous lovers had been selfish and perfunctory or inept. Even those affairs she remembered as exceptions were devoid of emotional content. But Jim Northcutt gratified her as no other man ever had. She was perpetually amazed that anyone his age could be such a practised lover. No, she often corrected herself, *practised* wasn't the right word. It implied studied, even contrived, proficiency. James Northcutt's lovemaking was spontaneous and uninhibited; he made a shared adventure of sex.

As Jim talked, Verna sensed the intensity of his desire for her. It excited her as any woman is excited when she recognizes an upsurge of elemental craving in a man of whom she is fond and with whom she enjoys making love. When he finished his whisky, they went upstairs to the two-room apartment she maintained for herself in the parlourhouse. Once they stepped across the threshold of what served as Verna's sitting room, Jim pushed the door shut with his shoulder. He drew Verna to him, crushing his mouth against hers while his strong hands searched out the curves and planes of her body

59

through the cloth of her dress.

Verna's response was instant and total. The pressure in Jim's loins was a torment. He finally spoke, his voice hoarse, his words unclear. But Verna understood and they hurried into the bedroom together. Jim undressed rapidly. His body muscles were taught, straining. Verna needed a few more moments to undress. At last she stood naked before him. She raised her hands to her head, removing the tortoise-shell pins from her long blonde hair so that it cascaded over shoulders and breasts.

Jim took the two steps separating them, lifted her bodily in his arms. Their mouths locked, and then they were on the bed and she moaned, arching her body up against his. They moved in unison, but not in any slow or gradual tempo, for that was not what either of them needed then. Verna's slender legs gripped his back. Her fingers clung to his flesh. Then, abruptly and to her astonishment she felt the first spasms build within her.

'Jim!' It was a cry of rapture – and of wonder. Verna could feel, but she could not believe. It had never happened to her like this. Never. Not even with Jim. He had been moving inside her for only seconds. Yet, she was already approaching orgasm. It built so swiftly and to such a peak that she clamped a hand over her own mouth to muffle the open scream of pleasure that broke deep from within her. Finally, the full force of the prolonged orgasm began to subside, but – incredibly – the initial sensations that promised another were even then pulsing, amplifying.

'Jim – don't stop!' Verna gasped. 'Please . . .!'

He continued to thrust, himself reaching a plane of feeling that transcended physical pleasure. When Verna climaxed again, the tightly wound springs inside him broke loose and his groan was long, ecstatic as his own orgasm burst through him.

Minutes passed and they lay close to each other.

'God, but I needed you!' Jim murmured, caressing her shoulder.

Verna Fletcher savoured the words. Any other man would have said 'God, but I needed *that*' – if he had said anything at all. But Jim admitted having needed *her*.

She smiled. 'More of the same?' She kept her tone light, almost flippant.

'More. Only not the same.' He kissed her lips and Verna

revelled in his touch, in the feel of him. 'Let's be slow, easy this time.'

Verna's built-in timing mechanism functioned perfectly. She knew the day would be important for both of them, and she awoke a few minutes after 10 A.M., fully alert. There was much to be done, and they could not be late for their noon appointment, but she indulged herself in a long affectionate look at Jim Northcutt, relaxed in sleep, yet strong and comforting against her.

We've lasted almost six months together, Verna reflected. It was a record for both of them. Her eyes with their long lashes were soft as they gazed at his rugged handsomeness in no way marred by the white scar on his chin or the slight misalignment of his nose that had been broken in some long forgotten barroom fight. They weren't in love with each other in any conventional sense of the word, and they both knew it, recognizing their relationship for what it was, a symbiosis of human need that had been previously lacking in their lives.

Verna knew she should wake Jim, but she delayed. Before the day was out, they would not only be lovers but business partners, too. Intuition told her this would cause their relationship to undergo a degree of change. But how great a degree and what effect would it have on them personally? Experience had taught her that even the most minor changes often had far-reaching effects, that nothing 'after' ever really remained exactly as it had been 'before'. Suddenly, and for no reason she could explain, Verna felt bittersweet nostalgia as she thought back to the first time she had met James Northcutt.

It had been shortly after Jim arrived in Osage County to work for the McMan Oil Company as a driller. He had a night off and visited Verna's bordello because he had been told it was the best of all the numerous parlourhouses and brothels in Logan.

Ushered into the parlour with its striped-paper walls, heavy velvet curtains and ornate couches and chairs protected by crocheted antimacassars, he found half a dozen men already gathered there. They were drinking and making the usual bawdy jokes with Verna's girls. Jim took an immediate interest in a lively chestnut-haired girl. It might have ended then, with Jim having a few drinks and going off to bed with her, but before he could, Verna Fletcher entered the parlour.

A beefy, hard-drinking man no one seemed to know, who said he was a lease broker from Texas, took one look at Verna and demanded that she spend the night with him. As owner of the bordello, Verna was under no obligation to entertain customers. If she went to bed with a man it was because she liked him, and the Texan repelled her. She refused. The lease broker assumed she was merely trying to pry some more money out of him.

'Piece of ass like yours is something special,' he sniggered, grasping her arm. 'You're worth a few extra bucks. Let's go.'

Verna tried to pull herself free. The other men saw that the Texan was brawny and vicious and were reluctant to interfere. Only Jim Northcutt got to his feet, stepping between Verna and the lease broker.

'Relax, mister,' Jim said, his voice deceptively affable. 'Leave the lady alone.'

'Lady?' the Texan sneered. 'Listen, any cunt that works in a whorehouse's got to fuck. Now beat it!'

Jim's answering smile was deceptive. He didn't move. The Texan shoved Verna aside, swung a wide haymaking punch. Northcutt ducked it easily, drove one big fist into the lease broker's whisky-bloated belly, rabbit-punched him with the other. The man spewed vomit, fell heavily to the floor and lay there unconscious.

'Somebody toss him out,' Northcutt said to the other men in the parlour, who were now only too glad to oblige.

Verna Fletcher was grateful to the tall, black-haired young driller. Although his face was youthful, it had been weathered by the sun and wind and cold of numberless God-forsaken drilling sites. His air and manner were those of a mature, self-sufficient man. She invited Jim to have a drink with her in the kitchen. They talked freely and openly. Each, they soon realized, was a loner and maverick. Yet each was lonely too, and hungry for close human companionship.

Later, Verna took Jim upstairs to her private apartment. He remained with her until the following afternoon, when he had to start back for the fields to work his night tour on a McMan Oil drilling rig. They had gratified each other fully while experiencing a fleeting sense of emotional reassurance.

'It was great,' Jim told her.

'That it was, my friend,' Verna agreed. 'That it was.'

Less than a week later, Jim moved in with Verna. He continued to work night tours while living and sleeping in her apartment during the day. The arrangement between them was without conditions or commitments save for the tacit understanding that the relationship would continue only as long as it remained satisfying to both. They grew close, yet avoided any deep emotional involvement that might breed its own self-destruction.

At least we've managed to keep it like that so far, Verna thought. She could no longer put off waking Jim. She wound some of his coal black hair around a forefinger, then tugged

'Time to get up, Jim.'

He mumbled something without opening his eyes. His right hand moved, searched, found one of her firm breasts, cupped it, the ball of his thumb rubbing the nipple, pressing it when it sprang erect.

'Not this morning.' Verna laughed, edging away. 'We've got other things to do – remember, partner?'

His eyes opened.

'Yeah,' he grumbled, then snapped awake and grinned. 'We don't have to rush, though.' He reached for her. Jim, too, realized that their relationship was about to take on an entirely new dimension.

'Abe said we should be at his place before twelve,' Verna said. 'By the time we get ready and dressed, we'll just about make it.'

'Wouldn't you rather . . . ?'

'Sure.' She laughed as she slid out of bed. 'But if we rathered, we'd be in bed all morning.'

Verna was right, Jim told himself, and now the tension returned. They would close the deal in the Peavey property that day, take care of all the preliminary formalities, so he could start drilling as soon as possible. That was what counted. He rose from the large brass bed and went to a washbasin standing on a commode. He filled the basin with water from a big glazed earthenware pitcher and began washing himself. He heard Verna laugh delightedly and turned to stare at her.

'It just hit me!' she said. 'I'm about to go into a legitimate business for the first time in my life!'

Her spirits remained high while they dressed and went downstairs. The girls were still asleep in their rooms. Only Celia, the pretty Negro maid, was up, and she made breakfast for them. After they'd eaten, Verna and Jim got into his Ford, parked in front of the house.

In 1921, Logan, Oklahoma, had a permanent population of some one thousand two hundred. However, an army of over seven thousand five hundred men working the surrounding oil fields could only choose between Logan and Stainesville when they wanted to have the use of a woman for an hour or a night or go on their payday sprees. The dismal town of Logan prospered mightily.

Logan proper clung precariously to the sides of Cedar Hill, a topographical freak rising unaccountably from an expanse of flatland forested with several hundred oil derricks. Its unpaved main street – Cedar Hill Avenue – was an implausible abomination. Straight and broad enough for a city fifty times the size of the three-year-old boomtown, it sharp-angled up one side of 'The Hill' and down the other. The steepness of its gradient required that the shoddy wooden sidewalks be terraced. At the end of every fifteen or twenty lineal feet of duckboard walkway there were steps, then another stretch of sidewalk and again steps. The walkways were set flush against solid rows of ramshackle, boxlike frame commercial structures. Most had only one storey, none had more than two – and of these, more than a few were false-fronted.

Jim Northcutt now had to retrace part of the route he had taken early in the morning, when he had come into Logan from the fields. He drove along the unpaved side street on which Verna's bordello and three other similar establishments were located, turned right onto Cedar Hill Avenue. At 11.30 A.M. on a Thursday, the town enjoyed relative peace and quiet, but the drive was neither pleasant nor quick.

The day when oilmen would recognize natural gas as an energy source no less valuable than oil was still in the future. In most fields, natural gas was considered a useless and potentially dangerous nuisance and flared off, burned at the wellheads. Millions of cubic feet of gas were flared in the fields around Logan every day, and layers of grimy black smoke hung over the town.

Along Cedar Hill Avenue animal hooves, iron-shod wagon and buggy wheels and automobile tyres churned up stifling clouds of dust. Traffic on Cedar Hill Avenue – the only route in or out of Logan – was a lunatic snarl. Scores of mule- or horse-drawn freight wagons moved in both directions. Those headed west were heavily loaded, bound for the drilling sites. Those going east were empty, returning to railheads and storage points where they would load additional supplies and equipment and take them to the fields.

Going uphill, the traffic stream crawled at a speed no faster than a crippled man could hobble. Moving downhill, it flowed a little more rapidly, but there was always danger that an overloaded wagon might get out of control and crush whatever was in its path.

Jim's Ford laboured up the eastern slope of The Hill. He cursed silently. Verna Fletcher tried to wipe grime and dust from her face with a lace-trimmed handkerchief. When he reached the summit of Cedar Hill, Jim felt better. The traffic ahead of him gathered speed. A few hundred yards farther on, he turned left onto a side street.

'Ten minutes in this town and you're dirtier than if you pulled a double tour on a rotary rig,' Jim grumbled. Like all oil field workers, he pronounced *tour* as *tower*.

'We're almost at Abe's place,' Verna smiled. 'Maybe he'll let you spend the afternoon paddling around in that museum piece he calls a bathtub.'

3

Abraham Schlechter's bathtub was justly famous in Logan, which could boast of having only six in the entire town. Three parlourhouses, including Verna's, each had one. There was another in the Sooner Hotel. A fifth belonged to Logan's best barber. But these were all primitive specimens compared to the regal model Abe Schlechter had imported from Chicago. Abe's bathtub was enormous, large enough for the tallest of men to immerse his entire body. The tub, which stood on gilt claw-and-ball feet, had shiny taps and spouts. Enamel nymphs and satyrs cavorted along its outside surfaces. A huge boiler provided hot water.

Abe Schlechter was the proprietor of the Schlechter Oil Well Supply Company. He dealt with small independent operators who bought drilling and pumping equipment in minimal quantities consistent with their immediate needs, often on credit. Every oil boomtown had such a small-scale supply house. More than a few wildcatters became millionaires only because dealers like Abe Schlechter carried them on the cuff until they brought in their first producing wells.

Local supply stores also served as places where oilmen could meet, trade gossip and rumour, start deals and close them. All had bulletin boards on which men could tack messages or notices announcing there was something they wished to buy, sell or exchange. Abe Schlechter had added other services and conveniences. These included an extra telephone and the huge, gaudy bathtub. Schlechter allowed free use of these amenities, and men from the fields frequently stood in line waiting their turn at one or the other.

Many oil well supply 'retailers' in the mid-continent fields were, like Abe Schlechter, Jewish. Very often, they were the only Jews in the boomtowns. Although accepted (even welcomed) as businessmen, they were frequently isolated (or even ostracized) socially. Abe Schlechter fared better than most. Veteran oilmen were amazed by his knowledge of drilling and production, grateful for the time- and money-saving advice and tips he gave them. The Jew, they agreed, sure as hell knew the oil business.

Abe was forty-seven. Before coming to the United States in 1901, he had worked in the Borislav oil fields of his native Galicia. There, wells had been drilled to three thousand five hundred feet and more when American oilmen were still inclined to abandon operations if they didn't hit pay sand at half that depth. Galician drillers had long since solved numerous technical problems that continued to plague Americans.

As an immigrant, Schlechter joined relatives in Chicago, where he went into the junk business, learned English and married. He progressed to trading in used machinery and fathered three children – a firstborn son, Samuel, and two daughters. By 1919 he had amassed a modest amount of capital and decided to combine old oil fields experience with what he'd learned dealing in machinery.

He set out for Oklahoma. However, he did not want his wife and children to live in a helldorado environment. He left them in Chicago, visiting them there several times a year. They would join him when he had made enough money to expand his business and settle in a larger, more stable community such as Tulsa or Oklahoma City. In the meantime, a man with a man's physical needs, Abe Schlechter patronized Verna Fletcher's bordello once each week. He invariably spent the entire night. Always with the same girl, a plump and good-natured brunette who, Schlechter guiltily admitted to himself, reminded him of his wife when she was younger.

Being a regular customer, Abe enjoyed a special status at the parlourhouse. He was well liked, for he was generous, held his liquor and never caused trouble. The lean, balding Jewish supply dealer with sad, almost spaniel-like eyes was a favourite client. Verna Fletcher often had long conversations with him. She enjoyed hearing his stories of life in Europe and of his experiences in America. She was also aware of his reputation as an expert on oil drilling and production.

Jim Northcutt had been living with Verna for only a few weeks when he first told her of his ambition to become an independent operator. She brought the subject up on several occasions after that, questioning Jim, learning that he had saved up a little over five thousand dollars towards a stake to finance the venture. It was a fair start, she knew, but by no means enough, for the costs of drilling an exploration well could run to twenty-five thousand dollars and even more.

Then, without Jim's knowledge, she had a talk with Abe Schlechter. She related all that Jim Northcutt had told her about his hopes and plans.

'Why tell me, Verna?' Abe asked, puzzled.

'Because I'd like your advice. I've been thinking I could do worse than invest a little of my own money,' Verna replied. She saw Abe's knowing smile, shook her blonde head. 'Wrong guess. I don't want to make any kept man out of Jim. I'm out for myself.'

Verna was a bordello madam only because she knew of no other way to make an equally comfortable living. She dreamed of one day having sufficient money to move elsewhere, become 'respectable', perhaps marry advantageously. Oil could bring wealth and much of it. An investment in a successful wild-catting venture could bring large returns.

'Do me a favour, Abe,' she went on. 'Talk to Jim. Find out if he's really got what it takes. I think he has, but I don't know anything about oil.'

Schlechter laughed. 'Only one thing is sure about the oil business. It's a gamble. There aren't any guarantees that you'll find oil when you drill. I'll do what you ask, though.'

During the next few weeks, Abe and Jim Northcutt had several long conversations about oil and the petroleum industry. Abe quickly realized that the young driller not only knew the business, but was ahead of his time.

Originally, American oilmen drilled where crude had seeped to the surface. Later, when most such areas had been exploited, they became fixed on the idea of drilling on anticlines, folds of underground strata in which the sides sloped down in opposite directions from a ridge at the peak. Sometimes they were right; sometimes not. In Oklahoma fewer than half the producing wells were on anticlines. The rest had been discovered by random – by 'hunch' – drilling. James Northcutt was one who refused to accept the anticlinal theory as an article of faith.

'Oil migrates through porous strata,' he argued. 'There's no reason why it can't be found in other structures and formations.'

'They've been thinking that in Europe for years,' Schlechter nodded. 'Found a lot of oil thinking it, too.'

Abe eventually narrowed down their discussions.

'Verna tells me you want to wildcat, Jim.'

'She's right. Soon's I have a big enough stake.'

'Where?'

'Here in Oklahoma. Not much more than twenty miles from where we're sitting right now, Abe. I've spotted a piece of land I figure is swimming in oil, and from what I hear, the guy who owns it'll grant a lease or lease option for next to nothing.'

Abe Schlechter eyed Jim sceptically. Leases on promising properties in Osage County were bringing three thousand dollars and more an acre.

'The big oil companies know every inch of ground in Osage County,' he pointed out. 'How come they haven't grabbed the bargain?'

'Simple. The property was prospected a year ago. Magnolia Petroleum drilled four test wells.'

'And?'

'They were all dusters. Magnolia gave up its lease.'

'An outfit the size of Magnolia doesn't make many mistakes.'

'It did in this case.' Jim lit a cigarette. 'The geology geniuses drilled in the wrong places. They were after anticlines. I'd drill further north. I'm certain there's oil there.'

'Certain?' Abe's tone was tolerant but dubious. 'Why? Who can be certain of oil?'

'How the hell can I explain it.' Jim exhaled smoke through his nostrils. 'It's a feeling. Call it creekology if you want.'

Creekology was a term coined by oilmen to describe an uncanny sense of surface geology that a few men possessed innately and a few others somehow managed to develop. It was undefinable, a mysterious instinct or intuition.

'A feeling like a twitch in the crotch, maybe?' Schlechter asked, his large dark eyes narrowing, his expression serious.

'That's it. Exactly.'

The supply dealer nodded. There were men who could sense the presence of petroleum even if it was thousands of feet below ground. Men like Tom Slick and T. N. Barnsdall and Lyman Stewart – and they had become multi-millionaires. Natural laws couldn't explain the wild talent that made some men natural oil dowsers. They responded to the hidden presence of crude viscerally, even sexually.

'Doesn't surprise me,' he mused aloud. 'In Galicia I saw men who got hard-ons when they walked across ground that had oil under it. It should happen to me. My schmuck is a real schmuck. From oil, it doesn't even get a tickle.'

Although Abe Schlechter spoke excellent and only slightly accented English, he occasionally used Yiddish words and expressions. Jim had never heard the word *schmuck* before but guessed its meaning and chuckled, nodding agreement. Actual sexual responses to oil weren't all that unusual.

'I've been around guys who actually came in their pants when a well blew in,' he declared. 'Happened automatically.'

Jim himself had never had that experience. However, well completions did arouse him sexually. When oil began to geyser or flow, his first impulse was to hurry from the drilling site and find a woman. It was a familiar reaction in the fields and oilmen spoke about it often. But then, countless oilmen were acutely conscious of the sexual implications inherent – and evident – in almost all phases of oil drilling and production.

Jim's mind raced ahead of the conversation, veered off on a tangent, and he shook his head.

'Oil, money, sex, power – they all seem to go together, don't they?' he said.

'A philosopher, yet,' Abe grinned. 'But you're right. They

do.' He paused, looked at Jim closely. 'And you want as much as you can get of all of them, Jim.'

Northcutt was silent for a moment. It was perhaps the first time he had been confronted by a conscious realization of his deepest desires.

'Yes,' he said. 'I sure as hell do.'

Abraham Schlechter came to have even more confidence in Jim's instincts and abilities than Verna Fletcher had. He decided that he, too, would gamble on James Northcutt. He announced his decision to Jim and Verna in mid-May.

'You have around five thousand in cash, Jim,' he said. 'Verna says she'll match that. I'll put up the machinery and equipment —'

'That'll be worth more than five thousand,' Jim interrupted. 'Closer to seven, seven-five, maybe more.'

'Maybe,' Abe shrugged. 'But you'll be doing the actual work. So let's make it a straight three-way partnership.' Then he laughed.

'What's funny?' Verna asked.

'Some partnership!' Abe chortled. 'Jim's an orphan who ran away from his aunt and uncle's home. You own what the upright citizens call a disorderly house – and me they call the Town Yid. A partnership between three *oysvorfs* with a *bissel* of *sachel* and a lot of *chutzpah*, as we say in Yiddish – three outcasts with a little common sense and a lot of nerve,' he translated.

Verna and Jim joined in the laughter. The description, they agreed, was perfect.

A few days later, they retained an attorney and had partnership papers drawn up. Then they began negotiations with George Peavey, the farmer who owned the land on which Jim wanted to drill. Peavey retained his own counsel, and the negotiations became somewhat complicated and drawn out. But final agreement was reached at last. That was why Jim and Verna were going to Abe Schlechter's store shortly before noon on 14 June 1921. George Peavey, his attorney and their own lawyer would be meeting there to close the deal on a lease option covering the property. All the necessary legal documents would be finally signed, sealed and delivered . . .

4

Jim Northcutt angle-parked in front of the flat-roofed, un-painted Schlechter Oil Well Supply Company store.

'I'll get Abe,' he said to Verna, kissing her cheek.

He got out of the car and went into the store. The interior was divided in two by a long counter. Behind it, floor-to-ceiling racks and bins were filled with tools, smaller spare parts and other items used in drilling wells and producing oil. The space in front of the counter was taken up by chairs, cuspidors, the traditional bulletin board and some tables piled with news-papers and magazines. On the right were a wall-mounted tele-phone and a door leading to the addition built to accommodate Abe Schlechter's renowned bathtub. Several oilmen lounged in the chairs smoking, chewing tobacco, reading, talking. Some had clean clothes and towels with them; they were waiting to use the tub. Jim exchanged greetings with two men he recog-nized.

'Hear you had some tussle last night,' one said.

Jim said nothing, hoping the subject would be dropped.

'Jack Donovan's saying you done a public service,' the man persisted. 'Guy you killed was wanted in six states.'

'That so?' Northcutt moved on towards the corner cubicle that was Abraham Schlechter's private office and found him busy with a customer.

'You and Verna go back to the house,' Abe said. 'I'll be there in a minute. The others should be along soon.'

Jim helped Verna down from the Ford. They walked around to the rear of the store. Fifty yards behind it was a frame house resembling an oversized packing crate, flanked on one side by a stable and on the other by a metal-roofed warehouse. Canvas tarpaulins covered bulky gear stored in the open.

They were greeted by Lily Sleeping Moon, an old and enormously fat Choctaw Indian woman who served as Abe Schlechter's housekeeper and cook. 'You come in,' Lily said. 'I make coffee.'

Lily Sleeping Moon evidently sensed the importance of the occasion. The spartan living room was freshly cleaned and dusted; there was even a vase with fresh flowers. Jim folded his big frame into a scuffed armchair. Verna went into the kitchen to ask for warm water and a mirror, to wash off the dust and rearrange her windblown hair.

Northcutt leaned back and closed his eyes. We sign today, he reflected. Then the real work begins, with all the usual risks – plus the time squeeze. George Peavey, the farmer who owned the land on which Jim wanted to drill, at first had seemed willing to grant a standard gas and oil lease on his 640-acre property. Then he had unaccountably changed his mind. He would grant only a sixty-day lease option. An exploration well would have to be completed in that period. If it was a producer, a regular lease would be granted automatically. If not, work would have to be abandoned.

The conditions had been accepted for three reasons. Peavey asked only one thousand dollars cash bonus payment. Jim Northcutt's hunch about there being oil on the land was overpowering. And, he felt confident he could complete the first well within sixty days.

Verna returned, her face clean and her hair neatly combed. Lily Sleeping Moon waddled behind her carrying a tray loaded with coffeepot, cups and saucers. She put the tray on a table just as the front door opened. Abe Schlechter ushered three men inside.

'Judge' Henry Kendall, the partners' attorney, was in his sixties and tall and distinguished. George Peavey, a leathery middle-aged farmer, wore clean overalls. His lawyer, Reese Lawson, was many years younger and had an air of impatience about him.

Jim had not met Reese Lawson before and took an instant dislike to him. Lawson's manner indicated he had little regard for his own client and even less taste for dealing with an ordinary driller, the proprietress of a brothel and the Town Jew. Lawson deals from the bottom of the deck, Northcutt's intuition warned.

The two attorneys passed around copies of the lease-option agreement, reviewing its provisions. Effective two days later, on 16 June, it stated that if oil was discovered within sixty days, the partners would have a regular lease and could drill additional wells. George Peavey was to receive royalties equivalent to one-eighth the value of all crude produced.

'Note that if no oil is found, the lessees must abandon all work,' Lawson pointed out. 'They must either move all equipment off the property, or Mr Peavey may permit them to sell it *in situ*.'

Northcutt picked up a note in Reese Lawson's voice. The first sign of sharks, he thought. Lawson hopes I'll find traces of oil without actually bringing in a producer. Then somebody he's fronting for will try to buy our rig for next to nothing and continue drilling. The bastards are going to be disappointed. I'll complete that well if I have to make hole by chewing down through the rock.

At last, the ritual of signing the papers was completed. George Peavey stood up.

'When do I get my money?' he asked.

'Right now, Mr Peavey.' Henry Kendall held out a cheque.

Peavey glanced at Lawson. 'Didn't Cade say we was to get cash?'

'It's a bank cheque,' Kendall told him. 'Good as cash.'

Peavey and Lawson left almost immediately. When they'd gone, Jim Northcutt frowned.

' "Didn't Cade say we was to get cash?" ' he repeated George Peavey's words. 'Who's Cade? What's he got to do with this deal?'

Abe Schlechter looked dour. 'Only guy I know by that name is Everett Cade, a lease hound who shows up in town every now and then.'

'That particular Cade's been involved in some phoney stock promotions,' Henry Kendall said. 'I had no idea he even knew Peavey. He could mean some kind of trouble —'

'Anybody who doesn't expect trouble shouldn't try wildcatting,' Jim shrugged. He got to his feet. The new 'Cade' element could be forgotten for the moment. 'Thanks for everything, Judge.' He turned to Schlechter. 'I'll see you early in the morning, Abe. Verna and I'll be moving along.'

'Wait, Jim,' Verna said. She went to her dresser, opened a drawer, took out a small box and gave it to him. It was embossed with the name of an Oklahoma City jewellery store. 'It's for luck, with an awful lot of' – she almost said 'love' – 'with an awful lot of high hopes.'

Jim opened the box. A tiny object gleamed against blue velvet. He plucked it out with two big fingers and saw an exquisitely fashioned replica of a gusher. Derrick and rig front were made of gold. Black onyx set above the crown block in a plume represented spouting oil.

'A sort of charm for your watch chain,' Verna said, smiling because he was obviously greatly pleased.

He took her in his arms. His kiss, tender and affectionate at first, quickly turned ravenous. God, but I need *you*, she wanted to say, but didn't. Instead, when they were undressed, she gently pushed him down on the bed.

'There, partner – flat on your back.' She kept her tone light and bantering. 'You need special care today.'

Hours had passed.

They had been napping. Not for long, though. Celia dropped something with a loud crash downstairs. The sound awakened Verna and her stirrings woke Jim. He kissed her neck.

'At least I know you don't have another girl,' Verna Fletcher said, her fingertips tracing patterns on his bare chest.

'Oh? Having me watched?'

'Uh-uh.' Verna had often heard a pair of oil field terms she thought would be fitting. 'I checked your flow meter and gauged your gallonage.'

Jim laughed. All the more because Verna's manner reiterated what he found so gratifying in their relationship. It had a free and easy quality without any attempt on Verna's part to be possessive.

Abe Schlechter appeared edgy when Jim arrived at his house shortly after seven the next morning. They drank coffee together.

'I spent yesterday afternoon asking questions,' Abe said.

'Get any answers?'

'None I wanted to hear. Reese Lawson and Everett Cade are like this.' Abe held up two closed fingers. 'The combination doesn't smell right.' He swallowed coffee moodily. 'Cade's a Texan. He's supposed to have a tie-in with some major company.'

'That figures,' Jim said with a casual shrug.

Crooked lease hounds operated in many ways. Sometimes they worked on their own account, obtaining gas and oil leases for little or no money and selling them at high prices to gullible buyers. At other times, they acted as front men for well-organized lease grabbers or even large oil companies that wanted to appropriate a small operator's holdings.

74

'Look, Abe,' Jim said, rolling a cigarette. 'We aren't exactly virgins in this business. Start hunting for oil, and you're bound to have thieves circling around.'

'With people like Cade, we could have real problems.' Abe's face, always thin, now seemed gaunt. He knew that lease grabbers cared about ends, not means.

'Don't get nervous,' Northcutt grinned. 'Anybody out to screw us will wait until we've done some serious drilling. Our only problem now is to spud in our well. Every day counts.'

Schlechter sighed, then became businesslike.

'I can have the first supply loads rolling tomorrow,' he said. 'I've also lined up a labour gang. You set with your drilling crews?'

Jim nodded. 'I signed on men I've worked with before. They're tough and I can trust them.'

Northcutt spent the day and early evening at Abe Schlechter's store preparing lists of supplies and equipment needed to begin operations. He excluded certain items that oil well supply dealers didn't stock – and besides, he didn't want Abe to know he felt they might be needed.

On his way back to Verna's, Jim stopped on Cedar Hill Avenue and went into the Logan Hardware Emporium. He bought two double-barrelled 12-gauge shotguns, a ·45 calibre Colt revolver and a box of ammunition for each weapon. Experience had taught James Northcutt that the surest means of avoiding trouble lay in being able to give more than others could dish out. When it came to insurance and ounces of prevention, nothing outweighed 00-shot and ·45 calibre lead slugs.

Across Cedar Hill Avenue and several doors down from the Hardware Emporium, lights still burned in the office of Reese Lawson, attorney-at-law. Bare bulbs dangling from the ceiling cast uncertain light, for Logan's electric generating plant was unreliable.

Reese Lawson's feet were up on his desk. He was talking to Everett Cade, telling him of developments that had taken place during Cade's most recent absence in Texas.

'. . . and they signed yesterday,' Lawson concluded his account.

Cade, short-necked and beefy, sprawled in a leather armchair.

'What've you racked up for us so far?' he asked.

'Seventeen leases covering about two thousand acres.'

'We'll make a bundle,' Cade said.

Their scheme was an oil fields perennial – a perfectly legal swindle. Cade had scented opportunity when he first heard that someone was interested in drilling on George Peavey's property. He sought out Peavey and befriended him, advising the farmer to grant only a sixty-day option and to retain Reese Lawson as his attorney. Since he was seldom in Logan, Cade then allowed Lawson to take over.

Many farms surrounding Peavey's had also been prospected by various companies in the past and judged to bear no oil. The companies had abandoned their leases. All rights reverted back to the disappointed farmers who owned the properties. Oilmen had no further interest in them. Only someone with a strong hunch about a particular tract – such as Northcutt had about the Peavey property – would gamble on further exploration. In such circumstances, speculators often offered landowners 'a dollar and other considerations' deals. They paid a token dollar for a lease covering an entire tract. While they made no specific commitment to drill, the owners were to receive royalties as, if and when oil was discovered on their lands.

Once he had been retained by Peavey, Reese Lawson stalled the negotiations with Jim Northcutt and his partners. He gained time to talk seventeen farmers who still dreamed of oil riches into granting 'dollar' leases to a dummy corporation he represented as a 'big Texas syndicate'.

Cade and Lawson had no intention of prospecting for oil. They were blowing a bubble. News of renewed exploration on the Peavey tract would spread fast and far and create a wave of oil fever. The value of leases on adjoining properties would skyrocket as credulous people would clamour to buy lease shares. Inevitably, they and the property owners would be cheated. Cade and Lawson would profit – and handsomely.

And, there was a chance that James Northcutt's hunch was valid. This is why Cade and Lawson convinced George Peavey he should not grant a standard lease. The sixty-day limit put Northcutt and his partners in a tight bind. If drilling indicated the presence of oil, any number of stratagems could be used to prevent the well from being completed before the deadline. Then Cade and Lawson could take over the lease, bring in the producing wells and make even more profits without having spent a penny on the initial exploration costs. It was, Everett

Cade gloated, all foolproof.

'Soon's a derrrick goes up on Peavey's land, the yokels're bound to go wild,' he said to Reese Lawson. 'They'll stampede to buy shares in those leases you bought for a buck apiece.' He shifted his bulk, sat upright. 'We been gabbing long enough. Let's find some booze and pussy.'

'I'm for that,' Lawson said. 'How about Verna Fletcher's?'

'Not there! Not on a bet!'

'Why not?' the lawyer asked, puzzled.

'Because I said no,' Cade replied. If Lawson hadn't heard how he'd been knocked unconscious there by some young driller one night, all the better. Memory of the episode still rankled.

Mention of Verna had set Lawson to musing aloud.

'Weird set-up,' he grimaced. 'All three were there to sign yesterday – the whore, the hebe and Northcutt. 'Course, he shacks with her —'

'Who does?' Cade asked.

'Northcutt. Ever hear how they got started?'

The lease hound said no, and Lawson laughed.

'Seems Northcutt breezed into her place one night about five, six months ago and slugged some drunk who was trying to lay her —'

'Hold on! I never met this Northcutt. What's he look like?'

'He's big. Over six foot. With black hair and grey eyes —'

'And a nose that must've been busted some time?'

'That's him,' Lawson nodded. 'Then you do know the guy.'

'Uh – not really,' Cade lied. 'Just seen him around.' Funny how things work out, he thought. So James Northcutt is the son of a bitch. Now I can pay him back double.

'Come on,' he said and got to his feet. 'There're other whorehouses in this town besides Verna Fletcher's.'

His eyes gleamed. He was contemplating how he could balance accounts with James Northcutt. And with Verna Fletcher.

5

George Peavey's land, located in the south-eastern corner of Osage County, was served by a barely negotiable farm road. Jim Northcutt, his men and the first wagon loads of material arrived at the property early on the morning of 16 June 1921.

They set to work immediately, and twelve days later much had been accomplished.

A stream had been cleared to provide water, an access road levelled and pine-plank bunkhouse, cook shack and storage sheds built. The steam engine to power drilling tools, draw works, pumps, electric generator and other machinery was installed and operational. A derrick had been erected over the spot where Jim intended to drill. Four timber legs stood upright, tapering from base to crown block, and were laced together with wooden cross-braces, forming a slender eighty-two-foot-high skeletal pyramid.

At dawn on 28 June, everything was almost ready for the spudding operation that marked the start of actual drilling. Jim gulped down his breakfast and spoke with Luke Rayburn, the driller he had hired, who was his number two man on the site.

'I'm going into Logan,' Jim announced. He hadn't been there since they'd started work. He had remained on the site and slept in the bunkhouse with the hired hands. 'Wrap up the loose ends. I'll be back this afternoon, and we'll spud in tomorrow morning.'

A rugged, pockmarked man of twenty-six, Luke Rayburn was an oil fields veteran and topnotch driller. He had worked with Northcutt on jobs with various companies in the past and did not hesitate to concede that, although five years his junior, Jim Northcutt was the better driller.

'No sweat,' Rayburn grinned. 'We'll be all set.'

The main Stainesville–Logan road was clogged with two-way traffic jolting painfully over ruts and potholes. There were animal-drawn freighters, farm wagons, buggies, Model T Fords, occasional Chevvies and Dodges – all uniformly shrouded with thick dust.

Jim could only drive at the speed set by the slowest vehicle in the line ahead of him, and eyed the countryside to right and left. The road was flanked by flush, proven oil fields. There were derricks everywhere. Others were being built at top speed, with agile riggers scrambling over the unfinished structures, racing to complete them.

The Law of Capture, Jim thought. This legal doctrine had shaped the nature of the oil industry. Established long ago by the courts, it held that oil in its natural state was like the wild beast in the jungle, belonging to whoever was the first to capture it.

An underground oil zone could extend beneath the properties owned or leased by any number of different firms or individuals. Since all drew from the same subterranean reservoir, which contained only so much crude oil, competition was frantic and fierce. The more wells an operator drilled, the better chance he had of bringing up – of 'capturing' – more oil than his neighbours.

No wonder the dividing line between Law of Capture and Law of the Jungle was often invisible in the oil business, Jim reflected. Yet, he breathed the smell of crude and, like all oilmen, found it stimulating, evocative, as sweet as the money and power it represented.

Jim was astonished to find the usual loungers in Abe Schlechter's store speaking in low tones and watching their language. The mystery unravelled when he went to Abe's cubicle office. There was a young woman with Schlechter. Apparently she was about to leave. To Jim's knowledge, no female other than Lily Sleeping Moon had ever set foot inside the store.

She wasn't more than twenty-three and dressed in mourning. Northcutt glimpsed auburn hair and hazel eyes.

'This is Jim Northcutt,' Abe said. 'Jim, Mrs Nancy Tappen.'

Her face was oval and her handshake firm, Jim noted.

'How do you do, Mr Northcutt.'

Their eyes met. Jim mumbled the appropriate words.

'I really must leave,' Nancy Tappen said. The hazel eyes seemed to convey some message, Jim thought, then decided he only imagined it.

Abe accompanied her out of the store, returning a moment later.

'Beautiful girl,' Jim said cautiously. 'Too bad she's in mourning. Friend of yours, Abe?'

'Her husband was a wildcatter, one of my customers. He died last month. She's settling up his account gradually.'

'Oh.' Jim busied himself rolling a cigarette. 'She live here?' God knows, I'd sure remember if I'd ever seen her before.'

'She lives in Pawhuska.'

Nancy Tappen had worn a light, fresh cologne. Its scent lingered. Northcutt made a conspicuous effort to ignore it.

'We're spudding in tomorrow,' he said.

'Terrific!' Schlechter beamed. 'You seeing Verna today?'

'Sure. After I leave here. Anybody using the tub?'

'Don't think so. Help yourself.'

'Will in a minute.' Jim cocked his right eyebrow. 'Heard any more rumours I should know about?'

'The whole county's been talking up a new oil boom ever since you started work on the Peavey property.'

'Because we're shoestringing an exploration well?'

'May be other reasons. Cade and Lawson bought up a lot of leases on surrounding properties. Claim they represent a big syndicate. They're hoping to cash in somehow.'

'I smell a phoney promotion,' Jim said, wrinkling his nose. Then he grinned. 'I smell myself, too. I'm going to take that bath.'

Freshly scrubbed and dressed in clean clothes, Jim went to Verna's.

'You best go straight up,' Celia, the maid, told him. 'Miss Verna's been moping like you been gone for months.'

He hurried upstairs and along the corridor that led to Verna's apartment. He was quiet, not wanting to wake the girls who were sleeping in the other rooms. Reaching her door, he rattled the knob.

'Celia?' Verna's voice was sleepy, indistinct.

'It's me, Jim.'

Seconds later, the door was unlocked, flung open. Verna took his hand, pulled him into the sitting room, and he was kissing her. She slid from his embrace, led him into the bedroom.

'Bed's been awful empty with just me in it,' she said. Her voice was throaty. 'How long can you stay?'

'Two hours at the outside.'

Her smile was mischievous.

'Not outside,' she said. 'Inside.' She laughed happily and her hands were unfastening his belt and the buttons of his trousers.

An oil well borehole had to be sixty feet deep before a full string of drilling tools could be suspended from the rig's walking beam and the task of punching down into formation rock begun in earnest. Drilling commenced with the use of a spudding bit. Attached to a jerk line suspended from the crown block, the bit was raised and dropped until the initial sixty-foot depth was reached. The first drop of spudding bit marked the actual beginnings, though.

'She dropped right,' Luke Rayburn observed, after the spudding bit took its first bite of earth. 'It's a good sign, Jim.'

'That isn't,' Northcutt said, pointing in the general direction of the farm road that led past the Peavey property. Although it was barely dawn, the vanguard of a parade of vehicles was turning onto the access road, coming towards the drilling site. In places as acutely oil-conscious as Oklahoma, word that a well was being spudded on unproven land always drew sightseers.

'Keep 'em the hell away from the rig,' Jim ordered two of his roustabouts.

They managed to keep all the gawkers away but one, a pudgy, self-important individual. He proclaimed himself the editor of the *Sentinel*, Osage County's leading weekly newspaper. He wasted half an hour of Jim Northcutt's time asking questions.

'Can't get the story in before next week's edition,' he said before departing. 'But it'll be on the front page.'

Jim couldn't quite see why his venture would rate front-page space, but shrugged and went back to work.

'That bastard!' Jim swore angrily a few days later when he saw a copy of the *Sentinel*. Luke Rayburn was standing nearby with Will Dubbs, a beetle-browed tool dresser with a heavyweight wrestler's build.

'You sound awful pissed off, Boss,' Will Dubbs said.

'Listen to this shit!' Jim snorted. 'Headline says "Big Syndicate To Prospect. Organizers See Huge New Oil Boom." What a crock!'

'So what?' Luke Rayburn said.

'I don't like being used to help chisellers screw the poor

dumb jerks who'll get taken, that's what.' Jim tossed the paper aside. It was obvious that Everett Cade and Reese Lawson were pulling out all stops in efforts to build public excitement.

Jim appeared at Abraham Schlechter's store on the morning of the eighth day after the well had been spudded in. He was hollow-eyed and grimy.

'I came in to take a bath and give you a list of gear we need,' he told Schlechter.

'You mean you came in to take a bath before seeing Verna,' Abe chuckled. 'See her first. Stop by later in the afternoon and we'll worry about the list then.'

Jim spent almost three hours with Verna Fletcher. They made love feverishly, speaking little, Then he eased himself from the bed and took his watch from the pocket of his trousers. Verna saw the gold-and-onyx gusher charm she'd given him on the chain. After he left, she felt a deep pang of loneliness.

Returning to Abe's, Jim was surprised to meet Nancy Tappen there again. She had evidently ended her mourning. She now wore a bottle-green dress that emphasized the exciting planes and curves of her body.

'Pleased to see you again, Mrs Tappen,' he said. Pleased – and then some. But I only left Verna half an hour ago – and I was drained.

'Call me Nancy.' Her smile was more than a smile.

'Nancy and I have a couple more things to talk about,' Abe said. 'Then she has to catch the train for Pawhuska. Mind waiting, Jim?'

'Not at all,' Jim spoke impulsively. 'It won't take long to go over our list, and if Nancy'll wait, I'll be glad to drive her home.'

'I hate to put you to any trouble – Jim.' Nancy's eyes transmitted a message that aroused Jim even further.

They left together in Jim's car at about three-thirty.

'The trees here are so dreary-looking,' Nancy said when they were a few miles outside Logan. 'What are they?'

'Blackjack and post oak, mostly,' Jim told her.

'We have beautiful trees back home in Rochester, New York. I grew up there – even went to normal school in Rochester.'

'Sorry.' Jim laughed. 'I can't see you as a schoolmarm.'

'Neither could I. That's why – but I don't want to bore you.'

'Won't bore me at all. Tell me.'

'That's why I married Ralph Tappen.'

'What was a 'catter doing in Rochester, for God's sake?'

'Visiting his family.' A sigh. 'He was over thirty. I wasn't even nineteen.' Need any more hints, Jim?

He didn't. He had seen a grove of trees well off the road. He slowed, turned and drove across open country into the grove. He stopped the car and reached for Nancy. She flung herself at him, seized his thumb and thrust it between her lips. Her tongue licked wildly even as her teeth nibbled at the flesh.

Jim pulled his thumb free and climbed out of the Ford. He took a blanket from the trunk and spread it under a tree. Nancy allowed him to lead her to the blanket and ease her down on it. She moaned in pleasure when he began undoing the fastenings of her dress.

Nancy Tappen's body was flawless. She moaned frequently and stammered unintelligible phrases.

What followed was even stranger. The instant they were together, Nancy began flailing her hips wildly against his. She uttered loud cries and raked his back and shoulders with her fingernails. Her movements were clumsy. She climaxed quickly and fiercely and then flung herself away from him and sobbed.

Jim felt both baffled and cheated. She stared up at him, her auburn hair uncoiled.

'I – I wasn't good, was I?' she asked. 'Ralph only did it to me like that five times. He always wanted it another way.'

'How?' Northcutt was genuinely curious. He was still kneeling beside her.

'I'll show you.' He needed only a second to realize that at this, she was anything but clumsy.

Much later, Jim drove Nancy Tappen into Pawhuska. It was after two in the morning when he drove back into Logan. He debated whether or not he should stop by to see Verna for a few minutes. He decided against it. There would still be customers in the parlourhouse. Besides, there were all the fingernail scratches and bite marks with which Nancy Tappen had covered his body. He considered it wiser to skip the visit and return to the drilling site.

6

After sleeping four hours, Jim took over from Luke Rayburn, who'd pulled a double tour while he had been gone.

'Last batch of cuttings the bailer brought up are over there.' Luke yawned before leaving the derrick floor and heading for the cook shack and breakfast.

'Cuttings' were the pulverized rock periodically removed from the borehole. Jim studied them for a moment. Pete Reilly was the day-tour tool dresser, and he was busy at his portable forge pounding a dulled bit with his sledge.

'Hey, Pete!' Jim called to the toolie. 'Have the grunts scare me up a big can and about thirty gallons of water.'

Two roughnecks brought a large galvanized iron can and filled it with water. Jim picked up a shovel and dumped several shovelfuls of cuttings into the can. He then turned his attention to the drilling rig.

The next morning, after having pulled his own double tour to even up with Rayburn, Jim inspected the galvanized iron can and its contents. Peering intently, Jim saw a tiny green-brown patch floating on the surface of the water. Luke Rayburn had arrived to start his regular tour, and Northcutt called him over.

'Take a gander,' he said. 'We might've run into a halo.'

'God damn, we might at that!' Rayburn exclaimed.

Jim had made a primitive and not very reliable test. Although oil may be locked thousands of feet below ground surface by layers of impervious rock, minute particles of it sometimes still manage to migrate past the barriers. They spread out through subterranean strata forming an almost impossible to detect ring of oil traces, a sort of halo.

If contained in certain types of clays or rocks – and provided all other conditions are favourable – when the clay or rock is immersed in water, the tiny particles may work themselves free. Oil being lighter than water, they will float to the top and be drawn together by capillary attraction.

The green-brown patch proved nothing. A halo could spread far and wide. The borehole might be thousands of feet from the mark of the pool in which the particles originated. The minute oil traces might even have come from an oil pool so small as to have no commercial value. Still, Jim had his first indication that his hunch was not entirely wrong.

It was inevitable. A roustabout went into Stainesville, got drunk and babbled far too much of matters about which he knew nothing.

'Northcutt's done run into oil traces,' he bragged to attract attention and when he did, went on to embellish and lie out-right. The baler was bringing up sand saturated with oil, he said. The well was a sure bet to come in at any moment.

Those who heard his tales embroidered them even further when passing them on. The next day brought large crowds to Jim's drilling site. The editor of the Osage County *Sentinel* came, too.

'Hear she's ready to blow in,' he said to Northcutt.

'Somebody's been stuffing your ears with horseshit, mister!' Jim rasped, grey eyes almost black. 'Now beat it before I break your God-damned neck!'

The editor fled.

James Northcutt's intuition told him that if there really was any trouble brewing, the rumours would bring it to a quick boil. He talked with Luke Rayburn, Will Dubbs and Pete Reilly, the three men on his crew whom he trusted most.

'There's a chance somebody might try to stop us from drilling and grab this lease,' he told them.

They were all veterans, familiar with the harsher facts of the oil business. When Jim unwrapped the two shotguns and the ·45 calibre Colt he'd bought some time before, they showed no surprise. They simply helped him clean and load the weapons.

'We'll keep one shotgun on the rig, the other by the forge,' he told them. 'The driller on tour carries the Colt.'

Reese Lawson's fingers drummed on his desk top.

'I discount the stories, Ev,' he said. 'Far as I can tell, they started with some boozed-up bum.'

'Northcutt must've run across some traces or there wouldn't have been any talk at all,' Everett Cade said. 'I'm telling you we can't afford to fart around any longer. If Northcutt hits pay sand before the option runs out, we're sucking hind teat.'

'Why? Hundreds of dopes are already begging to find out when "the syndicate's" going to sell lease shares. If Northcutt brings in his well, the fever'll only shoot higher. We'll clean up without taking over the Peavey lease.'

'Scared?' Cade asked.

'Just don't see sense in taking unnecessary risks. Why should we?'

'Because I want James L. Northcutt's hide even more'n I want that lease,' Cade said. 'Is that reason enough?'

'If you say so.'

'There's more reason, though, Reese.' Cade's eyes glittered with cunning. 'I been talking to some people from Jersey Crest.'

Lawson came alert. Jersey Crest was a major company, a giant. Its presence was felt almost everywhere that oil was produced. Jersey Crest was entrenched in most Oklahoma fields. But for some reason, it had been outmanoeuvred in Osage County. Its management had been trying to correct that situation, without much success.

'Jersey Crest is big potatoes, Ev.'

'Damned right. And the people I've been palavering with tell me if there's oil on that Peavey property, Jersey Crest wants the lease. They'll pay a pile – if we can deliver it.'

'How much?'

'Half a million, maybe more.'

'Christ, Ev, if there is oil on that land, the lease'll be worth more than that!'

'Maybe, maybe not. We deal with Jersey Crest, we not only got a heap of cash, we got one of the biggest companies in the business looking at us real friendly like. That's an asset Reese.'

Lawson had to agree. With Jersey Crest as their behind-the-scenes patron, they could make a fortune. None the less, he felt uneasy.

'Want to tell me just what you're thinking, Ev?'

'Sure. I'm thinking Northcutt won't complete that well.'

'Oh?'

'His rig ain't going to be working so good in a couple of days or so,' Cade said.

'I don't like it.' Lawson shook his head. 'Why should we —'

'Relax. You won't be mixed up in any of it. I'm handling the whole thing myself.'

After nightfall two days later, Everett Cade drove his new Model T sedan out of Logan and headed west. He drove for an hour, turned off onto a crude road and some thirty minutes later reached a remote farmhouse. He guided the car behind the house and switched off engine and headlights.

Cade entered by the back door and went directly to the kitchen, where three men were seated around a wooden table drinking moonshine whisky. A kerosene lamp burned on the table. Cade greeted the men by their first names. Slim was ropy, sallow-faced. Bud was of medium height, young and a towhead. Josh, the third man, was burly, with a full beard.

Slim poured whisky into a tin mug for Cade. Cade grimaced as he downed the raw whisky. Then he sat at the table.

'How we going to work this, Ev?' Josh asked.

'The easy way,' Cade replied, and proceeded to explain everything to them in detail.

Jim Northcutt went on night tour. Time dragged. After some hours, he checked his watch. The bare electric lights strung on the rig and near the tool dresser's forge provided all the light needed. He saw it was 11.34 P.M. A long night still stretched ahead.

'How you making it, Will?' he called to Will Dubbs, who was at his forge.

'Okay, Boss. Need any help on the rig?'

'Nope. I'm just bored and wanted to hear my own voice.'

'It sounds real pretty. Better than that guy Caruso.'

'He's a tenor, for God's sake!'

'Could be, Boss. I never heard him – just heard *of* him.'

Jim gave an inward sigh and checked the temper screw that secured drilling cable to walking beam.

Everett Cade drove his Ford along the farm road that led past George Peavey's property. He parked a good distance from the access road that went to Jim Northcutt's drilling site. He and his three companions got out of the car. Bud and Josh carried two dozen sticks of dynamite and lengths of primer cord.

'We head over there,' Cade said.

They walked about a mile. The countryside was flat, the night dark. Soon, they saw a faint glow in the distance. It was cast by the lights on Northcutt's rig.

'Josh, you and Bud circle left, go for the generator and the toolie,' Cade instructed. 'Slim and I'll go around to the right. We'll belly down close to the rig. When you douse the lights, we'll go in after the driller.'

Josh and Bud took off in one direction. Cade, Slim at his side, angled off across the untended farmland. Save for the chuffing of the steam engine and the occasional howl of a coyote, the night was silent. Their footsteps made hardly any sound. Eventually, they were within a hundred yards of the drilling rig.

'Close enough,' Cade whispered. He and Slim flattened themselves on the ground. The derrick and rig front were clearly visible, illuminated by the electric light bulbs. Cade saw one man on the drilling platform.

Five minutes passed.

Ten.

Then the lights went out, leaving a darkness that seemed blacker than the night itself.

Cade nudged Slim. 'Let's get going,' he said. He gripped a heavy lug wrench in one hand, a ·38 calibre Smith and Wesson revolver in the other, and he and Slim scrambled to their feet and began running towards the derrick.

7

Cable tool drilling is an extension of the hammer and chisel principle. A bit-tipped tool string weighing a ton or more is suspended in the borehole by wire rope. The rope hangs from one end of the walking beam, the hinged crossbar of a giant T it forms with the upright Samson post. It works off a crank on the band wheel. Powered by an engine, the wheel rotates. The walking beam see-saws, raises and drops the wire rope. On the downstroke, tool string and drilling bit hammer deeper into the rock and earth far below.

Jim Northcutt made another of the routine checks of working parts that all drillers conduct throughout their tours on a rig. The steam engine was behaving. The chain drive to band wheel clattered normally. Everything else was in order.

Suddenly, he was blinded. The rig lights blacked out.

'Will!' he shouted to Will Dubbs, his tool dresser. 'Check that generator!' It had to be the generator, for the steam engine continued operating.

Northcutt edged across the floor of the drilling platform to the derrick leg, where a flashlight was kept hanging from a nail. He moved cautiously. He had no wish to blunder into moving parts in the darkness.

Will Dubbs was also blinded. But he heard Jim's instructions and started off in the direction of the generator. He took only two or three steps. Then something hard and heavy slammed down on his head. He dropped without a sound.

'He's out?' the man named Bud whispered.

Josh bent down, checked. 'Cold,' he said. 'Maybe dead.'

'Then give me a hand.' Bud was already busy attaching dynamite sticks to the steam engine.

Jim couldn't find the flashlight. Someone must have borrowed and not replaced it. He cursed and called out to Dubbs.

'Hey, Will!'

There was no reply. Instead, Jim heard the scrape of boot-soles on the drilling platform behind him. He reacted instinctively, lunging for the shotgun that was where it should be. The action saved him. The lug wrench that Everett Cade swung missed his head, striking Northcutt's shoulder. The blow was painful and knocked Jim off balance. He hadn't yet found his feet, but he raised the shotgun and fired one barrel. The gun roared, bucking in his hands. His aim had been too high. He missed.

'Shoot the bastard!' The voice came from the darkness, off to the right. Jim's mind raced. There were obviously two intruders on the drilling platform. No telling how many more. He ducked behind the Samson post.

Jim had seen only a murky, indistinct form that appeared, then disappeared.

Cade, realizing he hadn't knocked out the driller and unnerved that the man had a shotgun, dived behind the bull wheel. He drew a revolver. Peering into the blackness, he tried to find his target. Before he could, there were two loud pistol reports. Slim had fired at the spot where he thought the driller was crouching.

Bullets thudded into the Samson post. Jim Northcutt saw the two spurts of flame from Slim's pistol muzzle. He pointed the shotgun, triggered off the second barrel. The gun blasted and 00-shot found its mark. Northcutt heard a scream, followed by the thud of a falling body. Then there were louder sounds as the wounded man cried out in pain and his arms and legs thrashed against the wooden derrick floor.

It was becoming more than Everett Cade had bargained for. Reasoning that the driller was armed with only a shotgun and had fired both its barrels, Cade sprang out from behind the bull wheel. The ·38 was in his fist. He pulled the trigger once, twice, a third time. Lead slugs cracked air close to Jim Northcutt's head.

Jim yanked his ·45 Colt from its holster. He crouched low, snapped off two shots at the shadowy figure leaping towards him. The second shot was good. The figure seemed to be slammed flat, the ·38 dropping to the wooden flooring, and lay groaning.

The bullet had caught Everett Cade in the thigh. Jim scooped up the ·38, then bent down, shoving the muzzle of his Colt into Cade's face.

'How many of you?' Jim demanded.

Cade was terrified that the driller would shoot. He muttered that there were two other men. Northcutt straightened up, sprinted towards the forge. If there were others, they had doubtless gone after Will Dubbs. That explained why Dubbs hadn't answered him a few moments before.

By then, Bud and Josh had fixed dynamite to the steam engine, run the fuse and crawled close to the derrick leg nearest them. They had heard the shots and the screams and groans, but assumed it was the driller who had been hit. Even so, they worked hurriedly, making a sloppy job of taping only one stick of dynamite to the derrick leg.

Then they saw a shape loom out of the darkness and realized it was the driller. That meant Cade and Slim must have been the ones hit. Bud pulled his gun, opened fire, pumping out bullets.

Jim dived to the ground. There were more shots. Northcutt fixed the location of the orange-yellow muzzle flashes in his mind, aimed and triggered the Colt.

There was a high-pitched screech as the bullet tore into Bud's stomach.

Only one left, Jim thought. By now, his eyes were becoming accustomed to the darkness. He recognized the outline of a man hunched near the base of the derrick leg. The man began moving, running away from the rig in a low crouch.

Jim sprang after the man, caught up with him and hurled him to the ground. As they both fell, Jim's hand encountered a full beard. He gripped the beard, swung the Colt so that the

90

barrel smashed across the man's face. Jim rose, started to drag the man back towards the rig.

'No!' Josh screamed and tried to struggle free. 'For Christ's sake – the fuse's lit!'

Dynamite, Jim thought. The men had come to blow up his rig. The charges had been set and would go off at any moment. He was seized by a murderous fury. Whoever they were, the men wanted to destroy the drilling rig and him with it.

Josh had his hands free and groped for his own revolver. Jim saw him take out the weapon. All his restraint vanished. He pointed the Colt, shot the bearded man in the chest. He ignored the blood spurting from the wound and heaved the man up onto the rig floor.

The dynamite had not yet gone off. The steam engine was running, operating the heavy duty chain drive to the band wheel. Jim did not think. His actions were motivated by primal impulses. He seized the wounded man's beard and thrust his face and head into the drive mechanism. Great revolving sprockets spiked into the man's skull and dragged it under the massive links of the chain drive. Head and neck were torn off and ground into a jelly of blood and brains and shredded bone.

The two explosions came simultaneously a moment later. Gusts of flame stabbed up in the darkness. The blasts were uneven, one much louder than the other, but they mingled and the steam engine was blown off its mountings into a thousand fragments of scrap metal and the derrick floor rocked and heaved. Jim Northcutt was flung to the floor of the rig.

It had all happened in a very few minutes. The men asleep in the bunkhouse had been awakened by the first shots. They had leaped from their cots and, pausing only to pull on their boots, had rushed towards the rig.

Slim and Josh were both dead. Bud would live only a few more hours. Everett Cade, whom Jim Northcutt now recognized, was badly, but not mortally, wounded in the thigh. Jim's main concern was for Will Dubbs. The toolie was unconscious.

Northcutt told Luke Rayburn and some other men to look after Dubbs and sent a roustabout off in his Ford to summon a doctor and notify the sheriff's office. Using a flashlight, he then surveyed the damage, and his heart sank. The steam engine was a total loss. Far worse, one derrick leg had been almost blown away at the base. The structure could never withstand the stresses of drilling operations.

Jim strode across the blood-soaked derrick floor to where Everett Cade lay and ordered him to sit up. For a moment, Jim thought of putting a bullet through Cade's head.

Dynamited oil rigs, drilling-site gun battles and their leftover debris of dead and wounded were hardly rare occurrences in Oklahoma oil country, even as late as 1921. Both the doctor who came from Stainesville and the Osage County deputies who arrived soon after him were hardened to such violent incidents.

The doctor ordered Will Dubbs rushed to the Stainesville hospital, pronounced Josh and Slim dead and declared that any attempt to save Bud's life would be futile. The deputies were equally methodical and unruffled. James Northcutt had been entirely within his rights to kill criminal trespassers. They arrested Everett Cade, made arrangements to remove the two corpses and the dying man and wished Jim the best of future luck.

By early morning, they were gone, and Jim and his men were able to make a closer survey of the damage.

'Engine's gone, but boiler and drive seem okay,' Luke Rayburn declared. 'If we get a replacement engine, we can operate again.'

'No chance,' Northcutt said miserably. 'We'll have to tear down and rebuild the whole God-damned derrick.'

'Maybe not,' Rayburn disagreed, inspecting the damaged derrick leg. 'Might use jacks and winched guylines to bring her back to plumb, then shore up. I saw it done once. Only took three, four days.'

'Possible,' Jim allowed, but without much hope. 'We'll give it a try. First we clean up the mess. Then we need power. Abe should have another engine in stock. I'll make a fast run to Logan.'

Reese Lawson worked quickly. He hurried to Pawhuska, the Osage County seat, where Everett Cade was being held under arrest.

Cade's wounded leg had been patched up. He had stubbornly refused to answer questions. Lawson instructed him to tell an improvised tale of having been forced to accompany the other three men at gunpoint. They were all dead and could not re-

92

fute the version, Lawson told him.

'But Northcutt,' Cade protested. 'He —'

'I'll pass out bribes, make sure you get bail. Then you'll cut out of the state.'

It worked as the attorney planned. Although Cade was in much pain and able to walk only with a crutch, Lawson drove him to Logan.

'I'll kill that bastard Northcutt!' Cade swore.

'Like hell you will,' Lawson said. 'I'm putting you on a train for Dallas. You'll damned well stay there.' He realized he was in command now, giving orders, and enjoyed it. 'You stay out of Oklahoma until I bring off our lease game like I wanted to in the first place.'

Cade's surly silence affirmed that he would do as Lawson told him.

Abe Schlechter did have another steam engine in stock. It was delivered to the site and operating within two days. As soon as they had a power source, Jim and his crew laboured feverishly to make the derrick usable again.

Luke Rayburn's idea seemed to be sound. Two winches were set out and firmly anchored. Steel ropes were secured to upper portions of the derrick, their free ends run to the winches. The heavy crossbeams nearest to derrick-floor level were reinforced to take great upthrusting pressures, and huge screw jacks were placed under them.

When all this had been done sweating men operated the jacks and straining winches spooled the cables taut. The derrick was brought back to perpendicular plumb, and it was firmly held.

The damaged leg was literally splinted. Upright timbers were placed against all four sides of the leg, secured with bolts and iron banding. The guylines were slacked off, the jacks lowered and the derrick was tested.

'She'll hold,' Jim said. Despite his bone-weariness, he was now eager to resume work on the well immediately. They had lost precious days. It was 29 July. The lease option had only seventeen days to run. The deadline was crowding in on him.

8

On Wednesday, 3 August, Jim read another article in the *Sentinel*.

SYNDICATE TO SELL PUBLIC LEASE SHARES

The story quoted 'Reese Lawson, attorney for a large syndicate of prominent Texas and Oklahoma oilmen' as saying: 'My clients have decided to give the general public an opportunity of participating in their multi-million dollar venture.'

Succeeding paragraphs referred to 'highly promising geologists' reports' and 'plans for drilling exploration wells'.

Northcutt grimaced sourly. Cade was out on bail and had disappeared from Osage County. Lawson was carrying the ball. They'd bring off their swindle, not much question about that. The world abounded with suckers. Crooks were always certain of their profits. Legitimate small-scale operators took the heavy gambles and could only hope.

Each passing day drew Jim Northcutt's nerves tauter. He and his men had been making hole at a remarkable rate considering the difficult undergound formations they encountered and the water seeps that required drilling to be suspended while casing was run. Yet, progress was infuriatingly slow compared to the onrush of the lease-option expiration date. His impatience and sense of frustration were intensified every time the bailer was run. The cuttings it brought to the surface strongly hinted the presence of oil somewhere below.

But where – at what depth? Would the pay zone be reached before they ran out of time?

Such questions were a source of agonized concern to Jim on 6 August, when only nine days remained before the deadline. That morning, the drilling log showed the borehole down to 2,305 feet, and the bailer brought up cuttings that gave definite encouragement.

'Looks like we're going into the Mississippi lime,' he told Luke Rayburn shortly before noon. 'We might make it.'

'I wish I was a praying man,' Rayburn said. 'One hitch, and we're finished.' Any stoppages or delays now would bring drilling to a halt a short distance from what Luke, too, felt was pay sand somewhere beyond the present bottom of the hole.

'Our bit's getting dull,' Jim said. 'We ought to change it.' He looked at his watch, unconsciously fingering the gusher charm Verna had given him. 'We'll pull the tool string now, eat and change bits afterwards,' he added.

Rayburn nodded. He released the chain-drive clutch. The walking beam stopped its see-sawing. Jim detached the temper screw holding the wire drill rope to the walking beam and signalled Luke, who fed power to the bull wheel. The wheel began turning, spooling cable and pulling the tool string up to the surface.

Eventually, the drilling tools – first rope socket, then sinker, the huge link-like jars, auger stem and finally six-foot-long drilling bit – emerged from the borehole. Pulverized rock and slimy clay spilled over the derrick floor. When the tools were clear of the hole and hanging several feet above the casing head, Rayburn cut the power. The two men headed for the cookhouse.

Steve Carter was a roustabout. The other men called him 'Peewee' or 'Four Eyes' because Carter was short, thin and wore thick-lensed eyeglasses. Despite his size, Steve Carter was strong and a good worker. He had one fault; he went on periodic drinking sprees. However, in the oil fields a man's drinking habits were overlooked as long as he remained able to do his job. Peewee Carter was one of those men who held up his end of the work even when drunk.

Carter had been drinking for two days, but he performed all his assigned tasks. At lunchtime, he avoided the cook shack and ducked into the bunkhouse. He drained the rotgut remaining in the jug he kept under his cot. Staggering slightly as he went out again, he almost collided with Pete Reilly.

'You need black coffee, Peewee,' Pete told him.

'Nah,' Carter mumbled, peering through his glasses.

Reilly shrugged and the little roustabout went off towards the drilling rig. When he got there, Carter stared around him in bafflement. The rig was deserted. He clambered unsteadily onto the rig floor, saw the tool string had been pulled. Odd, he thought.

'Hey, anybody here?' he called out. There was no reply.

Peewee Carter shook his head, instantly wished he hadn't. The movement made the inside of his skull throb and spin. He pulled off his glasses with one hand, rubbed at his eyes with the other and staggered forward a few paces. His boot soles splashed down on wet clay. His feet slithered out from under him. Carter tried to regain his balance, couldn't. Then he gave a horrified scream as his alcohol-fogged brain registered the realization that he had pitched over the lip of the casing head and was plunging headfirst down the borehole.

Luke Rayburn saw the pair of metal-rimmed eyeglasses when he, Jim Northcutt and Pete Reilly returned to the rig. He picked them up.

'Somebody must've dropped these,' he said.

Pete Reilly snatched the glasses out of his hand. Pete recognized them as Carter's – Peewee couldn't see a foot ahead of him without them.

'Jesus Christ, no!' he groaned, remembering the condition Carter had been in. He stared down at the rig floor, observed the streaks frantically floundering boot soles had left in the clay muck.

'Jim,' Reilly said in a whisper. 'I think Carter's down in the hole.'

Northcutt stared at Reilly, then snatched a flashlight that hung from a nail driven into a crossbeam. He bellied down on the floor of the drilling platform. Switching on the light, he lowered it down into the borehole. He could see nothing.

'Make sure Carter's not passed out someplace,' he said, getting to his feet. Premonition told him the search would be useless.

It was. The entire crew searched. The men returned to the rig, gathered around and reported there was no sign of Carter anywhere.

'We have to face it, Jim,' Luke Rayburn said softly. 'Peewee's down there, and he's dead.' Carter would have fallen more than one hundred feet before encountering casing narrow enough to wedge his body.

The men were silent. All old-timers in the fields, they knew of other such falls down boreholes. They also knew it might take days, even weeks to fish for the body with tongs and bring it to the surface – in chunks, for the tongs were made to fish for metal, not human bodies. And, they were aware that efforts to recover the corpse would eliminate any chance of completing the well before the deadline.

'Anybody friends with Carter?' Jim asked.

'I used to talk to him some,' Pete Reilly said.

'He ever tell you if he was married or had kids or —'

'Peewee was single,' Reilly said. 'Didn't even have a regular girl. He'd go to a whorehouse once in a while, that's all.'

Northcutt chewed at his lips. Carter had been a boomer who drifted from one job to another. Still, he had been a man. But if we fish for the body, I can kiss well and lease good-bye, he thought. And we're getting close to oil. I can feel it. The twitch in the crotch Abe Schlechter talks about. God damn it, we can't stop now!

'Wait here,' he told his men. He ran to the bunkhouse and opened his trunk. He took out three bottles of whisky and returned to the rig. The men watched silently as he opened the bottles and passed them around. They sensed the decision he'd made.

'Belt down what you can hold,' Jim said, his tone hollow. 'Then we'll change the bit.'

The men passed the bottles, drank deeply. The dulled bit was replaced with one freshly sharpened. Jim personally worked the controls and lowered the tool string back down into the borehole. Then he secured drilling rope to temper screw and let in the clutch on the chain drive operating the band wheel. The walking beam began its relentless see-sawing action.

When the bailer was run again, there were more traces of oil in the cuttings. But there were also wisps of clothing and shreds of human flesh and bone.

Abe Schlechter didn't touch the breakfast Lily Sleeping Moon set before him on the morning of 10 August, but he drank cup after cup of black coffee. He hadn't slept at all the night before. He couldn't after talking to Pete Reilly, who had telephoned him from Stainesville at around 9 P.M.

'Jim sent me in to call and tell you it looks good,' Reilly had said. 'We can almost hear the music.'

When a drilling bit punches down through the last layer of impervious rock to an oil reservoir, natural gas seeks escape under heavy pressure and makes a variety of sounds. These are transmitted up the borehole ahead of the gas and oil. Sometimes, the steel casing lining the hole resonates. Whether it does or not, many oilmen have called the noise of the gas 'music'.

Coffee only made Abe more jittery. I'll go out of my mind if I stay here, he thought. He telephoned Verna.

'The well may be coming in today,' he told her. 'I want to drive out to the site. Care to go along?'

'Of course.'

'I'll pick you up in an hour.'

He was almost ready to leave the store when Nancy Tappen arrived. She had been paying off what her dead husband owed in instalments, and she brought Abe a one-thousand-dollar cheque.

'I hate to rush you,' he said, 'but I'm heading out to the Peavey property. Jim thinks he may hit pay sand today.'

Nancy had not seen Jim since the day he had driven her to Pawhuska and they stopped and made love, but she had thought of him often.

'Can I go along with you?' she asked Abe.

Schlechter's instincts told him that Verna Fletcher and Nancy Tappen would hardly hit it off together.

'Sorry, Nancy,' he told her. 'It's impossible.'

Nancy was thinking rapidly. If Jim Northcutt brought in a big producing well, he'd probably become rich. Rich enough, at any rate. He would be fine husband material, worth the effort to trap.

'All right, Abe,' she said. She made up her mind she'd hire a taxi and go to the site herself.

Jim Northcutt and his men had worked straight through the previous night. All were caught up in the mounting excitement that accompanies the imminent completion of an oil well.

Shortly after 11 A.M., a rattletrap Dodge sedan with the words 'Logan Taxicab Service' painted on its sides drove up to the site. Nancy Tappen got out. The taxi turned around and left.

Jim was astonished to see Nancy and experienced a powerful sexual response. No wonder, he told himself, remembering that he hadn't seen Verna – or even been off the site – for over a week.

'I heard the hopeful news,' Nancy said. 'Thought I'd come out and root for you.'

'Look, I'm busy as hell on the rig,' he told her. 'If you want to stay around, go over to the cook shack.'

It was half an hour later that Luke Rayburn let out a loud bellow.

'God damn, Jim! She's busting loose!'

Jim heard and felt the rumbling sound of restless natural gas at the same moment. He lunged for the temper screw, detached it.

'Throw on the tug ropes!' he shouted to Pete Reilly.

The wooden rig floor shook and trembled beneath his feet.

Reilly had the bull wheel turning under full power, but the steam engine seemed to be racing even as drilling rope was being spooled up on the drum at top speed.

Northcutt suddenly found himself bathed in sweat. His heart battered against his ribs. The drilling bit had broken through the last layer of impervious rock and driven into an oil-saturated limestone stratum. Oil was trapped there under enormous natural gas pressure. Now the gas was bursting free. It was rushing up through the escape channel provided by the borehole. Its force and velocity were so great that cable and tool string were being driven upward faster than the bull wheel could spool up the slack. Wire rope was already kinking and looping on the derrick floor.

'Any more power?' Jim yelled to Reilly.

'No! Throttle's wide open!'

The wire rope loops on the rig floor were multiplying. No steam engine and bull wheel on earth could reel in cable at the rate it was being spewed from the borehole.

'Run for it!' Jim shouted.

He waited only long enough to make certain his men obeyed and then he leaped from the drilling platform and ran from the rig. He was still running seconds later when there was a deafening roar and the heavy string of drilling tools shot from the hole like projectiles fired from a cannon.

Propelled by tremendous natural gas pressure, the jointed tool slammed against the crown block. The string broke apart into its components which hurtled down, smashing cross-sills and spearing through the rig floor.

Now a dark column of oil spouted like an immense geyser.

Jim turned and stared at the rig. The derrick was almost invisible, all but the bottom section hidden by gushing oil that plumed out at the crown to spray in all directions. Within moments, he was drenched with oil.

Rayburn ran to him and pounded his back.

99

'Biggest spouter I've seen in years!' Rayburn yelled.

The two men stood in the downpour of crude oil and strained their lungs shouting triumphant whoops.

'Ten thousand barrels a day if she's giving an ounce!' Rayburn screamed, leaping around in a wild dance. 'I'll eat that rig if she ain't!' He stopped his dance abruptly. 'Christ, Jim! We got to cap that son of a bitch!'

That snapped Jim Northcutt back to his senses. A gusher was an awesome, a magnificent sight, and this was *his* gusher. But the crude spewing into the air was being wasted and lost. The well had to be brought under control, the oil spraying out of the hole diverted into field tanks and earthen reservoirs. A gate valve would have to be swung over the casing head, lowered down and secured to it.

'Yeah,' Jim panted. 'Round up the crew!'

Then he remembered Nancy Tappen. He swung around, rushed off to find her. She had run a short distance from the cook shack. She saw him, and came to meet him.

'Congratulations, Jim,' she said. 'I —'

'Don't say anything!' He grasped her hand, half led, half dragged her to his car. He practically thrust her into it, then flung himself behind the wheel. He turned on the ignition, ground the engine into life.

'Jim – where are we going?'

He didn't answer, but fed gas to the Ford, spun the wheel and drove off to the right, away from the rig. Nancy glanced at his face, looking craggier and harder now that it was splattered with crude oil. She understood and felt a tightening rush of response.

Jim drove the car across the open fields to a spot where a small rise of ground hid them from the rig, and cut the engine. He slid away from the wheel, seized her in his arms and his mouth crushed against hers. They tasted crude on each other's lips, and this somehow seemed to arouse Jim even further. The realization that it did increased Nancy's own desire.

He tore open his clothes. Then, surprised, she stared down at him.

'But you've already —'

'Yeah, when the well came in.' His voice was harsh, and he pulled her to him. His body had reacted involuntarily at the moment he'd seen oil bursting up out of the borehole. 'Don't let that worry you.' He was unfastening her dress. 'There's plenty more stored up.'

Abe Schlechter's Model T snapped a front axle in a pothole halfway between Logan and the drilling site. He and Verna had to wait an hour before an empty wagon came by amid the stream of loaded vehicles headed for the big proven fields. The mule skinner agreed to take them to the Peavey tract for ten dollars, but they did not arrive until after three o'clock in the afternoon.

Jim had long since sent off one of the roustabouts to drive Nancy Tappen to Stainesville in his car. He was busy with his crew, battling to cap the gusher.

He stopped working long enough to accept his partners' excited congratulations and several hungry kisses from Verna. Then he returned to the rig.

9

News of the oil strike flashed across Oklahoma. Once again, a hunch-impelled wildcatter had made fools of big-company geologists and opened up a new producing field where they'd said there was no oil.

The day after the well blew in and was still uncapped and gushing, Jim Northcutt had a visitor. He was Raymond Harper, a tall, well-dressed man whose business card identified him as a representative of the Jersey Crest Oil Company.

'We're interested in this lease,' Harper said.

Jim knew that Jersey Crest was a major oil company noted for its ruthless business practices. More often than not, independents dealing with Jersey Crest got badly burned. Indeed, the company was notorious for manoeuvring independent operators into untenable situations and then taking them over. On the other hand, he was also aware that Jersey Crest wanted a foothold in Osage County. Because of this, Jim thought, the company might make a straighforward deal and offer a fair price.

The conversation dragged on. Raymond Harper adroitly avoided mentioning any figures. Jim's patience wore thin.

'There's no use our talking business unless you make some kind of offer,' he said. 'My partners —'

'Ah, yes,' Harper said with a faint smile. 'Your partners. Now, I'll be frank. We know something about them. They're not oilmen. *You* are. You brought in the well over there —'

'So what?' Jim demanded, his eyes narrowing.

'So, suppose I mentioned *two* figures, Mr Northcutt . . .?'

Jim suspected what was coming next and his jaw tightened.

'. . . one you can discuss with your partners. Another that would be entirely between us.'

I guess he thinks I'll bite because I'm young, Jim reflected. The ancient ploy of trying to obtain a bargain by setting partners against each other, offering one a private payoff.

'Shag your butt off this land, Harper,' Jim said.

'Northcutt, Jersey Crest is a very large company. Co-operate with it, and you'll have co-operation in return. Be hostile, and you'll find that while large corporations may be impersonal, they have long memories.'

'If you're not out of here in one minute flat, I'll turn my roustabouts loose!'

Raymond Harper shrugged, returned to his chauffeur-driven car and left the well site. The report he would take back to Tulsa would be James L. Northcutt's first black mark against him in the Jersey Crest book.

The gusher was capped on the afternoon of 13 August. Jim went to Pawhuska where the offices of the Arbuckle National Pipeline and Refining Company were located. He needed an outlet for the crude being produced by the discovery well and for the oil that would be produced by other wells he would drill on the property. Under normal circumstances, Arbuckle would agree to lay gathering pipelines to the site and contract to buy all the crude produced. However, Arbuckle officials had other ideas.

'We'd rather buy your lease than your production,' David Kitson, an Arbuckle vice-president, told Jim.

Northcutt was not surprised by the proposal. Wildcatters opening up new fields could either produce crude and sell it or they could make huge, quick-turnover profits by selling their leases to large companies. The latter course provided capital for new ventures. He guessed that Arbuckle's eagerness to buy the lease was largely prompted by its desire to keep Jersey

Crest out of Osage County.

'That leaves one question,' Jim said. 'What's your starting offer, Mr Kitson?'

'A million dollars,' David Kitson replied smoothly, crossing one expensively trousered leg over the other. 'Cash.'

Jim Northcutt's thick black eyebrows rose high and he whistled. For a moment, Kitson thought Jim was staggered by the size of the sum. He quickly realized he was wrong.

'What's Arbuckle doing, looking for giveaways?' Jim pretended dismay. 'That's not an offer. It's a joke. Leases on *unproved* land near producing sites are going for anywhere up to three thousand dollars an acre. My partners and I have six hundred and forty acres under lease, and we're producing!'

Kitson looked closely at the young wildcatter. The ruggedly built, roughly dressed youth was shrewd, obviously tough, and he had the instincts of a hard-bargaining businessman.

'What do you consider a fair price?' Kitson inquired.

'Five million, maybe.'

'That's preposterous!'

'It is.' Jim's nod was affable. 'Only there's always a happy medium between bad offers and preposterous asking prices. All we have to do is haggle in a genteel way, Mr Kitson, and we'll find it.'

Negotiations continued for a few days. At last, Mr Kitson made what Jim sensed was Arbuckle's final offer: $2,850,000.

Jim, Verna and Abe held a meeting in Judge Henry Kendall's office.

Kendall stated that Arbuckle National had made a firm and formal offer of $2,850,000 for the Peavey lease. The partners would have to decide whether they wanted to accept it or not. Althought Jim had told Verna and Abe about it earlier, they still looked stunned.

'I – I can't really believe it,' Verna said. 'That's almost a million dollars apiece!'

'Yes,' their attorney said. 'However, you should bear one thing in mind. You could make much more money over the years by holding the lease and producing and selling crude oil.'

'Maybe,' Abe said. 'Or the property could run dry tomorrow.'

'It could,' Jim agreed. While the 'tomorrow' was something

103

of an exaggeration, wells – and fields – did run dry very suddenly at times. Oil was totally unpredictable.

'Do you want to sell the lease, Jim?' Verna asked.

The question demanded honesty and candour.

'Here's how I feel. The three of us – *oysvorfs*, you called us, Abe – went into this for pretty much the same reason. Each of us wanted enough money to leave Osage County and start out fresh someplace else. This is our chance. Yes, I want to sell.'

'You, Miss Fletcher?' Kendall asked.

'It'll give me more money than I ever dreamed I'd have. I say we should take the offer.'

'Mr Schlechter?'

'Sell. Definitely.'

'Then it's unanimous,' Kendall said.

Jim was exhilarated. With his share, he could organize his own company. He noticed Verna looking at him, long lashes hooding her eyes. Wonder what she's thinking, he mused, his own feelings conflicted by the realization they would soon go their separate ways. He would miss Verna. But he had his own plans, his own life to lead.

We're close to the end of the road, Verna Fletcher thought. My attachment to Jim is strong. Too strong. He was young and valued his freedom and independence above all else, even while driven by a fierce and determined ambition. But I have my own life ahead, my own dreams to fulfil.

Abraham Schlechter was lost in euphoric reverie. He and his wife and children would be together. They'd live like – like European nobility? No, Abe thought. Like American millionaires! He visualized the kind of house he would have in Tulsa. His children would attend fine schools. Especially his son Samuel – bright, eager to become a lawyer. Now I can even think of sending him to the Harvard Law School. Provided a Samuel Schlechter could be squeezed in on the school's Jewish quota. Then his mind flicked to images of a main supply store in Tulsa and branches located in various boomtowns . . .

Judge Henry Kendall broke into their thoughts. 'I presume you wish the partnership dissolved after the sale is completed?'

The long silence that followed was affirmation.

After all outstanding bills and obligations had been paid, Jim, Verna and Abe each netted slightly more than $900,000. Ironically their profits were less than those reaped by Everett Cade and Reese Lawson. Discovery of oil on the Peavey tract created oil fever. The value of the leases they held on nearby properties zoomed. Lawson sold leases to hundreds of credulous buyers, realizing almost $5,000,000. He divided evenly with Cade, who returned from Texas, was lavish with bribes and had all charges against him dropped.

James Northcutt observed that these developments followed familiar oil business patterns. It was an industry axiom that more money had gone into the ground in swindles than had been taken out of it in crude. He was no less philosophical about the perseverance with which Nancy Tappen sought to form a relationship with him. She made innumerable telephone calls to Abe's store and even Henry Kendall's office asking for him. She came to Logan and out to the well site. He realized that his new wealth was the real attraction, and he ignored her. Nancy Tappen had no further role in his life, no part in his plans.

Jim formed the Northcutt Petroleum Company and announced he intended going to Southern California. Huge new oil strikes were being made there. The state already accounted for 30 per cent of all the crude oil being produced in the country. It was, Jim believed, where his next opportunities lay.

In mid-September, Verna sold her parlourhouse to a competing madam who would take possession on the twenty-sixth of the month, a Monday. Verna had her own blueprint, at least for the immediate future. She would take Celia with her and travel for a time, perhaps go to Europe. Then she would find a place where she could settle under another name and achieve the 'respectability' she desired.

'We've got a long weekend,' she told Jim on the Thursday evening before the day she would have to turn her house over to its new owner. 'Let's spend it in bed.'

They did, and their lovemaking expressed the feelings both had but neither would – or could – communicate in words, alternating between frenzy and tenderness.

They tried to hide their emotions on Monday morning, but did not entirely succeed.

'It was great,' Verna said, repeating the phrase Jim had used after the first time they had gone to bed together.

'That it was, my friend.' He remembered her words, too, and when he repeated them, his voice was hoarse and uneven.

Everything that Verna was taking with her had been packed.

Jim drove Verna and Celia to the railroad station. She was starting her travels by making a visit to her native Philadelphia. Abe Schlechter came to the station, as did the parlourhouse girls.

'Let's keep in touch,' Jim said, giving Verna a final kiss before all the others crowded in to say good-bye.

'Of course, Jim.' She kissed him back fiercely. 'All the luck – my friend.' Her voice caught, tears formed in her eyes and she pulled herself away.

When the train pulled out of the station, Jim experienced a deep sadness, a sense of loss greater than he'd ever known before.

'Verna's quite a woman,' Abe Schlechter said to him as they walked from the platform together.

Jim was silent, then he seemed to shake himself.

'Come on, Abe,' he said. 'Let's go someplace and have a drink – maybe even get drunk.'

BOOK TWO

1

29 June

Presidential Advisor Arthur Gerlach and National Energy Resources Department Secretary Rowan Engelhardt met at Washington's Mayflower Hotel for lunch. They had purposely asked for a specific table. It was the one at which FBI Director J. Edgar Hoover had lunched daily for many years until his death in 1972. The table was secluded, beyond earshot of other diners, and they could talk there freely.

If Gerlach looked like an athletics instructor, Rowan Engelhardt gave the impression of being a fast-rising, fortyish banker, which was not too far removed from the truth. A one-time building-and-loan company vice-president, he had taken a Treasury Department post in which he'd been able to provide much aid to banks and bankers without ever openly compromising himself. On the contrary, he had established a reputation in government circles as a highly capable administrator. He was conservative in appearance and outward manner, rather humourless, and he owed his Cabinet appointment to Arthur Gerlach, who had brought Engelhardt's name to the attention of the President.

'I've checked over all the enabling laws and Executive directives establishing the Energy Resources Department,' Engelhardt said, sipping at his vodka martini. 'They're pretty broad.'

'They usually are when people hit panic buttons to set up a new department or agency,' Gerlach observed, eyeing but not drinking his own, Tanqueray gin, martini. The Department of National Energy Resources had been established in great haste after petroleum industry officials first began predicting that there would be another fuel shortage, worse than the last.

'We have all the authority we need for the Department to interpose itself between James Northcutt and the Chinese Government,' Engelhardt went on. 'For example, presidential directive four-twelve-dash-nine empowers me to refuse export licences on any drilling equipment the Department considers essential for use in increasing domestic production. Then, there's —'

'Don't bother.' Arthur Gerlach picked up his glass. 'Remember, I helped draft those directives. Cheers.' He swallowed some of his martini, smiled. 'Whatever powers you don't have for hamstringing Northcutt, State and Commerce and Interior do.'

'He has a loophole you may have overlooked, Art.'

'I doubt it, but tell me anyway.'

'He could conceivably bypass us by forming a foreign-based subsidiary or using one he already has.'

'No way.' Gerlach shook his head. 'One, Chou En-lai and his bunch want to deal with an *American* company that has full US Government backing. They won't mess around with any NIPCO subsidiaries, not when deals involve billions of dollars. Two, we can keep NIPCO so off balance here in the States with IRS, FTC, SEC and other headaches that Northcutt won't have time to look for loopholes. Three, the Jersey Crest consortium's own competitive programme is gathering momentum. That'll help keep NIPCO occupied, even pinned down.'

Rowan Engelhardt adjusted his dark-framed glasses and quietly cleared his throat.

'Any connection between that – ah – competitive programme and the difficulties NIPCO had a few days ago in Qantara?' he asked.

'I wouldn't know,' Arthur Gerlach replied honestly. 'I can suspect, though.'

'Do you?'

'Sort of. But I can't prove anything. I doubt if anyone could, least of all James Northcutt. If a company like Jersey Crest takes extraordinary steps, all tracks are buried. Deep.'

Engelhardt had some more of his drink.

'It all sounds a shade too easy,' he said. 'All the biggest battalions and God on the Jersey Crest side. Northcutt isn't exactly a helpless infant. He'll hit back.'

'Probably. Won't do him much good, however.'

'Damn it, Art. The other day, even you had doubts. You told me Northcutt had good congressional support and talked about the media and public opinion!'

'I've thought it all out, Rowan. Take Congress. It's going to tread softly with this new Administration for a while, give it a chance. Right?'

'Probably.'

'And the Northcutt image is vulnerable. He's an expatriate, hasn't lived in the United States for God only knows how long. We can hang plenty on that hook.'

'How?'

Arthur Gerlach chuckled.

'Try this for size. Can any American who refuses to live in his native land really have its best interests at heart? Can a billionaire who accepted a decoration from Charles de Gaulle be trusted to make huge deals with Communist China and not give the foreigners an edge?'

'It's good for openers,' Engelhardt agreed.

'Better than good.'

'I have a couple more questions.'

'Shoot.'

'Who do we have to worry about most on the Northcutt side?'

Gerlach frowned thoughtfully, finished his drink.

'My guess is his lawyer, guy named Samuel Schlechter.'

'Jewish?'

'Uh-huh.'

'Funny, oilmen don't usually have Jewish lawyers, especially not when they operate in the Middle East.'

'Northcutt seems to like being an exception to rules,' Gerlach said. 'As I hear it, Northcutt was friends with Schlechter's father way back when.'

'So he hired the son?'

'Hired, hell. Set Schlechter up in his own law firm. It's Schlechter, Bemmelman and Crane now. Big firm in New York.'

Engelhardt reached for a menu.

'My last question before we order.'

'I'm listening.'

'The million from Jersey Crest. Shouldn't part of it be up front?'

'Not part,' Gerlach said. 'All. I'll start making noises this afternoon and make it clear we want the money ASAP. In cash.'

Russell Peterson received the telephone call from Arthur Gerlach shortly after 2 P.M.

'We're all geared up,' Gerlach said. 'I'm wondering when we can expect to see the – ah – materials you mentioned.'

'I'll have to ask my boss,' Peterson told him. 'He may have to make more inquiries. It may take a day or two before I have the answer. Will you go ahead in the meantime?'

'Sure.' Arthur Gerlach laughed. 'Considering whom we're dealing with, I'll go along on trust for a couple of days. Even a week.'

Peterson went to see his employer, Guy Bannister, at his Radio City headquarters.

Bannister reacted to the report of the telephone call with an impatient scowl.

'God damn it, you should have told him he'll hear when he hears, period.' His irritation was part artificial, part real. Pretended dissatisfaction with Peterson's actions kept Peterson nervous about his job and $65,000-a-year salary. This, in turn, kept Peterson docile and obedient. But Guy Bannister was also genuinely annoyed that Gerlach and Engelhardt would be receiving a million dollars as their payoff. It was twice the total Bannister could hope to clear in fees for all the complex and extremely delicate assignments he'd been given by Powell Pierce.

'Gerlach's not a type you can toss around,' Russell Peterson said.

'Crap! A grafter is a grafter. You just didn't lean on him hard enough.' Bannister made a gesture that dismissed Peterson. 'All right. I'll pick up the pieces you dropped again.'

When Peterson had gone, Bannister relaxed his expression. He reached for his telephone, dialled a local number. When it was answered by a switchboard operator, he asked for Mr Charles Farrier, president of Italo-American Fidelity Realtors, Incorporated.

Farrier – whose English name was a literal translation of Carlo Maniscalco – came on the line. The two men exchanged cordial preliminaries. Then Guy Bannister, former CIA agent and more recently successful 'industrial security' specialist, asked the question for which Powell Pierce might conceivably want an answer.

'Found any more properties my client might be interested in?' Bannister inquired.

'We have,' Charles Farrier replied. 'One in Florida, another in New Jersey. Teams of our best appraisers will be looking them over. You should have reports tomorrow or the next day.'

Bannister had no difficulty obtaining an appointment with Powell Pierce for 4.30 that afternoon.

Bannister walked the few blocks to the Jersey Crest Tower on Madison Avenue. He took the elevator marked '57th Floor Only'. He arrived in the reception room of the Jersey Crest Oil Company's suite at 4.21. He was told to wait. He was ushered into Pierce's own office at 4.30 on the dot.

Pierce's rosewood desk gleamed softly. His snowy hair was, as always, immaculately trimmed and combed. He tipped his head a bit to one side, templed his fingers.

'I'd like to say that I'm impressed by the results you've obtained so far, Bannister,' he said.

'There should be more this week on the retail project,' Bannister said. First the good news, he thought, and waited to hear if Pierce wanted him to be more specific. Evidently, he did not. Now the bad news.

'We heard from Gerlach in Washington this afternoon,' he said.

'Oh!' Powell Pierce's expression remained unchanged. 'What did he want?'

'The money. In advance.'

'I expected that,' Pierce said.

'We're supposed to get back to him with some word.'

'Of course. Tell him payment will be made in full as soon as there is some tangible evidence that he and Engelhardt are co-operating.'

'Anything in particular you want them to do?'

'No. Any demonstration, no matter how minor, will do for the time being. The object is to have them actually commit themselves. Once they've taken some action, they *are* committed and can't pull out. A fact I'm sure Gerlach and Engelhardt will recognize.'

Shrewd, Bannister reflected. And true.

'I'll see to it Gerlach gets the message.' He made as if to stand up and leave.

'Wait a minute,' Pierce stopped him. 'The mechanics of payment will be complicated, as you probably realize.'

I certainly do, Guy Bannister thought. A million untraceable dollars would have to be obtained somewhere. With no paperwork that anyone could ever uncover. The task would not be simple, not even for a company the size of Jersey Crest.

'The money will be drawn in cash from a numbered Swiss bank account,' Powell Pierce said. 'It will then have to be taken to Washington and given to Gerlach.' He gazed at Bannister. 'I can't use anyone within the company to do the job. Will you take care of it?'

Bannister thought for a moment.

'Not personally,' he said. There were far too many risks involved. 'I've got a man I can trust who will, though.'

'That's satisfactory – provided you really are able to trust him.'

'I am.' Russell Peterson could run the million-dollar errand. He'd take the risks, ask no questions and do exactly as he was told.

2

30 June

James Northcutt had spent another long working day at Bonheur, his Cap d'Antibes estate. He was on the transatlantic telephone for hours with NIPCO executives, listening to their reports, demanding and receiving information. More hours were devoted to meeting with Samuel Schlechter and Mark Radford.

The overall picture that emerged was grim. Bad as the situation appeared, it would inevitably grow worse. Both Sam Schlechter and Mark Radford concurred. Worse surprises than even the sabotage at Qantara were bound to come in the future.

It was on that note that he left the two men in his study at 10 P.M. He went upstairs to Barbara Wallace's suite in the east wing of the mansion. He needed release from the pressures boiling within him.

Now it was almost midnight and Barbara Wallace lay cording her muscles and moaning in pretended pleasure. James Northcutt intuitively sensed she was shamming and eased himself away from her. He had no anxieties about his virility or his capacity to satisfy a woman. His sexual drive and prowess had always been lusty. They had remained so. Due, he admitted, in part to the Niehans cellular therapy rejuvenation treatments he underwent periodically. But they were more than adequate none the less. He knew the fault was not his. Barbara's pretendings were a very recent phenomenon.

Actually, she had lasted as his resident mistress longer than most of her innumerable predecessors, and with reason. He had found her witty, entertaining and capable of providing him with intellectual stimulation. She also possessed many qualities that counterbalanced what more than a few women had described as the dominant-male bastard ingredient in Jim Northcutt's nature.

But her attractions had worn thin. Whatever was genuine and spontaneous in her had been displayed again and again. Repetition made for overexposure and created boredom. Of late, she had begun resorting to crude tricks that Northcutt felt were an affront to his intelligence.

'You're marvellous, Jim,' Barbara sighed, her eyes closed and her full-breasted torso heaving with mimed post-orgastic pantings. 'That took everything out of me.'

He was silent for a moment. Yes, he reflected, she had provided release, satisfied him physically. He had achieved orgasm, but it had been a zestless mechanical release, not much more exciting than masturbation. And she had made it worse by feigning her own climax in a clumsy attempt to feed his ego. The hell with it, he decided.

'And you're lying,' he said with rancour. His expression was indifferent as he got out of bed and reached for his pyjamas and dressing gown.

Barbara Wallace's eyes snapped open, at first reflecting disbelief, an instant later rage. She sat bolt upright in the bed.

'Trying to dump me, Jim?' she demanded.

'The phrasing is yours,' he said evenly, putting on his pyjamas.

'You can't throw me out.'

'Your choice of words is bad.' He put on his dressing gown, knotting its belt. 'I don't like being told what I can – or can't – do.' He sat down in an armchair, his grey eyes steady but darkening. 'As you should know by now. And it's not my habit to "throw out" any woman I've been involved with.'

'No, it isn't your habit, is it?' Barbara glared at him. Her normally attractive face was distorted by anger. 'Not you, the

115

oilfield bum turned perfect gentleman! Only you didn't really change. You're a shit, Jim. A self-centred, woman-using shit!'

He stared at her impassively. He'd been through similar scenes with women before. Best let her rage spend itself.

'The big tycoon – and all prick!' Barbara ranted. 'What you can't grab or toss away, you buy or sell. Including women. We're all cash-and-carry gadgets, aren't we, Jim?'

Her hands grasped the bed sheet and clenched into fists.

'Then you pay to have us clear out. Generous Jim Northcutt! I suppose my cheque's already made out and your Jew shyster's drawn up the get-lost contract...'

Like most very rich men, James Northcutt had learned through bitter experience that the ending of an affair had to be treated as a business transaction if future problems were to be avoided. Money had to change hands, legal documents had to be signed.

A mistress being discarded was given a lump-sum payment and required to sign a meticulously spelled-out agreement. She would receive a regular monthly cheque (usually from a NIPCO subsidiary on whose payroll she was placed in some 'advisory' capacity). The cheques would continue, as long as she lived up to the terms of the agreement. These specified she was waiving all claims against her former lover and would bring no lawsuits against him. There were other non-molestation clauses. The ex-mistress agreed not to visit Northcutt unless invited. She would grant no interviews to the media and write no books or articles about him or their relationship and otherwise refrain from causing him any annoyance or embarrassment.

'... what's my payoff, Jim? How much was I worth? Do I get the standard —'

'That's enough,' Northcutt said. Even her tirade bored him. 'Any more hysterics, and I will have you thrown out – and there won't be any payoff, as you put it.'

Barbara did not know if he was bluffing, and she did not dare push him further. She would need whatever money he gave her. She had no doubts she would eventually find another wealthy lover, but it might take time. Of course, she would never find one nearly as rich as James Northcutt, and Barbara was painfully aware of this. It made her feel even more frustrated and infuriated. Making a supreme effort to regain her self-control, she lapsed into a sullen silence.

116

'I'll see you in the morning,' Northcutt told her. He stood up, left her suite.

After he had gone, Barbara flung herself out of bed and rushed into her bathroom. She took two Seconal capsules from a vial in the medicine cabinet and swallowed them with a little water. Then she returned to bed.

While waiting for the Seconal to work, Barbara let her mind dwell on the various ways she might get back to Northcutt. Despite the legal documents she would sign, there were many weapons she could use. The prospects themselves were a palliative, and she was smiling as the pills took effect and she finally fell asleep.

Kathy Northcutt had gone up to her own suite early. She had spent the day swimming and sunning herself, and she was languidly tired. Besides, there were a few letters she wanted to write, and this was something she preferred doing in bed with a writing stand propped over her body.

She bathed, wrote the letters and went to sleep.

A knock on the door brought her awake. She turned on her bedside lamp and glanced at the small clock next to it. A few minutes after two in the morning. She stifled a yawn and smiled. She knew it could only be her father. James Northcutt had never needed much sleep. He frequently read – business reports and correspondence, technical journals, books of all kinds – far into the morning hours. When Kathy was visiting Bonheur, he would often come to her suite, sit and talk for an hour or two.

'Feel up to conversation?' she heard him ask from the corridor outside.

'Sure, Dad.' She sat up and piled pillows to support her back.

He entered and grinned at his daughter. Light from the bedside lamp made her loose, coppery hair gleam. Even without makeup, her fine-boned face was lovely. He went to a chair facing her bed and folded his large frame into it.

'What's your excuse this time?' Kathy asked, smiling. 'Run out of reading matter or suffering from eyestrain?'

'I just got through cutting some knots for myself.'

Kathy's expression was comprehending. She could pick up her father's moods and inflections and if not actually read, then deduce, his thoughts.

'I take it Barbara's joining your army of exes.'

'You psyched that fast.'

'Who needs ESP? I've been seeing the signs ever since I got here. Your ennui has been showing. Anyway, congratulations.'

'You don't like Barbara, do you?'

'Nope. It's a woman thing. She may be fantastic in bed —'

'She is – was.'

'– but she's a bitch.'

'Aren't all you females bitches?'

'Uh-huh. Only we usually come in three grades, Junior, Regular and Super. Juniors just take a painful nip when they bite. Regulars sink their teeth in deep, gouge out big chunks —'

'And Barbara?'

'A Super. Fangs instead of teeth, and they're poisoned.'

Jim Northcutt laughed.

'How about you, Kath? What's your category?'

'I'm a Grade Four. Giant Economy Size. There aren't many of us, thank God. We have built-in selector switches. We flick 'em to suit – make ourselves Juniors, Regulars or Supers. Depending on what – or who – we're after.' Kathy's eyes were grey like her father's, and she had his right-eyebrow-angling mannerism. It slanted up now. 'Like father, like daughter – whatever a male version of a Grade Four bitch is called.'

'I'm curious. Why rate Barbara lower – or would it be higher?'

'Look, thanks to you – not just because you're rich, but for a lot of reasons – I have a choice. I can afford to act or react any way I please. Barbara can't. She's trapped in the feminine mystique, totally dependent on whoever is keeping her around as a house pet. That makes for rigid patterns, Dad, and even more rigid responses.'

'My daughter, the Women's Liberationist,' Northcutt chuckled.

'In a sense, yes,' Kathy agreed. 'But the whole male–female thing is all ass-backwards. Women like Barbara think they're using men. It's the other way around. Think about it sometime.'

Jim Northcutt snorted derisive protest.

'If you had any idea what women have cost me —'

Kathy's laugh was hearty. 'Cancel everything I said. *Don't* think about it, Dad. Not ever. You'd freak out if you did. I

118

guess you must be the ultimate male chauvinist. But I'll forgive you.'

'Should I say thanks?'

Kathy ignored the question. Her expression had abruptly turned serious, searching. She knew about what had happened at Qantara. Television, radio and newspapers had all carried accounts of the incident. However, she sensed there was something else, and she had to find out. It was her first chance to ask her father privately.

'Dad?'

'Hmm?'

'You're in a bad jam, aren't you?'

Northcutt was startled. He hesitated before replying and when he did, avoided giving a direct answer.

'Do I strike you as having a worried look?'

'Come off it. There are heavy vibes all over the place. You and Sam and Mark Radford overplay the supercool bit, then lock yourselves away for hours. I can tell you're sweating!'

'It's only business.'

Kathy stared at him reproachfully. She shook her head, her red hair a shimmering halo.

'*Only* business!' she exclaimed. 'Any time unflappable Jim Northcutt gets jittery about business, it has to be God-damned serious.'

Northcutt rubbed his jaw and sank into thought. Kathy's perception amazed him at times, and he recognized many of his own traits and qualities in her. However, there was one inescapable drawback. Kathy was his daughter, intelligent and shrewd, but still a woman.

I should have had a son, he mused. We should be working together, sharing in the benefits – and the problems – of what I'd always hoped would be a family business. Christ, I once even had dreams of establishing an honest-to-God dynasty!

Jim Northcutt looked up at his daughter. Maybe I'm not so bad off, after all, he reflected. Kathy was far more than a consolation prize. True, she had been spoiled and pampered throughout her twenty-nine years of life. Yet, she had remained an individual with a mind and spirit of her own, and there was steel in her.

He sighed, raising and lowering his broad shoulders, and at last repsonded to her comments.

'You're right, Kath,' he said, making the admission impulsively. 'I have got a load of problems, and they are God-damned serious.'

She waited for him to say more. When seconds passed and he remained silent, she spoke.

'Go on, Dad, tell me what it's all about.' Her voice was low and reassuring. 'I'm a big girl.'

He nodded, began to speak, and as he did, he found the bond between them growing stronger.

3

1 July

Barbara did not come downstairs in the morning. Jim North-cutt first assumed she was sulking. Then Medding relayed a message. She had commandeered the services of two maids and was packing. She would be finished with the task by mid-afternoon.

'Miss Wallace asks that you have the papers ready by then, sir,' Medding concluded. 'She says you know what she means.'

Northcutt felt relieved. Apparently Barbara was going to be reasonable and leave quietly, without histrionics. He took Sam Schlechter aside and told him he was ending the affair with Barbara. Schlechter made no comment. He was all too familiar with the oilman's habits. Northcutt would find a successor to take Barbara Wallace's place soon enough, and the cycle would begin all over again.

'Grab one of my secretaries and have her run up the usual good-bye and good-riddance agreements, will you, Sam?' Northcutt asked. The documents were all but form-letter stan-dardized.

'You haven't mentioned any figures,' Schlechter said.

'Fifty thousand lump, a thousand – no, better make that fifteen hundred a month.'

'The fifty being a personal gift from you, as usual?'

'Yes. For the monthly payments, pick a subsidiary and put her on the payroll as a marketing consultant or some damned thing.'

Schlechter raised a protesting hand.

'I advise against that, Jim. Make them personal payments.'

'Why, for God's sake?' Northcutt scowled. 'Your law firm brought in the tax experts who worked out that gimmick years ago. You've never been squeamish before.'

'We didn't have problems like we have now, either. I don't trust Barbara.' And she's likely to be vengeful. 'Suppose she talks and someone discovers how you've been retroactively subsidizing your sex life with corporate funds? We have enough difficulties at the moment. Why ask for another that could balloon into a major scandal?'

Northcutt's scowl deepened.

'Eighteen thousand a year,' he muttered. 'All taxable to me.'

Schlechter shook his head ruefully and laughed. Northcutt was again displaying one of the more ludicrous paradoxes of his makeup. *Time* Magazine had estimated that his income was $10,000 an hour, 24 hours a day, 365 days a year, and Schlechter knew this to be reasonably accurate. Yet Jim had the classic billionaire's phobia about paying from his own pocket for anything that could be charged to one of his companies. And the mere mention of personal income taxes often sufficed to trigger a tirade that lasted for hours.

'You're buying insurance,' Schlechter said as though soothing a distressed child. 'It's damned cheap.' Not even pennies by Northcutt's financial standards.

The scowl on the oilman's face began to fade.

'Do whatever you think best,' he agreed grudgingly.

Sam Schlechter and Mark Radford were to meet with James Northcutt in his study at eleven. They arrived a few minutes early. When Northcutt entered shortly afterwards, he had Kathy with him.

Schlechter was taken aback. Kathy had never participated in her father's business discussions before. In fact, Jim Northcutt had often expressed his determination to keep Kathy far removed from matters concerning NIPCO. Sam had tried to change this attitude, arguing that Kathy should be allowed to familiarize herself with the organization of her father's empire.

'Why?' was Northcutt's invariable rejoinder. 'Oil is an all-male business. You learn it from the ground up, out on the drilling sites, not by having people tell you what's going on – and who the hell ever heard of a woman roustabout?'

'Jim, use your head,' Schlechter would plead over and over.

'After you're gone Kathy will own or control your stock. It's going to be *her* business. She'll be NIPCO, the same as you've been and are!'

'Not really,' Northcutt countered sadly. 'The days when one man can still run a multi-billion-dollar business are almost over. The time when one woman can do it hasn't arrived. When I check out, NIPCO becomes another drag-ass corporation. It'll be managed by hired-hand executives who don't dare take a shit unless they have committee approval and don't *give* a shit about anything but their bonuses and stock options. That's the future, Sam!'

'Whether you're right or not, Kathy should have a chance to find out what she'll be up against,' Schlechter persevered.

'Nonsense. She won't be up against anything. We've established foolproof trusts and foundations, picked the best executors, administrators and trustees and boxed them in so they won't be able to pull any fast stunts. Kathy's interests are protected.'

This had been Northcutt's stand through the years, Schlechter reflected. Was it possible that Kathy's unexpected presence at the meeting was an about-face in Jim's attitude?

Mark Radford, watching Kathy curl her slender body into a wing chair, wondered if he would find her presence distracting. Yes, he thought, taking in the snug fit of her lime green bodyshirt and blue Levi's, it'll be hard work trying to keep my mind off *that*.

'Kath got the whole story out of me,' Northcutt announced, planting his rangy frame behind his desk. 'She took it without a tremor and raised hell until I said she could join us.'

That's it, Schlechter thought. Northcutt had never been able to refuse his daughter anything she asked for. But there must be more.

'I should've listened to you, Sam,' Northcutt continued. 'Did you know Kath's been studying NIPCO financial statements and annual reports for years and can practically quote 'em by heart?'

'No, I didn't,' Schlechter replied.

'Neither did I. Not till around five this morning.'

Northcutt quickly riffled through the stack of Telexes, cables and letters a secretary had placed on his desk earlier. Under normal circumstances, they would have been considered important, requiring immediate attention. Now they could wait.

'Let's get started.' The oilman thrust the papers aside. 'Give me a rundown on the latest.'

Schlechter and Radford had worked far into the night, contacting key company personnel in both hemispheres.

'I milked my Washington sources,' Sam said. 'We guessed right. Jersey Crest's making the most of their clout with the Administration. The wheels are starting to run. Against us.'

'Any details?'

'More than a few, I'm sorry to say. The word is your Chinese deal will be blocked. Every delaying tactic will be used to stall until the Chinese run out of patience. Then they'll be told it's because NIPCO couldn't really live up to the agreements —'

'But that the Jersey Crest consortium can – and fast – is that the ploy?' Jim Northcutt broke in.

'Right. The consortium wants the trade with China – and more. It wants to get rid of NIPCO. Permanently.'

'We figured that, too.'

'Pierce and his people have reached figures close to the top of the Administration. Even the National Energy Resources Department has been lined up.'

'There must be some damned big payoffs,' Northcutt muttered.

'Unquestionably.'

'Can't we raise the ante?'

'No. The deals have been made. We have to go for the flanks.'

'Meaning what?'

'The Jersey Crest consortium has bought up people in the Executive branch. We have friends in the Senate and House, and you and NIPCO stand well with the press and public. We can use them all to build backfires. Unless you want me to stay here, I'll fly to Washington tomorrow and start manoeuvring.'

'Good.' Northcutt turned to Mark Radford. 'What've you got?'

Mark felt Kathy's grey eyes on him. He ran the fingers of one hand through his sun-bleached sandy hair.

'The latest out of Qantara is almost encouraging,' he began. George Needham, who had taken over as acting resident manager, had a firm grip on the situation. The storage-tank fires were under control. The installations were seriously dam-

123

aged. However, Needham had Telexed the home-office that with all-out efforts, they might be back in near normal operation within two months. NIPCO executives in New York were doing everything to fly needed supplies to Qantara. And, there was no critical personnel problem on the island.

Contrary to early fears, relatively very few NIPCO employees had panicked and quit their jobs. This, Radford emphasized, was due to George Needham's success in restoring confidence and morale.

'I'd like to recommend you send Needham a personal letter of appreciation, J.L.,' Mark added.

'He'll get that – and a big bonus,' Northcutt said. He drummed his fingers on the desk top, his eyes narrowing, and asked, 'Any hint on who was directly responsible for the wrecking job?'

'The Arab press is blaming it on Israeli commandoes —'

'Horseshit!' Northcutt snorted. 'Why would the Israelis care about the Qantara fields?'

'Needham suspects Gerhard Hohenberg, an ex-SS man who set up shop in Istanbul around 1950. Hohenberg is an expert at high-priced assassinations and industrial sabotage.'

'I should've smelled Hohenberg right off,' Northcutt said.

'You know him?' Kathy asked.

'Know about him,' her father replied. 'He's the son of a bitch who engineered Enrico Mattei's murder, among other things.'

In the 1960s, Enrico Mattei headed the nationalized Italian petroleum industry. He outwitted – and outbid – several major international oil companies in contests for Middle Eastern and North African drilling concessions. The Majors decided he had to be eliminated. The 'contract' went to Gerhard Hohenberg. On 27 October 1962, Enrico Mattei's private executive aircraft exploded in mid-air, killing him and everyone else aboard. It was deliberate sabotage, but no arrests were ever made.

'Go on, Mark, what else?' Northcutt prompted.

'I spoke with Keeley last night.' Peter Keeley was the president of NIPCO and headquartered in New York. 'Some more NIPpy-brand service stations have been destroyed or damaged by "mysterious" fires. Local police haven't got anywhere. Keeley's done some checking, and I've called my own sources. The arson is professional. Whoever's footing the bills has hired an experienced, organized mob.'

'No surprise there,' Jim Northcutt observed acidly.

'As I see it, that's one I can do something about,' Radford said, a grin forming on his sun-seared face. 'I'm flying out, too – to New York. Maybe Pierce and his friends will find themselves having to file a few fire-insurance claims of their own.'

Kathy Northcutt uncurled herself, sat up straight and leaned forward, her eyes blazing.

'Are you saying you want to imitate them?' she demanded. 'Maybe even start a gang war?'

Radford blinked uncertainly. He looked at Northcutt, hoping for some hint as to what kind of answer he should give Kathy. Jim avoided meeting his glance. In that case, screw it, Mark thought and gazed squarely at Northcutt's daughter.

'It's exactly what I'm saying,' he told her, bracing for a horrified reaction. Instead, she offered an enormous smile.

'And I've been sitting here thinking you've all gone soft!' Kathy exclaimed. 'Thank God I was wrong!'

James Northcutt's afternoon meeting with Barbara Wallace was brief. She accepted the cheque for fifty thousand dollars without comment, signed all the copies of the agreement that Schlechter handed her.

'I have some of my bags in my car,' she told Northcutt. 'Please have the rest of my things sent to the address I've left with Medding.' She folded her copy of the agreement, put it into her Gucci handbag along with the cheque. 'You can reach me there if you want me for anything, Jim. I don't know whether to say *au revoir* or *adieu*. So I've just said both, and you can take your choice.'

Barbara drove out of the Bonheur estate grounds and into Cap d'Antibes, then headed her Mercedes towards Paris. The lump-sum payment was just about the amount she had expected. The monthly payments were somewhat more liberal than she had thought they would be. But these weren't the reasons why she smiled as she wove the Mercedes in and out of traffic.

Barbara Wallace was thinking ahead. Once the fifty-thousand-dollar cheque had cleared, she would begin concentrating on ways and means to make Jim Northcutt squirm.

4

2 July

National Energy Resources Secretary Rowan Engelhardt provided tangible evidence of co-operation by issuing a statement to the news media.

'Trade talks have been conducted recently in Peking between officials of the People's Republic of China and Mr James L. Northcutt. These have aroused much comment in the press. Mr Northcutt, a United States citizen long resident in France, has been negotiating on behalf of his Northcutt International Petroleum Company, an American corporation.

'The agreements under discussion involve a sum of over eight billion dollars. The figure is large. The implications of the talks are far-reaching. The matter demands close study by United States Government agencies, particularly the Department of National Energy Resources.

'There is, as we are all acutely aware, a critical shortage of gasoline, heating oil and other petroleum products in this country. There is no question but that we must increase the production of crude oil and other energy sources. However, we must also be certain that capital, industrial effort and vitally needed plant facilities are deployed in areas and concentrated on programmes that will provide maximum benefits for all Americans.

'I wish to give the public my assurance that the Department of National Energy Resources will examine the proposed Chinese–Northcutt International Petroleum agreements in light of these considerations. All factors will be weighed carefully with the sole objective of safeguarding national interests.'

On its face reasonable and even reassuring, the statement served to kindle the first sparks of public doubt. More important, it served between-the-lines notice that the Department of National Energy Resources was set to create bureaucratic obstacles that would gravely hamper James Northcutt and NIPCO.

Arriving in Washington, Samuel Schlechter went directly to

see Senator John Bosworth. They were old friends. Bosworth was a three-term veteran of the Senate. Campaign contributions from James Northcutt – and, before such contributions became illegal, from Northcutt companies – had helped win his elections. Senator Bosworth sat on important committees, and he did not forget past favours.

'If you need me, holler,' he told supporters and meant it. 'I deliver.'

Schlechter sat in Bosworth's office.

'We need you, John.' Schlechter parodied the backwoods speech patterns Bosworth affected to win votes in his largely rural home state. 'Came to ask that you join a posse.'

'You talk good shit-kicker English for a New Yorker.' Bosworth laughed.

'I should. I was brought up in Oklahoma.'

'Funny. I know that, but I always think of you as Mister Manhattan himself, Sam.' The Senator spoke normally. He offered Schlechter a cigar and when the attorney refused, took one himself and lit it. 'I knew what you needed when you phoned from France. The rumours have been seeping down. Arthur Gerlach and Rowan Engelhardt are lowering the boom on Jim and NIPCO.'

'They're only dummies, John. The real voice you hear belongs to Powell Pierce, and he has Western Impex and Richland Consolidated tied into a consortium with Jersey Crest.'

Bosworth took the cigar from his mouth and whistled.

'That adds up to a lot of money and power, Sam.'

'Too much for you to buck?' Schlechter asked.

'Nope. I don't owe that bunch anything.' Bosworth puffed at his cigar again. 'We can gather support in both houses. The three companies have their own stable. Still, we ought to form a fair-sized group. We can make noise and raise mighty embarrassing questions. Might even be able to start an investigation or two.'

He squinted at Schlechter through a haze of cigar smoke.

'I'll see to it we push hard,' he said. 'But there won't be instant results – and it won't be cheap.'

'The thought never crossed my mind,' Sam said. 'In this case, money is no object.'

'It couldn't be. Northcutt stands to lose everything.' Bosworth's expression was knowing. 'One minor point, Sam.'

'What's in it for you?'

'You're reading my mind.'

'Name a figure, John.'

Bosworth shifted his cigar. 'Northcutt's always helped me. I won't hold him up. Others will, though. I'm warning you of that now. Make it fifty thousand, and I'll ride along to the end of the line.'

'You've got it,' Schlechter said, thinking, fifty thousand dollars. The cost of buying a United States Senator and of buying off a shopworn mistress was the same. Right to the penny. 'What's our next move, John?'

'We go about twenty yards down the hall to see Richard Hurley,' Bosworth said. 'He's chairman of the Senate Energy Resources Committee. Dick and I roll a lot of logs together. He'll be damned useful to you.'

Mark Radford landed at Kennedy Airport at 11 A.M. He was met by Peter Keeley, who had a NIPCO limousine waiting.

'Learned anything about who's burning down our dealers' stations?' Mark asked as they rode into Manhattan.

'Not officially,' Keeley replied. 'The police claim they haven't been able to find any evidence of arson, much less clues as to who might be responsible.'

'But unofficially?'

Keeley said he had managed to establish some contact with underworld sources. In return for several thousand dollars, he had been given a hint that perhaps an 'organization' operating under the name Italo-American Fidelity Realtors was conducting the fire bombings.

According to his informants, the real estate company was the front for the Farrier *famiglia*. This Mafia gang controlled a number of gambling and loan-shark rackets in New York. However, it was known to specialize in protection, labour intimidation, other strong-arm operations – and insurance-fraud arson. Carlo Maniscalco, or Charles Farrier, as he preferred to be called, headed the organization.

'Their offices are on Third Avenue,' Keeley said.

'Let me off there,' Radford directed. 'Then have the driver take my luggage to the Drake. I have reservations there.'

'You're jumping into this with both feet awfully fast,' Keeley observed. 'Shouldn't you —'

'I shouldn't do anything but what I just said,' Mark told

128

him. 'We haven't any time to fool around. The sooner I check out this Farrier and his operation, the further ahead we'll be.'

Italo-American Fidelity Realtors, Incorporated, had an elaborate suite of offices in a gleaming new high-rise building on Third Avenue and Forty-eighth Street.

'If Mr Farrier's in, I'd like to talk to him,' Radford told the bosomy and sloe-eyed receptionist. He handed her a NIPCO business card with his name on it. The receptionist telephoned to an inner office, spoke in a tone too low for Mark to hear what she said. After a moment, she hung up.

'Somebody'll come out for you, Mr Radford.'

A man appeared, led him through a frosted glass door, down a corridor, to a glossy-modern office. A slender, grey-haired and conservatively dressed man was seated behind a free-form palissandre desk. He scrutinized his muscular, six-foot-three visitor in the manner of a pawnbroker appraising a diamond. A cheek muscle twitched.

'Take a chair, Mr Radford.'

Mark noticed that Farrier's manicured fingers flexed, betraying a trace of nervousness.

'Is your company interested in buying or selling real property?' Farrier asked. There was a slight grating edge to his voice.

'Neither,' Mark said. 'We're interested in fireproofing some of those we already have.'

Farrier's lips were full, but now they drew tight.

'I think you made a mistake and walked into the wrong office, Mr Radford.' The grating edge had become more obvious. 'That's not in our line of business.'

'Isn't it?' Mark's blue eyes showed surprise. 'I've been told your firm sells offbeat, high-risk insurance as a sideline. I heard that if premiums are large enough, you can insure that things will happen – or not happen.'

Farrier's expression and manner had become bland.

'Talk to the wrong people and you're liable to pick up some wild tales, Radford.' His omission of the 'Mr' was pointed. 'This is a fully licensed real estate firm. Check Dun and Bradstreet. We're rated. Three-A, I believe.'

'Let's stop fencing, Farrier' – no mister for you, either, you gold-plated hood – 'to D and B and maybe most of the world you're a successful real estate broker. I know otherwise, and I have a purely commercial proposition to put to you.'

A smart bastard, Farrier thought. However, no matter what Radford knew, there was nothing he could prove. There was no risk of loss, possibly a chance of gain, in listening.

'Go on, Radford.'

Mark chose his euphemisms carefully.

'Let's assume you have a client who is one of NIPCO's competitors, and assume further that your firm is performing certain services designed to weaken NIPCO's position. Our proposition is simple. Drop the present client and take on the NIPCO account instead. At double whatever fees you're now being paid.'

There it was, Mark Radford thought. James Northcutt had wanted him to make one all-out attempt at buying off the fire bombers. If it succeeded, Jersey Crest and its intermediaries would no doubt hire another gang. But that would take a little time – time that NIPCO needed desperately. If it didn't work? Then other action would have to be taken.

Charles Farrier gave the proposal a moment of concentrated thought. He dealt with Guy Bannister and his Federpol Industrial Security firm, but was aware that Bannister merely acted as a front for some very large and rich corporate client. A major oil company, Farrier reflected. The prospect of receiving doubled fees was tempting. But a contract was a contract, especially when it was with the more powerful group, the one that would most likely end up the winner.

'Sorry,' he said at last. 'We'll hold on to our present account.' There was a cold finality in his tone.

What I figured would happen, Mark told himself. At any rate, I've managed to confirm that Farrier and Italo-American were conducting the terror campaign against NIPCO dealers. At least one enemy force had been pinpointed. He knew what to do next.

5

2 July

James Northcutt and his daughter were in the main drawing room at Bonheur a little after 10 P.M., when Medding entered to announce that Mark Radford was telephoning from New York.

'I'll take it in my study,' Jim said.

Kathy was more than a bit surprised to find herself tense with excitement. She followed her father, telling herself her eagerness to hear news of Mark Radford was only because he was fighting to save Northcutt International.

'I really didn't expect you'd get anywhere,' Northcutt said after hearing Radford's account of his meeting with Farrier. 'What's the outlook for getting help from the authorities?'

'Bleak,' Radford told him. 'I've been over the question with Keeley. These people are highly organized professionals. They know how to cover their tracks. Besides, we would have to get co-operation from the local police departments in every town where there are NIPCO dealers.'

'Adds up to hundreds,' Northcutt said.

'And most of the police departments are either impotent or bought off or both.'

James Northcutt exhaled. It sounded like a sigh of resignation.

'Appears we have no choice, Mark,' he said. 'See what you can do on the alternate plan we discussed before you left France.'

When the conversation ended, Jim Northcutt cradled the receiver and gazed moodily at a Raoul Dufy seascape hanging near his desk.

'Dad?' Kathy said.

Her father didn't shift his eyes.

'You're sending Mark to Steve Kostis and Lloyd Birdwell for help.'

'That's the idea. The three of us were good friends in the old days.'

'More like a trio of buccaneers,' Kathy said, smiling.

'How would you know?' Northcutt turned his head, staring at Kathy, his grey eyes widening. 'That all happened before you were born – most of it even before I'd met your mother.' He, Steven Kostis and Lloyd Birdwell had their Southern California salad days in the 1920s and '30s. Kathy hadn't been born until World War Two was almost over.

'My God! They were Uncle Steve and Uncle Lloyd when I was a kid and we lived in L.A. They'd come over to the house in Bel Air and all of you would sit around drinking whisky and trading stories. Don't you remember?'

A feeling of nostalgia swept over him. After Kathy began to walk and talk and while his marriage to her mother, Pamela, lasted, the girl had been constantly at his side whenever he was home.

'Why, I wasn't even six when Steve Kostis taught me how to stack a poker deck.' Kathy laughed. 'My hands were so small I could barely hold the cards, but he managed to teach me just the same.'

'Christ, that's right. I'd forgotten.'

'I can still deal after your cut and give you four aces and myself a straight flush.'

'Now you've got *me* started.' Her father's mood had turned reminiscent. 'Wasn't there a night when Lloyd Birdwell came over roaring drunk and swearing off women for life because his affair with Veronica Lake had broken up?'

'There sure was. The servants blew their minds. He came in barefooted with those awful tennis shoes he usually wore slung over a shoulder. He was raving that all women were two-faced tramps —'

'Then he noticed you.'

'And got solemn the way some drunks do. He handed me a nickel. "You're the exception," he said. "Use the nickel to call me the minute you reach the legal age." I didn't really know what he meant, but I kept the nickel for years.'

'You did?'

'Sure. I thought he was very handsome and dashing – even if he was kind of a kook and a millionaire.'

Jim Northcutt's right eyebrow slanted.

'Lloyd was always eccentric as hell, but what did his being a millionaire have to do with it? You must've known I was, too.'

'I did. But you and Lloyd Birdwell were the only rich men

I'd ever seen who weren't uptight about it.'

'Wait a minute. You liked Steve Kostis, and he had more money than either Lloyd or me back in those days.'

'It didn't show. Kostis was always so good-natured – kind of a young Santa Claus with a trace of Greek accent. Besides, there weren't any newspaper stories about him like there were about you and Birdwell. It was a long time before I ever managed to figure out what Steve Kostis did for a living.'

'Were you shocked?'

'Hardly. He became one of my favourite folk heroes along with you and Lloyd.'

Kathy studied her father carefully. Yes, she decided, I've taken the right approach, injected precisely the right tone. He's as receptive now as he'll ever be.

'Dad.'

'What, Kath?'

'Sending Mark Radford to ask Kostis and Birdwell for help adds up to a very big order. Mark is smart, reliable and knows his business. Still, he's a hired hand. And you're sending him to talk on your behalf with two very powerful men you haven't seen personally in ten, twelve years or more.'

'I'd go myself, but —'

'I think I can understand why you don't. But consider this, Dad. Steve Kostis is retired, keeping a very low profile. Lloyd Birdwell has been playing hermit since the early nineteen sixties. Suddenly, they get a visit from a NIPCO employee – an executive and your representative, but an employee all the same. Suppose they consider Mark merely a flunky and give him a brushoff?'

Northcutt remained silent, then finally spoke.

'We'd find other means —'

'Maybe. But even if you did, it would take more time, and that's one commodity we don't have in any great supply.'

'What's the point, Kath?'

'That I catch the next plane – or take yours – meet Mark Radford in New York and go to L.A. with him. My old "Uncles" Steve and Lloyd are bound to welcome me with open arms. They'd be less likely to say no if I was along than if Mark came alone.' Kathy gazed at her father with shrewd, level eyes. 'Every man is a sucker for a damsel in distress.'

Northcutt had to admit that Kathy's arguments were logical. Kathy could bring it off, he told himself, but I'd be using my own daughter to save myself.

Kathy easily tuned in on her father's mental conflict. It was what she had expected, and she smiled gently and chose her words carefully.

'You and Sam Schlechter keep telling me I'll have control of NIPCO someday,' she said. 'If NIPCO goes, you and I both go along with it.' She raised her right eyebrow. 'Your ambivalence about women is too much!'

'What in the hell does that mean?'

'I'll drag a family skeleton out of the closet to explain. You've told me how you got your start. One-third of your financing came from a woman you lived with. She ran a whorehouse —'

'Jesus Christ! What does that prove?' Northcutt demanded.

'What I mentioned before. Your ambivalent attitude towards women. You were having an affair with Verna Fletcher. From the way you've talked about her, I suspect you were in love with her ...'

I was, Jim Northcutt agreed silently. I didn't realize it in time. Afterwards – but why dredge up those memories now.

'... but that didn't stop you from taking her money to use in your business. You treated her as a person. I happen to be your daughter. I'm not a person to you. I'm Miss Fragile. You're terrified that if something ever touches me, I'll crumble. It is, *mon cher père*, the stupidest – and shittiest – attitude you could take.'

'A man doesn't send his daughter to soft-soap other men!'

'For God's sake!' Kathy protested. 'I won't be sleeping with Lloyd Birdwell or Steve Kostis or even using what *you'd* probably call sex appeal on them. I'll be exploiting the same nostalgia factor that had us both dewy-eyed a few minutes ago.'

Her eyes were steady now.

'Can't you see I'll be helping to save what's mine as well as yours?'

Verna Fletcher's reaction would have been precisely the same, Northcutt reflected. And so would that of Kathy's mother, Pamela. Strange how the women who are important in a man's life seem to share certain basic qualities.

Northcutt's hand strayed to his watch pocket. The big turnip pocket watch he carried in Oklahoma had been discarded decades before. However, he had never stopped carrying a

134

looped chain with the gold-and-onyx gusher charm Verna had given him. He put two fingers into his pocket, lightly rubbing the charm. Not out of superstition, but because touching the tiny, tangible link to the past seemed to give continuity to the present.

'Use my plane,' he said to Kathy, his jawline taut. 'Pick up Radford in New York. I'll put through a call and tell him to wait for you.'

6

3 July

Energy crisis, economic recession and international developments made any prospect of early congressional adjournment for the summer unlikely. Therefore legislators streamed out of Washington to take full advantage of the long Fourth of July weekend vacation.

By mid-afternoon, Capitol Hill was almost deserted and temperatures hovered around the 90-degree mark.

Samuel Schlechter could accomplish nothing further by remaining in Washington. He had completed his intensive bargaining and mobilized an impressive force of Senate and House mercenaries who had agreed to ally themselves with NIPCO. He returned to his Shoreham Hotel suite with Senator John Bosworth. There they relaxed and drank Jack Daniel's while Bosworth smoked one of his inevitable Montecruz panatelas.

Their mood was cautiously hopeful.

'You must've obligated Jim Northcutt for close to a million,' Bosworth said.

'Not quite.' Schlechter sipped his bourbon. 'A shade less than eight hundred thousand.' He gave Bosworth a candid look. 'It's cheap – *if* we obtain results.'

'We will,' Bosworth assured him, savouring the Montecruz. He had drained his glass earlier and refilled it now from a bottle on the table beside his armchair. 'The lineup is good, with some top rankers. You have Dick Hurley —'

'Thanks to you,' Schlechter broke in.

'Won't deny I helped,' Bosworth shrugged. 'The thing to remember is that Senator Hurley's influential, and we do have him steamed up. He's never liked Arthur Gerlach, and he voted against Rowan Engelhardt's confirmation. When Hurley unlimbers his committee, he'll be out for blood.'

'Don't be overoptimistic,' Schlechter warned. 'Hurley won't be able to move too fast, and we might all be miscalculating the impact a Senate committee can have on Powell Pierce and his war against NIPCO.'

'God damn, but you're a cheerful cuss, Sam.' The Senator gulped bourbon. 'Can't you look at the bright side?'

'Certainly I can,' Schlechter said, finishing his own drink. 'When I *know* it's there.'

James L. Northcutt's private Boeing 727/100 landed at Newark Airport in the early evening.

Kathy Northcutt, the sole passenger aboard the craft, disembarked and found Mark Radford waiting for her. He had come to the airport in a chauffeured NIPCO limousine.

'J.L. didn't mention where you'd be staying for the night,' Mark said. 'Are you going to your own apartment?'

'No. I closed it up before I left. I have a reservation at the Pierre.'

A porter deposited a single Vuitton bag on the front seat. Kathy had left the rest of her luggage aboard the plane. Crew members would clear it through customs for her, then reload it for the flight to Los Angeles in the morning. Radford gave the driver instructions, and the gleaming limo pulled away from the kerb.

'The Pierre, huh?' Mark mused aloud, leaning back in the rear seat. The hotel was elegant and luxurious, but its ultra-staid atmosphere somehow didn't seem to fit with Kathy's personality. 'Why there of all places?'

'Because I always stay at the Pierre when I need a hotel in New York.' There was a note of reprimand in her tone, as though Mark had overstepped some boundary line by asking. Her tone softened when she added, 'Um – like when my own place is being decorated or painted.'

Mark was silent. He looked at Kathy's delicately moulded face and once again knew that he liked what he saw. But he had heard Katherine Northcutt's caustic remarks about her last lover while he was at Bonheur, and had observed the eas with which she had assumed an equal role during the conferences he and Schlechter had with James Northcutt. She could prove to be a very tough young lady, he thought, perhaps too tough.

The limousine eased into the Lincoln Tunnel, surfacing on the Manhattan side.

'You booked for the evening?' Kathy asked suddenly.

'Nope. I was hoping you would have dinner with me.'

'I was waiting for you to ask.'

'Any particular place?' he asked.

'Let's make it the Pierre We're flying early tomorrow. That way, I can go right up to my suite afterwards.'

Mark dwelt on business matters throughout dinner. He discussed the specific commitments they would try to obtain from Steve Kostis and Lloyd Birdwell and the alternatives if one or both of the men refused them. Kathy's impatience, tinged with boredom, showed itself when coffee was served.

'We can talk about all that tomorrow,' she said. 'It's more than four hours to the coast.'

'Okay,' Mark shrugged. 'Would you care for a cognac or shall I call for the bill?'

'The bill,' Kathy said. 'We'll have the cognac up in my suite.'

On the thirty-fourth floor, Kathy handed Mark her doorkey. He unlocked the door and followed her inside.

'I'll have room service send up the cognac,' he said, moving towards the phone in the sitting room.

'I don't really want a drink. Do you?'

He paused, looked at her.

'No.'

She was lovely. Her coppery hair gleamed softly in the subdued light, and her eyes were frankly erotic. Christ, why not, Mark thought. She wants me and I want her, and why should I be a damned fool? Hangups about sex with the boss's daughter went out with the first Horatio Alger story — if they ever existed at all.

He went to Kathy, took her in his arms. Her response was volcanic, her body enveloping his. Her mouth was feverish, her tongue thrusting deep. She gripped his shoulders and moved against him. Then her muscles tightened. She moaned. The moan built to a cry. Her body strained, shuddered violently

137

and then she went limp in his arms.

'Christ – oh, Christ!' she said unevenly and eased herself from his embrace. She brushed loose strands of hair away from her face, recovered her equilibrium and smiled. 'I was on the thin edge all through dinner.'

She reached for his hand.

'We have too many clothes on,' she said, leading him into the adjoining bedroom. The bed had been turned down by the night chambermaids. Mark began undressing her, his hands and lips caressing her as he did.

'Don't make me wait,' Kathy gasped.

Mark thought he was jarred by a note in her voice, but he could not identify it. She pulled herself free and hurriedly removed the rest of her clothing.

He tossed his jacket on the back of a chair and unbuttoned his shirt. He watched her movements. Her body was supple – lovely.

'Anyone ever told you that you're not the worst-looking woman in the world?'

'Not recently.' Her smile was on and off. 'For God's sake, hurry up.'

The grating note was there again.

When he was undressed, Kathy went to him, then released him abruptly, sat down on the foot of the bed. She lay back on it, her feet touching the thick-carpeted floor, and opened her thighs.

'Take me!'

Mark took a step forward. He was ready to kneel on the carpet. But vague and fleeting impressions now registered fully, and he stopped dead. He had no inhibitions about, indeed he delighted in all forms of sex with women.

He stopped because he had now identified and was able to define the discordant voice-quality that he had noticed before when Kathy spoke. Her tone was clearly imperious, demanding. She expected instant, unquestioning obedience. He stared at her, his blue eyes narrowing. His look turned angry.

'I said —'

'I heard you.'

'Then why . . .?'

Kathy's words trailed off as she sat up and saw that he was already reaching for his clothes.

'You picked the wrong guy, Miss Northcutt,' he said over

138

his shoulder. 'I'm not a hired stud.'

'You rotten bastard!'

Mark dressed rapidly. He didn't speak until he was fully clothed and on his way out of the room.

'See you on the plane tomorrow at eight,' he said. Before she could call out to him, he was gone.

7

4 July

Mark Radford had no idea of what Kathy Northcutt's attitude would be towards him, and he didn't much care. He arrived at the Newark airport at 7.30 A.M. and boarded the Northcutt International Petroleum Company Boeing. The four flight-crew and four cabin-crew members were already aboard. The pilot said he had filed their flight plan. All was ready for take-off at eight sharp, provided Miss Northcutt arrived before then.

There was a lounge-conference room amidships in the palatially appointed 727. Mark took a seat there. He opened his attaché case and began making notes on a legal-sized memo pad. The steward and a saucy, mini-skirted stewardess treated him deferentially and when he asked for coffee, they brought it in a sterling silver pot.

Kathy Northcutt boarded at ten minutes before eight. The crew members acted as though she were reigning royalty. Which she was, as far as they were concerned, Mark reflected, watching the performance.

'Good morning.' Kathy's greeting to him was crisp, impersonal but without any trace of rancour. She sat down in one of the white-leather-upholstered lounge chairs facing Mark and buckled her seat belt.

'I told the pilot to take off right away,' she said. She nodded towards the papers Mark had spread out on a tabletop. 'Anything there I should read?' Cabin doors were being thumped and sealed shut while the four Rolls-Royce jet engines whined into life.

'We ought to go through everything together,' Radford said,

securing his own seat belt. He handed her the papers. 'If you have questions, I'll try to answer them. Later, I'd like you to tell me about Birdwell and Kostis. The more I know about them that isn't public information, the better chance I'll have of being convincing.'

The Boeing had begun taxiing to its assigned runway for take-off.

Kathy's right eyebrow slanted.

'I'm afraid you have the wrong idea about this jaunt, Mark. I'm the one who'll be doing the convincing. Your job is to look up brightly and reel off facts and figures. When and if they're needed.'

Damned if you aren't the last word in ball-breakers, Radford thought. If I didn't feel that I owed your father loyalty, I'd dump this whole mess in your lap and walk out.

The three top buttons of Kathy's nubby-textured raw silk St Laurent shirt were open. When she leaned forward even slightly, Mark could see the tops of her breasts. No bra, he observed. Nothing subtle about her post-rejection teasing.

Mark Radford was forced to make many modifications in his assessment of Kathy's character during the flight. No doubt she was a pampered brat grown into a woman who needed to dominate others. But that had nothing to do with her ability to grasp a difficult subject.

Kathy first speed-read the reports and papers he had given her. Then she culled out those of greatest importance and concentrated on them. Her comments and requests for elaboration were trenchant. Her capacity for quick comprehension of even technical complexities showed a high degree of intelligence and an astute business sense.

Mark had to admit to himself that he was impressed. She *is* Daddy's Girl in more ways than one, he mused.

They ate lunch while overflying New Mexico and Arizona.

'At least you don't have to call for a bill this time,' Kathy said archly when steward and stewardess had cleared the table.

'No, but I will have a cognac,' he said. 'And I do want it.'

Neat parry and better than I expected, Kathy granted silently. Seems I'll have to flick my bitch controls up a notch. And you, Mark Radford, will end up sliced and skewered into manageable chunks. I guarantee it.

The Boeing touched down gently. Its engines roared as the pilot applied reverse thrust. Moments later, the aeroplane was taxiing smoothly towards an apron parking area assigned by the Los Angeles International Airport control tower.

'A NIPCO Western Division car's meeting us,' Mark said.

'Use it to send our luggage straight to the hotel,' Kathy said. They had two bungalow reservations at the Beverly Hills Hotel. 'Tell the steward to take care of it.'

'What do we do, walk?'

'Hardly. I phoned Steve Kostis last night. He's sending one of his cars for us.' Kathy's smile was smug and only a shade from being condescending. 'Being able to call the country's biggest racket financier "Uncle Steve" does have its advantages.'

Especially if you happen to have one of the world's richest men as a father, Mark commented to himself. Kathy was clearly out to put him in his place. With a vengeance.

Kathy remembered that years ago, the men who worked for Steve Kostis seemed to be uniformly sullen and hard-faced. Now, they were met by a man who introduced himself as Kostis's 'administrative assistant', and he was of an entirely different breed. From his appearance and manner, he might have been a Security First National Bank middle-management executive. He led them to a waiting Lincoln Continental limousine, the body of which was obviously custom-crafted. A uniformed chauffeur was poised beside it, ready to open the door.

'I'll ride up front,' their escort said.

Kathy and Mark got into the back seat. The chauffeur closed the door. The sound of the door shutting resembled none that Kathy had ever heard before. She said as much to Radford. 'Like a steel cargo-hatch.'

'Make that a tank hatch and you'll be closer. This thing is armoured. Look at the windows. Bulletproof glass.'

Kathy Northcutt was hardly the type to giggle, but she did now – with delight. She had always enjoyed the offbeat. The Lincoln made fast time on the Freeway, then turned off on Beechwood Drive, headed into the Hollywood Hills. After much turning and twisting the car made its way to Mulholland Drive. Steve Kostis's home stood atop a conical peak high above the Mulholland Reservoir and overlooked all of Los Angeles. On this smog-free day one could see across the sprawl of the city to the Pacific and even glimpse the bluish blob that was Catalina Island.

The limousine halted before steel-barred gates set into a thick stone wall encircling acres of landscaped grounds.

'San Quentin?' Kathy quipped.

A watchman in a dark blue suit was posted just inside the gates. He recognized the Lincoln and pushed a button. The limousine drove through as the gates swung open.

The Kostis house was enormous, about the same size as James Northcutt's mansion at Bonheur. But it was built of grey stone. This further emphasized the fortress – or prison – effect. Inside, the contrasts were startling. Steve Kostis evidently had a taste for the flamboyant and garish. A cavernous entrance hall featured a twelve-foot-high waterfall that cascaded into a pool twenty feet in diameter. The pool was surrounded by tropical plants. Concealed multi-coloured lights heightened the Miami Beach hotel-lobby flavour.

Two men dressed in street clothes, with the air and carriage of bodyguards, appeared. Kathy saw they were of the same sort of hard-faced men who had attended Uncle Steve Kostis when she was a child. Somehow, it made her feel better. A Steve Kostis who had grown effete would have been a grave disappointment.

'If you'll follow us. Mr Kostis asked that you be taken straight in.' The executive type who had met them at the airport spoke, and he and the two bodyguards led Mark and Kathy down one corridor, then another and finally a third. Double doors walled it off at the far end. In answer to their knock, a wheezing voice called out that they should enter.

The room was huge – and darkened. Heavy, opaque drapes were drawn across the windows to shut out sunlight. Illumination came from dimmed, concealed lights. Any furniture that was visible in the gloom was stridently modern.

A man was propped rather than sitting in a large oddly shaped chair. He was immensely fat and looked to be in his mid-seventies, even though it was difficult to believe anyone so obese could have lived that long.

Kathy took a few steps into the room and tried to focus her eyes. It was only with effort that she recognized the mountain of fat as Steve Kostis.

'Uncle Steve,' she said and crossed the room.

Kostis sensed her stunned reaction.

'Not what I used to be, Kathy?' he rasped. His breathing

was laboured. Kathy reached his chair. His once-florid Greek face was hideously bloated, but she leaned down and kissed him on the cheek.

'Uncle Steve, this is Mark Radford. Dad tell you about him?'

'He did. On the phone. Glad to know you, Radford.' He extended his hand. Mark took it. He had expected it to be limp and was surprised by the strength it retained. He saw Kostis more closely. Weak eyes that were pained by direct light peered from surrounding folds of fat. A thick-lipped mouth grotesquely parodied a smile.

'Sit down,' Kostis said, wheezing in air. 'Both of you.' His eyes focused on Kathy. 'Still able to handle a deck?'

'Want to check me out? High card cut for ten thousand?'

Steve Kostis responded with a hacking cough. 'Eat? Drink? Anything else I can offer?'

Kathy shook her head.

'I knew this redhead when she was this high,' Kostis said to Mark Radford. 'I used to tell Jim. He was proud of being a wildcatter. I said Kathy proved he was. She was like a wildcat even then.'

Kostis swung his head back in Kathy's direction.

'How's your dad?'

'All right,' Kathy replied. Not fair to tell him that Jim Northcutt's in great shape. It might make Kostis envious. 'He sends you his best.'

'Jesus! When I think how long I've known him. Ever since the twenties! Even before I started bankrolling the guys who ran the rum boats.'

Kathy laughed.

'I didn't find out until much later, but by the time I met you, Uncle Steve, you were financing half the gambling in Las Vegas.'

'Not half, redhead. Three-quarters. Only it wasn't any fun by then. Too much like big business. The fun was back in the days between the two big wars. That's when your dad and Lloyd Birdwell and me played with characters like Ed Doheny and Carl Laemmle and Sam Goldwyn and even that over-stuffed asshole, Willie Hearst.' Kostis fell silent, gasped for air, spoke again. 'Your dad ever tell you how Hearst caught Lloyd Birdwell with Marion Davies one night?'

'No, he didn't.'

'It's a big party. At Clara Bow's place. Everybody's drunk or coked up – except Hearst, of course. Marion disappears. Hearst goes looking for her. Finds her in the bushes with Lloyd. Starts yelling in that squeaky voice that he's going to ruin Birdwell by running exposes about him in all the Hearst papers. Lloyd just laughs. Hearst had a lot of notes and mortgages hanging over his head by then. Lloyd says he'll buy them up out of petty cash and foreclose.'

Kostis had another coughing spell. It passed, and he went on.

'Anyway, poor Willie's so mad, he raves that's he going to have Birdwell knocked off. Lloyd stops laughing and puts on a straight face. "I'll be damned," he says. "I just told Marion how Jim Northcutt and I were going to hire some of Steve Kostis's boys to bump you off, Willie. That way, Jim and I can share her easier between us." Hearst hears that and dumps right on his butt. He starts to bawl like a baby. "Go ahead, have me killed," he yowls, "but keep your hands off Marion!" '

The mountain of fat that was Steve Kostis's body shook violently as he broke into laughter. Then the laughter stopped.

'Yeah,' he said, his tone much subdued. 'Your dad and Lloyd and me had some times together.'

He and Kathy talked for almost an hour. Eventually it became apparent that Kostis was tiring.

'Redhead, Jim told me on the phone you and Radford were coming to see me because he's in trouble.'

'That's about it, Uncle Steve. Let Mark tell you.'

Mark rapidly outlined the problem. Then he narrowed down to the arson campaign being conducted against NIPCO retailers on the East Coast.

'. . . and the actual dirty work is being done by a New York Mafia outfit,' Radford finished.

'Whose?' Kostis demanded.

'The *capo* goes by the name of Charles Farrier.'

'He must be small-time or new. I never heard of him.'

'His real name is Carlo Maniscalco.'

There was an almost imperceptible change in Kostis's face. 'You talked to him?'

'I did.' Mark related his conversation with Farrier. 'Offered double whatever he was being paid. He turned it down. Flat.'

Steven Kostis lapsed into silence. He had spent his active life as moneylender, grubstaker, factor and financier for bootleggers, gamblers and other assorted racketeers. In California and several other states, he had been widely called the mobster's A.P. Giannini. Along the way he had amassed a hundred-million-dollar fortune. With the millions, he'd made countless enemies – and some friends.

He counted Jim Northcutt as a friend. But I've retired, Kostis reflected, pulled out of the deals and rackets and the headaches. I've got what? Two years to live, five at most if the doctors are'nt lying and I'm lucky. What's the sense of getting myself involved?

He stared at Kathy.

'Tell me, redhead,' he rasped. 'You got any good reason why I should stick my nose in this mess?'

'Dad predicted you ask me that.'

'Yeah, he would. And how you should answer?'

' "We stay friends either way." That was all.'

Northcutt meant it, too, Steve Kostis mused, and his mind went back over the years. Jim did me favours – including a couple of very big ones. The noises Kostis made in his throat might have been a chuckle.

'You Jim's field man on this deal?' he asked Mark.

'Yes.'

'Okay,' Kostis said. 'Give one of my boys all your New York phone numbers and addresses. I still got connections and swing some weight. Somebody'll get in touch with you.'

Kathy stood up, put her arms around Kostis's neck and kissed him.

'Thanks, Uncle Steve.'

'Forget it, redhead.' The melancholy ghost of what had once been a bawdy leer contorted his features. 'Too bad you weren't born fifteen-twenty years sooner. I'd've laid you for sure.'

'If I hadn't raped you first, cardsharp.'

Kostis wheezed, coughed, wheezed again.

'When you seeing Lloyd Birdwell?' he asked.

'We have an appointment for tomorrow,' Kathy replied.

'Give the crazy son of a bitch my regards.'

He paused, and added, 'Be careful. You're playing with some very tough characters.'

Kathy and Mark purposely avoided each other that evening. Kathy telephoned some old friends who lived in and around Los Angeles and gave an impromptu dinner party in her

145

Beverley Hills Hotel bungalow.

Mark went to the Polo Lounge, where he met a minor television actress. She saw he was deeply tanned and well tailored and assumed he was a producer, at very least a director. When, over dinner, he finally managed to convince her that he was neither, she no longer cared what he did for a living.

Later, in Mark's bungalow, she gave a display of sexual virtuosity that left her – and Mark Radford – contentedly exhausted and asleep in each other's arms.

8

5 July

Mark regretted the six-thirty call that woke him. He regretted even more that he had to shower, shave, dress, eat breakfast and be ready to leave for Lloyd Birdwell's estate by eight.

'Will you phone me?' the girl he had met the night before asked over their large room-service breakfast.

'Sure,' he promised.

It was only after he and Kathy Northcutt left the hotel in the NIPCO Western Division limousine that he realized he had forgotten the girl's last name and neglected to obtain her telephone number. When the chauffeur drew up at the gate to Lloyd Birdwell's Malibu estate, Mark and Kathy had a sense of déjà vu. Countless photographs of the estate had appeared in newspapers and magazines, all taken from the outside. A twenty-foot-high concrete wall topped by multi-strand barbed-wire barriers surrounded Birdwell's fifty acres. The gates themselves were solid steel, guarded by two uniformed men wearing open-holstered ·45 calibre automatics on belts festooned with extra cartridge-clips.

An elaborate, obviously much practised ritual began. One guard walked to the chauffeur's door.

'Driver's licence and vehicle registration.'

The second guard stood to the right of the limousine, very much alert and wary.

The chauffeur produced the requested papers, gave them to the first security man, who walked away to check the registra-

146

tion licence numbers against those on the car plate. Satisfied, he returned, gave the papers back to the chauffeur. Then he stepped to Mark's passenger compartment window.

'ID papers, please.'

Mark had his passport out. Kathy offered hers. He gave both to the guard, who studied them, paying special attention to the passport photos.

'I'll have to call in for clearance.' The guard walked to a sentry box built against the massive wall.

'You'd think we were trying to get into the CIA code-room,' Mark said. 'I've been reading and hearing about Birdwell most of my life. He's the world's richest hermit. What's he afraid of, anyway?'

'According to Dad, Lloyd started to have phobias way back,' Kathy replied. 'He just got progressively worse, until he was afraid of everything. For no real reason.'

'He must be a nut.'

'In some compartments, maybe. But not in the ones that count for him. Look at the influence he has in the oil business.'

True, Mark reflected. The Birdwell Equipment Company manufactured two-thirds of all the drilling tools used by American oil companies.

'And then there's everything else he owns,' Kathy said.

Also true. Despite eccentricity – or even partial insanity – Lloyd Birdwell had put together one of the world's largest and most diversified industrial conglomerates. Birdwell companies manufactured military aircraft, prefabricated houses, ballistics missiles, pleasure boats, electronics gear, space-exploration rocket components, computers, earth-moving machinery – the list was almost without end. His real estate holdings were enormous. He owned an assortment of banks, book publishing companies and insurance companies. He also controlled a large motion-picture studio and had now bought an important television-film producing organization.

Television reminded Mark of the actress with whom he had spent the night. He shot Kathy a sidelong glance, saw she was gazing through the window on her side and wondered if she had slept alone.

The security man emerged from his sentry box.

'They're okay, Hank,' he said to his colleague, who nodded and, for the first time, relaxed.

'Start your engine,' the first guard told the chauffeur. 'Be ready to drive through. The gates are controlled from the inside. They'll open in a minute, but close automatically thirty seconds later. Don't drive over fifteen miles an hour on the grounds.'

The chauffeur nodded and started the engine. The great steel gates opened. The limousine rolled through. Mark Radford's eyes widened in astonishment. There wasn't a tree or a shrub to be seen. The grounds were entirely carpeted with grass – no, he corrected himself, looking more closely. Not grass. Jesus Christ Almighty, he thought – fifty acres of Astroturf!

Two men wearing uniforms identical to those of the gate guards stood, watching the limousine. Mark counted a dozen slender steel towers thrusting up from the expanse of Astroturf. These were topped by cross-arms on which were mounted powerful searchlights and rectangular boxes. Mark correctly guessed the latter were closed-circuit television cameras.

Lloyd Birdwell's house crowned a rise, the only one on the otherwise table-flat grounds. But it didn't look like a house at all. Formally institutional in design, the large three-storey structure had been built with concrete, stainless steel and glass. It resembled a pharmaceutical company's ultramodern research laboratory or even a hospital.

'Weird,' Mark Radford muttered.

'Pure Lloyd Birdwell,' Kathy said.

Another uniformed security man met them at the entrance. Once inside, the hospital atmosphere became even more pronounced. The foyer was spotless, its gleaming white-tile walls antiseptic.

'Miss Northcutt, Mr Radford, in here, please.' The security man held open a door. Another sterile room, unfurnished, but with blue circles inlaid in the otherwise white-tile floor. Above each circle what appeared to be a spotlight was suspended from the ceiling. 'Each of you please stand inside a circle.'

Kathy and Mark obeyed. The security man opened a wall-mounted switch box, flicked levers. Ultraviolet light flared down from the ceiling for two or three seconds, then went out.

I've read about this someplace, Mark remembered. Lloyd Birdwell has a germ phobia and believes that ultraviolet light is the universal bactericide. Ushered into yet another room, he and Kathy were given calf-high white cloth boots and instructed to put them on over their shoes.

148

Kathy and Mark were led down a white-tiled corridor lined with white doors to a three-car elevator bank and taken to the third floor. Stepping from the car, they could hear the muted clack of electric typewriters from behind closed doors. Otherwise, the third floor was a replica of the first.

'Quiet today,' their escort commented. 'Almost everybody's off for the Fourth of July weekend.' He opened a door that looked like all the others and stood back carefully so as not to cross the threshold while Kathy and Mark entered.

The prophylactic room was divided down the middle by a waist-high, counter-like stainless steel wall surmounted by solid sheet glass that reached to the ceiling. There were comfortable chairs upholstered in white plastic on the near side of the counter. Two-way microphones were set into the glass at intervals.

A uniformed man sat in a corner. He, too, wore white cloth boots.

'Don't try talking to Mac,' their escort said from the doorway. 'He's deaf and dumb. Mr Birdwell has him sit in on all conversations as a guard. Just sit wherever you'd like Mr Birdwell should be with you in a few minutes.' He left, closing the door behind him.

Mark nodded to the deaf-mute guard, who made no response, merely staring at Radford and Kathy as they sat in adjoining chairs. Perhaps five minutes passed. Then a door on the other side of the stainless-steel and glass partition opened. A tall, thin man wearing blue-and-white-striped pyjamas entered. He was completely bald. His eyes were coal black, intense, burning. The eyes of a genius – or a madman.

Lloyd Birdwell. In the pyjama-clad flesh.

He walked with quick, jerky steps, moving up to the partition on his side. He sat in a chair directly facing the one occupied by Kathy and leaned forward to speak into the microphone. His face looked permanently haggard. Mark saw through the glass that Birdwell's hair and eyebrows had been shaved off. He wondered if the billionaire's trichotillomania extended to his body and pubic hairs. Did he shave his armpits, chest, pelvic area?

'I'd never recongize you as the Kathy Northcutt I knew.' Birdwell spoke his first words, his voice surprisingly strong and resonant. 'Except for the hair. And you do have Jim's eyes.'

'How are you, Uncle Lloyd?' Kathy said into the mike on

149

her side of the glass. She held up a five-cent piece. 'Bet you don't remember. You once gave me a nickel to call you with when I reached the age of consent.' She laughed. 'I'm long past the jail-bait stage.'

'I gave you a nickel, did I?' Birdwell said. 'Shows how long it's been. I understand you can't make a call from a pay booth for a nickel any more.'

My God, Mark thought. He really doesn't *know*. He only 'understands'. He's been away from the outside world for that many years.

'Inflation,' Kathy said. 'Get's worse all the time.'

'Historical inevitability.' Birdwell showed the glimmer of a smile. 'Money values erode. Just like people.' He waved a hand. Mark saw that the fingernails were chewed down. None the less, the fingers were graceful and long. 'Let's not go into that, Kathy. I can only spare you fifteen minutes.' He glanced in Mark's direction. 'You're the Radford Jim mentioned?'

'Yes, Mr Birdwell.'

Black eyes shifted back to Kathy.

'Jim always handled his own scrapes before. Is he eroding, too?'

'He's outnumbered,' Kathy replied evenly.

'How badly?'

'Explain it, Mark.'

Radford felt rather than saw the penetrating black eyes fix on him through the glass partition. He reduced the account to its bare essentials. There was no comment from Birdwell until Mark first mentioned the Jersey Crest Oil Company.

'So Jersey Crest is still after Jim,' Birdwell broke in. 'The continuity of corporate hatred defies understanding. It survives whole generations of management, handed down from one to the next like a family vendetta.'

Lloyd Birdwell fell silent. When Radford made as if to speak, Birdwell made a gesture, addressed Kathy.

'You've seen Steve Kostis?' he asked.

'Yes, yesterday,' Kathy said.

'And?'

'He promised to help.'

'Shall we get down to cases? What does Jim want?'

Kathy glanced at Mark, signalling for him to reply.

'Jersey Crest, Western Impex and Richland Consolidated have formed a consortium to ruin NIPCO,' Radford said.

150

'They buy their drilling tools and machinery directly from Birdwell Equipment Company —'

'If Birdwell Equipment refuses to sell them drilling tools,' Birdwell interrupted, 'they'll be seriously hurt. Once they find out why they've been cut off, they'll ease up on NIPCO. Is that correct?'

Mark shook his head. 'J.L. isn't asking that you do anything so drastic.'

'Good. If he were, I'd be forced to refuse.'

'However, if deliveries on some crucial items could be delayed, say ninety days or so . . .'

'Yes.'

Mark interrupted the 'yes' as simply an affirmation that Birdwell followed the argument and wanted him to continue.

'J.L. will underwrite any financial losses sustained by Birdwell Equipment —'

'Hell, man, I already told you yes,' Birdwell declared. 'For ninety days.'

'Uncle Lloyd —'

A buzzer sounded. Mark suspected that Birdwell had activated it himself.

'I'm sorry,' he said, smoothing the front of his pyjama top. 'I have another appointment. Good-bye, Kathy, Radford. There's a man posted outside. He'll escort you downstairs.'

Kathy and Mark said almost nothing to each other until they had removed their cloth boots, and entered the limousine, which then passed through the gates.

'The whole business is freaky,' Kathy finally said. 'We ask two powerful men to take big risks for us. I figured we would get some arguments, even some excuses. Instead they agree to help us, as if they were presold. It was too easy.'

'They *were* presold,' Mark replied. 'Kostis and Birdwell owe your father debts of some kind.'

'Dad mentioned nothing about being owed —'

'He wouldn't. Not to us or to them. He gambled they would remember without being presented with the bills. So he asked for help without pleading and without mentioning what he had once done for them. That's the way a man does it, a man with real pride. Think about it.'

Kathy did and then she looked at Mark with new interest. 'God,' she said, 'how I'd love to know the whole story.'

So would I, Mark reflected. I'll bet it's one hell of a yarn.

1

'... and you broke all records for pissing away a fortune. Now you're bust. Let's be honest. That's why I'm here.'

It was a rainy afternoon in January 1922. Jim Northcutt finished a blunt review of the information he'd gathered about Lloyd Birdwell. They were sitting in Birdwell's downtown Los Angeles office.

'You certainly found out a great deal about me,' Lloyd Birdwell muttered. Lanky, with a boyish face, he rocked nervously in his squeaking swivel chair. He could not deny that at the age of twenty-three, he had already reached a dead end. And it rankled that James Northcutt, a man who said he was a year younger, was so self-confident, obviously successful and in a position to call the shots.

'Wasn't difficult,' Northcutt shrugged, rolling a cigarette. 'Oil business in California is no different than it is in Oklahoma. You can't keep any secrets.'

Jim had been in Southern California several weeks, scouting for opportunities to resume his wildcatting operations. He believed that Lloyd Birdwell's tiny, foundering Birdwell Golden State Oil Company was ideal for his purposes. He had come to the company's three-room headquarters in a Figueroa Street office building to make Lloyd Birdwell a proposal.

'I never even tried to keep secrets,' Birdwell said. A compulsive nail biter, he gnawed at a finger end. 'Another mistake I made.'

He had made a very large number of mistakes, all serious.

A native of Houston, Lloyd Birdwell was in his junior year at Harvard when his father died in 1919, leaving him a fortune. Lloyd Birdwell inherited more than a million dollars in cash and government bonds, plus 92 per cent of the stock in the Birdwell Equipment Company. Founded by his father, the Texas firm manufactured oil well drilling tools. Lloyd Birdwell would be rich.

Unfortunately, he spent the first million during an eighteen-month marathon of womanizing, gambling and general hell raising. He had then used his stock as collateral for a $1·5 million bank loan, an amount less than half the stock's true value.

'I'm sorry, Birdwell,' Jim Northcutt said, suddenly reversing his earlier tack. 'I shouldn't have battered at you like that.' He lit his cigarette, looking at the nervous young man. He found himself liking the rich man's son. Lloyd Birdwell had a potential – if only someone could find and exploit it.

'Hell, don't apologize.' Birdwell stared gloomily at his desktop. 'I screwed up. By myself. Nobody held a gun to my head.'

When more wild spending sprees had shrunk the borrowed $1·5 million to $500,000, Lloyd Birdwell had moved from Texas to California. He hoped to recoup by investing in the Los Angeles Basin oil boom. He organized the Birdwell Golden State Oil Company, acquired seven leases, drilled five wells, all of them dry holes. He and his company were now on the verge of bankruptcy.

'One thing I can't figure out,' Jim Northcutt said. 'You're in a spot. But you still control Birdwell Equipment —'

'Wrong. I gave up my voting rights. The bank has them.'

'You're kidding!' Jim Northcutt's leathery features registered disbelief.

'Wish I were. The bankers wouldn't lend me money unless I did. They were afraid I might run the company into the ground. They had a point. I think I'm smarter now. Unfortunately, it's too late.'

'Not necessarily,' Jim said. 'As I hear it, Birdwell Golden State's in debt for about a hundred thousand bucks.'

'Yes.'

'You hold seven leases and drilled test wells on five.'

'Right,' Birdwell confirmed, biting at a forefinger. 'I imagine you've heard all about those leases.'

I have, Northcutt thought, and I've looked them over myself. Geologists and lease brokers claim they're worthless. But California geologists are even bigger assholes than those in Oklahoma and all lease hounds are liars and thieves. True, three of the leases aren't worth shit. Three others are possible. One – out in Huntington Beach – looks so good it gives me the old crotch-twist.

'I have my own company, Northcutt Petroleum,' Jim said. 'I'll make you an offer for Birdwell Golden State. I want to buy the company, merge it into my own.'

153

Birdwell took a cigarette from a pack of Murads, lit it with a hand that shook slightly.

'Northcutt Petroleum will take over your company's debts,' Jim went on. 'It'll also pay you twenty thousand in cash and you'll receive ten per cent of all excess recovery or other profits made from your leases.' He stubbed out his cigarette. 'You will also go on the Northcutt Petroleum payroll as a vice-president at five thousand a year.'

Lloyd Birdwell's symmetrical and aristocratic face showed disappointment, relief and incredulity in equal parts. The effect was comical, and Jim laughed.

'Confused?' he asked.

'My company's drilling equipment alone is worth —'

'*Was* worth,' Jim corrected him. 'Try selling it off. This is a cut-throat business, Birdwell. Oilmen will wait until you go under and buy your gear at the sheriff's sale for practically nothing.'

'I don't understand why you're offering me a job,' Birdwell said.

'It's a sweetener.'

'What would you expect me to do?'

'Two things. You're educated, polished – or would be if you didn't go at your fingernails like some damned beaver working at a log. You could take care of the office. Later, you can handle some of our purchasing.'

'What purchasing?'

'Drilling tools, mainly. Whatever else Birdwell Equipment manufactures. You'll get them for us at rock-bottom prices.'

'I told you the stock's out of my hands.'

'You'll have it back sooner or later. We'll figure a way.'

Lloyd Birdwell stared hard at Northcutt. The offer wasn't spectacular, but he knew it was better than he could hope to receive from anyone else. And, there was something about Jim Northcutt that inspired confidence. Birdwell felt almost as though the casually stated promise that he would recover his stock was already accomplished fact.

'Make it twenty per cent of excess recovery and other profits, and you have a deal.'

Good, Jim thought. There is a horse trader buried somewhere inside Lloyd Birdwell.

'I might consider going to fifteen per cent.'

'Twenty.' Birdwell's tone had a determined edge.

'Fifteen per cent of any clear profit. Take it or leave it.'

Lloyd Birdwell drew on his Murad, inhaled deeply. James Northcutt's expression was adamant, his grey eyes unwavering.

'You have a deal,' Birdwell said.

I sure as hell have, Jim mused as they shook hands. The Huntington Beach lease alone should pay out the whole purchase price a hundred times over. I won't have to invest much in drilling rigs since Birdwell has already bought the necessary equipment. And there are six other leases. I'll unload the three duds and give the three possibles a closer check. A fine package for the amount involved, and as a bonus, I'm also buying Lloyd Birdwell. If I rawhide him a little, he'll make money for the both of us.

When Jim made the handshake deal with Lloyd Birdwell, he had been in Southern California more than two months. He had arrived from Oklahoma the previous November and found that Los Angeles suited him perfectly. Already a horizontal urban sprawl with over half a million population, the city offered the amenities of a metropolis, but served them up in a casual, informal wrapper. He recognized that for anyone with money Los Angeles came close to paradise.

And he did have ample money. His share of the profits from the sale of the Peavey lease was virtually intact. He had almost $900,000. Two-thirds was in personal bank accounts. The remainder was the capital in his Northcutt Petroleum Company, Incorporated, and he owned all the stock.

Jim had done some personal splurging. He acquired an extensive new wardrobe and bought a new La Salle coupe. He lived in a two-room suite at the Hollywood Hotel on the corner of Hollywood Boulevard and Highland Avenue. It was expensive, even by Oklahoma standards, but he felt the cost was justified. There was a streak of the glamour-struck country bumpkin in him, Jim admitted to himself.

Numerous motion-picture-industry personalities stayed at the Hollywood Hotel, actors and actresses, producers and directors. And the presence of film notables drew droves of attractive young women who dreamed of being 'discovered'. James Northcutt had his pick of those not currently demonstrating their talents in producers' or directors' beds. Then, of course, the hotel was serviced by the best and most reliable bootleggers. This was no small consideration. Most of the booze being peddled in Los Angeles was – Jim had learned – worse than gut-searing Oklahoma moonshine.

But Oklahoma and Osage County seemed far away in space and time. Jim received two letters from Abraham Schlechter and one from Verna Fletcher. Abe rhapsodized about a house he had bought in Tulsa; he would soon move his family there from Chicago. Verna had written from New York City. She and Celia were sailing for Europe. They would be gone two months, possibly longer. The tone of Verna's letter was warm, friendly, without any mention of the passion they had once shared.

For Jim, however, all personal thoughts and involvements were a digression, for he was driven by a furious urge to be on a drilling rig again. California already produced more oil than any other state and was creating more oil millionaires as new oil fields were being discovered and developed almost daily.

Royal Dutch Shell had opened up the Signal Hill field only months before, and the great race was on to suck the field dry. A forest of over five hundred derricks were already pumping, and riggers worked around the clock to erect others so that additional wells could be drilled by the operators who had purchased new leases.

At first, James Northcutt scouted for promising properties but found none. Then he heard about Birdwell Golden State Oil Company, a tiny independent firm that was in serious trouble. Jim discounted the opinions he heard from various oilmen who said that Lloyd Birdwell's leases were worthless. He learned where the properties were located and inspected them personally.

Instinct told him there was oil on Birdwell's Huntington Beach lease, and that there might be oil on three others. Common sense told him he would be buying more for less if he took over Birdwell Golden State than if he bid for his own leases and then purchased drilling rigs and equipment.

Two weeks were needed to complete the legal formalities involved in taking over Lloyd Birdwell's company. Before the last papers were signed, Jim sent telegrams to Luke Rayburn, Pete Reilly and Will Dubbs in Oklahoma, offering them jobs. They were crack men and would form the nucleus of North-

156

cutt Petroleum's field crews.

Pete Reilly had boomed on from Osage County, leaving no forwarding address. But Luke Rayburn and Will Dubbs replied immediately. They would be in Los Angeles within a week.

2

Will Dubbs and Luke Rayburn had been in Los Angeles only two days when Jim Northcutt gave them their first assignment.

'Hell, Boss, I figured we'd get a chance to live it up a little,' Luke complained in Jim's suite at the Hollywood Hotel. 'There's sure a lot to see out here.'

'There're dames sitting outside who'd make a dead man come in his coffin,' Will Dubbs remarked, his beetle brows darting.

The hotel had a broad, veranda-like porch facing Hollywood Boulevard. Many who had achieved cinema success would sit there in comfortable chairs, displaying themselves to passers-by. Hopefuls would sit there, too, on the chance they might be able to meet and speak with someone who had influence at a studio.

Jim had filled three water tumblers with Old Taylor. 'In the morning, we'll drive out to a place called Huntington Beach. I'm itching to get started,' he said, raising his glass.

'Shit, those fancy new clothes ain't changed you at all,' Luke commented.

'Nope.' A few drops of whisky spilled onto Jim's trouser leg. He dabbed at them with a pocket handkerchief. The back of his hand brushed against the charm dangling from his watch chain. 'I'm busting to bring in another gusher.'

Not *another* gusher, a voice said inside him. A dozen. A hundred – a thousand gushers. Jim put the full glass to his lips and drank down the whisky.

The Huntington Beach lease was one of the seven Northcutt acquired when he bought the bankrupt Birdwell Golden State Oil Company. The lease covered four acres of ground on the Pacific coastline some fifty-five miles south-east of the Los Angeles civic centre.

The land, covered by sand, was barren save for a derrick, drilling rig, two utility shacks and a pile of equipment. With beach and surf only a few hundred feet distant, metal at the abandoned site had begun to rust in the moist, salt-laden air.

There had been important oil discoveries in the Huntington Beach area. However, the property covered by the lease and adjoining properties were considered to lie outside the boundaries of the underground pool. Test wells had been drilled on several adjoining tracts. All proved to be dry holes.

Jim, Luke and Will stood beside the abandoned drilling rig.

'Everybody sinking test wells around here has quit at twenty-three hundred feet, maximum,' Northcutt said. 'Birdwell's crews abandoned at two thousand.'

Jim's intuitive responses told him there *was* oil beneath his feet. Not at 2,000 or even 2,300 feet, but farther down.

'We have four acres, we'll drill four wells,' he announced.

'Run four strings at once?' Will asked.

'That's the size of it. You two are going to be the tool pushers.' Tool pushers were men who superintended two or more drilling rigs and crews. 'One of you on day tours, the other on nights.'

'Who've you signed as drilling super?' Rayburn asked.

'Me,' Jim told him.

'You?' Luke stared at Northcutt. 'You made yourself close to a million bucks in Oklahoma.'

'Nobody else,' Jim said. 'You'll have me rawhiding you.'

Most underground formations in California required the rotary method for drilling wells. Instead of hammering down through rock, the drilling bit turned, gouging and grinding. The bit rotated at the end of screw-jointed hollow steel rods called drill pipe. Drill pipe came in thirty-foot lengths. These were screwed into sixty- or ninety-foot segments, known to oil field workers as 'doubles' or 'thribbles'. When the bit dulled, the pipe had to be drawn up from the hole. Each segment was unscrewed as it emerged and was stacked inside the derrick. When the dulled bit finally surfaced, it was removed and a new one substituted. Then the process was reversed, the drill being lowered and successive segments of drill pipe attached.

It was more complex and costlier than cable tool drilling and expenses went even higher because two-man crews could not handle rotary operations. Four, even five, men were required for each tour on a rotary rig.

'Won't be cheap,' Jim agreed. 'But Birdwell has rigs on other properties. We'll tear them down and set 'em up here.'

Luke examined the derelict rig.

'Won't take much to get this working again,' he said. 'A few new parts and some elbow grease and we start where the last crew left off, just go deeper.'

'Got any hunches about how much deeper?' Northcutt asked.

'Sorta. I figure we may get someplace if we chug down another eight hundred or a thousand feet.'

'Then that's what we'll do,' Jim said. 'We start tomorrow.'

The abandoned drilling rigs on Birdwell Golden State's other leases were disassembled and trucked to the Huntington Beach lease, where three new derricks had been erected. Jim designated the original well as Northcutt Number One, the others Northcutt Numbers Two, Three and Four. After some 3,500-barrel field tanks had been set up, drilling on Number One was resumed, and the other three wells were spudded.

The beginnings were not auspicious. A bit twisted off on Number One at 2,200 feet. Many days were lost while drillers fished blindly for the bit at the bottom of the hole. At last, using rotary jars and overshots, they worked the bit loose and brought it to the surface.

The delay on Number One had no effect on the drilling of the other three wells. The crews continued boring down. Many of the men expressed doubt regarding Jim Northcutt's judgement. Indeed, some wondered if he might be mad.

But those who had worked for such wildcatters as Tom Slick, or who had seen the uncanny instincts of Union Oil Company's Lyman Stewart prove correct time and time again, wondered if Northcutt might be one of those rare species, a natural oil man.

3

Northcutt Number One came in for 6,600 barrels daily production on the evening of 2 April 1922. Pay sand had been reached at 3,350 feet.

James Northcutt began contracting major oil companies to sell the crude. The answers he received were unanimous. All refused to deal with him.

'We're not interested.'

A lie. Major companies were always interested in buying additional supplies of crude oil.

'We have all we need.'

A bigger lie. The company making that claim badly needed crude to feed its refineries.

'Your crude doesn't meet our standards.'

The biggest lie of all. Northcutt Number One was producing sweet high-gravity crude that tested 37·7 on the Baumé scale for measuring the gravity of oil. That particular company had been buying crude testing as low as 32!

After two days of futile telephoning from the drilling site, Jim drove into Los Angeles. Northcutt Petroleum had taken over Birdwell Golden State's offices on Figueroa Street. Jim rushed into the office occupied by his paper work vice-president, Lloyd Birdwell, and told him the story.

'If you've got any friends anywhere in this business, get on them,' Jim urged. 'Otherwise, we may have to drink our production!'

'I'll try everyone and everything,' Birdwell promised.

Two more days of effort accomplished nothing.

On 7 April, Northcutt Number Two came in at 3,290 feet. Its initial daily production: 4,100 barrels.

Jim should have been elated. Instead, he was deeply worried. The field tanks were almost topped off by the production of Number One. In another twenty-four hours, his men would have to dig open pits in the ground to store the crude pouring up to the surface. He had already stretched his financial resources by drilling four wells simultaneously. If he could find no outlet for the oil being produced on the lease, he would be pushed into bankruptcy no less surely than Lloyd Birdwell had been. And Birdwell had produced no oil at all.

'I can't understand it,' Birdwell told Jim. 'I've called dozens of people. Nobody will touch our crude!'

Earth reservoirs were dug.

Northcutt Number Three reached 3,150 feet on 10 April, and came in for 4,200 barrels a day.

Frantic now, James Northcutt canvassed the surrounding

area. He found an independent refinery that had gone out of business. Its storage tanks remained intact. They had a combined capacity of 250,000 barrels. He leased the tanks. The crude oil being produced by his three Huntington Beach wells would have to be trucked ten miles to the tanks – at high cost. But at least the oil would not be lost.

By then, the properties adjoining the Northcutt Petroleum Company site were swarming with oil workers. Ground was being levelled, access roads were being built and derricks were already going up. Other operators, seeing that Northcutt had struck oil, were rushing to tap the subterranean oil reservoir by drilling offset wells.

Northcutt now realized that he was facing a classic petroleum industry squeeze play. A very powerful oil company wanted his Huntington Beach lease and had passed the word to its peers and lesser firms. Northcutt Petroleum was to be shut out. No refining company would buy a drop of oil it was producing. Northcutt could – literally – drown in his own oil unless he complied with as-yet undelivered ultimatums.

Proof came the day after the Number Three well was completed. Between noon and four o'clock in the afternoon, sixteen calls for Jim came in over the phone installed in his field super's shack on the drilling site. All the calls were from lease brokers; each made essentially the same spiel as the first.

'I represent a principal who'd like to remain anonymous, Mr Northcutt. I've been authorized to make you a proposition. My principal is ready to buy your lease.'

The price named was always the same: $300,000.

The offer was absurd. There were three highly productive wells on the property. The four-acre lease was worth an absolute minimum of $4 million.

By petroleum-industry standards, Northcutt Petroleum was among the smallest of pygmies, and it had opened up a rich new field. Clearly, one of the Majors was determined to smash the upstart independent and force Northcutt to sell the lease for almost nothing.

The Number Four well came in on 12 April and made 3,200 barrels a day initial production.

Lease brokers made more calls to Jim. Instead of increasing the price they quoted for the lease, they dropped it to $250,000, unquestionably on the assumption that Northcutt was backed into a corner. Labour costs, the expenses of trucking and storing the crude being produced and other continuing outlays were rapidly draining the tiny company's resources. Working through the lease hounds, the anonymous principal was tightening the screws.

'We're licked,' Lloyd Birdwell told Jim. 'There isn't a crack, anywhere. Some Major big enough to make all the refiners follow its orders wants that lease. If I were you, I'd take the offer before it goes even lower.'

'Bullshit!' Northcutt exploded. 'I don't care who's behind this. I'm not throwing in my hand.'

Jim himself did not know how much of his gut reaction was genuine determination and how much sheer bravado. The leased tanks would soon be full. There were no other storage tanks available. His total cash reserves had dwindled to less than fifty thousand dollars, enough to continue operating for a week, perhaps ten days. After that, not only his company but he himself would be broke.

'You can't beat the Majors when they gang up,' Lloyd Birdwell warned. 'They've got the business by the balls. Small companies either go under – or else.'

'Maybe,' Jim said. 'I'll see you later.'

He still had a few ideas. One that had the greatest promise also involved the risk that he would be leaping from one fire into another.

Edward L. Doheny was among the most ruthless of the rugged individualists in the western US petroleum industry. Many had labelled him the 'worst of the robber barons' and classed Doheny with Jay Gould and William H. Vanderbilt. Doheny had been a central figure in the rape of the great Mexican oil fields. His piranha tactics had earned him millions – and the hatred of countless people he trampled and ruined in the process of amassing his immense fortune.

But Doheny was a maverick. He made no permanent alliances with anyone, took on all opponents and challengers with supreme self-confidence. A consummate manipulator of both state and national politicians, he was not only above the law, but even above the superlaws by which the major oil companies controlled the petroleum industry.

Jim Northcutt telephoned Doheny, asking for an appointment. A secretary had him wait for several minutes, then came back on the line.

'Mr Doheny would like to know if you're the James North-

162

cutt who brought in the Huntington Beach wells,' she said.

'Yes, I am.'

'Then Mr Doheny will see you tomorrow at nine in the morning.'

When Jim Northcutt entered Edward L. Doheny's office, Doheny followed a fixed habit for which he was noted. He took a large turnip watch from his pocket, glanced at the face and said, 'It's eight fifty-nine. You've got exactly five minutes to say your piece.' Then he placed the watch on top of his mahogany desk and stared at it.

'I don't need five minutes, Mr Doheny,' Jim said. 'I hold a lease on four acres in Huntington Beach. I've brought in four producing wells. They're making around twenty thousand barrels a day. And I'm getting screwed. Nobody'll buy my crude. Somebody wants my lease – for a quarter of a million. That's the story.'

Doheny studied the young wildcatter. Doheny himself had started out wielding a pick and shovel, and he mentally gave Jim a few points. He also saw that Northcutt had come wearing work-clothes instead of a business suit and sensed that he had done this on purpose – and added more points for shrewdness.

'You're being screwed and you want me to help you get unscrewed?' Doheny asked.

'Yes.'

Doheny scooped his watch from the desk and shoved it back into his pocket.

'You're a lucky bastard, Northcutt,' he said smiling. 'You know who's after your lease?'

'No.'

'Jersey Crest.'

'And that makes me lucky?'

'In a roundabout way, it sure as hell does. For some reason, you're on the Jersey Crest Oil Company shit list. And, at the moment, Jersey Crest happens to be on mine.'

Edward Doheny smiled. 'Relax, son,' he said. 'The shaft is as good as out of your ass. One of my companies will take your production. I'll have crews laying gathering lines to your site tomorrow.'

Just like that. Jim blinked and heaved an enormous sigh of relief and gratitude.

'Thanks, Mr Doheny.'

'I said you were lucky, Northcutt. I'm doing this because right now Jersey Crest and I are tangling, not because I'm doing you any favours. Don't come to me the next time around!'

'I'm hoping there won't be a next time,' Jim said. 'I'll try to learn how to play in the big leagues.'

'Oh, there will be a next time,' Edward Doheny laughed. 'The first lesson you'd better learn is that an independent is never safe in the oil business. You'll be fighting somebody bigger than you are until the day you die of old age – if you don't get battered to death sooner.'

He rang for a secretary.

'Take a memo of agreement,' he told her. 'It's between Doheny Refining and Northcutt Petroleum...'

4

With Edward L. Doheny's help, Jim had broken the boycott. Jersey Crest Oil put another black mark against Northcutt's name. Some day that James Northcutt would be put in his place. 'Back where he belongs – as a driller on somebody's payroll,' one Jersey Crest executive said.

Six months after the boycott was broken, Jim Northcutt could count himself a multi-millionaire. The net realizable assets of his company exceeded $4·5 million, and he continued to be the sole stockholder.

Profits from operations conducted on what had originally been Birdwell Golden State leases were high. Lloyd Birdwell collected almost $750,000 as his 15 per cent share. He used the money to make partial payment on the loan he had obtained from a Dallas bank by pledging his Birdwell Equipment Company stock as collateral. But he still owed again as much. The Texas bankers insisted on holding all the stock until the entire loan was paid, as they could under Texas law and the terms of Birdwell's loan agreement.

'For God's sake, get yourself out of hock,' Jim told Lloyd Birdwell. If Lloyd regained his stock, he would again control the Birdwell Equipment Company. Northcutt Petroleum would then enjoy a great advantage in purchasing drilling tools and equipment. 'I'll lend you the rest of the money.'

'I'd just have to give you the stock as collateral, and I'd be no better off than I am now,' Lloyd said.

'Balls!' Jim Northcutt snorted. 'I'll make an unsecured note. Your signature's enough.'

'How much interest?'

'None. Not in terms of percentage. Once you're in control of Birdwell, I'll take the interest in discounts on tools and machinery.' Northcutt's grey eyes suddenly gleamed. An association of ideas had made him think of Abraham Schlechter. 'There's one other string.'

Jim produced a Bull Durham sack, went on rolling a cigarette. Millions or no millions, he still preferred rolling his own to smoking tailor-mades. 'I want to help a friend of mine, a guy named Abraham Schlechter. Runs an oil well supply company out of Tulsa. He helped grubstake me. I want him to become Birdwell Equipment's exclusive agent for Oklahoma.'

'We already have one. He's a man who's represented Birdwell Equipment ever since my father started the company.'

'Do you owe him anything special?'

'No.'

'Then there's no problem,' Jim shrugged. 'You'll be owing me seven hundred and fifty thousand. I owe Schlechter plenty – in gratitude.' He cocked his right eyebrow. 'One hand doesn't wash, it greases the other, Lloyd.'

'Okay,' Birdwell said after a moment's reflection. 'The minute I have my stock back from the bank, Schlechter is Birdwell's new Oklahoma rep.'

Although Abraham Schlechter had written several letters over the months, Jim had not answered them. He had been busy and besides, he abhorred writing personal letters. Now, he placed a long-distance call to Tulsa – and wondered why he hadn't thought of doing so long ago.

Schlechter sounded flabbergasted.

'What's wrong, Jim?'

'Nothing. Why should there be?'

'Uh – that is, your calling me and...'

'Abe, you're a Jewish hysteric.'

'Is there another kind?' Schlechter laughed, recovering his equanimity. 'Fact is, I've been hearing all kinds of good things

165

about you.'

'I haven't done too bad out here. And how goes it with you?'

'Fine. The family's healthy and happy. You should see my son. Samuel's at the top of his class in school. Business is pretty good too. I got the main store here in Tulsa, a branch in Cushing, and the old one's still going strong in Logan. Complain, I can't.'

'Listen, Abe. You know the Birdwell Equipment Company?'

'Do I? They manufacture the best drilling tools.'

'How'd you like to be their Oklahoma sales agent?'

'You need to ask? I'd get a swelled head, to say nothing of what it'd mean to my bank account.'

'You'll have it,' Jim said and gave Schlechter a rundown. Then, he asked: 'By the way, you heard from Verna?'

'Got some postcards from Europe.'

'So did I. Anything else?'

'Nope. Not for three, four months.'

'Strange. Neither have I. Sure hope she's okay.'

'If she wasn't, Celia would have got in touch with us.'

She would have, Jim reflected. Still, it was odd that there had been no word at all from Verna Fletcher for so long.

Northcutt was amazed when Lloyd Birdwell repaid the money he had borrowed within a fortnight.

'What did you do, stick up that bank?' Jim asked.

'I found a gold mine,' Lloyd replied. 'Birdwell Equipment had a three million cash surplus I didn't even know about. Shows how dumb I was about business when I took that loan. Anyway, I fired the directors and president. I proposed myself as Board Chairman *and* president and voted myself a million-buck bonus. Since I was holding a ninety-two per cent stock interest again, I didn't get much argument.'

'You're learning,' Northcutt laughed.

'I've learned.' Birdwell gnawed at a finger.

'What's bothering you, Lloyd?' Jim asked.

'I want to sell my rights to fifteen per cent of the profits from my old company's leases.'

Northcutt's right eyebrow shot up in bewilderment.

'Why?'

'First of all, every time I get a cheque from you, it reminds me how I flopped on my own. Second, I'm resigning as a vice-

166

president of Northcutt Petroleum. I don't want to work for anybody. I want to run my own show. Can you understand how I feel?'

Jim nodded. It's exactly how I feel, he reflected. I hate reminders of failure and a business is either mine with no one to give me orders – or the hell with it. Lloyd Birdwell had grown up.

During the next few days, the two men arrived at a mutually satisfactory figure of $225,000. Birdwell gave his word that Northcutt would enjoy preferential price quotations from Birdwell Equipment and that Abe Schlechter would be the firm's exclusive Oklahoma sales representative.

'I'm going to start parlaying now, Jim,' Birdwell said. 'As I see it, no better place for it than Southern California.'

Jim grinned and nodded. He, too, intended to parlay.

Enormous fortunes were made in Southern California during the 1920s. The greatest wealth flowed from the two industries that outwardly seemed to form worlds in themselves: motion pictures and oil. Few outsiders realized the extent to which the two worlds were conterminous, even overlapping.

Successful oilmen were often far richer than the most highly publicized movie moguls. They frequently financed the production of films – hoping for profit or merely as big-time spenders' larks. On the other hand, moneyed cinema folk would invest heavily in oil ventures – or speculations.

The movie world had many attractions for lusty oilmen with large appetites for pleasure. 'Hollywood' parties were elaborate and uninhibited. Women were beautiful and readily available.

Not yet twenty-three and one of the youngest of the California oil millionaires, Jim Northcutt tired of hotel suites and furnished rented houses. In December 1922, he bought a twelve-room Spanish hacienda-style home in Los Angeles. It was located on Wilshire Boulevard near Rossmore Avenue, an elegant and exclusive neighbourhood. He retained a decorator to furnish the house, hired a three-member domestic staff and moved in during the last week of February 1923.

Jim enjoyed the motion-picture world's social life. He attended parties and gave them himself. He had affairs and one-night adventures with actresses and aspiring actresses. One night in May 1923, he went to a party given by Jesse Lasky and was introduced to Louise Condon. Like Jim, she was raven-haired. And, she was among the lovelier of the film industry's second-string ingenues.

They left the party together. Jim drove Louise to her house. She sat close to him in the Duesenberg that had replaced the La Salle.

Her home was on Adams Boulevard, one of the large, staid mansions that had originally belonged to Old-Money Angelenos. People who had not quite arrived rented such homes in an effort to show that they too had achieved success. Jim wondered how Louise Condon could afford to rent and maintain the house.

'Come in for a drink,' she said.

A maid served them bourbon, then vanished.

'You've got a good bootlegger,' Jim said, tasting his drink. 'This is real stuff – and he didn't cut it.'

'Can you?' Louise murmured, her sloe eyes holding his.

Her bedroom was ornate, the bed immense and round.

When they had undressed she stood close to him.

She has a beautiful body, Jim thought.

'You like mirrors?' she asked. 'I love to make love in front of one.' She led him to her dressing table, turned to face the mirror over it. She leaned over, watching herself in the mirror.

He gripped her, and soon she cried out in pleasure.

Jim did not leave until long after dawn, and he saw Louise Condon several times after that. One day she asked him to take her to a party.

'It's being given by Steve Kostis,' Louise told him.

The name rang a bell in Jim's mind, but he couldn't place it. He agreed to go.

Kostis's house was only a few blocks from the one Louise Condon lived in, but even larger and more luxuriously furnished. Over two dozen guests were already present when Louise and Jim arrived.

She evidently knew their host well. A stocky man of about twenty-five, Steven Kostis had a somewhat hard face and black, oiled hair. He spoke with an accent. Greek, Jim guessed correctly.

'There's plenty of good booze – have fun,' Kostis said after being introduced to Jim. 'See you later.'

After two hours, someone mentioned a poker game.

'Can anybody get in?' Jim asked.

'All you need is money, friend. We play high stakes.'

'Go on,' Louise urged Jim.

'Okay,' he said. 'I'll play a few hands.'

He followed four men into a library. Two were film producers, one a director and the last a highly successful comedian. Steve Kostis was seated at a table covered with green felt.

'The usual?' Kostis asked. 'Dealer's choice, no limit. Everybody buys five thousand chips to start.'

The four film-industry men sat down at the table. Jim took the last chair. The men produced chequebooks. He did the same.

'Who do I make this out to?' he inquired.

'Leave the payee blank,' someone told him.

The comedian dealt first. Five-card stud. Betting was high. Jim lost $600 on the hand. He also lost on the next two. It was the director's turn to deal. He called for draw with a $50 ante. Jim caught a pair of tens, but folded.

They continued to play for almost an hour and Jim found himself down to $470 in chips. The comedian signed another cheque. One producer had dropped out. The other had about $1,000 remaining. The big stacks of chips were in front of the director and Kostis. Jim's grey eyes had been darkening steadily. It was his turn to deal again.

'Five cards, face up, no draw,' he announced, shoving his chips to the centre of the table. 'Four hundred seventy bucks.'

The director grumbled, but he and the others remaining in the game matched the bet. Jim shuffled the deck, slapped it down for the cut. He grinned enigmatically and dealt five face-up hands very fast. His opponents had nothing higher than low-number pairs. He had three aces and a pair of jacks. He ignored the stunned looks.

'Can I see you alone for a minute, Mr Kostis?' he asked.

Steve Kostis gave a curt nod, stood up and led Jim into an adjoining room. He closed the door behind them.

'I'll take my cheque,' Jim said quietly.

'What the hell you talking about?' Kostis demanded.

'You and that director aren't the only people who can stack a deck,' Jim laughed. He held out his hand. 'My cheque, pal.' He now remembered Kostis's name. He had heard talk about poker parties given by the 'lucky' Greek.

Kostis glared at him venomously.

'You got a big mouth. I got guys who can shut you up —'

'Send 'em around. My roughnecks'll bust their heads open!'

Kostis blinked.

'You ain't a movie guy? You're in the oil business?'

'You win the cigar.'

'That dumb bitch!' Kostis blurted.

'I've figured that, too,' Jim grinned. 'Louise helps bring in the suckers. That's how she affords that house and all the rest.'

'I tell her, bring movie guys,' Kostis muttered. 'Oil guys are trouble.'

'Sure. There isn't a roustabout who hasn't played more poker than fifty of these assholes put together. So my cheque.'

'Hey,' Kostis said. 'You got big money?'

'Why?'

'Shit. If you needed dough, we could do okay together. You make a deck talk real good.' He took some cheques from his pocket and sorted through them. 'Northcutt, right?'

'Yup.'

'Here.' Kostis gave Jim his cheque – and an amused look. 'You don't scare. I like that. I think maybe I even like you.'

'Thanks.'

'Drop around some other time. Just for drinks and laughs.'

'I will,' Jim said. Crooked or not, the young Greek was a good loser and had a sense of humour. Besides, he thought, one never knew when it might be useful to be on friendly terms with Steve Kostis.

The two men shook hands. Jim started for the door, then stopped.

'What do you give Louise for bringing in the fish?' he asked.

'Ten per cent of what they drop.'

'In that case, I'll give her five hundred – ten per cent of what I *might* have dropped,' Jim said. 'As a farewell present.'

'Before or after you lay her tonight?'

'After. What do you take me for, a sucker?'

They both laughed.

5

There was good reason why Verna Fletcher had stopped writing to Jim Northcutt and Abe Schlechter.

She was married. And, since November 1922, she had been living with her husband in Pasadena, California.

Verna wanted some time to pass before contacting either Jim or Abe. She felt she needed it to make the final transition from past to present, to put what had happened in manageable perspective and acclimate herself to her new life and environment. Only when these goals had been accomplished would she be sufficiently self-confident and emotionally secure.

Verna had met Andrew Harkness while returning from Europe aboard the *Carinthia*. He was thirty-five, handsome enough, cultured and well bred. He had been a major during the war, was obviously well-to-do and a bachelor.

Harkness attached himself to Verna during the Atlantic crossing. For him, it was love at first sight. Verna was much less certain that she was falling in love, but she liked Harkness and enjoyed his company. He had no doubts that Verna Fletcher was anything but what she represented herself to be: the daughter of a Philadelphia businessman who had died and left her a fortune. His manner was considerate, even courtly, and he made no attempt to take Verna to bed.

Arriving in New York, Verna decided to stay there a few weeks. She and Celia checked into the Astor. Andrew Harkness changed his own plans and also stopped over in New York. He took Verna everywhere. When, inevitably, he proposed marriage, she accepted. She realized that marriage to Andrew Harkness was her best chance for achieving the respectability and social position she so earnestly desired.

They were married in New York and went to California, taking Celia with them. Harkness came from an Old-Money Southern California family. His own income derived from an inherited estate, and he owned an elaborate mansion on Orange Grove Avenue in Pasadena, the street known locally as Millionaires' Row.

Pasadena was the most quiet and conservative city in the

entire state, perhaps even west of the Mississippi. By then, Verna had discovered that her husband was charming and delightful socially, but very much inhibited and unimaginative as a lover. Now she found that his main interests were polo, golf, tennis and deep involvement in what the ultraconservative local newspapers called 'civic' and 'cultural' affairs. Determined to make her marriage work, Verna made herself share his enthusiasms.

'It's all so dull, and the people are so stuffy,' she confided to Celia.

'You want to be doing something yourself,' Celia observed shrewdly. 'You still ain't flushed that Jim Northcutt out of your system.'

Yes to the first, no to the second, Verna conceded silently.

Lloyd Birdwell's experiences had matured him and awakened all his latent instincts as a businessman and industrialist. And, it developed, he was more far-sighted than he realized.

Lloyd had learned to fly an aeroplane in 1919, being taught by a barnstorming pilot who owned a rickety war-surplus DH-4. His interest in flying and aeroplanes had lain dormant for more than two years. Now it was rekindled. He sensed there would be great expansion in the aviation industry. As the first step in what he had described to Jim Northcutt as 'parlaying', he organized the Birdwell Aircraft Corporation. He leased factory space in Glendale and hired a small but select team of engineers, technicians and skilled workers.

'Concentrate on two models,' he told the engineers. 'A fast pursuit plane for the army and a transport for civilian use.'

One project somehow seemed to lead to another. Lloyd directed the affairs of the Birdwell Equipment Company in Houston as he had said he would, by 'remote control'. He ordered the development of new, advanced oil field machinery. Oilmen had long been hampered by the basic design of drilling rigs. These were clumsy, bulky and had to be completely dismantled if they were to be moved from one location to another. Even reels had to be dismounted from their bearings and the links of chain drives broken.

'Aim for maximum portability,' Lloyd wrote in one of the terse memos that Birdwell Equipment Company executives soon came to regard as imperial edicts. 'All equipment has to be completely utilized for quick tear-down and rig-up. Sub-

172

assemblies must be within present truck-loading capacities.

His nervous energy was still not satisfied. Birdwell bought the ailing Sentinel Films and its ramshackle Culver City studios. Ownership of the studio enabled Birdwell to combine business with pleasure at many levels. Women hunted him, avidly prepaying sexual quid for what they hoped might be the quo of a 'break'. But while he enjoyed his sexual largesse, Lloyd Birdwell had a keen and discriminating eye for the types of feminine beauty and personality that would appeal most to the movie-going public.

Birdwell was his own talent scout. He went often to see performances given by the myriad little-theatre groups in Southern California. The first signs of the personal eccentricity for which he would later become famous had begun to show themselves. He invariably went alone, wearing baggy rumpled suits and sometimes tennis shoes, and slumped down in back-row seats to remain incognito.

This was why, in May 1923, he attended an opening-night performance of *The Tempest* given by the Pasadena Community Playhouse. Organized by Gilmour Brown and heavily subsidized by Pasadena's wealthy residents, the Playhouse had bred much talent in the past.

Birdwell sat through the first act. The performers were mediocre. During the intermission, he slouched into the lobby, leaned against a wall and lit a Murad. He gave the other people in the lobby, all of them in evening dress, a sweeping, cursory glance.

'Jesus Christ!' he exclaimed, letting the Murad drop from his fingers.

The girl appeared to be in her early twenties. She was a natural blonde with deep blue eyes and wore a simple, even severe, black gown. But her face was exquisite. It combined earthy sensuality with angelic innocence, and her figure was breathtaking. She stood in a group of five or six people. She was with a man whose face and build were those of an athlete, but whose air and manner were haughty, bordering – it seemed even from a distance – on the pompous.

Birdwell made his way across the lobby.

'Excuse me,' he said. 'I'm Lloyd Birdwell . . .'

Most of those in the group stared at him with expressions that ranged from disdain to outright annoyance. The blonde girl alone appeared to take the interruption in stride and

173

smiled pleasantly.

'. . . and I'd like to speak to the young lady a moment.'

'Who did you say you were?' the athletic man demanded as he stared at Birdwell's unkempt clothes.

'Lloyd Birdwell. I own Sentinel Pictures, among other things.'

The faces relaxed. A little. There had already been items in the newspapers about Lloyd Birdwell. The athletic man unbent sufficiently to introduce himself.

'I'm Andrew Harkness. The "young lady" you wish to speak to is my wife, Verna.' Then he introduced the others.

Birdwell was interested only in Verna Harkness.

'Mrs Harkness, Sentinel is casting a new picture —'

'Oho!' Verna laughed. 'Don't tell me this is the screen-test offer I've heard so much about!'

'You won't even have to make a test,' Birdwell said. Her face was fabulous. Instinct told him it would be even more so on the screen and that Verna Harkness could easily become a top-flight star. Overnight. 'I'm willing to offer you a contract, right now.'

'I'm flattered,' Verna said, 'but I'm not an actress.'

Andrew Harkness appeared to be uncomfortable.

'All women are natural-born actresses,' Birdwell said.

Verna's laugh was throaty. Her husband glowered. Being a patron of Community Playhouse capital-'D' Drama was one thing. Having his wife appear in Hollywood films was quite another.

'You can't be serious, Mr Birdwell,' he said.

'Can't I?' Birdwell, ignoring Harkness, spoke directly to Verna. 'My starting offer is a thousand dollars a week for a year. With options and escalation clauses —'

'A thousand dollars a week!' someone in the group exclaimed.

Even Andrew Harkness was impressed. The figure itself was high enough to be an earnest indication that Lloyd Birdwell intended to cast Verna in important roles. He found himself wavering. He and Verna did not have any real need for the money. However, provided he could personally guide her career and insure that her dignity was maintained, there would be a certain cachet to having a wife who was a film star.

'Could you and your husband come to the studio tomorrow, Mrs Harkness?' Birdwell asked.

'Certainly not tomorrow,' Verna replied. 'Maybe not on any day. I'll have to think about this very carefully – and talk it over with Andrew.'

'Please call me whenever you've made a decision.' Lloyd Birdwell gave one of his business cards to Andrew Harkness. 'I hope it will be soon. We want to start rolling on the picture I mentioned. Within a few weeks —'

'You aren't joking at all, are you?' Verna asked.

'No, I'm not.' Birdwell smiled inwardly. She's intrigued, he thought. Her husband is weighing the pros and cons and already seeing more of the former than the latter. Verna Harkness won't be able to refuse in the long run. And I'd best make my exit now – for maximum effect. 'Glad to have met you all,' he said. 'Good night.' He turned, walked to the exit doors and out into the street.

'Verna,' Andrew Harkness said when Birdwell had gone. 'Are you . . .'

'I don't know, Andrew,' Verna replied, staring at the doors through which Birdwell had disappeared. I think I will, she added to herself. For ever so many reasons.

6

By May 1923, Northcutt Petroleum boasted assets of over six million dollars. Yet James L. Northcutt, sole stockholder, was far from satisfied.

In the petroleum industry, a $6 million company that was limited to prospecting for oil and producing it, selling the crude to refiners, was still highly vulnerable. Only continuing expansion could provide any hope of survival.

One day the Union Oil Company announced it had brought in an exploration well on previously unexplored land near Geary, a forlorn hamlet located about midway between Los Angeles and Long Beach. The well had come in at 4,200 feet, was making 2,500 barrels a day.

Jim and Luke Rayburn drove to the site in Northcutt's sleek, black Duesenberg. Large crowds of people had come to see the well, as they always did when someone opened up a new field. Many were oilmen and lease hounds. Some had fanned out across properties surrounding the site and were inspecting them carefully. Here and there, surveyors were peering through tripod-mounted transits.

'The big lease scramble's started,' Rayburn said. 'Funny how everything's happening south of the road, nothing on the north side.'

Jim pulled the Duesenberg off the road into an open field and cut the ignition.

'The hotshot geologists figure the whole pool must be located on the south side.'

He stared through the windshield at the terrain. It appeared to be table-flat farmland. But terrain appearances could be deceiving. Suddenly, he grabbed Luke Rayburn's shoulder.

'Take a look at that.' A mile or so ahead of them, a Southern Pacific Railroad spurline track crossed the road at an angle. A long, heavily loaded freight train was moving along the track, going north-west. It moved slowly, the engine straining hard. 'That train's going uphill. The grade's so gentle and gradual you don't notice it's even there just by looking at the ground.'

The train laboured past the crossing, strained on for another thousand yards or so and began to gather speed.

'Dome structure,' Jim stated flatly.

Dome structures are geologic features created in long past millennia by great masses of salt. These pushed upward and deformed surrounding underground rock formations. Multitudes of oil traps were created by dome structures. The richest oil reservoirs were often in subterranean strata below the crest of the dome.

'Top of the dome's way over there, a mile and a half from where we are now,' Northcutt said, pointing to where the freight train had reached the invisible summit and had begun to pick up momentum on the downgrade of the reverse slope. 'That's where you'll find the centre of this pool.'

He switched on the ignition. 'Let's haul ass and start shopping for leases.'

Gas and oil leases for properties above what Jim judged to be the crest of the dome and immediately adjacent to it were available at very low prices. Northcutt Petroleum acquired leases covering two hundred acres at an average cash bonus payment of $615 an acre. To the south of the road, asking prices for leases had already soared to $300,000 an acre.

The next time Jim and Luke went to the Geary area, Jim paced his property silently for almost an hour, meticulously studying every topographical feature down to the smallest folds in the ground and the most insignificant rock outcroppings. At last, he stopped. 'We'll spud Number One here,' he announced.

'Your crotch twitching, Boss?' Luke said.

'Practically oscillating,' Jim said.

Jim Northcutt saw the item – and the photograph – in the motion-picture pages of the Los Angeles *Times*.

'Lloyd Birdwell, the Sentinel Films mogul, says he has discovered a new star. She is Verna Harkness, a blonde beauty married to Pasadena socialite-sportsman Andrew Harkness. Birdwell states he has signed Verna to a one-year contract and that she will be the female lead in *Strange Breed*, a big-budget Sentinel production . . .'

Jim stopped reading and stared at the photograph.

It couldn't be. The face smiling out of the blurry newspaper halftone was that of Verna Fletcher. He tried to reach Lloyd Birdwell, finally got him on the telephone at his Birdwell Aircraft Company offices.

'Congratulations on your new find,' Jim said, choosing his words cautiously. 'Saw her photo and the story in the *Times*.'

'She's fantastic,' Birdwell said.

'You sound bewitched, pal.'

'I'm not far from it.'

'I read the publicity crap in the paper. What's the truth about her being married to some Pasadena stuffed shirt?'

'That's the straight story. She is – and he *is* a stuffed shirt, take it from me.'

When their conversation was completed, Jim slowly hung up the receiver. Verna. He took out the watch-chain charm she had given him and toyed with it. He very much wanted to see Verna again.

No, he thought. Forget it.

He put the charm back into his pocket.

Verna had made her break with the past, and she had married. He couldn't blame her. She had every right to be Mrs Andrew Harkness and, if Lloyd Birdwell was right, become a successful motion-picture star. The last thing in the world she needed was to have James Northcutt or anyone else intrude into her life as a reminder of what she wanted to forget.

Strange, Jim mused. I'm curious as hell about what Verna saw in Harkness and whether she was content and satisfied with being his wife.

'It's none of my business,' he muttered. He got up from his desk and stalked out of his office.

'I'm going down to the Geary site,' he told his secretary.

'What if anyone calls, Mr Northcutt?'

'Say you don't have any idea when I'll be back.' He made an odd face. 'I don't have any idea either,' he added, more for his own benefit than hers and not quite sure what he actually meant.

Arriving at the Geary site, Jim changed into denim shirt and trousers and heavy boots. The Number One well had been spudded in a few days earlier. He personally took over as driller on the rig and worked thirty-six hours straight without sleep. After that, he felt exhausted – but unspooled inside – and drove to his Wilshire Boulevard home. Still wearing sweat-stained and mud-splattered work-clothes, he fell into bed and slept for eighteen hours.

Jim had never got around to visiting Steve Kostis again. Though he had thought of the young Greek gambler once or twice over the months, he had had too many other things to do. He was surprised, therefore, one morning in July, when Kostis called his office and asked for an appointment.

'Ask him if he can drop by this afternoon,' Jim instructed his secretary.

Steve Kostis arrived promptly at 3 P.M.

'Hello, Mr Northcutt.'

'Suppose we two cardsharps start off on a first-name basis.'

'Okay, Jim. I like that. Anyway, I got a proposition for you.'

'Oh?' Northcutt's eyebrow rose slightly. 'A job dealing for you, maybe?'

Kostis laughed.

'You own property right down to the water in Huntington Beach, right?'

'Don't own it, Steve. I lease it. Have wells there.'

'Same thing.' Kostis offered a cigar case. Jim shook his head, reached for a Bull Durham sack on his desk. The Greek lit one of his own cigars.

'It's like this. I ain't running my game no more. I made a

pile of dough and quit. Got into something better. That's how come my proposition.

'You got a dock at Huntington Beach. You let two boats pull in at the dock a couple of times a week and unload some stuff, and I'll pay you ten thousand a month. Adds up to a hundred twenty thousand a year. That's money, even if you are a millionaire, Jim.'

Northcutt grinned. 'Booze.'

Kostis gave Jim a level look.

'I'm bankrolling some runners. The boats come in at night. They need a place —'

'Steve, what I don't know can't hurt me.'

Jim Northcutt considered Prohibition the ultimate absurdity. He could not bring himself to view any bootlegger as a criminal. He knew that large freighters with liquor crammed in their holds lay off the three-mile limit. Small boats went out, loaded and brought the liquor to shore. At least it was honest booze, brought in from abroad, not the raw – and often deadly – alky cooked up by domestic moonshiners.

'Far as I'm concerned, your boats can pull up at the dock. and you don't owe me anything – except send me a case of something special once in a while,' Jim said. 'You make whatever deals you want with the guys on my night crews.'

His grey eyes narrowed.

'But God help your ass if there's any slowdown in work or oil production. I'll break you in half myself.'

'I owe you, Jim.'

'I may be in a spot where I'll have to come around and collect some day. Now beat it, Steve. I've got work to do.'

7

Lloyd Birdwell's interest in Verna Harkness was that of an entrepreneur. He was certain her face and personality would have instant box-office appeal, which would mean great profit for Sentinel Films. She was a property to be exploited.

Birdwell accepted without question Verna's story that she was the orphaned daughter of a wealthy Philadelphia businessman, and the Sentinel Films publicity department made the most of it. While playing down the fact that she was married, studio flacks poured out press releases about 'Sentinel's Main Line, millionairess find'.

A week after Verna signed her contract with Sentinel Films, Birdwell gave a lavish press party for her at the studio. Although she was accompanied by her husband, Lloyd managed to persuade Andrew Harkness that he should remain in the background.

Birdwell invited several of his personal friends to attend, Jim Northcutt among them. Jim debated with himself for a long time whether he should go. In the end, his desire to see Verna again – and his curiosity about her husband – prevailed.

Verna was not aware that Birdwell knew Jim or that Northcutt was coming to the press party. When Lloyd brought Jim over to meet her – as he believed, for the first time – she was surrounded by reporters and fan-magazine writers.

'Verna,' Birdwell said, 'this is a friend of mine.'

Oh, dear God, Verna thought, looking up and seeing Jim Northcutt's face. She felt herself turn pale. Jim! Her breath caught.

'... Verna Harkness,' Birdwell was saying.

'How do you do, Mrs Harkness,' Jim said, holding out his hand.

She took it, and there was gratitude in her blue eyes, and she began to breathe again. I should have known Jim wouldn't say or do anything that might give me away, she told herself. Memories and emotions were awakened as she took his hand, and the expression in her eyes changed to one far more complex than mere gratitude.

'Have – have you and Lloyd known each other long?' she asked.

'A couple of years.' Jim held her hand for a moment and found it difficult to keep his voice even and casual. 'I met him a little while after I got out here. From Oklahoma.' He released her hand. 'Right, Lloyd?'

'Jim and I were in business together,' Birdwell said. 'To tell you the truth, I wouldn't be in business at all today if it weren't for him.'

'We're all in business because of somebody,' Jim said, and Verna got the message that he hadn't forgotten.

They might have said more to each other, but the reporters were growing impatient. Lloyd and Jim moved off, shouldering their way through the crowd.

'I'll be damned if I didn't get the feeling Verna recognized you from someplace,' Birdwell said.

'If she thought she did, it was a case of mistaken identity,' Jim said. 'I never saw her before. I'd sure remember if I had.' He took a glass of bourbon from a tray being passed around by a white-jacketed Filipino waiter.

Finishing his drink, Jim decided he would leave. He felt someone touch his arm.

'Thanks, Jim,' Verna said.

He said nothing for the moment, afraid that if he did, he might betray the longing he felt.

'How's Abe?' Verna asked, her lashes lowering for an instant.

'Fine.'

'Will you send him my best?'

'Sure. And I'll explain things.'

She stared at some unseen point midway between them.

'Jim – and how are you, Jim?'

'Just great, Verna. I —'

A studio official interrupted, took Verna by the arm and led her away. Jim gazed after her for several seconds, then left the party.

Lloyd Birdwell telephoned Jim three days later. He sounded greatly agitated.

'Can I see you right away?' he asked. 'It's important.'

'Come on over to my office. I'll wait for you.'

Birdwell arrived less than half an hour later. He entered Jim's office and closed the door behind him. He refused to take a chair, paced the floor nervously.

'You knew Verna Harkness in Oklahoma, didn't you, Jim?' he asked.

'She tell you that?' Northcutt evaded a direct answer.

'No. The studio got a call. Somebody claims he was in Logan, Oklahoma, in 1921. Says that Verna Harkness was Verna Fletcher then, and she ran a parlourhouse.'

'Even if she did, so what?'

'This bastard threatens to spread the story around.' Birdwell stopped pacing, chewed hard at a fingernail. 'He wants twenty thousand bucks to keep his mouth shut.' Lloyd finally sat down. 'Believe me, Jim. I don't give a damn what Verna Hark-

181

ness was – not personally I don't.'

'Then why all the panic?'

'For God's sake! If anything like that gets out, Sentinel will be massacred by the press. As for Verna, we'd have to drop her – and her marriage would be finished. Can you imagine what that shithead Harkness would do?'

Birdwell stopped biting his fingernail, lit a Murad, took two puffs and stubbed it out in an ashtray.

'If we pay off, it's only the beginning,' he said. 'There'll be more demands.'

'Verna know anything about this?' Jim asked.

'Nothing. So far, it's been between this guy and the studio.'

'You got his name?'

'He says it's Edward Fraine. Mean anything to you?'

'Nope, but that doesn't count. Hundreds of guys went to Verna's place in Logan.' There was no use trying to hide the truth. If there was a blackmailer, Lloyd needed to know it. Jim was glad to see that Birdwell took the confirmation without a flicker of reaction. 'Any one of 'em might have recognized her from the publicity photos plastered all over the newspapers.'

Jim fell silent, thinking.

'Sit tight a minute,' he said and reached for his telephone. He had four numbers for Steven Kostis. He located the Greek on his third try.

'Doing anything important, Steve?'

'Depends, Jim. Why?'

'A friend of mine needs a favour. He's here now. If you could drop around . . .'

'Be there in fifteen minutes.'

The rapport that Jim had established with Steve Kostis immediately included Lloyd Birdwell.

'So what's your problem?' Kostis asked.

Lloyd told him.

'That's no problem,' Steve said.

'The hell it isn't!' Lloyd protested. 'Whoever Edward Fraine is, he can —'

'Only he won't. You got a way of getting in touch with him?'

'I think so. He left a telephone number.'

'Call him. Say you'll send a couple of men to pay him the dough wherever he wants. This afternoon.'

'But —'

'Go on, Lloyd,' Jim urged. 'Do what Steve tells you.'

Birdwell made the call and spoke for a few moments. Then he listened, wrote an address on a piece of paper and hung up.

'That's where he'll be at four-thirty,' Lloyd said, holding out the piece of paper. 'Now I'll get the money —'

'What for?' Kostis broke in. 'Just gimme that paper and tell me where I can reach you around five, five-thirty.'

'I'll be at the studio,' Birdwell said dubiously.

'Okay, Lloyd. You'll hear from me.'

He got up to leave.

'I still owe you,' he said to Jim. Grinning at both men, he was gone.

Lloyd Birdwell got the promised call from Steve Kostis shortly before five-thirty that afternoon.

'No more sweat,' Kostis retorted. 'My boys had a long talk with Fraine. He'll be in the hospital for a month or two.'

Jim Northcutt, Steve Kostis and Lloyd Birdwell saw each other often after that. As Lloyd Birdwell was to remark many years later, none of them quite understood how or why, but they got along remarkably well together and became fast friends.

8

Jim had installed the first of what would be a long succession of resident mistresses in his Wilshire Boulevard home. She was Madeleine Knight, a svelte brunette who had been the protégé of Warner Brothers studio director Frank Borzage.

The Sentinel Films production of *Strange Breed* starring John Gilbert and Verna Harkness was released in February 1924. Jim attended the premiere with Madeleine Knight. He was happy to see that Lloyd Birdwell's instincts regarding Verna were correct. She was ravishing on the screen, a natural actress and certain to be a success.

Birdwell gave a huge post-premiere party at the Cotton Club, in which Steve Kostis owned an interest. Verna was again surrounded by dozens of people, and Jim managed to speak with her for only a moment.

'You really liked it?' Verna asked him.

'I liked you,' he said. 'You were great.' He intended the comment to convey its message on two levels, and Verna understood.

'You're my favourite critic,' she said, flashing him a warm look, then averting her eyes.

Madeleine Knight was standing beside Jim and picked up an undercurrent between him and Verna.

'How long have you known her?' Madeleine asked later.

'Verna Harkness? Oh, I met her last year, not long after Lloyd signed her to a contract.'

'You're a liar.'

'For Christ's sake, why should I lie?'

'I don't know.' Madeleine glared at him. She used the issue as an excuse to start an argument that lasted until dawn. It was only the latest in a series of growing irritations that made Jim Northcutt realize that the affair had about run its course.

In the beginning, Madeleine Knight had been overjoyed to be the mistress of a young and handsome oil millionaire. Then she gradually began to discover that life with James Northcutt wasn't quite what she had anticipated. He was much too pre-occupied with business, and she had expected their relationship to be one of constant and luxurious leisure.

'You're rich,' she complained to Jim. 'We should be travelling, having fun.'

But he was building Northcutt Petroleum, and there was no lessening of his concentration on business. Madeleine Knight's boredom increased, showing itself in frequent quarrels such as the argument over whether Jim had previously known Verna Harkness.

That particular battle ended their affair as far as Jim was concerned. Within the next few days, he got in touch with a real estate broker and bought a bungalow on Colgate Avenue in Madeleine Knight's name. Then he called on a moving company to come for her clothes and personal possessions and gave her a cheque for ten thousand dollars.

'You won't get away with this!' Madeleine stormed as she left the Wilshire Boulevard house. 'I'll sue for breach of promise!'

Northcutt stopped payment on her cheque. Only when Madeleine finally agreed to sign a document waiving all claims against him did he pay her the money. He had learned another lesson. He resolved that in the future discarded mistresses would sign first and receive their consolation prizes afterwards. He made this abundantly clear to Louise Padgett, who became Madeleine's successor, and she took the stipulation in stride.

Jim reorganized Northcutt Petroleum. The corporation was capitalized at $4 million, had assets exceeding $12 million. There were 40,000 common shares issued, each with a par value of $100. Jim gave Luke Rayburn and Will Dubbs 100 shares each, holding the other 39,800 himself.

The company's offices were moved to the new, nine-storey Phelan Building on Seventh and Flower streets in downtown Los Angeles. James Northcutt was president and Chairman of the Board. The administrative staff was held to twenty-eight people. There were, of course, many times that number of field and operational personnel, for the company owned fifty-two leases, thirty-nine of which were producing. Test wells were being drilled on five others. Eight remained to be developed, and Jim was constantly scouting for promising new leases.

Louise Padgett lasted barely five months as Jim's mistress. By the end of 1925, he had established and ended two other semipermanent affairs. For the time being he'd had his fill of any but the most casual relationships with women. This led him into even closer contact with his friends, Lloyd Birdwell and Steven Kostis, neither of whom ever formed any but the most cursory liaisons. The three followed patterns common enough among wealthy young bachelors.

Although each found his own women, they often shared their more spectacular discoveries. One man, tiring of a particularly accomplished bedmate, would pass her on to the next. Since their interest in any female was usually short-lived, they frequently took turns bedding the same girl within a short period of time. This created complications in some cases.

There was Lila Turner. Steve Kostis won her from John Barrymore one night in a drunken crap game at the Ambassador Hotel. Steve spent three nights with Lila, found that she was magnificent in bed but inclined to drink too much and become troublesome. He bequeathed her to Lloyd Birdwell at a party. Birdwell found Lila Turner entertaining for a weekend. He then told Jim Northcutt that she was remarkably acrobatic when sober, and Jim bedded her for two nights. On the second morning after, he sent Lila away with a bottle of genuine

185

Scotch under her arm and two hundred dollars stuffed into her beaded handbag.

About a month later, each of the three men received the same telephoned complaint from Lila Turner on the same day.

'I'm pregnant, and I don't know which one of you guys did it.'

That evening, the men met at Jim's house. After several rounds of cocktails, they arrived at a solution to their predicament.

Lloyd Birdwell had never mastered the art of stacking a deck of cards. Thus he could be trusted to deal honestly. Northcutt and Kostis watched while he shuffled a deck and dealt three five-card poker hands.

Kostis had the lowest hand. As they had agreed, the loser would pay for what a private Santa Monica hospital euphemistically called an appendectomy and give Lila Turner five hundred dollars to put up with the inconvenience – and to keep quiet.

'Poetic justice,' Birdwell observed with mock piety. 'You brought her into the circle.'

'Next time, I'll put condoms on you bastards myself,' Steve snorted, tossing his cards back to Lloyd and drinking another martini.

9

Jim Northcutt's business sense told him that the high oil prices and Great Bull Market of 1927 had no firm foundation. 'Everybody's talking prosperity,' he said at a Northcutt Petroleum Board meeting. 'It's phoney. God damn it, look at the statistics. Nearly sixty per cent of all the families – the *families*, mind you – in this country have incomes of less than two thousand dollars a year.'

Northcutt Petroleum now had producing fields in New Mexico and Oklahoma in addition to California. Although falling crude prices reduced its gross income, efficiency kept its profits high and assets had increased by 30 per cent in two years.

Just the same, Northcutt Petroleum remained a company

engaged exclusively in oil exploration and production and, as such, still highly vulnerable. In order to survive in the long run, the firm would have to become an integrated company – transport, refine and market its own oil and petroleum products.

Tens of millions of dollars would be required to fulfil this ambition. More, any efforts to build such a new integrated company would encounter heavy opposition from the Majors who now largely controlled the industry.

'We need more capital,' Jim told his directors. 'Much more.'

Northcutt Petroleum was again reorganized, now as a public stock company. A total of 1·8 million shares of stock were issued, with 600,000 shares being sold publicly at ten dollars a share. This added $6 million immediately to the company's capital. Jim kept almost 1·2 million shares himself.

The company reported good earnings, and the price of its stock rose steadily, to 11½, then 13, then 15.

To the surprise of his executives, Jim held off on expansion programmes. He used a majority of the company's new capital to buy United States Government bonds.

In March 1928, the bull market moved into its most frenzied phase. There were new orgies of buying and, on 9 June, Northcutt Petroleum hit 25½.

Jim, who had been carefully watching stock prices, now fed 500,000 shares of his own stock into the market – for over $12·5 million. The next month, there was a sharp market break. Northcutt Petroleum went down to 17. Jim repurchased his 500,000 shares. He was left with a clear profit of $4 million. He bought government bonds with the money.

Over the next two years, after twice repeating this tactic of selling his shares high and buying them back low, Jim's overall profits were in the neighbourhood of $30 million. Each time, he bought government bonds with the money. Considering the company's assets, he was now worth more than $60 million personally. In mid-January 1930, he decided to launch his expansion programme.

'There's a long depression ahead,' he predicted to his directors and executives. 'The oil business is in for a murderous beating. But we have ready money. When others bail out for whatever they can realize, we'll buy!'

When other oil companies began to cut back operations, lay off personnel and reduce wages and salaries, Northcutt Petroleum did none of these things. As a consequence, Jim earned the fierce and underlying loyalty of his employees – and more hatred and resentment from his competitors.

'The bastards are not going to shaft us!' Northcutt raged at a Board meeting one morning in September 1930.

Northcutt Petroleum had acquired a 3,600-acre lease in the recently discovered Tubman Hills field in Ventura County, north of Los Angeles. Jim bought the lease at a give-away price of $300,000 because, as he had foreseen, with money in short supply, ready cash would purchase many times its face value.

Early test drilling indicated the field would be one of the richest ever discovered in the state. But other leases on the land were owned by large oil companies that were feeling the effects of depression and the overproduction of oil. Oil was selling for as little as fifteen cents a barrel in Texas. Under these circumstances, the big companies had got together to limit production in the Tubman Hills field.

They had formulated a unit-operation agreement: All individual interests in the field were to be considered as being pooled and undivided. Each lease owner could only drill so many wells for every hundred acres covered by its lease, and only a part of the entire field could be developed.

The area of the Tubman Hills field in which development would be allowed was outlined in blue pencil on the map Jim spread on the boardroom table. It was a masterpiece of gerrymandering. Each big oil company had large-sized tracts inside the blue line. Northcutt Petroleum had less than 200 of its acres inside, over 3,400 acres outside.

The agreement would not go into effect until formally ratified at a meeting in Santa Barbara the following month.

'There's eleven big companies holding leases in Tubman Hills,' Jim said, slamming his big hand down on the map. 'They'll vote down any proposal we might make. Northcutt Petroleum's the runt, and they're out to strangle it!'

Jim recited slowly the names of the other companies involved. Nine were giants. Two – Barrow and Creager Oil and Western Shore Petroleum – were large integrated independents.

'Barrow and Creager stock is selling for two fifty a share,' he said. 'Western Shore's at three bucks. Trouble is, each outfit has at least half its stock in the hands of management or management's friends. Otherwise, I'd buy up the majority of stock in one or the other. As it stands, I'll have to settle for good-sized minority blocs. Enough for leverage.'

He instructed his brokers to start buying the same day.

The Tubman Hills Oil Producers Association met on 30 October at the exclusive El Camino Reale Hotel in Santa Barbara. Jim Northcutt came with Luke Rayburn and several attorneys.

The others at the meeting included representatives of such oil-industry behemoths as Standard, Gulf and Jersey Crest, lesser Majors and the two big independents. They greeted James Northcutt with indifference and relegated him and his companions to the last seats in the conference room.

As a democratic gesture, the operators had made Theodore Creager, president of Barrow and Creager Oil, chairman of the meeting. There were few preliminaries. Creager, a sallow-faced man who looked more like a mortician than an oil company president, spoke.

'You are all aware that the unit-operation plan we are voting on today was formulated by leading California petroleum-industry experts. If there are any last-minute proposals —'

'There sure as shit are!'

Shocked faces swung towards Jim Northcutt, who was standing now, feet planted wide, glaring at Creager.

Theodore Creager's already thin lips grew thinner.

'Ah – Mr Northcutt, I believe?'

'In the pissed-off flesh, Mr Chairman. For your information, Mr Creager, Northcutt Petroleum owns twenty-seven per cent of the stock in your company.'

'Mr Northcutt, I don't see what that has to do —'

'Northcutt Petroleum also owns twenty-one per cent of Western Shore Petroleum's stock,' Jim continued. 'I can raise holy hell with your two companies – and with your Tubman Hills compact,' Northcutt said. 'If Barrow and Creager and Western Shore vote for this agreement, I'll take them both to court for screwing Northcutt Petroleum, a minority stockholder in both companies.'

Jim sat down and calmly started rolling a cigarette. Theodore Creager hurriedly went into a huddle with delegates of the three largest Majors. Their whisperings lasted a few moments.

Creager cleared his throat and stood. 'Gentlemen, this meeting is adjourned for half an hour,' he said, his voice ragged.

'Some of the other representatives and I will have a short, informal conference with Mr Northcutt.'

The Tubman Hills unit-operation map was redrawn. Northcutt Petroleum was allowed 1,200 acres inside the blue line, the same proportion of total lease acreage as was allotted to the larger companies.

'You made a clean sweep,' Luke Rayburn commented on the drive back to Los Angeles.

'Not quite,' Jim said.

'Jesus! What else do you want?'

Northcutt grinned.

'The Barrow and Creager Oil Company,' he replied. 'And I'm going after it. We'll have an integrated set-up. From wells right down to corner gas stations.'

There was no longer anything Jim Northcutt could say or do that would surprise Luke Rayburn. His pockmarked face creased into an easy smile and he reached for his hip pocket. He pulled out a silver flask, unscrewed the cap and offered the flask to Jim.

Northcutt took one hand from the steering wheel and drank deeply.

10

President Herbert Hoover spent a great deal of his time expressing confidence in the future. So did Andrew Mellon, who had been US Treasury Secretary for almost a decade.

They and their confidence were like Canute and his broom.

Depression deepened. Unemployment soared. General industrial output dropped by almost 50 per cent. Automobile production fell a shocking 75 per cent. During 1930–31, a total of 4,601 American banks closed.

The US petroleum industry had its own crises. Crude prices crumbled to all-time lows. Mid-continent producers were forced to sell their crude for as little as three cents a barrel.

Some independent producers refined their own gasoline, sold it for whatever they could and precipitated catastrophic price wars. In some parts of the country, gasoline sold for eight seven, even six cents a gallon at roadside pumps.

There were instances in which the Majors retaliated by hiring good squads to terrorize small independents and wreck their refineries. A number of operators were badly beaten, shot and killed. Oklahoma and Texas declared martial law in certain oil fields. Armed National Guardsmen took over the fields to insure that crude production was reduced. These efforts were an attempt to achieve some degree of price stabilization that would protect the investments and the income of the Major companies.

Countless independent operators went bankrupt or sold out for whatever was offered – or simply abandoned their leases, rigs and wells. Majors with Rockefeller, Mellon or other limitless fortunes behind them grew even larger as they swallowed small companies by the dozens.

James Northcutt was able to view the chaos around him with comparative equanimity. His foresight in investing large sums in government bonds provided ample capital reserves. He could continue his campaign to gain control of the Barrow and Creager Oil Company.

But the campaign abruptly reached what seemed to be an impasse. Jim had acquired about 31 per cent of Barrow and Creager's stock and elected two men to B and C's nine-man Board of Directors. They were, of course, overwhelmingly outnumbered – and suddenly, there were no more Barrow and Creager shares available on the market.

The reasons for this soon became clear. Those who held sizeable blocs of B and C stock were front men for the Jersey Crest Oil Corporation, which was controlled by the Roetenhaffer family, a powerful American industrial-financial dynasty. The Roetenhaffer interests had all remaining B and C stock transferred to Jersey Crest.

Northcutt went to New York City, to consult with stock-market experts, brokers and corporation lawyers. After weeks of meetings and conferences, he had to admit he had made no headway in his struggle to gain control of Barrow and Creager.

The Roetenhaffer dynasty moved to put more obstacles in Jim Northcutt's path. Its agents hastily formed the Temple Corporation, a holding company to which Jersey Crest transferred its majority stockholdings in Barrow and Creager. The new Temple Corporation stock was scheduled for distribution to

Jersey Crest shareholders on a pro-rata basis. This would disperse B and C stock so widely that any possibility of gaining control of the company be put far beyond Northcutt's reach.

Jim conferred with more New York attorneys, received more discouraging answers. He'd exhausted all sources when, one night, he took a girl to Sherman Billingsley's Stork Club. Located on Fifty-eighth Street, it was one of Manhattan's more expensive speakeasies.

The girl was immediately forgotten when Jim saw Verna seated at a table with a number of other people. They were in evening clothes, and Verna was the centre of attraction. Northcutt could not take his eyes from her. Over the years he had followed the course of her career and personal life closely.

Verna had gone from one professional success to another. She had proven to be one of the relatively few silent film stars whose voice registered well on a sound track. The transition from silents to talkies had made her even more of a box-office attraction, and she was rated as one of Hollywood's top ten female stars.

Her personal life had been considerably less successful. Though she retained the professional name Verna Harkness, she had long since divorced her first husband. She had married a second time, and that marriage had also ended in divorce.

Verna herself had not changed, Jim told himself, staring at her across the room. Let's see, he mused. I'm thirty-one, almost thirty-two, and she's three years older, but I'll be damned if she looks it. Same blonde hair, same great blue eyes with the long lashes – and Christ, I still want her. More than that. Right now, I need her. The way I used to when things got tough back in Oklahoma.

'Sorry,' he said to the girl with him. 'There's somebody here I have to talk to – about business. It may be my only chance.'

The girl pouted and protested, but Jim sent her home in his hired limousine. Then he went over to Verna's table.

'Jim!' Verna was apparently delighted to see him. 'Funny that I didn't notice you before.' She flashed him a well-remembered smile. 'And you're hard to miss, friend. Even in a crowd.'

She introduced him to the others and a waiter placed a chair at her right for him. Someone told him the gathering was a 'sort of farewell party' for Verna.

192

'Oh?' Jim turned to her. 'Farewell to what – or whom?'

'New York,' she replied. 'I've been here two months. I'm going to Chicago tomorrow.'

'On the *Twentieth Century*?' Verna Harkness would hardly travel aboard any but the crack VIP train.

'Yes.'

'No press agents and business managers?'

'Only Celia.'

They were interrupted as waiters served more champagne. The others at the table were taken aback when Jim pulled a sack of Bull Durham from the pocket of his expensive dinner jacket and began to roll a cigarette. Verna only smiled. Fondly.

Jim had intended to stay in New York another few days, but changed his plans. Early the next morning, he checked on that evening's *Twentieth Century Limited* and was told the train was completely booked. Three fifty-dollar bills solved that problem. Suddenly, a bedroom–drawing room suite became available. In the same car aboard which Miss Verna Harkness had similar accommodations.

Half an hour out of Grand Central Station, Verna and Celia were having dinner in their compartment. When the door handle rattled, Celia started for the door. Verna stopped her. Verna's feminine intuition told her there was only one possibility.

'Hello, Jim,' she said, grinning as she opened the door. 'Two things you never learned. To smoke tailor-mades and to knock. Come in.'

They sat in the drawing room. Jim ordered champagne. The three of them talked and drank.

'Almost like old times,' Jim said, a bit awkwardly.

'Not quite, Jim,' Verna said. 'We've all changed.'

Have we, Jim wondered, staring moodily into his glass.

'You're in some kind of trouble,' Verna said suddenly.

His right eyebrow shot up. 'Word gets around fast.'

'I didn't hear a thing, Jim.'

'Then how—'

'We used to know each other pretty well. The signs show.'

He emptied his glass. 'Not the kind of trouble we used to know.'

'Tell me.' She avoided his eyes. 'After all, we were partners once.'

'That we were,' Jim said and sketched out his problems with Jersey Crest. 'So, while I can't really lose, I can't win, either,' he concluded glumly.

'You *have* changed,' Verna said. 'You never worried about odds in the old days, and you never settled for anything less than a win.' Not in business, at any rate. Memories make for nostalgia and nostalgia stirs up old feelings, she added to herself, wanting him.

Funny, Jim thought. Somehow Verna made the odds seem less impossible. He stood up to pour more champagne. It was then that Verna noticed the gold-and-onyx gusher charm hanging from a chain in his vest pocket.

'You – you still have that?' Verna asked, pointing.

'Sure,' he nodded. 'Always kept it.'

Now Verna stood up, too, took the champagne bottle from Jim's hand and started towards the compartment door.

'Get a good night's sleep, Celia,' she said over her shoulder. She looked at Jim. 'Let's make it your place, friend.' She tried to keep her tone light, but the undertones of old longings came through.

They entered Jim's compartment and the champagne bottle Verna was carrying fell from her fingers and spilled its contents on the carpeted floor. They ignored it, for they were in each other's arms, their mouths locked.

Jim's hands moved over the curves and planes of her body and to his amazement, experienced total tactile recall. It was as if there had been no intervening years, not even months or days.

Verna clung to him and to the reality of his touch, his lean body and the feelings that rose within her. She didn't speak.

'Verna.' Jim's voice was hoarse. 'I —'

'No speeches, Jim. Let's just make love.'

Moments later they were undressed and lying together. Her moan was a scream she would not have been able to stifle even if the noise of the speeding train hadn't covered it.

'Go on,' she begged, gasping. But there was no need for her to urge him. There was limitless craving in his movements. Her body was wracked by violent spasms as she climaxed again and he with her. He did not move away, and he grew inside her again.

'My God!' Verna sobbed and arched her body, holding him even more tightly.

They made love again and again until midnight, dozed in each other's arms for perhaps half an hour. Their desire seemed inexhaustible, but by dawn it had finally spent itself. They lay together, listening to the click of the wheels and the occasional blast of the locomotive whistle.

It was Jim who spoke first.

'Verna.' He coiled a strand of her hair around a finger as he had in the distant past. She turned her head, blue eyes enigmatic as they studied him.

'Umm?'

'You know, I'm almost thirty-two.'

Verna sensed the direction in which he was leading.

'And I'm older,' she parried. 'I always have been.'

He seemed not to have heard her.

'I'm still single,' he blurted.

There it was, Verna thought. After more than a decade.

'You should always stay single, Jim,' she said softly.

He stirred, propped himself up on an elbow.

'Why? Because I screw around so much?'

'Only partly. The main reason is that you'd never stop doing the things you'd have to give up if you wanted to stay married.'

'That's not an answer.'

'Promise to tell me the truth?' Her smile was soft, almost maternal.

'Yes.'

'We've been making love for hours, and it's been wonderful —'

'God, yes —'

'I haven't asked my question. Now tell me. Since we've been here in your compartment, how many times have you thought of your company and Jersey Crest and the company you're trying to take over?'

'Hell, I don't know,' Jim growled impatiently. 'Five times. Maybe six. What difference . . .'

He stopped, realizing that his words had revealed a great deal about him.

Verna sat up, using a doubled-over pillow for a backrest.

'You'll get married one of these days,' she said, her smile

195

still gentle.

'But you don't think it'll last?'

'No,' Verna replied honestly. 'Too much of you is business, Jim. Or call it oil, if you want. There's not much of you left over for people.' She deepened her smile. 'Wives want a lot more. Besides, you'd never allow any woman to tie you down.'

Jim couldn't deny the truth of what Verna said. There was his past performance to consider. The long string of mistresses. Each having a strong initial attraction. Each beginning to wear on him quickly, especially when they showed the first signs of becoming possessive.

'Verna, maybe we could —'

'Not a chance, Jim,' she said. 'Not in a million years.'

I've always held an idealized Jim Northcutt image in my mind, Verna reflected. But you can't be idealized, Jim. A woman either takes you as you are, or she'd better forget it. She'd lose, no matter what she did. If she were pliant and submissive, you'd be bored. If she tried to share your life, your obsession with personal independence would finish the relationship.

'I'm in no rush to get back to the Coast,' Jim said. 'So I'll stop over in Chicago, and we can —'

'*We* can't do anything in Chicago. Not together, Jim.'

'Why the hell not?'

'Because I'm going to Chicago to get married. I'm making a third try.' With someone who isn't at all like you. It just may work.

'But last night and this morning – you and I . . .'

'Call it catharsis, Jim.'

The locomotive whistle let loose with several sharp blasts. To Northcutt, they were like exclamation marks tacked on to her words.

Catharsis.

Maybe, he thought, but he doubted it, and when the locomotive whistle blew again, it sounded strangely sad and dismal in his ears.

11

The encounter with Verna left Jim Northcutt emotionally perplexed. Instead of going on to Los Angeles, he decided he would pay Abraham Schlechter a visit in Tulsa. He had not seen Abe for almost five years, when Schlechter had brought his family to California on a vacation.

Abe was beginning to show his age, Jim noticed. He was almost bald, and his face, always thin, was now gaunt and etched with deep lines.

'You haven't changed much, Jim,' Schlechter said.

Abe and his wife Sarah insisted that Jim stay with them. They took him upstairs to one of the guest rooms, and Abe proudly showed Jim the connecting bathroom.

'Look – you'll remember this.'

Jim burst out laughing. Abe had closed down his original supply store in Logan a few years before and had shipped to Tulsa the huge, gaudy bathtub that had been used by so many oilmen. It was installed in the bathroom.

'You might like to soak in that again,' Schlechter said.

'I will,' Jim nodded. Perhaps that might even create the illusion that he was soaking off the years along with the grime he had collected on the train from Chicago.

The Schlechters had invited their married children to join them in the dinner prepared in Jim Northcutt's honour. Abe's son Sam was among them. Sam had obtained his law degree some years before and was a practising attorney in Tulsa. When his father asked Jim what he had been doing in New York, Sam listened intently as Northcutt gave a short résumé of the problems he was facing in his campaign to take over Barrow and Creager.

'I got nowhere in New York,' Jim finished.

Sam Schlechter leaned forward.

'You say Jersey Crest formed the Temple Corporation as a holding company?' he asked.

'That's the size of it,' Jim nodded.

'But the Temple stock hasn't yet been distributed to Jersey Crest stockholders?'

'No.'

'Have they been formally notified they'll have rights to a pro-rata distribution of Temple stock?'

'Yes, I think so. About three weeks ago.'

'Seems to me there are two things you can do,' Sam Schlechter said. 'First you should find someone who owns a big bloc of Jersey Crest stock. Make him an offer for his rights to Temple Corporation stock. If you can buy them, you have that much more of an edge – plus a psychological advantage.'

'By God, you're right.'

'Then, file an action calling for Jersey Crest to distribute the actual Barrow and Creager stock – rather than shares in the front holding company – to its stockholders.'

Jim blinked. Sam Schlechter was young – although not that much younger than I am, he reflected – but he made sense.

'It's bound to have a strong effect,' Sam continued. 'The general climate isn't good for such games by outfits the size of Jersey Crest.'

Northcutt was thoughtful. The young attorney's suggestions were excellent. He'd doubtless already learned much about the realities of corporation – and especially oil-business – law in Tulsa, the toughest of all petroleum battlegrounds.

Jim made an intuitive decision.

'I've been paying six-figure fees to law firms in California and New York,' he said. 'And you just came up with the first constructive suggestions.' He toyed with his coffee cup and cocked an eyebrow. 'How'd you like to take over?'

'I'm afraid I don't follow you.'

'Come out to California, Sam. You'll be the Northcutt Petroleum house attorney and a member of the Board. You can also have your own private practice. I'll foot all the bills and guarantee that you'll make double whatever you're making now.'

Before he left for Los Angeles two days later, Jim Northcutt reached an agreement with Samuel Schlechter. It was the beginning of an association that would last for decades and make Sam a multi-millionaire in his own right.

Jim returned to Los Angeles, renewed in his determination to defeat Jersey Crest.

Between 1880 and 1910, the American petroleum industry had been run by virtually one man – Jordan B. Roetenhaffer. Using tactics that were seldom ethical, and very often crimi nal, he built a huge trust, National Crest Oil Corporation, that controlled America's oil transportation and refinery facilities and its oil marketing outlets. Competing oil interests and the US Supreme Court eventually loosened National Crest's stranglehold on the industry. J. B. Roetenhaffer, forced to dissolve the trust, broke it into more than forty separate companies, keeping firm control over the largest, Jersey Crest Oil.

Upon Roetenhaffer's death, his oldest son, J. B., Jr, as he was called, inherited an estimated $175 million. He retained the stock in Jersey Crest and other Roetenhaffer companies that were part of his inheritance. But he took no active part in the management of the companies. This he left to his many brothers, sons and nephews.

When James Northcutt went over the names of those who owned sizeable blocs of Jersey Crest stock, the one name that stood out most prominently was Jordan B. Roetenhaffer, Jr. He held a total of 11 per cent of Jersey Crest's common stock. This entitled him to an equal percentage of shares of Temple Corporation, the new holding company to which Jersey Crest had transferred its majority stockholdings in Barrow and Creager. When the Temple Corporation shares were distributed, J. B., Jr, would have control over 11 per cent of Barrow and Creager stock.

Jim learned that J. B., Jr, was staying in Colorado Springs. He went there immediately and arranged for a meeting.

Bored as ever by business details, J. B., Jr, quickly agreed to sell his rights to the Temple Corporation stock when he heard Jim's generous offer. Northcutt left Colorado Springs to all intents and purposes owning 11 per cent more Barrow and Creager stock. Added to all his previous purchases, his holdings in the company now topped 42 per cent.

The Roetenhaffer name had a power all its own. When other Jersey Crest stockholders learned that J. B., Jr, had sold his rights to Temple Corporation shares, many assumed that he had inside knowledge that had made him dubious about the holding company. Several Jersey Crest shareholders followed his lead.

Within two months after Samuel Schlechter's arrival in Los Angeles, Jim managed to buy up other blocs of Temple Corporation stock. By mid-1932, Northcutt Petroleum owned 57 per cent of the Barrow and Creager Oil Company.

Jim now had the basic structure on which to build what he had so long desired, a vertically integrated oil company.

The 1932 national election resulted in an overwhelming victory for Franklin Delano Roosevelt. Most of the country considered it a foregone conclusion that Prohibition would be repealed soon after Roosevelt took office early in 1933. The prospect generated intensive rivalry among bootleggers who wanted to be ready for Repeal and establish themselves in other lucrative enterprises. The rivalry frequently caused violence and murders.

One night in December, Jim Northcutt and Steven Kostis were drinking and dancing with two girls at Nestor's, a speakeasy and nightclub on La Cienega Boulevard. Shortly after midnight, they paid their bill and walked towards Jim's car, parked half a block down the street.

Northcutt had his car keys out and was a few feet ahead of Kostis and the two girls. Perhaps that was why he first saw the dark sedan that turned out of a side street and headed towards them, gathering speed.

Jim never knew what sixth sense caused him to react as he did. But, when the car was still some fifty yards distant, he spun around, spread his arms wide and flung himself at Steve and the women.

'What the hell!' Kostis shouted, and the girls cried out in dismay as Jim Northcutt hurled all three of them – and himself – to the sidewalk.

By then, the dark sedan was abreast of them, and there was a volley of shots. Bullets punched into the sidewalk and cracked overhead. All missed, thanks to Jim's swift act. The sedan roared on into the night.

'They were after me,' Steve said while he and Jim helped the two now-hysterical girls to their feet. 'After this, I don't just owe you. I'm in hock to you for the rest of my life.'

BOOK THREE

1

6 July (Morning)

The inert mountain of flesh that was Steve Kostis seemed revitalized by the visit that Kathy Northcutt and Mark Radford made to his Mulholland Drive mansion. Kostis issued orders, sent several of his men out to deliver messages, made a number of telephone calls.

'You're acting twenty years younger,' Nicholas Loues, Steven's closest aide, observed.

'I feel forty years younger,' Kostis said. Even his breathing was easier. 'I've been squatting here, doing nothing except feeling sorry for myself. Now I've got something to do again.'

Nick Loues looked at him dubiously.

'Sure you want to get mixed up in Northcutt's mess?' he asked. 'The people you sent for might not want to go along. They've been out of the rough stuff for a long time.'

'Yeah. Only they're good for their IOU's, Nick. I owe Jim Northcutt. They owe me.'

Now the eight men who had received Kostis's message began arriving. Each came in a chauffeured limousine. All appeared to be highly successful businessmen, and all knew one another.

Steven met them in the same dimly lit room where he had talked to Kathy and Mark two days before. He got to the point quickly.

'Friend of mine needs help,' he said. He related what he had been told about the arson campaign being waged against Northcutt International Petroleum's retailers on the East Coast.

'Jersey Crest's behind it,' Kostis summed up. 'Charles Farrier – Carlo Maniscalco – in New York is doing the demolition work.'

There was a moment's silence.

'Farrier's backed by the Moretti family,' one of the men – a prominent San Francisco importer-exporter – said finally. 'Anyone interfering with Maniscalco will have the whole Moretti mob on his neck.'

'So what?' Kostis growled. 'Listen, George. When you had

problems with Bugsy Siegel and his outfit, you came to me. Right?'

A grudging 'Yes, Steve, but that was —'

'Years ago? And if Siegel hadn't been hit, George, it would've been you.'

Another silence.

'God damn it, Steven, we can't afford to get involved.' It was Frank Zeller. According to the *Journal of Commerce*, Zeller was Missouri's leading real estate and public-transportation tycoon.

'Your memory's short, Frank,' Kostis declared, a sharp edge to his voice. 'I couldn't afford to get involved in fifty-one, either, when you asked me to pull Charles Binaggio off your back. But I arranged it, even though Binaggio was the Governor's buddy. It wasn't easy, Frank, since I got to remind you. I had him and two of his triggermen blown up right in the Democratic party headquarters in K.C.'

'Fifty-one isn't now,' Zeller protested. 'We're all legit. We mix with a bunch of oil companies, and we're begging for big trouble. The federal government'll come down on us.'

'Crap!' Kostis sneered.

'Who foots the bills if we have to buy?' a third man asked.

'Northcutt,' Steven said. 'He's never welshed in his life.'

'You say so. Only we don't know him.'

'*I* know him, and you know me. I'm guaranteeing.'

'Personally?'

'Personally.'

The eight men looked at Kostis.

'You always went along with us, Steve,' Zeller said, speaking for all. 'We'll go along. I just hope you understand that Maniscalco – or Farrier, if that's what he's calling himself – has the Moretti outfit behind him. And the Moretti bunch has a lot of its own friends. This might turn into one hell of a big war.'

'Yeah,' Steven Kostis agreed amiably. 'It sure might.'

Lloyd Birdwell, clad in his customary blue-striped silk pyjamas, stood before one of his bedroom windows. The glass was bulletproof and tinted blue. He gazed outside and nodded his clean-shaven head approvingly. Men riding what appeared to be hybrids of golf carts and dune buggies were going about the daily task of cleaning the acres of Astroturf that covered the grounds of his Malibu estate.

All the windows in the building that served as Birdwell's home and the nerve centre of his business empire were hermetically sealed. Nevertheless, Lloyd Birdwell was still afraid that dirt or litter on the Astroturf might produce germs. And germs might filter inside. He turned from the window towards a stainless-steel console covered with an array of switches and buttons. A bony hand pushed a toggle switch forward. A light glowed and a voice came over a loudspeaker.

'Yes, Mr Birdwell?'

'Altkirk available?' Thomas Altkirk was his chief lieutenant.

'Yes, sir.'

There was a moment's silence.

'Tom here, Lloyd.'

'Dial the computer to the central-records section of Birdwell Equipment in Houston. I want complete print-outs showing what they're doing on every current order we have from Jersey Crest, Western Impex and Richland Consolidated.'

'I'll have them in fifteen minutes.'

'Bring them up to me when you do.' The papers would be sprayed with a germicidal gas and then exposed to ultraviolet light before Birdwell saw them.

Less than twenty minutes later Thomas Altkirk buzzed and was admitted. He was ramrod straight, wore a crew cut and might have passed for a marine drill sergeant who was still in peak condition at forty-five. Like everyone who went beyond the main-floor reception rooms of the buildings, he wore white cotton boots held tight at mid-calf by drawstrings.

'Shall I wait?' Altkirk asked, placing a thick accordion-folded stack of computer print-out sheets on a table.

'No, thanks.'

After Altkirk had gone, Birdwell sat down in a white leather armchair and began studying the print-outs. An odd smile played over his almost cadaverous face.

For many years, he had been a recluse, insulating himself not only against dirt and bacteria and the world at large but also from memories. He had become practically an automaton concentrating solely on his financial affairs.

But Kathy Northcutt's visit the previous day had activated forgotten memories. Yes, Jim Northcutt and Steve Kostis and I were good friends, he reflected. And, if it hadn't been for the breaks Jim gave me in 1922 when he took over Birdwell Golden State Oil, I might be penniless today. Having once made

205

the admission, he knew he could not leave Northcutt in the lurch.

As soon as Kathy Northcutt and Mark Radford had gone, Birdwell had issued instructions. Now he studied the print-outs and saw that his directives were being carried out. Already orders for drilling tools and other equipment from the three companies ranged against Northcutt were being sidetracked. The companies would begin to feel the lack of equipment in about thirty days. If Northcutt and NIPCO managed to hold out until then on their own, that pinch would help them by hampering and confounding their opponents. Lloyd Birdwell was satisfied. He had done all he could.

2

6 July (Afternoon)

Kathy Northcutt and Mark Radford boarded the NIPCO 727 for their return flight to New York at 9 A.M.

They had obtained what they had sought and now shared a sense of accomplishment. This feeling established a considerable degree of outward rapport between them. However, beneath the surface, injured female and angry male sexual prides continued to sulk.

Kathy still seethed over her rejection by Mark on the night before their departure from New York. No man had ever left her as Mark had when he stalked out of her Hotel Pierre suite. For his part, Mark Radford wanted Kathy. But *not*, he told himself, if she persisted in being the imperious female for whom sex was a form of exploitation.

The undercurrents were not evident during their flight. Their conversation was friendly but impersonal. Kathy guided it into a discussion of the oil business and began asking questions. Mark recognized that she was seeking to fill gaps in her knowledge, some of which was surprisingly elementary, considering that she was the daughter of an oil billionaire.

'I thought you'd been studying NIPCO's annual reports and financial statements for years,' Mark said. 'At least, that's what your father told us at Bonheur.'

'Oh, I'm familiar with how NIPCO itself operates,' Kathy said. 'What I'm hazy about is the oil business as a whole and how NIPCO fits into the overall pattern.'

'Any particular place you'd like to start?' Mark lit a Salem.

'With my own changing perspectives. I had always thought of NIPCO as a big company. All of a sudden, I realize it's not so big after all.'

'Depends on how you measure things,' Mark said. 'NIPCO has about three billion in assets. The company made almost a hundred and forty million profit last year. That's big, all right, if you're not talking about the oil business. But compare it, say, to Exxon, with almost thirty billion in sales and two and a half billion in profits annually. Then NIPCO doesn't seem so big.'

He inhaled deeply, allowing the smoke to drift from his nostrils.

'Next, you have to remember that Exxon and six other multi-national giants – seven companies in all – control eighty per cent of all petroleum production, refining and marketing outside the Communist countries. That's a good chunk of the world, Kathy. An independent company like NIPCO has to scramble if it's going to stay in business.

'Now let's focus on the United States. We're the world's biggest user of petroleum products. Do you realize that four cents out of every dollar the average American consumer spends goes for gasoline and motor oil? Four cents out of every one of the seven hundred billion plus dollars consumers spend in this country every year.'

Kathy blinked. 'I never dreamed it was *that* much!'

Radford grinned. He was enjoying his role as a teacher to this beautiful and quixotic girl. 'Five companies – Exxon, Mobil, Gulf, Texaco and Jersey Crest – account for over sixty per cent of *all* petroleum sales in the US. You can translate that into six out of every ten gallons of gasoline or jet, diesel or heating fuel – or any petroleum you can name.'

'Mark.' Kathy was very serious now. 'If a few Majors are so enormously rich and powerful, how has NIPCO managed to last this long?'

'Because your father built an independent oil company that's integrated, well to pump, and doesn't have to rely on the Majors for anything. NIPCO produces, transports and refines its own crude and sells the products through its own marketing organization. Northcutt International Petroleum is self-sufficient in the same way as the giants or the lesser – but still large – major companies like Union Oil or Tenneco. None the less, NIPCO has to fight to stay in existence.'

'Dad has antagonized them all, hasn't he?'

'That's putting it mildly,' Mark laughed. 'He's always refused to go along with their price-fixing schemes, underselling them at the pump. NIPCO wouldn't play the fuel-shortage game the last time, and we're not playing it now, either.'

'Just how phoney is the shortage, Mark?'

'Tough to say. Any available figures come from the National Petroleum Council, and that's completely dominated by the Majors. There *are* some production and refining shortfalls, but nowhere near what the Majors would like people to believe. They've blown it all out of proportion.'

'So they can raise their prices even higher,' Kathy said.

'That's one aim. Another is to get rid of all environmental controls. Another is to obtain still greater tax benefits and indirect federal subsidies. Then, they're hoping to push the last remaining independent refiners and marketers out of business. They want to expand that shared monopoly and give the public an even bigger screwing.'

Kathy didn't appear entirely convinced.

'Mark, economists and experts —'

'Please! Ever hear your father on the subject of economists and experts? He calls them God-damned fools who juggle statistics they don't understand to make them fit any theory they're paid to rationalize.'

He grimaced.

'The oil industry isn't even one hundred and twenty years old. In that time, there have been God only knows how many panics that the world was going to run out of oil overnight. It hasn't. It won't. Not in our lifetime.'

'You sound awfully sure.'

'I am. Most existing fields aren't producing to capacity. There are new fields being opened up in Africa, Alaska, Canada, right here in the United States. Then you've got offshore and deep-sea reservoirs that are only now being tapped.'

Kathy's eyes suddenly glowed.

'And when NIPCO starts exploring and drilling in China —'

'Now you're getting the idea – and the fever,' Radford said. 'Those drilling concessions your father went after should produce more crude than anyone ever dreamed existed. If his deals with Peking go through, not even the Majors will be able to bleat about oil shortages.'

'Still, there are shortages now.'

'I said there are shortfalls. The critical shortage scare is mainly a swindle. Use your head, Kathy. Sure, oil consumption has been rising steadily from one year to the next. But what happened a couple of years ago and again only recently? Bang! All of a sudden you're expected to swallow the argument that there's been a quantum jump in demand from one day to the next. Good morning, everybody. At oh-six-hundred hours today, there's an oil famine. Can you actually bring yourself to believe it?'

'No,' Kathy said. 'When you put it that way, I guess I really can't.'

She lapsed into a deep, thoughtful silence. She was beginning to understand why mavericks like James L. Northcutt were hated and considered pariahs by the Majors.

Arriving in New York, Kathy and Mark went directly to Samuel Schlechter's office.

'We'll place a conference call to Jim in France,' Schlechter said. 'I'll have Peter Keeley listen too.' Keeley, the president of NIPCO, had offices uptown in the NIPCO Building. 'Then you'll have to go through the story only once.'

It took fifteen minutes to set up the conference call and establish contact with James Northcutt at his Cap d'Antibes estate.

'Good or bad?' they heard Northcutt's deep voice inquire.

'Good, Dad,' Kathy replied. 'Kostis and Birdwell are with us.'

'What're the mechanics, Mark?' Northcutt asked.

'Birdwell simply does what you suggested for ninety days. Kostis will have people coming to see me in a few days. They'll take care of the actual work. I'll be a sort of overseer.'

'Sam, Pete, Radford – keep me posted. Phone me every ten minutes if you feel it's necessary. Now I'd like to talk to Kathy privately.'

When the others had replaced their receivers and Kathy was alone, she said, 'Yes, Dad.'

'A question first. Did you or didn't you?'

'Did I or didn't I do what?'

'Seduce Mark Radford the first night you were in New

209

York.' Kathy heard her father chuckle. 'I made a bet with my-self.'

'You won't believe it, but I can't honestly answer yes or no,' she said. 'Not yet, anyway.'

Northcutt grew serious. 'When are you coming back to Bonheur?'

'I thought I'd stay here a week or so.'

'Please fly over tomorrow.'

'Why so soon, Dad?'

'Because I'd like to have you here. For moral support.'

He means it, Kathy thought. It was the first time in her life that he had ever asked that she adjust her plans to suit his wishes.

'Of course, Dad. I'll leave in the morning.'

When Sam Schlechter and Mark Radford heard that North-cutt had asked Kathy to leave for France the next day, they guessed the real reasons behind his request. Jim Northcutt didn't want his daughter to be in New York when the dirty infighting began. Naturally, neither made any mention of this to Kathy.

Kathy and Mark left Schlechter's office together.

'Dinner this evening?' Mark asked. He didn't know when he would see her again.

'Yes,' she said. 'When and where?'

'You're still at the Pierre. Let's return to the scene of the original crime.'

'Your crime or mine?'

'Maybe if we try hard enough, we'll find out.'

3

6 July (Evening)

Mark met Kathy in the Hotel Pierre's L-shaped, muted rococo lobby at eight that evening.

'I made sure we'd have the same table,' he told her as they went into the Café Pierre.

The meal was a game of sexual chess, the opponents playing for the same prize, but each uneasy about how it might end.

You bastard, Kathy thought as they ate and Mark chatted

amiably. All my systems are GO. I'm melting all over the table-cloth. But I'll be damned if I let you know. Not this time. If you do the heavy male-aggressor bit, it's going to be my turn to refuse and reject. Even if I have to spend the rest of the night alone, clawing my way up and down the walls.

'Coffee and a *digestif*?' Mark asked when they had finished dinner.

You surprise me, Kathy applauded silently. I expected you to order coffee and cognac for both of us.

'What are you having?' she asked.

'Double espresso, double Remy.'

'I'd like a regular coffee and a Grand Marnier.'

'That's out of character.'

'Oh?' Kathy's right eyebrow rose slightly. 'How?'

'You're hardly the Grand Marnier type.'

'Observant man.'

'Then have the cognac you really want. I won't read any symbolic act of surrender into it.'

Smartass, Kathy thought. 'All right,' she said. 'Remy for me, too.'

The coffees and cognacs were served.

'You're leaving early in the morning,' Mark said, raising his snifter in a toast. 'Happy landings.'

'Thanks.'

Their eyes met.

Anyway, you're one of the coolest bastards I've ever seen, Kathy mused. They drank. He was silent.

'Say something,' she said, watching him closely.

'The Surgeon-General has determined that cigarette smoking is dangerous for your health.'

'You're freaking out.'

'Nope. You told me to say something. I did. Here it is. Printed right on my pack of Salems. Care for one?' He offered the pack.

'No, you idiot.' Kathy realized she was smiling – and losing ground. She caught herself and tried to regain the initiative. 'You're not so observant after all. I seldom smoke, and never menthols. Haven't you noticed?'

'I've noticed.' Mark lit a cigarette. 'Just wanted to see if your habit patterns can be altered.' He slipped the pack into his pocket. 'Being of the old school, I warned you of the risks first.'

'Your old-school tie may strangle you, friend. Any more of my habit patterns you'd like to alter?'

'A couple.' Mark leaned forward. 'Your bedroom manners for one.' He had decided to take the offensive, but there was a strong hint of affectionate humour in his voice.

'Independent research laboratories have made astounding discoveries lately,' he went on, grinning, before Kathy had any chance to make a comment. 'When there are two people, sex has to be two-way. Otherwise, it's masturbation for one, like nowhere for the other.'

Kathy glared at him. Then her look began to change. He was getting through to her. He's got pride in himself, she thought. Other men . . .

'You're a person, Kathy,' he was saying now. 'So am I – I hope.' He stubbed out his cigarette. 'The last thing you need is a wind-up gigolo in bed. Unless, of course, you've got some sort of dominatrix hang-up, in which case I'm not —'

'I don't have anything of the kind!' Kathy found herself protesting – and also found herself conceding that Mark Radford had reached her finally.

'I have a dry throat,' she said, picking up her water goblet.

'Kathy —'

'Please call for the bill, Mark.'

The moment they entered Kathy's suite, the telephone began to ring.

'Must've tripped a switch when we opened the door,' Mark observed unhappily.

'I'll make it quick,' Kathy said, moving towards the sitting room telephone. She picked it up on the third ring.

'Kathy! I'm so glad I managed to reach you!'

Charlotte Wrightman, Kathy recognized the voice and made a face. She cupped her hand over the transmitter.

'A woman I've known for years,' she told Mark. 'She went through a divorce trauma a month ago. I made the mistake of calling her when I got here from France.'

She took her hand from the mouthpiece.

'I've been in California, and I'll be leaving for Europe again early tomorrow, Charlotte,' Kathy said. 'Very early.' She hoped the hint would shorten the conversation.

'Kathy, I'm horribly depressed. If I don't talk to somebody —'

'Shouldn't you – umm – like call your analyst?'

'Oh, I stopped going to him. He wasn't helping...'

Kathy put her hand over the phone again.

'Mark, I could blow my brains out, but this might take a few minutes.' She silently cursed Charlotte Wrightman, her ex-husband, ex-psychiatrist and Alexander Graham Bell. She sat down in an armchair and braced for Charlotte's woeful recital.

'... and then Bryce, this man I've been seeing...'

Mark Radford was nervously moving around the room. Kathy's eyes followed him and she smiled, slipping off her shoe. She spoke occasionally, vainly seeking to stem her friend's monologue.

'You say you didn't know he was married until last week?'

'No. You see, Kathy, he and his wife have been separated, but it's not a legal separation...'

Charlotte's voice droned on. Kathy only half-listened as she continued to watch Mark's restless pacing. She tipped her head to the left, her long hair a cascade of burnished copper. She held the telephone between hunched shoulder and ear. Her slender body contorted as she reached with both hands to open the zip fastener at the back of her dress.

'... so I couldn't go on and on with that situation...'

The try for the zip failed. The telephone almost slipped and fell. Kathy clutched at it with her left hand, covering the mouthpiece with her right.

'Mark,' she murmured, twisting her torso so her back was facing him. She craned her neck down. 'I can't reach.'

He stopped pacing and sat down on the arm of her chair. His fingers brushed against her cheek and neck before moving to the zip and gently easing it open.

'... and then Bryce told me he and his wife were both into encounter therapy. Together. So I had to do something...'

'You're better off getting out of the affair,' Kathy said, hand off the receiver again. Mark Radford's hands were stroking her shoulders and upper back. The sensation was galvanic. She could not suppress a gasp of delight.

'Hey, what's the matter, Kathy?' Charlotte asked.

'Uh – nothing.' Except I wish you'd get the hell off the phone.

'Anyway. I don't know if I'm better off or not. That's why I had a battle with my analyst...'

Oh, God, Kathy thought.

Marks hands had slipped under the fabric of her dress. She wasn't wearing a bra, and he was caressing her breasts. She gasped, louder than before and hurriedly clamped her hand over the mouthpiece.

She turned her torso to the left again and held her hand and arm out and shrugged her right shoulder so he could slip her dress top off.

'. . . three years. That's how long I'd been going to him, and he said I was being immature . . .'

Kathy switched the telephone to her right hand, stretching out her left arm so that Mark could ease off the top of her dress. He kissed her shoulder, brushing his fingers against her straining nipples. Strands of her red hair framed her breasts.

'I may just vaporize right here,' he whispered, his tongue flicking her ear.

'. . . and I still want Bryce. What do you think I should do?'

'Oooh – uh, why – why not look around for another psychiatrist?' Kathy stammered.

'I'll be needing one myself in about ten seconds flat,' Mark whispered.

'Another one? God damn it, Kathy, I want . . .'

Kathy continued to hold the telephone, but she stood up. Her dress fell to the floor around her feet. She stepped out of it.

'Charlotte, dear, I've had a murderous day. I'm beat —'

'So am I! But let me tell you what else happened . . .'

Kathy's lips silently formed the words, oh shit. She slid one hand under the elastic top of her panti-hose, eased it down towards her hips. Mark stood up from the chair arm and went to her. The panti-hose were down to her thighs. She sat down again. Mark leaned over her and removed them. He kissed her upper thighs, felt her body quiver and then arch. He straightened, took a step backwards and stood relishing the beauty of her body. His desire for her was a throbbing ache.

Kathy covered the mouthpiece with her hand once more.

'I'll get her off the line and be in the bedroom in two minutes – or I'll throw this phone out the window,' she said, her voice hoarse.

'Make it a minute and a half,' Mark said. He kissed her neck and started for the bedroom.

'. . . Bryce called me last night. He said that his being married shouldn't make any difference . . .'

214

'What did you do?' Kathy asked, standing up.

'I hung up on him.'

'Charlotte! That's the biggest goof you could have made. Call him. Now!'

'You think —'

'I'm certain. And I'm going to hang up myself. Before you lose another minute!'

She replaced the phone for a moment, lifted it again, told the hotel switchboard to put through no more calls. Slamming down the receiver, she hurried into the bedroom.

Mark met her inside the doorway. He took her in his arms and kissed her. Her response was instantaneous. Then her lips pressed against his chest, kissing his flesh. She tilted her head back and stared up at him.

'Please. Let's go to bed.'

They moved to the large bed together. He freed himself from her grasp, lowered her gently onto the bed.

'Mark.' It was a whisper.

'Yes?'

'Is this really what you want?'

'Yes, now.'

'Then together. Please.' Her hands moved to his waist and thighs, urging his body up on the bed.

He lay beside her. Her orgasm was swift and intense.

Then she was no longer coherent.

His own orgasm was volcanic.

'Like never,' Kathy murmured afterwards.

A little later, they made love again. And then yet again. When they fell asleep, he was holding her close to him.

Kathy awakened when she became aware that Mark was calling her name.

'Kathy. Got to get up.'

'Why?' It was a sleepy mumble against his shoulder. She had thrown a leg across his body while she slept. She became aware of the pressure of his body against her. Her eyes opened. 'Maybe I would rather wake up. We'll spend the whole day —'

'You're flying this morning.' He kissed her. 'Remember?'

'I can fly tomorrow.'

'You promised your father. And I've got work to do.'

Kathy burrowed her head deeper against his shoulder.

'What time is it?'

'About six-thirty.'

'Too early.'

'That's why I woke you. So we'll have time to make love again.'

'Mark?'

'Uh-huh.'

On second thought, Kathy decided not to say what she had been thinking.

'Just make love to me, Mark.'

Like never, she told herself. Not like this, with Mark. Good God, I think I may even be falling in love.

4

7 July

Peter Keeley leaned wearily against the edge of his desk in his office on the fifty-seventh floor of the NIPCO Building.

'So far, one hundred and thirty-eight of our independent dealers have served notice they want to cancel their contracts with NIPCO,' he declared. Sam Schlechter and Mark Radford sat facing him and made no immediate comment. Keeley, a slender, wiry man in his late fifties, appeared deeply worried.

NIPCO's retail marketing organization, practically unique in the industry, was being seriously threatened.

Most American motorists who patronize major-brand filling stations believe the myth that they are dealing with independent businessmen. They think the man who is called the 'owner' of the station actually owns it.

He very seldom does.

The typical major-brand service-station operator is a tenant – indeed, very much like a tenant farmer. His landlord is the major oil company whose products he must sell exclusively, and at established prices. The company owns the service-station facilities. The operator has a short-term lease. If he breaks any of the myriad fine-print rules spelled out in his lease-contract, the so-called 'independent dealer' finds that his rent is suddenly raised – sometimes doubled or even trebled – or that his lease is cancelled.

When the Northcutt International Petroleum Company began organizing its retail marketing network, it went directly
counter to the trend established by the Majors. NIPCO sought
to have its products handled by as many genuinely independent businessmen – actual filling-station owner-operators – as
possible. Its contracts were far more liberal than those drawn
by the major oil companies. NIPCO offered its retailers many
incentives and had built up a strong and loyal retail marketing
operation that sold NIPpy products through more than two
thousand seven hundred service-station outlets.

Now dealer loyalty was eroding.

'Under the circumstances, I can't say that I blame them for
cancelling,' Keeley went on. 'Counting last night's incident in
Tallahassee, we've had fourteen service stations totally or par-
tially burned down. Our retailers have got the word. If they
continue to handle our products, they'll be taking big risks.'

'Have any stated openly that they've been threatened?'
Mark asked.

'No.' Keeley waved a hand at a stack of papers on his desk.
'Reports from our regional managers. The dealers who want to
break their contracts don't give explanations – only transparent
excuses. Family considerations, personal health —'

'Personal health *is* the reason,' Samuel Schlechter commented grimly. 'They want to stay in one piece.'

'The working formula isn't hard to imagine,' Radford said.
'The Farrier mob burns down a NIPCO station in some town.
In the next day or so, other dealers in the area are visited by a
couple of guys who make it plain they're tough bastards. They
tell the station owners to break their contracts with us – or get
broken themselves. They also warn the dealers to keep their
mouths shut about having been visited.'

'One bright spot,' Schlecter said. 'All things considered, the
number of deserters is still low.'

'Pocketbook psychology,' Keeley declared. 'Our dealers have
been making a lot of money recently. We're the only company
of any size that hasn't slashed gasoline allocations to retailers.
With the Majors cutting supplies to their dealers, ours have
been selling every drop. Since we allow them a hefty profit,
they're hanging on.

'I'm afraid that bright spot is going to fade soon, though,' he
continued, sitting down. 'The sabotage on Qantara will inter-
rupt the flow of crude supplies from there. We'll have a twenty-

four per cent shortfall. We won't be able to maintain normal refinery output. In another two weeks at most, we'll have to reduce gallonage allocations to retailers. Then the dam is going to burst. We'll lose dealers by the hundreds.'

'Not if there aren't any more incidents or threats,' Schlechter said, his brown eyes radiating confidence. Peter Keeley's morale needed bolstering, Sam thought. If he loses his nerve, it will be a more damaging blow than if a dozen filling stations all went up in flames at once. 'We can also plug the dam by temporarily allowing our retailers an even greater profit margin. We'll swallow the losses. That'll keep our dealers in the fold until Qantara gets back into full production.'

'If and when,' Keeley muttered.

'Keep the faith,' Mark said with a smile of assurance. 'Things should start breaking in our favour before long.'

'I wish you could guarantee that, Mark,' Keeley said.

'I have guaranteed it,' Radford told him. 'To myself.'

After the meeting, Schlechter returned to his Lower Broadway law offices. There were several messages waiting for him. One, his secretary said, seemed particularly urgent.

'A Mr Dwight Farquhar called. He'd like a personal appointment with you. At the earliest opportunity and on a matter of utmost importance,' she told Schlechter. 'Those were his words. He made it sound like a Doomsday thing.'

He would, Sam reflected dourly. Dwight Farquhar was an attorney – and notorious in the legal profession. He was nimble enough to stay a short step from the disbarment proceedings. Farquhar's speciality was thumbscrewing corporations with largely manufactured minority stockholders' suits or other nuisance suits. The actions seldom had any merit; they were more in the nature of legal blackmail.

But many companies preferred to avoid long, costly court battles. They settled with Farquhar and his clients for a fraction of their original demands. Schlechter could not imagine what sort of scheme Farquhar was hatching, but thought it wise to talk to him quickly and be rid of the distraction.

'Try and get him back for me,' Sam told his secretary.

Farquhar was on the line moments later.

'I'm Dwight Farquhar, Mr Schlechter,' Sam heard a cool, abrasive voice saying over the telephone. 'I don't believe we've met.'

218

'We haven't. What can I do for you?'

'Maybe I ought to tell you I'm speaking on behalf of a client. Miss Barbara Wallace.'

Schlechter cursed silently. He had intuitively sensed that Barbara Wallace, James Northcutt's most recent cast-off mistress, would cause some kind of trouble, despite the signed agreement, $50,000 lump sum settlement and $1,500 monthly stipend.

'Oh?' he said into the telephone. 'I saw Miss Wallace only last month in France. Please give her my best regards.'

'I'll do that. Now would you care to hear more over the phone or should we have a face-to-face meeting?'

'There's no harm giving me some of the details,' Sam said.

'That'll be for you to decide after you hear them, I imagine,' Farquhar said. 'Miss Wallace returned to the United States two days ago. She retained me because she's worried. Her conscience is bothering her, and she's afraid that she might have made herself a party to certain illegal acts.'

'Isn't that her problem?'

'The Internal Revenue Service would very probably consider it James Northcutt's problem,' Dwight Farquhar said.

'What's that supposed to imply?' Schlechter asked.

'It seems from what Miss Wallace tells me that your client, Mr Northcutt, may have developed a deplorable habit. Of having his – ah – lady friends charge their rather lavish shopping bills to corporate accounts.'

Sam Schlechter's belly knotted. Jim Northcutt did insist on paying his mistresses' personal bills out of the funds of one subsidiary company or another. So did most other extremely wealthy businessmen, but it was always kept very quiet, hidden on company books. Now, with various federal agencies seeking to find ways of harassing Jim and NIPCO, Barbara Wallace had a menacing weapon. The I.R.S. would listen eagerly. There could be criminal charges against Northcutt.

'Miss Wallace has talked to me about going to the tax authorities and giving them the whole story in hopes of clearing herself,' Farquhar went on. 'I've convinced her to wait – until I can discuss the matter with you and perhaps determine if there are any valid bases to the allegations.'

Schlechter easily read between the spoken words. Dwight Farquhar would demand a huge settlement of some sort in return for Barbara Wallace's silence. But, Sam knew, even if

Northcutt paid whatever was asked, there would be no real guarantee that Barbara would keep her end of the bargain.

'We should have a private talk, don't you think?' Farquhar asked, his voice soothing now.

'Yes.' Dwight Farquhar was too shrewd and seasoned for Sam to fence with him further. 'Yes, I do, Mr Farquhar.'

'Ten sharp tomorrow at your office?'

Other appointments would have to be cancelled, Sam thought. This new and totally unexpected threat to Northcutt could prove as explosive as any dynamite charge.

'All right,' he said. 'Ten sharp. I'll be here.'

Schlechter put the question of Barbara Wallace into his mental suspense file until the following morning and had his secretary call Senator John Bosworth in Washington. He wanted to learn if Bosworth had made any progress since their meeting just before the Fourth of July holiday.

'I've got good news and bad, Sam,' Senator Bosworth said. 'Dick Hurley and his Senate Energy Resources Committee will start considering an investigation into the Administration's attitude and apparent delays on the NIPCO–Chinese negotiations. I'll be making a speech on the floor myself in the next few days. Three of my colleagues, whom you met . . .'

And paid off, Sam interjected silently.

'. . . will also say their piece on the subject.'

'Thanks, John. And the bad news?'

'I'm afraid Arthur Gerlach and Rowan Engelhardt of the Energy Resources Department got wind of what we're planning. Engelhardt is going on TV next week. The excuse is a report to the public on the energy crisis. As I understand it, he'll make a passing reference to the pending NIPCO trade agreements with China. My grapevine has it that he'll call them potentially more ruinous than the grain deal with Russia back in seventy-two.'

'Cheerful prospect,' Schlechter muttered. 'Do you have any suggestions, John?'

'Only that we keep punching.'

Arthur Gerlach, chief presidential advisor, made a personal visit to the New York offices of Federpol and its head, Guy Bannister.

'I'm not pushing you, Mr Bannister,' Gerlach said. 'But I've been talking to your man, Russell Peterson, and he hasn't given me any definite answers.'

Guy Bannister's smile was inquisitive.

'Afraid I can't supply any answers until I know what questions you asked Peterson,' he said.

Gerlach's expression was affable as he went along with Bannister's pretence that he didn't know.

'Peterson came down to Washington representing you, and therefore your client, whose name I don't suppose it's necessary to mention.'

'No, it isn't,' Bannister said. The less said about Powell Pierce and Jersey Crest Oil, even in his office, the better.

'We made an arrangement,' Gerlach went on. 'Then I checked with Peterson about when and how Rowan Engelhardt and I would get the consideration '

'The million dollars.'

'Exactly. The million dollars. Peterson said he had to talk to you, and that you had to talk to your client. Then Peterson got back to me. He said that as soon as there was – I quote – "tangible evidence of co-operation" on our part, your client would deliver.'

'I'm aware of all that,' Guy Bannister admitted.

'On July second, Engelhardt made a statement to the press. He took a slap at Northcutt International Petroleum and at James Northcutt. He raised official doubts about the trade talks Northcutt had with China.'

'Yes, I'm aware of that, too. So is my client. He was, I might add, quite satisfied. Pleased, even.'

Arthur Gerlach flashed a smile, then just as quickly turned it off.

'We didn't hear anything further,' he said. 'And Rowan Engelhardt's gone ahead with plans for a television speech next week. He'll do whatever he can to further your client's aims, Bannister – provided there's some, uh, tangible evidence from your client's end.'

'In other words, you and Engelhardt want the money beforehand.'

'It would certainly make us both feel more determined to be fully co-operative,' Gerlach said.

Guy Bannister thought for a moment. It was evident that Gerlach and the Energy Resources Secretary were becoming impatient. They would have to be paid.

'Do you mind waiting outside for a couple of minutes, Mr

Gerlach?' Bannister asked.

'Not at all,' Gerlach agreed.

When he was alone, Bannister telephoned Powell Pierce. Since both their lines were swept daily for electronic eavesdropping devices, they were not reluctant to speak quite freely.

'Gerlach's here,' Bannister reported.

'With his hand out, I presume,' Powell Pierce said.

'Very much so. What shall I tell him?'

There was a moment's silence.

'The cash will have to be picked up in Switzerland – from a numbered account in a Zurich bank,' Pierce said. 'I'm hesitant to send any of our own people, as I told you before. And I think you said you had a man you could trust.'

'I have one. Russell Peterson.'

'You're sure of him – after all, the sum involved is hardly small.'

'I am. He's been ground down and trained – and he's a married man with a house in Westchester and all the trimmings. He's completely reliable because he's completely predictable.'

'Good,' Pierce said. 'Now then, once I issue an order to the Zurich bank, how quickly can you complete the entire transaction?'

'Depends on where you'll want Peterson to go from Zurich,' Bannister replied.

'Directly to Washington, where he'll make the delivery.'

'Less than forty-eight hours – how much less depends on airline schedules.'

'That's fine,' Pierce said. 'I'll be in touch with you in a day or two. In the meantime, you can assure Gerlach that he and Engelhardt will have their money within four days.'

5

8 July

Mark Radford had been given office space on the fifty-third floor of the NIPCO Building. Although he rated more elaborate accommodations, he insisted on having an isolated two-room suite. The less NIPCO employees saw of him, the better. Officially, he was in New York to co-ordinate efforts to restore full production in Qantara. If he remained in the background, the fiction could be more easily preserved.

The second morning after Kathy's departure for France, Mark received three visitors. Two of them were bodyguards of the third. They did not look their parts, but then Robert di Lorenzi didn't look at all like a man who had bodyguards, either.

Slender, well tailored, Robert di Lorenzi had an angular yet pleasant face and a western Mediterranean complexion. About four inches shorter than Mark Radford's six feet three, his manner and speech were those of a rising young executive. His men waited in the outer room.

'I was told you have a project, Mark,' di Lorenzi said when Radford had closed the door to his private office. 'The word I got from the Coast was that I was to work with you – provided we got together on the price. I guess you know that what you need is liable to be expensive.'

'My boss is aware of that, Bob. I'm authorized to negotiate and close. Want to talk figures?'

'Not yet. I'd like to hear details first.'

Mark told di Lorenzi what he knew about the arson attacks on NIPCO service stations and related his conversation with Charles Farrier.

'We tried buying him off, but got nowhere,' Mark concluded. 'That leaves us one alternative. Your organization.'

Robert di Lorenzi's face showed no expression.

'How far are you people willing to go?' he asked.

'As far as necessary.'

'There could be complications. No matter what happens, you'd have to keep us supplied with the money until the project was finished – or you called it off.'

'How much do you need in advance?'

'Two hundred thousand for now.'

'Cheque or cash?' Mark asked.

'Cheques. Plural. We have a legitimate management-consultant operation as a front. We'll invoice you a hundred thousand for a retainer fee, another hundred thousand for a special organizational study. That makes everything neat and tidy.'

'When do you start?'

'This afternoon. The invoices will be here an hour or so after

I leave.'

'Anything you want from me – besides cheques?' Mark asked.

'God, yes. Everything you have on the stations that were fire-bombed. Including copies of insurance-investigation reports. A complete list of all your dealers, with their home addresses. Another list of those who want to cancel their contracts. That's for starters.'

'I figured you'd need all that,' Mark said. 'I've got everything here. Want to go over the stuff with me?'

'Sure.' di Lorenzo laughed. 'Any time you want a good job, call me. Our management-consultant company can always use an efficient executive.'

Samuel Schlechter also received a visitor that morning, at 10 A.M. He was Dwight Farquhar. Sam judged him to be about forty-five, and he was stocky and surprisingly ruddy-faced. He hardly looks his type, Schlechter reflected, but then not too many people do.

'I know you don't want me to waste your time,' Farquhar said, seating himself on a couch in Schlechter's office. 'And I won't. I'm here representing Miss Barbara Wallace.' His voice was warmer than it had been on the telephone. 'She's worried that she may somehow become involved in a tax-fraud case – even though she herself did nothing illegal.'

He looked at Schlechter as though waiting for some comment.

'Please go on,' was all Sam said.

'Of course. Miss Wallace was Mr James Northcutt's good friend and companion —'

'She was his mistress,' Schlechter broke in. 'She lived with him in France. That's public knowledge, so we don't have to pussy-foot around with euphemisms.'

Farquhar opened a briefcase, took out some notes and glanced at them.

'My client says Mr Northcutt arranged for her to make numerous purchases of personal items for herself. She also says he had the bills for these items paid by one or another corporation he owns or controls.' Farquhar riffled the notes. 'Care to hear any of the specifics?'

'Please,' Sam said. 'I'm very interested.'

'I think one example should be sufficient to give you an idea

224

of how detailed Miss Wallace's information is. Take this item.' He looked at the notes. 'On December twelfth last year, Miss Wallace bought a diamond bracelet at Cartier's in Paris. The price was twenty-one thousand dollars – billed in dollars rather than francs, at what Miss Wallace says was Mr Northcutt's request. The bills for that bracelet went to Northcutt International Petroleum France, S.A., which is a wholly owned subsidiary of NIPCO. The bill, I have been informed, was paid by the company.'

Farquhar paused, put the notes back into his briefcase.

'Miss Wallace's other purchases made on the same basis are documented in similar detail,' he said.

Schlechter kept his face impassive.

'May I ask a question?'

'Certainly.'

'Why hasn't Miss Wallace gone directly to the appropriate authorities?' Let's see what she and Farquhar are really after.

'Miss Wallace has a very deep affection for Mr Northcutt,' Dwight Farquhar replied. 'She first wants to make sure that she has her facts straight and thus avoid any possibility of causing him any unwarranted embarrassment.'

'I see.' The usual preliminary rigmarole.

'Then, of course, she hopes that if she *is* right, Mr Northcutt may be able to settle matters amicably with the tax authorities.' Farquhar's friendly smile was patently bogus. 'Her hope is that he can work out some arrangement to pay the back taxes due plus interests and penalties and thus avoid prosecution...'

Schletcher stopped listening. Farquhar was getting redundant, droning on without coming to the point. The threat that Barbara Wallace posed had been stated. It was greater than either she or Dwight Farquhar realized. With Administration figures like Gerlach and Engelhardt gunning for Northcutt, the I.R.S. would be certain to make a major tax-evasion case out of her information.

The question was what did Barbara Wallace want?

It was a multi-million-dollar question. A tax scandal involving Northcutt and NIPCO would cause incalculable losses in public confidence, in stock values and in terms of general damage done to the NIPCO image. And if the I.R.S. brought criminal charges and Northcutt was convicted, the result would be total disaster.

'. . . of course, a firm assurance from Mr Northcutt that she was mistaken . . .'

Sam turned back in. Farquhar was circling closer to the key point.

'. . . would put Miss Wallace's fears to rest.' Farquhar cleared his throat. 'She feels that since there was one large misunderstanding between her and Mr Northcutt, this entire matter may be another resulting from a lack of communication. If the close communication they once had together could be re-established . . .'

I get it, Schlechter thought. The answer is painfully simple. Barbara Wallace wants to be reinstated as Jim's mistress – and to make it seem that Jim begged her to return. After that? Two possibilities. One, she would remain long enough to twist a great deal of money out of Northcutt and then create the impression that she was walking out on him. Two, she might even demand that he marry her.

I always knew Barbara was a vindictive bitch, Sam reflected, but I underrated her.

'Miss Wallace would be most pleased to hear any comment you might have to make,' Dwight Farquhar finished.

Schlechter spread his hands.

'You're an attorney,' he said. A shakedown artist is more like it. 'You know as well as I do that the only comment I can make is that I'll inform James Northcutt of our conversation.'

Farquhar nodded and got to his feet.

'How soon can I expect to hear from you?'

'In about a week.'

'Good Lord, don't tell me it'll take you that long to get in touch with your client?' Farquhar's tone was mocking.

'I can reach my client in about five minutes flat,' Schlechter said, jabbing a slender forefinger towards his telephone. 'Only he won't be inclined to make any snap decisions in this matter. And I'll have to think this out. As you would, under the circumstances.'

Nothing to be gained by pushing too hard – yet, Dwight Farquhar thought. Actually a week's wait would probably be an advantage. The more Northcutt and Schlechter mulled and stewed, the more they would sweat. Then they'll start making Barbara Wallace settlement offers that can be jacked highe

226

and higher. Whatever the final figures, I'll have my one-third contingency fee. I can afford to wait.

Jim Northcutt took the call in his study at Bonheur.

Schlechter related his conversation with Dwight Farquhar.

'Barbara's detailed rundown of her personal purchases charged to NIPCO subsidiaries can create extremely serious I.R.S. problems,' Sam concluded glumly. 'Any intensive audit will confirm them and uncover similar items charged by her predecessors.' His voice turned bleak. 'There could be criminal charges, Jim.'

Northcutt glowered into the phone.

'Suppose we predate paper work and show the amounts as loans the companies made to me,' he said. 'I'll repay them. That's the way these things are usually handled, isn't it?'

'Sure. It's what people in your position generally do when they're afraid the tax auditors might be getting warm.' Schlechter inhaled deeply. 'Only we don't have the time. Gerlach is bound to push the I.R.S. to act fast. It would take our accountants months to go back over all the books and find and hide every item. We don't have months. As of now, we have a week. After that, Barbara is liable to pull the plug.'

'Give me a day to think it over, Sam.'

There's no end to it, Jim thought, slowly replacing the receiver.

Northcutt usually followed his own instincts. Now, he felt he had to talk to someone. I've been doing that more and more, recently, be reflected. Maybe I am getting too old for all this.

He called Kathy into his study and told her what he had heard from Schlechter.

'I'll probably have to settle with Barbara on her terms,' Northcutt declared, his tone dismal.

'Come off it, Dad. There must be some way —'

'We're fighting too many battles already,' her father said. 'Barbara's charges could be the final push that brings everything down. With an almighty crash.'

'Aren't you exaggerating?'

'Look, Kath. Pretend you're managing investments for a pension or mutual fund. The I.R.S. starts auditing the books of NIPCO and its subsidiaries. Then there's an announcement I'm under investigation for tax fraud —'

'Now I see. Sure, I'd start selling off NIPCO stock. So would everyone else. The bottom would drop out.' Kathy studied her father's weathered features. 'Your negotiations with China are the real key to all this, aren't they? I mean, the Majors want the concessions and contracts for themselves. That's why there's so much pressure on you and NIPCO.'

'It's the immediate reason,' Northcutt agreed.

'Suppose you stepped aside and let Jersey Crest and the others take over the dealings with the Chinese? Wouldn't that resolve everything?'

Northcutt's face hardened.

'Jersey Crest and the others would ease off,' he said. 'But I'm not giving up the Chinese deal. God damn it, Kath, I want it for NIPCO! It's the biggest single project I've ever tackled – the capstone of my career, if you want to get flowery about it. Once those agreements go through, NIPCO will be right up there with the Majors.'

Kathy understood. James Northcutt equated personal success – and even survival – with the fortunes of NIPCO. He was finally on the verge of realizing his highest ambitions. His pride – in himself and the company he had built – was not only deeply involved, but at stake.

'I'll go back to New York,' she declared. 'Between us, Mark Radford, Sam and I should find a way to take care of Barbara Wallace.'

'No!' Jim Northcutt said. He began reeling off arguments why Kathy should not return to New York. He found they were futile. She countered or rejected them all.

Kathy's reaction did not entirely displease Northcutt. He had learned much about his daughter. She could be as obstinate as he, and he had come to realize that her obstinacy was often reasoned determination. And, he discovered himself conceding, female or not, she had inherited his instincts and drives.

What had she called herself, Northcutt reflected. Oh, yes. He remembered. A Grade Four, giant economy-size bitch. 'Like father, like daughter,' she had said, adding that he was 'whatever the male version of a Number Four bitch is called'. He made a swift decision.

'We'll leave together in the morning,' he told Kathy.

'We?' She registered astonishment – and concern.

The global web of Northcutt's empire was organized so that Bonheur was its real nerve centre. It was there that final decisions were made and orders were issued. By James L. North-cutt. Under normal circumstances, Northcutt's absence from his Cap d'Antibes estate would be considered just another top-level business trip or simply a vacation.

But the present situation was a different matter.

Northcutt's absence from Bonheur would leave the head-quarters of his empire without its commander. It would excite comment and could lower the morale of those executives who directed the numerous NIPCO operating divisions and sub-sidiaries. Worse, his sudden and unscheduled appearance in New York was likely to be taken as a sign that he felt the opposition was gaining the upper hand, a sign that he was running scared.

Kathy said all this and more to her father. Northcutt merely raised his right eyebrow and repudiated her objections.

'I've been sitting here on my ass while everybody else's been carrying the can for me,' he said. 'I may be an old fart, but I'm neither helpless nor senile. The wolf pack that's formed up against us is going to find that out. The hard way.' His look softened abruptly, and he grinned at Kathy.

'We'll kick the shit out of them all,' he said. 'Together.'

Kathy experienced a surge of elation.

'You closed up your apartment, didn't you?' he asked. She nodded. 'Then we'll use the house on Sutton Place.'

Kathy Northcutt's large co-op apartment was on Park Avenue. Her father owned a townhouse on Sutton Place that was fully staffed and kept ready for immediate occupancy.

'I'd rather stay at the Pierre,' Kathy said.

'Because of Radford?' Northcutt asked. Kathy's smile was an affirmation. Another trait we share, her father thought. We somehow always find a way to mix business with pleasure. 'Okay,' he nodded. 'Stay wherever you want.'

6

9 July

Northcutt International Petroleum had its own powerful radio transmitting and receiving facilities on the eastern tip of Long Island. These were used mostly to maintain direct communications with remote drilling sites and deep-sea drilling rigs. It was this station that received a message from James Northcutt's 727 when the aircraft was still several hours out over the Atlantic.

'Inform Mr Samuel Schlechter that Mr Northcutt and his daughter are en route,' the pilot said. 'Our ETA at Newark is 1530 hours.'

Sam and Mark were stunned to learn that Northcutt and Kathy were coming to New York.

'Maybe he figures we haven't been getting results fast enough,' Radford suggested.

Schlechter shook his head.

'Jim's coming for only one reason. He wants to wade into the scrap personally – thank God.'

'You sound pleased,' Radford said.

'I am.'

'For Christ's sake, Sam! He'll only be begging for more trouble by being here. It'll put him in easy reach of everyone from hostile reporters to process servers. Then there'll be all the rumours flashing around the industry and Wall Street. The smartass consensus will be that he's flown over because he's panicking.'

'Take it easy,' Schlechter laughed. 'I know Jim a little better than you do. He functions at his peak when he's in direct charge. That'll offset any of the possible drawbacks.'

'He's no youngster,' Mark said.

'Watch him. He's liable to amaze you.'

The four-way conference began in Schlechter's office shortly before 5 P.M., and Mark was amazed. James Northcutt displayed the vigour of a forty-year-old as he asked questions and made terse comments.

'Anything further from Washington, Sam?'

'Nothing since my last report to you.'

'I'll be going down there to do some prodding on my own,' the oilman said, turning to Radford. 'Mark, what's the latest on the business with Farrier?'

'You really want to know the specifics?' Radford glanced at Kathy as if asking whether she should hear.

'God damn it, yes!' Northcutt said.

'Steve Kostis kept his promise. We've retained a management consultant who specializes in these problems. I'm dealing with a Robert di Lorenzi —'

'You trust him?'

'Yes.'

'What's he done for us so far?'

'Two of Farrier's thugs have been put out of commission. Permanently. There haven't been any more NIPCO station fires since the night of July sixth. di Lorenzi says it's only a lull. He expected Farrier to call in reinforcements, but he's set and ready for that.'

'What are the chances of di Lorenzi's activities being traced back to us?' Northcutt demanded.

'Virtually none. Of course, there can always be slip-ups.'

'In anything,' the oil tycoon growled. However, he was evidently satisfied. At least for the moment. 'Barbara,' he said to Schlechter. 'Any further word from her?'

'No,' Sam replied. 'I've had Barbara Wallace placed under twenty-four-hour surveillance by private detectives. Beyond that, I've done very little. I've been waiting for you to call the shots.'

Northcutt nodded and Kathy made no comment.

'Am I needed for anything else?' Mark asked.

'Neither of you are,' Northcutt said with a glance at his daughter. 'I'll see you in the morning.'

Kathy and Mark left.

'Think she's in love with him, Sam?' Northcutt asked when they had gone.

'She shows all the signs,' Schlechter said. Was Kathy in love with Mark? Schlechter harboured certain reservations. Kathy was too much like her father. 'Anything else on your mind, Jim?' he inquired to change the subject.

Northcutt chewed at his lower lip before answering.

'I did some heavy thinking last night,' he said. 'I want Peter Keeley's resignation as President of NIPCO. Today.'

Schlechter's brown eyes widened.

'You can't be serious, Jim. You chose Keeley yourself. You've always said he was the best man for the position.' Then Sam's expression changed to one of searching inquiry. 'Or have you run across something that's escaped me?'

'In a sense, yes. We need a sacrificial lamb – or goat, if you prefer. Pete Keeley is it. The news he's been kicked out will spread through the industry, through Wall Street, even to Washington.'

'Mind telling me what you expect to accomplish?'

'The confusion of our enemies, Sam. When people hear that I've fired Keeley, they'll jump to all the wrong conclusions.'

'For instance?'

'Oh, hell. That Keeley's policies have been the cause of many NIPCO problems. That I'm cleaning house as a prelude to offering peace terms all around. Or that I've lost my mind. There's no limit to the range of theories that'll sprout up.'

'Keeley has a five-year contract.'

'Buy it at face value. No questions, no arguments.'

'He knows everything there is to know about NIPCO and what we're trying to do,' Schlechter warned. 'Aren't you afraid he might do a lot of talking?'

'Ideally, I hope he goes straight to Jersey Crest or Western Impex or Richland Consolidated and tells everything he knows – to date. The people he talks to will think they're hearing the latest inside details, and they'll act accordingly. Our competitors are bound to get overconfident. They'll overestimate themselves, underestimate us. We'll hit back from directions they don't expect.'

'It'll be damned hard on Keeley personally. He's given a great deal to the company.'

'So have you. So have I. From my viewpoint, I'd rather have a disillusioned Peter Keeley than a dispossessed James Northcutt. Corporate axes do swing, Sam. Most companies are built on severed heads.'

Schlechter had to admit there was validity in Northcutt's proposed gambit, and he could hardly deny the more brutal facts of corporate life. Even generals had to die on the battlefield, not for God and country, but to further the strategic goals of their commanders-in-chief. While Peter Keeley was a fine executive and held a high position as president of NIPCO, by Northcutt's yard-stick he was simply another pawn – and expendable.

'Who'll take Pete's place?' the attorney asked.

'Just before I went to sleep last night, I made a mental list of candidates qualified to replace Keeley. Then I held an election and voted my shares. I'll be a son of a bitch, but one man won by a landslide. Me.'

'You slept well afterwards?'

'Like a baby, Sam.'

Guy Bannister had been to see Powell Pierce. Now, back in his Federpol offices in Rockefeller Center, he issued instructions to Russell Peterson.

'You take a plane to Zurich,' Bannister said, using the condescending tone that his years of CIA experience had taught him would remind subordinates that they must obey orders without question. 'Once there, you go straight to the Schweikert Kreditbank on the Bhanhofstrasse. Ask to see the Herr Direktor personally. He speaks English.'

Russell Peterson boiled inwardly. Bannister is treating me like a bottom-rung flunky, he thought. But then, he usually did. Peterson wished he could rebel, tell Bannister to take his assignments and shove them, quit his job with Federpol. But he knew that he could not. The $65,000-a-year salary was its own prison. And he and his wife Mae lived up to every dollar of it – and beyond. The bloody mortgage payment is a week overdue again, Peterson reminded himself. And Bloomingdale's had been sending them increasingly insistent reminders about their charge account, on which they'd made no payments for more than three months.

'Check, Guy,' he said. 'And then?'

'You give the Herr Direktor this authorization.' Bannister held out a slip of paper. 'You'll be given a million dollars in cash. In hundred-dollar and fifty-dollar bills.'

'Do I sign a receipt?'

'Only by number, not with your name. The number is on this card. Memorize it and then destroy the card.'

'Check. What after that?'

'You fly back – to Washington. Make sure you fly an airline that uses X-ray or sensor equipment for security checks. Avoid any that still relies on actual search of hand luggage.'

'Right.'

'When you get to Washington, telephone Gerlach. He'll tell you where to meet him. When you do, hand over the money.'

'Is he supposed to give me a receipt for it?'

'Not in writing, for God's sake. You're both to telephone me. He'll say something like everything's in order, and that's that. You come back up to New York.' Bannister gave Peterson a patronizing look. 'Any more questions?'

'Only one. When do you want me to leave?'

'You're booked out on a 10 A.M. Swissair flight for Zurich tomorrow morning. Anything else?'

'No.'

Russell Peterson drove his Buick Le Sabre along the Sawmill River Parkway, and he was deep in thought. Every gasoline filling station that he had passed was either closed or jammed with automobiles whose drivers were waiting to buy their five-gallon limit. The scenes served to remind Peterson how deeply he was involved in some of the manoeuvrings that helped create and perpetuate the gasoline famine.

Jersey Crest Oil reported almost two billion dollars in profits last year, he reflected. On the following day, he would be in Zurich, putting a million dollars of that money into his attaché case for delivery to Arthur Gerlach. A million, he thought, a fortune – but only a two-thousandth of Jersey Crest's annual profit. Only one-twentieth of 1 per cent of what the company made in a year.

He had put the withdrawal authorization into his inside jacket pocket. He was conscious of it being there and became increasingly so as he drove and continued to think.

When Russell Peterson reached his home in Pelham Manor, he parked the Buick in the driveway. Mae, his brown-haired and pretty wife, was waiting for him in the living room. She had the ritual evening martinis ready.

'The maid isn't around today, is she?' he asked, drinking his first cocktail.

'No, it's her day off – and we were going out to dinner, remember?' Mae Peterson said.

'Well go out later, honey,' he told her, pouring himself another martini. 'Right now, you and I are going to have a long talk.

7

10 July

James L. Northcutt sat at the head of the long conference table. More than a dozen NIPCO vice-presidents were seated in chairs ranged along the sides of the table. Samuel Schlechter sat at the foot, opposite Northcutt.

'How much crude do we have in storage above ground?' Jim Northcutt asked.

'Very little,' a vice-president replied, studying a computer print-out in front of him on the conference table. 'A shade over a nineteen-day supply.'

Oil companies engaged in refining and marketing maintain above-ground reserves of crude oil to meet such contingencies as delayed deliveries, production stoppages or other anomalous situations. These reserves are stored in tanks, usually situated very near their refineries.

Actually, a nineteen-day supply did not compare too unfavourably with the all-time industry-wide low averages that had prevailed since late in 1973. Considering energy-crunch conditions, it might even have been considered satisfactory, save for the fact the loss of Qantara production had slashed the crude replenishment rate by 25 per cent. Thus, in effect, NIPCO had only a fraction more than a fourteen-day supply.

Northcutt took the information calmly.

'Notify all our wholesalers and retailers that we're increasing their product allocations by ten per cent, immediately,' he said. 'And I don't give a damn what kind of miracles you have to perform in the refineries to boost output.'

The NIPCO executives stared in dismay. Only Sam Schlechter showed no change in his expression.

'J.L., did you say a ten per cent *increase*?' a subdued voice asked.

'Yes.'

'But that only means we'll run out of reserves just so much faster. With no crude coming in from the Middle East, it'll be simply a matter of weeks before we have nothing but current production from other sources to refine. Then we'll have to reduce allocations —'

'That's my worry,' Northcutt said. 'Your headaches are to get refinery output boosted.' He laid his large, powerful hands on the tabletop and gazed at the men around him. An eyebrow rose and a lopsided grin formed on his craggy face as he saw that most were still staring at him in disbelief.

'I'll give you another shock,' he said, the grin deepening. 'Two weeks from today, we're going to *increase* our dealer allocations another ten per cent.'

Northcutt's weather-beaten features appeared twenty years younger and his grey eyes gleamed.

'Gentlemen,' he said, 'when I started in as a wildcatter, I had a partner – Sam Schlechter's father. He taught me the Yiddish word *chutzpah*. It means nerve, guts, audacity – and more. This company has got slugged here and there of late. It's now going to load up on *chutzpah*, and come out slugging.'

Northcutt knew precisely what he was doing. He was placing the blame for all of NIPCO's problems on Peter Keeley, who had been the company president until the day before. It was a dirty trick, a form of *chutzpah* in itself. The executives had to believe they were making a new – and winning – start.

'I want you to think about the effect an announcement of an allocation increase will have,' Jim went on. 'The minute it's made, everybody from our own file clerks to bank presidents and securities analysts will have new confidence in NIPCO. There'll be a complete turn-around in climate and attitude. As for our dealers – hell, I don't have to tell you how they'll react.'

The expressions of those around him were no longer stunned. All that Northcutt said made business sense. But his logic held only to the point at which the law of diminishing returns would leave NIPCO without above-ground crude reserves. The company would then have to rely on current production from its fields elsewhere than in Qantara. This would supply only 75 per cent of even normal refining needs. There would be a 25 per cent shortfall, at very least.

'I know what's on your minds,' Jim told them. 'How do we close the gap? I mentioned that before. It's *my* worry.'

Northcutt pushed his chair away from the table, unfolded his tall, big-boned frame and made as if to leave.

'Oh, one more thing,' he said. 'You're all on the NIPCO payroll, and I want each and every one of you to stay there.

But if any of you have been paying attention to rumours and are scared that you're aboard a leaky boat – get out now.'

His eyes swept over the men at the table. Their expressions told him they would stick. Thank God, he told himself. I managed to bring it off. They're sold, all of them.

The news of Northcutt's return to the United States and of his taking over the NIPCO presidency after Peter Keeley's resignation brought immediate reactions.

Most major oil-company executives took it as a sign that Northcutt finally realized he was cornered. They guessed that he had come to New York to capitulate and save what he could from the inevitable wreckage.

A Jersey Crest senior vice-president expressed this view while speaking to Powell Pierce.

'Northcutt will be coming around, hat in hand,' he predicted. 'He'll probably start with Exxon or Mobil and work his way down the list looking for an ally.'

'Well, he won't find one,' Pierce said. 'I can guarantee that.'

Wall Street apparently agreed that Northcutt was demonstrating weakness rather than strength. During the July tenth trading session, NIPCO stock dropped six points.

'If Northcutt feels he has to play fire brigade personally at his age, there must be something damned wrong,' stockbrokers and securities analysts told each other – and their clients.

The *Wall Street Journal* commented:

'Northcutt International Petroleum is generally conceded to be the world's largest independent integrated oil company. Less than two weeks ago, unknown saboteurs wrecked its port facilities on the Persian Gulf island of Qantara.

'The company is said to obtain one-quarter of its total crude requirements from Qantara. Until its installations on the island are repaired and again in full operation, NIPCO is certain to feel the pinch.

'In the meantime, it has been persistently rumoured that the company's troubles have been multiplying. Many observers see at least partial confirmation of this in the abrupt resignation – some say summary dismissal – of NIPCO's long-time president, Peter Keeley. His place is being taken by James L. Northcutt, who owns over 60 per cent of the company's stock.

'A septuagenarian and perennial stormy petrel of the oil industry, Northcutt has recently conducted controversial trade negotiations with the Chinese Government in Peking. According-ing to some sources, it was Peter Keeley's opposition to deal-ing with China that led to his resignation ...'

The blonde virago, Dwight Farquhar thought as he asked his client, Barbara Wallace, to take a chair near his desk.

'Has Schlechter called you yet?' she asked.

'No,' Farquhar replied. 'I told you. I said we'd wait a week.' She was attractive enough, he reflected – if one liked the statu-esque dramatic type. He didn't.

'You've heard that Jim is in New York,' Barbara said.

'I have.'

'Do you think he came back because of me and the tax thing?'

'It might have been part of the reason,' Farquhar replied. 'I doubt if it was the only one, though. From all I can gather, Northcutt seems to have a very full plate at the moment.'

'Why don't you demand to see him personally?'

'Because that is not how these matters are handled.'

'Look,' Barbara said, her full mouth drawing tight. 'I don't care how you do it. But Jim Northcutt has to understand I'm not playing games. He either gives me a third of his stock in NIPCO – or I talk my head off to the Internal Revenue people. Did you make that clear to Schlechter?'

'No, I didn't,' Farquhar said blandly. 'I said nothing specific about your demands.'

'Why the hell not?'

'Common sense. Your demand is, to put it mildly, stagger-ing. It would be foolish to hit them with it until they're suffici-ently worried about the damage you can do. Besides, if I'd told Schlechter you were after Northcutt's stock, he might have started transferring it out of Northcutt's name – into some trust or foundation we couldn't touch. Now do you begin to understand?'

Barbara Wallace sullenly muttered something to the effect that she did.

Kathy Northcutt lay in Mark Radford's arms, and she was euphoric.

I'm past the what-am-I-getting-myself-into-stage, she thought, her hand caressing Mark's shoulder. I've reached the God-I'm-glad-I'm-in-it level. I even know why. Mark truly enjoys making love to me. He's not trying to prove anything. It's a mutual, equal interchange.

'You're awfully quiet,' Mark said, his blue eyes amused.

'Mmm.' She stirred her body closer to his. 'I'm having my private energy crisis.'

He nuzzled her flame-coloured hair, kissed her temple.

'You drained me,' she murmured. 'Dry.'

His hand moved along her thigh.

'Christ!' Her hips moved reflexively. 'All you have to do is touch me.' She shuddered with pleasure, but moved his hand away. 'Let's wait a little.'

He held a strand of her hair, tickled her nose with it.

'Mark,' she said. 'Know what I think about when we make love like we just did?'

'Let me guess. Flying saucers, maybe?'

'I'm serious. Or trying to be. I wonder if you're inside me or I'm around you.'

'That sounds like Grade-B Zen. Anyway, it's not original. You read it in a book.'

'Bastard.' She kissed his mouth. 'How did you know?'

'I read the same book, and I thought it was lousy.' He gave her firm buttock an elaborately sympathetic pat. 'You're letting your emotions show. It's out of character. Didn't you tell me once that sex is nothing but friction?'

She sucked his lower lip between her teeth, bit it.

'Hey, that hurt!'

'Serves you right. I never said anything of the kind. You're mixing me up with one of your other women.'

'Kathy, old buddy, you've just defined the impossible.' His palm brushed her nipples, then he cupped her right breast and fondled it gently.

Her tongue flicked his ear. 'How?'

'No man could ever mix you up with any other woman.'

'Oh,' she couldn't resist asking. 'Why not?'

'I refuse to answer that question on the grounds I might incriminate myself.'

'Coward,' Kathy said.

'Craven.'

'Quoth the craven nevermore?'

'How about once more?'

'Lunatic!' Her mouth covered his, and he drew her to him.

239

8

11 July

The oil shortage and energy crisis preoccupied the public. Nevertheless, so many conflicting statements had been made in Washington that a large segment of the population had given up trying to reconcile them. Consequently, Senator Richard Hurley's announcement caused only a mild flurry of interest in the media.

Chairman of the Senate Energy Resources Committee, Richard Hurley declared there would be a new investigation into the Administration's policies and actions in coping with the energy crisis. He decried what he termed the 'inconsistently selective' approach the Executive branch had taken towards 'privately owned companies seeking to ease the energy crunch.'

'On the other hand, the largest major oil companies are once again reporting record profits,' Hurley declared. 'Yet the Administration is pressing for them to be given additional tax incentives and other indirect subsidies. On the other hand, smaller companies that have sought to take positive steps to help solve critical shortages are apparently receiving scant co-operation from federal agencies.'

Senator Hurley cited the case of the Northcutt International Petroleum Company as a specific example. NIPCO, he said, was on the verge of concluding an unprecedented agreement with the Chinese Government. Under its terms, the United States would eventually obtain vast quantites of crude oil and LPG – liquified petroleum gas such as propane and butane.

'Immediate approval and implementation of this agreement should be a top-priority aim of the Administration,' Hurley stated. 'Unfortunately, there seems to be evidence of intentional foot-dragging in key Executive branch quarters.'

Asked about these allegations, Administration spokesmen avoided making any direct comment.

'Mr Rowan Engelhardt, Secretary of the Energy Resources Department, will make a nationwide television address in a few days,' was all that was forthcoming. 'He will discuss Administration policies on the energy crisis and clarify the issues raised by Senator Hurley.'

All this was greatly overshadowed by NIPCO's own announcement that it was raising all petroleum-product allocations to dealers and wholesalers by 10 per cent. NIPCO was the only oil company to make such a move since the second energy crisis began. Wall Street reacted sharply. NIPCO stock regained all it had lost the previous day and went up an additional half-point.

Northcutt and Schlechter did not permit themselves to become overly optimistic. They knew Rowan Engelhardt would be certain to do damage with his television address, and then NIPCO stock prices would drop again. Besides, they were embattled on many other fronts, and the outcomes of these clashes were very much in doubt.

Mark Radford paid no attention at all to Senator Richard Hurley's statement or its possible implications. Anything that happened in Washington was far outside the limits of his responsibility and interest. He had much more immediate concerns. The fifteenth NIPCO service station had been burned to the ground, this one in Baltimore.

Robert di Lorenzi came to Mark's office, accompanied – as always – by his two bodyguards.

'We'll hit another of Farrier's men tonight,' di Lorenzi said. 'It's all set up.' He frowned. 'But I might as well warn you. The grapevine has it that Farrier's calling in a bigger organization to beef up his outfit.'

'Where does that leave us?' Mark asked.

'It leaves my organization and me in a bad spot, unless I can get help,' Robert di Lorenzi replied. 'That means your people will have to pay more. There's no telling how high your bills might go.'

'Would you need any further okay from Steve Kostis?'

'No. All I'll need is word from you – and more money.'

'You've got the word from me,' Mark said. 'You'll have the money within an hour after you tell me how much.'

di Lorenzi frowned and rubbed his jaw.

'Ever stop to think we may be going at this the wrong way?' he inquired and continued without waiting for an answer. 'Maybe we'd get a hell of a lot further if I sent my guys right after the people who hired Farrier. We could blow up a few Jersey Crest stations —'

241

'No,' Mark shook his head. 'Not yet, at any rate.' That would escalate the conflict too rapidly. Compared to NIPCO's resources, those of Jersey Crest were limitless. The struggle had to be contained until there was no alternative but to retaliate against Jersey Crest's dealers.

Guy Bannister was having his own conversation with Charles Farrier.

'Northcutt pulled a fast one we didn't expect,' Bannister said. 'NIPCO raised its dealer allocations ten per cent.'

'I heard,' Farrier nodded.

'Those NIPCO retailers are going to be harder to scare now,' Bannister went on. 'They'll be making more money than ever. Joe Doakes running a NIPCO station in Atlanta won't be in any hurry to cancel his contract just because another NIPCO station burns down in Poughkeepsie. You'd better expand your operations.'

'I've lost men,' Charles Farrier said. 'I've already made arrangements for reinforcements.' He paused, eyed Bannister coolly. 'I think you ought to check this out with your client.'

'I have.'

'And?'

'I've only been telling you what he told me.'

'Did he tell you anything else?' Farrier inquired.

'You mean about your – ah, fees?'

'What else?'

'They'll be covered.' Bannister smiled.

'Then we have no problems,' Farrier said.

Powell Pierce, Chairman of the Jersey Crest Board, conferred with members of the company's management committee.

'Northcutt is bluffing,' one top-level executive said. 'That ten per cent allocation increase will get him headlines and improve his public image – but for how long?'

'It's not important,' a second committee member said. 'We know how much crude NIPCO produces and what it needs for its refineries. Without Qantara production, the company is twenty-five per cent short of normal requirements. A ten per cent across-the-board boost in dealer allocations makes things much worse for NIPCO.'

'Northcutt might have increased production elsewhere,' someone hazarded.

'Not by the seventy to eight thousand barrels a day needed to close the gap,' Pierce declared. 'The whole industry would know about it if he had.'

'Could he have made a deal somewhere for enough crude to cover him until Qantara's back in full production?'

'That's utterly impossible,' Pierce said. 'We've had every sizeable quantity of available crude pinpointed. There's none that he's bought – or can buy.'

Oil producers do not generally own the properties on which they drill their wells. For the most part, they merely lease the natural gas and oil rights on a given tract of land. They pay the owner a cash bonus for the lease and a percentage of the oil produced or its cash equivalent as a royalty.

Crude oil from several wells having the same ownership is usually piped to storage tanks – called 'lease tanks' – on the property. The crude is purchased by a pipeline, refinery or integrated major oil company that has laid gathering lines to the lease tanks.

Purchase contracts for crude are most often made at posted prices. In the United States, these are literally the notices posted on the bulletin boards of major oil companies, stating what prices will be paid for various grades of crude oil. A major company can easily determine how much crude oil producers are selling and to whom.

'Then he's playing for time,' a Jersey Crest vice-president said.

'Very probably,' Pierce murmured. 'But we won't give him time.' The various machineries that had been set into motion would insure it.

Mae Peterson was pale and extremely nervous as she passed through the purely symbolic immigration and customs checks at the Zurich air terminal.

Her husband was waiting for her.

'Russ,' she said, clinging to him. 'I'm scared!'

'Don't be,' he said. 'I've got it.'

'God, Russ, are you sure about all this?'

'Absolutely. By tomorrow afternoon, we'll be all set.'

Later that evening, while she stared at a dinner she could not bring herself to eat, Mae Peterson asked her husband again.

'You're really sure?'

'Look,' he told her. 'There's nothing anybody can do. Not without breaking the whole stink wide open. Get this, Mae. There aren't any receipts. No records. My name isn't on anything.'

'What about Guy Bannister?'

Bannister was their only problem, Russell Peterson admitted to himself, but he believed he had that solved.

'We just lay low where he can't find us for a while,' he said. 'Long enough for everybody to get tired of looking. Then it'll be you, me – and a million bucks.'

9

12 July

Guy Bannister glared at his desk calendar. Russell Peterson had left for Zurich on the morning of the tenth, two days before, and there had been no word from him. By now, he should have at least telephoned from Washington to confirm that the money had been delivered to Arthur Gerlach and Rowan Engelhardt.

'You heard anything from Peterson?' Bannister asked his secretary.

'No, sir.'

'Call the White House. I want to talk to Mr Gerlach.'

Gerlach was evidently busy. An hour passed before he called back.

'Peterson been there yet?' Bannister inquired.

'I haven't seen or heard from him.'

'He should be there at any time,' Bannister said uneasily.

Guy Bannister next telephoned the Schweikert Kreditbank in Zurich. Yes, an officer of the bank told him, Herr Peterson had been there. The day before. Yes, he had obtained what he was sent after and no, he had said nothing about where he was going.

Bannister tried Russell Peterson's home in Pelham Manor. There was no answer. The years Guy Bannister had spent in the CIA before he organized Federpol, his 'industrial security service', had taught him many lessons. He kept a file of the telephone numbers of all his employees' next-door neighbours.

244

His suspicions growing, he telephoned one of the numbers he had listed under Russell Peterson's name, that of a Mr and Mrs George Knebel. He spoke to a woman who identified herself as Mrs Knebel.

'I'm terribly sorry to disturb you, Mrs Knebel,' Bannister said. 'But this is Lieutenant William Rourke of the New York City Police Department. I'm trying to reach your neighbour, Mrs Peterson. Her husband has just been very seriously injured in an automobile accident.'

'Oh, my God! And Mae's gone off on a trip!'

'What was that?'

'I said Mae Peterson is on a trip. I saw her putting suitcases in her car early yesterday morning – just as I was getting breakfast for the kids. I asked her where she was going – but how about Russ, what happened —'

'Mrs Knebel, what did Mae Peterson tell you?'

'She – she said she and Russ were going on a long trip and —'

Guy Bannister slammed down his receiver. There was no longer any question in his mind.

'The dirty bastard!' he muttered.

Russell Peterson had run out. With one million dollars in cash. With Jersey Crest Oil's money. And he, Guy Bannister, would be held responsible. He had personally guaranteed Peterson's reliability to Powell Pierce.

'Jesus Christ!'

Bannister prided himself on knowing people and being able to predict exactly how they would act and react in given situations. He had seldom been wrong, and he had never been more certain of anyone's predictability and response pattern than of Russell Peterson's. It was utterly impossible that Peterson would abscond with the money. Yet, he had.

Bannister realized he had to face the fact – and that he would have to tell Powell Pierce. His mind worked, reviewing his options. They were limited. He could not notify police authorities. Official investigation would reveal existence of the secret Jersey Crest account in the Schweikert Kreditbank and thus involve his client in what could develop into a major scandal. There were only two things he could do – inform Pierce and then take his own steps to trace and find Russell Peterson and the missing million dollars.

* * *

245

Powell Pierce was remarkably unruffled.

'Have you told Gerlach what's happened?' he asked Guy Bannister.

'No, not yet.'

'Then do so today.' Pierce's look was that of a professor mildly reproving a student. 'Of course, Bannister, I am holding you accountable for the money.' He toyed with a letter opener. 'And for Peterson.'

Bannister swallowed. He and Federpol were successful, but refunding the million dollars was out of the question.

'I don't mean that I expect you to return the money yourself,' Pierce said, reading Bannister's thought. 'I'm assuming that you have your means for tracking down this man Peterson and forcing him to return what he has stolen.'

'I'll get him – and the money.'

'I believe you will.' Pierce pushed the letter opener aside, templed his fingers. 'Now I have no choice but to send one of my own people to obtain more money from Switzerland so that Gerlach and Engelhardt can be paid. Tell Gerlach that.'

'Yes, Mr Pierce. Is there anything else?'

'Only this. How you locate Peterson and what you have done with him after he returns the money are entirely your affair. However, I hope you realize that unless there is restitution of the full amount, I'll see that you're put out of business.'

Powell Pierce and Jersey Crest could destroy him and his business very easily, Guy Bannister realized as he left Pierce's office. Pierce would need only pass the word that he and Federpol could not be relied upon, and then there would be no more industrial clients and fat fees.

Bannister went to Charles Farrier's offices.

'You have people affiliated with you in Europe, don't you?' Bannister asked.

'Naturally,' Farrier nodded.

'I have a job for them.'

Bannister related the story of Russell Peterson. He had photographs of Peterson and his wife and more than enough additional information for identification purposes.

'We want the money,' Bannister concluded.

'Suppose my European friends get it back but decide that Peterson and his wife should disappear – permanently?'

'That,' Guy Bannister said, 'would be the ideal solution.'

246

1

By March 1937, James Northcutt had a fully integrated oil company. Two months later, he acquired his first foreign exploration and drilling concession, and the name of the company was accordingly changed to Northcutt International Petroleum Company – NIPCO.

Northcutt's newly expanded company required larger administrative headquarters and additional employees. Jim kept the best men in what had been the Barrow and Creager management and hired new personnel to replace the others.

Retail marketing presented its own problems. Barrow and Creager owned a sizeable chain of service stations along the West Coast, but had not been overly enterprising in this area. Its gasoline and motor oil sold under the brand name 'B.C.' Jim believed that a more aggressive sales programme was needed and that the company's products should have a brand name consumers would remember.

A Los Angeles advertising agency was retained to make suggestions and plan a campaign. None of the ideas it submitted had any appeal to Jim and his aides.

'Econogas.'

'Northcutt – the Premium Brand.'

'NIPCO, Quality Products for the Smart Motorist.'

'And we're paying good money to these morons,' Jim snorted at a Board meeting.

'Hold on, Jim,' Luke Rayburn spoke up. 'You started as a wildcatter. Damned near everybody associates wildcatting with the oil business. Why not use a wildcat as a trademark? The name's right. NIPCO. Call the wildcat NIPpy. Think of what people want in their gas. They want it to make their cars run better, give 'em more power.'

Luke grinned. 'NIPpy – the power-packed wildcat,' he said. 'Beats the hell out of what Standard, Shell, Gulf or most of the Majors have.'

'I like it,' one of the directors declared.

'I just bought it,' Northcutt said. 'Send those morons at the

247

ad agency a memo. If they give us any static, we'll find another outfit.'

An artist designed the trademark. A wildcat crouching, ready to spring. NIPpy, the Power-Packed Wildcat, soon became familiar to motorists in California, Oregon and Washington. It appealed to the public. Sales figures began to climb.

On 7 December 1941, the Japanese attacked Pearl Harbor. America was at war.

Jim toyed briefly with the idea of obtaining a commission in one of the armed forces. He made inquiries. Since he was forty-one with no previous military experience, he was not qualified for any of the combat arms.

'You can have a commission as a lieutenant colonel, but only in some branch like the quartermaster corps,' he was told.

'And spend the war counting blankets in a warehouse?' Northcutt sneered. 'Shit.'

Northcutt obtained an appointment with the Secretary of War, Henry L. Stimson.

'Your company is making an important contribution to the war effort,' Secretary Stimson said. 'Why not content yourself with managing it?'

'Managing what?' Jim laughed. 'Mr Secretary, we both know that oil companies are being managed by the orders that come out of Washington. My executives are capable of carrying out those orders. They don't need me.'

Stimson reflected for a moment.

'We do need an experienced oilman to confer with British officials about Britain's postwar civilian needs for petroleum products,' he said. 'Would you be willing to go to England?'

'When do you want me to leave?'

'Within the next two weeks.'

2

Northcutt was assigned billets in the Chesham, a bastard-Bauhaus structure off London's Belgrave Square. Built just before the war, the Chesham was London's newest hotel and second-highest building after St Paul's. It had been requisitioned from its owners by the British Government to provide housing for upper-rank American military and civilian officials on war-connected assignments.

Jim very quickly experienced a feeling of disillusionment with his fellow countrymen at the Chesham. They seemed oblivious to the reality of war and conditions around them. London had been battered and gutted by high explosive and incendiary bombs dropped by the Luftwaffe. All Britain lived under the most rigid austerity. Foodstuffs were severely rationed. Meat, sugar, butter and even tea were doled out weekly in quantities measured in ounces. Clothing was almost unobtainable for Londoners, gasoline for private cars was non-existent. A fresh egg or rasher of bacon were seldom-seen luxuries.

Yet Americans at the Chesham lived on a scale that even Northcutt, a multi-millionaire, considered extravagant. In uniform or out, American officials dined regularly on enormous steaks, ordered three and four fresh eggs for breakfast, roared through London streets in Packard limousines – which they called 'staff cars' – traded nylon stockings and five-pound cans of coffee on the black market. These luxuries – and countless more – were brought to England by US ships or even military aircraft for the benefit of high-ranking US contingents.

The cargo space used to transport the luxuries could have been put to far better purpose, Jim thought. Every side of beef, crate of eggs or Packard car shipped from the States meant that much less munitions and other vitally needed items for Britain. Yet Jim's fellow residents at the Chesham flaunted their material riches and sent unending streams of additional requisitions – all marked URGENT – to the United States.

He had been in London only a few days when Brigadier General Norris Penton, US army officer serving as a liaison officer with the RAF Bomber Command, invited him to a party in Penton's suite at the Chesham.

'We're having fresh lobster,' Penton told him. 'Flown in from Maine.'

Northcutt's first reaction was to make a caustic remark and refuse, but he changed his mind. He wanted to observe Penton and his guests at first hand.

'Thanks, General. I'll be there.'

Jim conferred all that day and into the evening with British Fuel Board officials. He arrived quite late for Norris Penton's party. About a dozen US army officers and as many attractive young women were talking, laughing and drinking heavily. The air was stifling. Cigarette or cigar smoke filled the room and all the windows were tightly closed and covered with thick blackout curtains.

'Sorry I'm late,' Northcutt muttered to his host.

'This is James Northcutt, one of our important oilmen,' Brigadier General Penton announced.

A US army enlisted man in a white waiter's jacket, one of Penton's three orderlies, stepped forward. 'What would you like to drink, sir?'

'Give the man bourbon,' General Penton said. He turned to Jim. 'Had twenty-four cases flown over last week. Old Grand-dad. There's Southern Comfort, too, if you'd like – ah, excuse me.' He moved off to join a brassy, big-breasted blonde who was talking rapidly in a grating cockney accent.

'So you're in the oil business?' the question came from a full colonel who had the flaming-bomb insignia of the ordnance corps on his uniform lapel and, Jim thought, the face of a constipated spaniel. 'My name's Raynor. Albert Raynor. Call me Al. You really in the oil business?'

Jim nodded. The orderly brought his drink on a tray. 'Been over here long, Colonel Raynor – Al?'

'Two months. One party after another. How about yourself?'

'I arrived this week.'

'Wait'll you get your feet wet and your stick dipped,' Raynor said, chortling. 'These English dames are wild. All you have to do is look at 'em and they'll lay.'

Seeing the kind of women you have here, I wouldn't doubt it, Jim thought. A grab-bag assortment of London tarts.

'Who're you with – some company like Standard?' Raynor asked.

'No. I have my own company.'

'Well, I'll be damned. What's the name of your outfit?'

'Northcutt International Petroleum.'

'NIPCO? Say, I have heard of it. Seen your gas stations when I was at the Presidio of San Francisco. Got any good stock-market tips? I figure I might as well make a few bucks out of this war, too.'

'Buy war bonds, Al,' Jim said, walking away.

A very drunk full colonel was trying to feel a dark-haired

girl's breasts. Penton was voicing his opinion about the blundering inefficiency of the British High Command to a knot of officers and women.

'... we'll have to show these Limeys how to fight...'

A girl in the bathroom was screaming. Another young woman lurched towards the bathroom door, apparently to offer help. An air corps lieutenant colonel stopped her.

'Wait'll she passes out,' he said.

Jim didn't finish his drink and he didn't bother speaking to his host. He left Penton's suite, returning to his own much smaller bed-sitter on the seventh floor. He undressed slowly and reflected that he was fortunate to be a civilian. The thought of having to say 'sir' to men like Penton and Raynor and obey their orders revolted him.

Jim found his assignment remarkably simple. The British officials and civil servants with whom he talked had all the necessary figures at hand. They presented their statements and arguments calmly. There was none of the hard sell he would have expected in similar situations in Washington.

The extent of Great Britain's postwar civilian fuel needs depended on imponderables. It was assumed that the Axis would be beaten – whether in two years or four or ten. But would British oil fields in the Middle East remain intact? Or would Axis bombers wreck them and other installations? Then, would Britain's oil refiners at home and abroad remain operable – or would they be damaged by bombings? As for transportation, no one could possibly predict the state of Britain's – or the world's – tanker fleets at the end of the war. German submarines were taking a staggering toll.

'My trip here has been useless,' Jim bluntly declared at what he had decided would be his last conference. 'Obviously no one can possibly estimate your requirements at this stage of the war.'

The British officials with whom he was meeting glanced at each other in embarrassment.

'Your visit has been – ah – perhaps a bit premature,' Trevor Crewe, a middle-aged economist, murmured. Crewe had left his teaching position at Oxford to serve on the British Government's Board of Natural Resources Allocations.

'You mean that this survey I'm supposed to be conducting was dreamed up at our end?' Jim interrupted.

Crewe had taken a strong liking to Jim during their meetings. The American oilman was perceptive and more a realist than most of his countrymen, who had been invading Britain on various assignments.

'No need for any apologies,' Crewe smiled. 'Governments do tend to muddle about somewhat when they first get involved in wars. Our own positively floundered for almost two years after the Germans invaded Poland.'

Trevor Crewe accompanied Jim to the street, where one of the ubiquitous American Packard staff cars waited.

'When will you be going back to the States?' Crewe asked.

'Soon as I can arrange air transportation through the army.'

'Today's Friday. I doubt if you'll be able to obtain all the necessary clearances and orders before Monday or Tuesday.' Crewe's smile was warm. 'I'd be delighted if you could spend the weekend with my daughter and me at our home in Oxford. There are a number of things I'd like to talk over with you.'

'Thank you, Mr Crewe. I can't refuse.'

Jim took a train to Oxford Saturday morning. Aware of the food problems all British families faced, he brought half an American ham, two dozen fresh eggs, a pound each of coffee and sugar. All came from the US commissary maintained for the VIP contingent at the Chesham. He would have brought more but realized that would only embarrass his host and arrogantly underscore the gulf between British austerity and American plenty.

Crewe met him at the station in a tiny Austin sedan. Jim put his overnight bag and parcels in the back and somehow managed to cram his big-boned six-foot-two frame into the front seat.

They drove less than two miles. Trevor Crewe's home was a small, delightful two-storey house dating from the Edwardian era. There was a lush green front lawn and numerous rose bushes. A drive curved in a semicircle from the road and led to the entrance. Crewe turned into it. A young woman stepped outside the front door to greet them.

Jim Northcutt could not help but stare wide-eyed.

'My daughter Pamela,' Crewe said.

Pamela was a common enough English girl's name. But there was nothing else commonplace about Pamela Crewe. Tall, red-haired, with lively Meissen blue eyes, her features were as finely honed as those of a Reynolds portrait. Her complexion was perfect, in the English manner, and she was deep-breasted and long-limbed.

'How do you do, Mr Northcutt.' Her voice was a clear contralto. 'So you're Daddy's favourite American.'

She stepped forward and held out her hand. Her movements were graceful, her handshake firm. Her manner was that of a well-bred daughter accustomed to meeting her father's many friends and making them all feel welcome.

Jim glanced reflexively towards her left hand. No, she did not wear a wedding or engagement ring. He studied her face for a moment. She was twenty-five, at most twenty-six.

'I'll get my things out of the car,' he said.

'Don't bother,' Crewe said. 'I'll bring them along. Go on inside with Pam. She'll mix you a drink.'

Northcutt looked at Pamela again.

'This way, Mr Northcutt,' she said, for some reason averting her eyes.

3

Trevor Crewe's wife had died in 1930, and he had never re-married. Until the outbreak of the war, he had devoted himself to teaching economics at Oxford and raising his two children, a boy and a girl. The son, now twenty-four, was an RAF meteorologist serving in Australia. Pamela was twenty-six, and had managed the household since she was sixteen.

Intelligent and highly educated, Pamela was devoted to her father. Although she had countless suitors, none appealed to her. The younger Englishmen she'd met were usually callow and languid. The older ones tended to be stuffy, stubbornly adhering to long obsolete Old School Tie traditions.

The young woman was not prepared for the impact that James Northcutt made on her. The big American radiated an independence and vitality she had not previously encountered. After their first half-hour together, she began to tell herself that he was the type of man about whom she had so often fantasized.

Jim was impressed by Crewe's encyclopedic knowledge of the international petroleum industry. The economics professor was intimate with the Byzantine intrigues of British and Continental oil cartels. He talked freely throughout the afternoon. It became apparent that he disapproved of many oil-industry practices and, more to the point, had had a specific purpose in asking Jim to spend the weekend at his home.

'I feel it's only fair that you be informed what our own oil men are doing,' Crewe said. 'For them, it's still business before patriotism. They're looking far beyond the end of the war. You are, of course, aware of the oil finds our British oil cartel made in Kuwait during 1938?'

'Yes. The Burghan field is supposedly the richest in the world.'

'It is.' Crewe's blue eyes, a shade darker than those of his daughter, were openly sardonic. 'Every well drilled there has been prolific. Millions of barrels of sweet, high-gravity crude have been produced by the Burghan field.' He paused, lit a scarred briar pipe and puffed at it for a moment. 'Last week, orders were issued halting all Kuwaiti operations until the end of the war.'

'That's insanity!' Jim snapped. 'British oil companies have Middle Eastern refineries. Your forces there and in North Africa need fuel —'

'Jim, the order shutting off Kuwaiti production came from the British army. Ostensibly from fear that the Germans may seize or bomb the fields. Pure poppycock. The real reason is that our British oil cartel doesn't want the Burghan field's reserves depleted.'

Their conversation was interrupted by Pamela, who came to tell them that dinner was ready. The meal, served by a middle-aged cook-housekeeper, was predictably spartan, save for a large omelette made with the eggs Northcutt had brought.

'Cook gawked when she saw the eggs,' Pamela said, flashing Jim a bright smile. 'She's saving the ham for tomorrow.'

Jim's mind was far from eggs and hams – or even Kuwaiti oil. There was much about Pamela that attracted him.

'Where did I leave off?' Trevor Crewe said. 'Oh, yes. Our oil men want the Burghan reserves intact for postwar profits.'

Jim forced himself to concentrate on Crewe's observations.

'The reasoning is sound, if amoral,' Trevor Crewe went on. 'You Americans have come into the war on our side. You're going all out, sending us enormous quantities of petroleum products. Some of it is in the form of free gifts. The rest might

254

as well be. No rational person expects Britain will ever repay the loans and credits extended by the United States. In effect, you'll be depleting your own petroleum reserves to keep us supplied. When the war ends, our British cartel will have its enormous Kuwaiti supplies intact and will be in a position to dominate the European oil market.'

'Are you suggesting that we shouldn't give Britain any oil for civilian use after the war?'

'I don't suggest anything, Jim. I simply feel you're entitled to complete information, not just fragmentary data.'

The conversation continued, and Northcutt grew increasingly thoughtful. I didn't see beyond the end of my lopsided nose, he reflected. I ran across a few penny-ante chisellers like General Penton and Colonel Raynor and jumped to the conclusion that we Americans are buzzards feeding off the bleeding body of Britain. Sure. The average Britisher is having a hell of a tough time and fighting what's our war, too. But there are British chisellers, too – and they're worse because they're cannibals, devouring their own. The British oil cartel was no different from the Majors at home. War or no war, it was all a matter of business – and profits.

'You seem glum, Mr Northcutt,' Pamela remarked over coffee.

'I am. And please call me Jim.'

'Shouldn't wonder that he's glum,' Trevor Crewe said with an impish glance at his daughter. 'Our friend has been an oilman for a long time. I'm certain he didn't think he had any more illusions that could be shattered.'

'But you did, after all – Jim?' Pamela asked.

'I should have known that nothing as minor as a world war could change the oil business,' Northcutt answered.

'*Plus ça change, plus c'est la même chose*,' said Crewe.

Jim found sleep difficult that night. He reviewed all Crewe had told him. But what actually kept him awake was the knowledge that Pamela's bedroom was only two doors down the hall from his own.

Pamela could not sleep either. She was thinking of Jim Northcutt.

'I'm booked on a transport plane flying ferry pilots back to the States on Tuesday,' Jim said at breakfast Sunday morning. 'But I'm cancelling.'

255

'Oh?' Pamela looked at him, then away. 'Staying in England longer than you'd planned?' There was a note of something more than merely polite interest in her tone.

'For a while,' Jim replied. His first-flush patriotic fervour had evaporated. The war had to be won. But NIPCO would make substantial contributions to the war effort through oil production and refining whether or not Jim returned to the United States and to personally directing its operations.

Over the weekend he had discussed with Trevor Crewe the possibility of taking advantage of business opportunities now present in Europe.

'I'll do my postwar shopping early,' he said. 'There are thousands of refugee businessmen here from every country on the Continent.'

Pamela weighed what he had said. Why shouldn't Northcutt do what so many others were doing? He was a millionaire. Men didn't become millionaires unless they could be coldly objective, even ruthless. He was obviously a man who had taken what he wanted. The thought excited her.

Northcutt took a late afternoon train for London. He and Crewe were to meet there during the week, and Jim happily accepted Pamela's invitation to visit with them at Oxford over another weekend. Soon.

Jim placed a transatlantic telephone call to War Secretary Stimson on Monday. He told Stimson he was mailing his report and would remain in London as a private citizen.

Jim moved from the Chesham to the Dorchester Hotel, and let it be known he was in the market to purchase European properties. In the days that immediately followed, he found himself besieged by businessmen and government officials who had fled to England from countries overrun by the Nazis.

Many of the businessmen had no faith in ultimate Allied victory. More than a few indicated they wished they had stayed in Europe and collaborated with the Nazis. They apparently believed Hitler was invincible and offered their abandoned holdings at ridiculously low prices.

Jim was dejected when he lunched with Crewe on Thursday. The economist was sympathetic and asked him to spend the weekend at Oxford. Jim eagerly agreed.

'Have you bought up the entire Continent yet, Jim?' Pamela

256

asked as she served tea for her father and Northcutt.

'Haven't bought anything,' Jim replied, stirring a single lump of sugar into his tea. 'I've listened to hours of complaints and heard some wild offers and demands, but that's about all.' He drank some of his tea. 'Matter of fact, I'm not going to do anything further until I find someone to help me.'

'Help you?' Pamela asked. 'How?'

'I can't handle all these people by myself. I need someone to take down information, then check out the claims they make. There isn't anyone available, though. Seems every person in London who can read and write is either on a government payroll or frozen into a war-industry job.'

There was a moment's silence. Pamela looked at her father.

'I don't have a job,' she said. 'I do a few hours of volunteer work a week, and that's all. I could help Jim. I'd like to.'

Trevor Crewe hid his smile.

'Consider yourself hired, Pam.' Jim said. 'When can you start?'

'Monday?'

'Fine with me. I'll book a room for you at the Dorchester. You can stay in London during the week and come home Friday evenings.'

Trevor Crewe pretended not to see the look his daughter gave James Northcutt.

4

For anyone with American dollars, London had been an enormous bargain basement since 1938. Fine paintings, antique furniture, jewellery, rare coin, book and stamp collections – all were sold for whatever panic prices they would bring at auctions or in urgently conducted private transactions.

Many of the treasures belonged to the refugees, Jew and Gentile, who had fled to England before the Nazis annexed or overran their countries. Others were offered for sale by Britons who sought American-dollar hedges against what they feared might be an Axis victory. More than a few wealthy US citizens founded or expanded their own collections by taking advantage of the bargains.

Northcutt's idea was to acquire property in Europe from

refugee owners in order to make NIPCO a truly international company in the postwar period.

Pamela was fascinated by the concept of business-empire-building – just as she was personally fascinated by James Northcutt, the empire builder. She felt that while Jim's basic idea was sound, it needed considerable modification. She sensed too that he would have to be guided rather than forced into changing his concepts.

Her first move was to arrange meetings between Northcutt and international-law experts, political scientists, Foreign Office officials.

After almost two weeks passed, Northcutt had lost much of his enthusiasm. Pamela decided he was ready for a gentle push in the right direction.

'Perhaps you should forget refugees and deal with British subjects,' she suggested.

'Pam, the object is to acquire properties on the Continent.'

'Exactly. British companies and individuals have enormous investments in European countries that have been taken over by the Germans. Many of the richer Britons doubt that we'll win the war. They would listen to ridiculously low offers for their sequestered properties on the Continent.

'If you deal with Britons on British soil, you won't have any postwar problems about ownership,' Pamela went on. 'They'll have to live up to their agreements. Once our side wins, your property rights will have to be recognized by the European countries.'

'You may be right,' Northcutt said. 'Let's have dinner together and talk about it some more.'

Pamela and Jim were sharply aware of their strong physical attraction for each other. Yet Jim Northcutt was curiously reticent about making what was obviously the next move. He could not understand the reasons for his hesitancy which he tried to rationalize by noting to himself the difference in age of fifteen years as well as his friendship with her father. But he sensed there was something else that held him back.

'Pick me up in my room in an hour,' Pamela said. She glanced at her wristwatch. 'That'll be seven forty-five. All right?'

'Fine. I'll be starved.'

* * *

When she opened her door he was amazed to see that she wore only a light robe, loosely belted and open at the throat. Her feet were bare and her red hair was tousled.

'Oh, I'm sorry, Jim,' she said apologetically. 'I must have been tired and fell asleep.'

Her eyes were strangely bright.

'No disaster,' he said, edging towards the corridor. 'Let's make it in another half-hour.'

'No!' Pamela's normally soft voice had a panicky, almost shrill edge. 'It won't take me that long.' She reached for his hand. The gesture showed none of the supple grace that always characterized her movements. 'I – I can hurry and dress in the bathroom.'

Her fingers closed around his wrist. He stepped into the room and locked the door. He reached for Pamela, drawing her to him. She was in his arms instantly, her head upturned.

Jim's desire for her soared at the abandon of her response, but he was aware of an off-key, almost jarring quality in her kiss and in the frantic way her hands clutched at him.

He drew his head back, stared at her, saw that her eyes were tightly closed.

'Take me to bed. Make love to me.' It was a litany.

The bed was single, and Jim held her straining body against his, his hands caressing her breasts. She moaned, her muscles flexing.

He parted her thighs, his fingers brushing against softness. Her hands groped blindly, but they did not guide him, and he withdrew.

'Pam!'

'Yes?' she whispered. 'Yes, Jim?'

'You've never been with a man before.'

'No.' She avoided looking at him and buried her head in the hollow of his shoulder. 'Don't be angry.'

'Why didn't you tell me?' he asked.

She was silent for a moment.

'Would you and I have got this far if I had?'

'I don't know. But we're here.' He was surprised by the tenderness in his own voice. He touched her cheek, stroked it. He bent his head and kissed her hair.

'You do want to make love to me?'

'Yes. Very much.' But the discovery that she was a virgin had done something to his physical and emotional mechan-

259

isms. Blood receded from his loins.

He suddenly comprehended that his feelings for Pamela somehow transcended the purely sexual. He knew that all too many women had been sadly disappointed in their first sexual experience because of their partner's lack of sensitivity.

'Pam,' he murmured. 'We'll take our time.' He stroked her soft bare shoulders.

He used his hands and lips gently, adroitly, and he was ready again.

'Keep your arms around me and kiss me,' he said. His right hand moved down her body in a gentle motion. Her muscles grew taut and she cried out ecstatically.

'Oh, my God!' she gasped, shuddering as the sensation subsided into a tingling afterglow. 'Jim ...'

But he was kissing her breasts. She did not resist. She moaned and experienced spasms of pleasure as his tongue flicked.

He kissed her for several minutes, his hands fondling and caressing her body before moving himself over her, very slowly, very carefully.

Initially he was gentle and when he felt her wince, he paused and waited. His arms were around her and his weight was on his elbows and knees and he murmured softly.

'Relax, darling,' he said over and over. 'Don't strain.'

He felt her resist, then give. Her moan was of delight, no pain.

'Jim – was that – did you ...'

He enveloped her mouth with his, muffling her words. She gripped him violently and her hips moved against his.

'I love you!' Pamela all but screamed when he brought her once more to climax.

Jim was caught in the pleasure tide of his own completion, but he heard her, and he was dismayed by the realization that he wanted to say, 'I love you, too.'

Later that evening, he did.

Pamela was certainly in love with Jim for the man that he was. But she was also excited by the power and wealth he represented and exhilarated by the knowledge that she was helping him increase both.

Pamela's comprehension of Britain's laws and customs and her wide acquaintance among influential people proved invaluable. Jim found himself relying more and more on her advice and guidance. Before long, he had acquired British-held ownership rights to several business properties on the Axis-held European Continent. These included an oil refinery in the south of France, a wholesale marketing facility in Belgium and an entire block of commercial buildings in Milan. He paid ridiculously low prices. The companies and individuals from whom he bought the properties had abandoned hope of ever recovering their Continental holdings. In fact, they considerd Northcutt a rich American fool who was very easily parted from his money.

5

In later years, James Northcutt would look back on his marriage to Pamela Crewe in the Kensington Registry Office as almost an incidental aside. It happened and marriage was what they both wanted at the time. They were by then lovers constantly in each other's company. The brief ceremony legalizing their relationship seemed a minor incident against the backdrop of war and their joint preoccupation with Jim's business affairs.

Trevor Crewe wanted to give a wedding reception for his daughter and new son-in-law, but they vetoed the idea. On their wedding night, Pamela and Jim took a train to Birmingham where, on the next day, they met with an industrialist and began negotiations for the purchase of his controlling stock interest in a chain of Austrian gasoline stations. The negotiations fell through after a few days. The Northcutts returned to London and Pamela openly moved into Jim's suite at the Dorchester.

Jim sensed that the bargain-basement days ended in November 1942. The Red Army was encircling the German forces in Stalingrad. American forces joined the British in the battle for North Africa. In the Pacific, US marines were breaking the back of Japanese resistance on Guadalcanal. No one thought the conflict would soon be over, but these battle-field developments instilled new hope and confidence in eventual Allied victory. Men and firms who had been eager to sell

European holdings for trivial sums now changed their minds.

'We'll go back to the States,' Jim announced in early December.

'Can we go after Christmas?' Pam asked. 'I'd like to spend it with Dad. Who knows when I'll be seeing him again.'

'We'll stay until after New Year's.'

The easy exchange over a matter of importance indicated the quality of their relationship. Pamela accepted Jim's decisions in principle. Yet she felt free to ask that he alter them when she believed there was a valid reason, and he almost always acceded to her requests. They were not only lovers, and husband and wife, but also equal partners, and James Northcutt thought that he had never been happier.

'You know, we've got something extra,' Jim remarked one night after he and Pamela had spent hours making love. 'Be interesting to isolate the X-factor.'

'Blame it on the war,' Pamela said with a sleepy laugh. Then she became serious. 'I can tell you – I think.'

'Oh?' He stroked her red hair.

'Seems to me that some couples are in love. Other husbands and wives love each other —'

'We don't?'

'We do. Both. We're in love and love. The extra is that we really like each other. The three are all different, and when all are present – but haven't you had them all with a woman before?'

Yes, I did, Jim said to himself. I had them all with Verna Fletcher.

'No,' he said aloud and kissed her passionately as if to make amends for the lie.

Pamela and Jim spent the Christmas holidays with Trevor Crewe in Oxford. Jim used his influence to obtain air transportation back to America on 5 January 1943. They planned to remain in New York two weeks, for Pamela was eager to see the city, and Jim was no less eager to show it to her.

They went to the Pierre, then New York's most luxurious hotel. Northcutt chose the Pierre because it had been recently purchased by his old friend and fellow maverick wildcatter, J. Paul Getty.'

'Is your friend very rich?'

'Paul's worth three, maybe four, times more than I am. He

could sign a cheque for a hundred and fifty million – and while it might clean him out, it wouldn't bounce. But then, he had a head start.'

Pamela blinked. She had known that Jim was well off but the extent of her husband's wealth amazed her. In a roundabout fashion Jim had just told her that he was worth in the neighbourhood of $50 million. And, beyond that, he was casually suggesting that some day his fortune might equal that of the older oilman, J. Paul Getty.

Coming from England, Pamela could not help but shake her head when New Yorkers complained about wartime hardships.

The city's halfhearted brownout seemed like a blaze of lights compared to the total blackouts she had known. Despite gasoline rationing, traffic was heavier than she had ever seen in London, even before the war. Shop windows displayed immense arrays of foods, merchandise, luxuries. Only the great numbers of men in uniform gave visible indication that America was actually at war.

But she loved New York, and she enjoyed shopping at Bonwit's, Saks, Bendel's and the other exclusive stores and shops. She revelled in the knowledge that Jim was a multi-millionaire and that she could spend without restraint. He spent even more on her. Representatives from Cartier's and Van Cleef and Arpels brought jewellery to the Pierre so that Pamela could pick and choose. To her own astonishment, she felt no hesitancy or self-consciousness about selecting items with five-figure price tags.

Jim had told Pamela he owned a home in Los Angeles, but he had never described it in detail. Pamela didn't quite know what mental image she had formed of the house. However, it was nothing like the reality she encountered when they arrived in Southern California.

'How on earth did you manage to live alone in so many rooms?' she asked, wide-eyed.

'I always had the servants,' Jim said. He didn't think it wise to mention that he was rarely alone in the Wilshire Boulevard mansion. 'And I gave a lot of parties. Which reminds me, once we get settled in, we'll give more.' He grinned. 'What the hell, maybe I'll even buy another house. Bigger. With all the swimming pool and tennis court trimmings.'

Pamela made no protest. In fact, she was already delighting in thoughts of the luxurious life Jim's wealth would provide.

For more than a month, life for the James Northcutts was an endless round of dinners, parties and shopping expeditions. Some of their time was devoted to house hunting. They soon found a twenty-seven-room Monterey-style mansion in Bel Air. It had been completed only a few months before Pearl Harbor, but was never occupied. The house had spacious grounds and gardens and the swimming pool and tennis court that Jim seemed to think obligatory.

'Like the place?' He asked Pamela.

'I love it!'

Northcutt instructed Sam Schlechter to arrange for the purchase of the house. He told Pamela she could have carte blanche to decorate and furnish their new home. Then, abruptly, Northcutt once again began to concentrate on business.

6

Early in 1942, to meet war needs, the US Government launched the 'Big Inch' project – a 1,254-mile-long pipeline that carried crude from Texas to New Jersey. A second pipeline project, 'Little Big Inch', two hundred miles longer, was soon under way. It had a peak throughput of 240,000 barrels daily and pumped 100-octane aviation gasoline across the country for shipment to Europe. Both projects were backed by federal funds but carried out by consortiums of major oil companies.

NIPCO had not been invited to join either of the consortiums, and this caused Jim considerable worry. He feared that once the war ended, control of the two great pipelines would revert to the Majors.

'The Majors will shut out the independents,' he told Sam Schlechter. 'The bastards will get around all the rules governing common carriers by one means or another.'

He then outlined his plans for protecting NIPCO.

'The government wants connecting lines built from various areas to the Big Inch and Little Big Inch systems. We'll build some of those connecting the lines even if we have to lose a few million doing it. Then we'll be in a position to horse-trade after the war. We'll give the Majors a fair shake on using our connecting lines if they give us the same treatment on the main transcontinental systems.'

'Sounds fine,' Sam Schlechter remarked. 'But the decisions are made in Washington.'

'They'll be made in our favour,' Northcutt declared. 'I'll pull the strings and lay out the cash.'

Pamela Northcutt was dismayed by the change and not at all sure that she could adjust to it.

She had been accustomed to having Jim with her ever since she went to work with him in London. Now, suddenly, she found herself alone most of the time. Her husband was constantly on the move – to Washington, Texas, Oklahoma, New Mexico, back to Washington. He telephoned her frequently, but by no means daily. She saw little of him even on those occasions when he returned to California. There were meetings, conferences, a thousand and one tasks that had to be given priority.

'Sorry, honey,' he would apologize. 'There's been a War Production Board foul-up.' And then he would be gone again.

Pamela said nothing for almost six months. The decoration and furnishing of their new Bel Air home kept her busy. Then, when all was completed and they had moved in, she became restless and dissatisfied. She spoke to Jim on one of the rare nights when he was in Los Angeles and home for dinner.

'I'm lonely, Jim,' she said. 'Isn't there some way —'

'For Christ's sake!' he exploded. 'I'm working on projects that mean the difference between life and death for NIPCO. And you're bitching about being lonely!'

'Jim —'

'God damn it, don't nag me, Pam!'

Part of his anger stemmed from guilt. There had been several affairs with other women during his trips to Washington and elsewhere. He wondered if Pamela suspected. She didn't, but she had sensed a subtle change in the quality of their relationship and determined she would restore it to what it had been.

Pamela knew Jim harboured hopes of establishing a dynasty and wanted children. The answer, she felt, was to become

265

pregnant. She did, in September 1943. Three months later, she miscarried. The experience terrified her. After that, she went to great lengths to avoid another pregnancy.

Jim continued to be away frequently and for periods of two weeks or more. Lonely and bored, Pamela gravitated into the snobbish clique of Hollywood's 'British Colony', composed of British actors, actresses, directors and producers. Most drank heavily and spent their spare time waxing nostalgic about England and making caustic comments about their American colleagues in Hollywood.

Large numbers of Britishers now began to frequent the Northcutt home in Bel Air. Pamela gave parties and held benefit affairs for various British and American war-relief agencies. Jim was a generous host when he was at home, but mainly he viewed Pamela's activities with good-natured tolerance.

The Birdwell Aircraft Company held a contract to produce a new top-secret experimental fighter plane for the army air force. It's revolutionary XP-119 engine was to be fuelled by upgraded propane, a liquefied petroleum gas. Lloyd Birdwell had insisted the fuel be produced by Northcutt International Petroleum. The contract was awarded to NIPCO's San Pedro refinery.

The XP-119 engine was ready for testing in May 1944. Jim happened to be in Los Angeles. He accepted Birdwell's invitation to witness the tests and observe the performance of the NIPCO fuel. When he arrived at the Birdwell Aircraft plant in Burbank, Lloyd accompanied him to a vast, hangar-like building. The engine was mounted on a great concrete test block in the centre of the floor.

'Who designed that monstrosity?' Jim asked. 'Rube Goldberg?'

'God knows,' Birdwell replied glumly. 'Some double-dome working for the army. We just got orders to build it – and the air frame it's supposed to get off the ground and keep in the air.'

Lloyd was obviously far from optimistic about the future of the XP-119 – and little wonder, Jim reflected. The engine was oversized, oblong and studded with an array of cumbersome fittings. Nearby was a horizontal pressurized bullet tank containing the propane fuel.

'Kind of risky having that tank indoors,' Jim observed.

266

'That's how the army wanted it for the test.' Birdwell shrugged, agreeing. 'Simple common sense tells me it's a hazard.'

Birdwell Aircraft employees and Army Air Corps officials, in uniform and out, bustled about, preparing for the test. After almost two hours, someone announced that everything was ready.

Engineers and technicians clustered around the test block. Jim and Lloyd stood several yards away to avoid interfering with other men who scurried back and forth with clipboards and testing gear.

A bell rang. There was a long, shrill whine, followed by some tentative splutters and finally a full throated roar as the XP-119 caught.

Then someone turned the wrong valve. Propane gas jetted from a bleed line on the tank. Volatile vapours ignited, a line ruptured and the entire tank blew.

A great sheet of flame lashed through the building, and fragments of steel tank and fittings sheared off the engine were hurled in every direction by the blast.

A piece of metal struck Jim in the right leg, and as he fell another smashed against his head. He was only vaguely aware of Birdwell groaning and falling on top of him, and then he lost consciousness.

Five men were killed, eighteen others injured. Northcutt and Birdwell were rushed to Cedars of Lebanon Hospital in Los Angeles. Jim suffered a compound fracture of the right leg and head injuries. Birdwell had several broken ribs and was badly cut by metal fragments. The two men were anaesthetized and given immediate treatment, after which they were placed in adjoining rooms.

Jim came out of the anaesthetic to find his right leg in traction and his head bandaged. Pamela sat by his bedside. She had been weeping. He grinned and held her hand.

The doctor was summoned. 'You're doing fine, Mr Northcutt,' he said.

'Bullshit!' Jim retorted loudly. 'I won't be fine until I'm out of here. How long will that be?'

'About ten days. After two or three quiet weeks at home you can start getting around with a walking cast and crutches.'

Jim remembered that Lloyd had been with him when the

267

propane tank exploded. 'How is Birdwell?' he demanded.

'Just as pissed off as you are,' Lloyd's voice came from the next room. The doors to both rooms were open. 'Hey, there's somebody here who wants to see you.'

'Who is it?' Jim called back.

'Me,' a woman's voice said from the doorway. 'The radio made it sound as though you were both dying.'

Jim stared, wide-eyed and disbelieving. It was Verna Fletcher.

My God, he thought. I haven't seen Verna since 1932, when we were together on the *Twentieth Century Limited*. She hasn't changed – and for Christ's sake, I'm still reacting.

Verna had remained a star. Jim had seen many of her motion pictures over the years. He had even taken Pamela to one at Grauman's Chinese Theatre and told her he knew Verna – through Lloyd Birdwell. But he made no mention of their relationship in Oklahoma. Only a year or so before, he had read that she was divorcing her third husband. Verna was single again.

'I'll be damned,' he said, a little nervously. 'So you have to think Lloyd and I are dying before you pay us a visit.'

Manners, he reminded himself, and introduced Pamela to Verna.

'I've seen ever so many of your films,' Pam said. 'You've been one of my favourite actresses ever since I was a little girl.'

Uh-oh, Jim thought. Pamela was much too clever and quick-witted for that remark to have slipped out. Her female intuition must have picked up something.

'I *have* been around a long time,' Verna laughed. She studied Pamela from under her lashes. A beautiful and intelligent woman, but there's a faint off-key note.

'Anyway, Jim, since neither of you seems to be dying, I'll run along,' Verna said.

'Please stay,' Pamela spoke up.

Northcutt had recovered his equilibrium.

'Don't go yet,' he said. 'As I told Pam, we've known each other since you started in pictures with Lloyd.'

'Yes, please stay a while,' Pam said. She stood up and brought another chair close to the bed.

The nurse entered to say that there were several other visitors waiting to see Jim – Samuel Schlechter, Luke Rayburn,

Steve Kostis.

'Then I *will* be going,' Verna said.

'Can you come back again?' Pamela asked.

Verna hesitated. 'Yes,' she finally replied. 'Tomorrow or the next day.'

'And please come to our house after Jim is home.'

'Of course,' Verna said.

Verna came to the hospital again, and, in spite of her better judgement, did visit the Northcutts' home later.

Oddly enough, she and Pamela became friendly, but there was still a mutual reserve.

'You and Jim had an affair, didn't you?' Pam asked one afternoon.

'Not exactly,' Verna replied, lying for Jim's sake, but aware that Pamela's intuition was too good for her to lie wholly. 'Jim was one of my customers.'

'Customers?'

'I was in a parlourhouse in Logan, Oklahoma, where Jim got his start as a wildcatter.'

'Oh. Why didn't he tell me?'

'He's trying to protect me,' Verna said with a smile. And I'm trying to protect your marriage, she thought. 'Now you know the big secret.'

Pam felt much more comfortable with Verna after that, but sensed that she had not heard the entire story. She observed Jim and Verna closely when they were together. Verna may have been in a parlourhouse, she thought, but Jim had not been merely a customer.

When Jim's leg was fully healed, he resumed his work and travels. Pam continued to see Verna Fletcher occasionally. The belief that there were still strong bonds between Verna and her husband grew, and it engendered feelings of anxiety over the solidity of her marriage.

A baby, Pam told the reflection in her dressing-table mirror one morning. Jim wanted a child. She would have to overcome her fears of another miscarriage.

For some reason, it proved difficult to do. Months, then more than a year passed, and she still had not become pregnant. This only increased her determination.

7

The high-sounding slogans of World War Two had begun to pall for James Northcutt by 1943. Once the tide of battle began to turn against the Axis, the entire character of the war had changed. It became a struggle for postwar control of oil-rich areas around the globe. The major oil companies took over as the real formulators of strategy.

President Franklin D. Roosevelt had surrounded himself with advisors and policy makers whose ties with the Majors were close. By mid-1943 men like Edwin Pauley, James Forrestal, Patrick Hurley and Herbert Hoover, Jr, not only called the tunes, but wrote much of the music that was being played.

Many of their manoeuvrings were aimed at the Middle East, over which the United States and Great Britain were fighting a grimly determined behind-the-scenes war.

In 1943, ARAMCO, a consortium of American oil companies, demanded full US Government support for its position in Saudi Arabia and quickly received formal assurances from the State Department: 'This Government will assist you in every appropriate way.' President Roosevelt funnelled more than $100 million in money, goods and credits to the Saudi Arabian Government and showered Saudi Arabian King Ibn Saud with gifts and honours.

The American consortium was safe – for the moment. But British oil interests were manipulating and prodding their own government. Although American and British servicemen were fighting and dying side by side on the battlefields, the major oil companies of each country pitted their respective governments against each other.

James Forrestal, Undersecretary of the Navy, openly accused the British Government of committing acts hostile to the United States in the Middle East.

'The British have five hundred people in Saudi Arabia posing as naturalists who are trying to prevent a locust plague,' Forrestal charged. 'They are in Saudi Arabia for no other reason than to see what the hell we are doing and what we've got there.'

Forrestal and others close to Roosevelt made even more

serious accusations. They claimed Britain was attempting to buy and coerce Ibn Saud and his ministers into taking oil concessions away from American companies and giving them to British firms.

American OSS agents were ranging over Mid-east countries in which British oil companies held concessions and large numbers of American troops and civilians were in Iran. Whatever their ostensible assignments, they had really been sent to pry oil concessions away from British companies and have them awarded to American Majors.

In London, Trevor Crewe was also watching the situation with increasing distaste. He managed to evade wartime censorship and keep his daughter and son-in-law informed.

'It will become much stickier,' Crewe wrote. 'Feeling runs high here. Our oil companies want to oust American interests from the Middle East at any cost. I've been informed that the War Cabinet will soon request top-level talks with the American Government in an effort to prevent the clash of oil interests from causing an open breach between Britain and the United States.'

Pamela shook her head after reading the letter. 'How unlike Daddy. He was never one to go into a flap or exaggerate —'

'He's not exaggerating,' Jim told her. 'It's all being kept supersecret, but Britain and the US are in their own separate, private battle. They're fighting to see who gets the biggest prizes after the war.'

'Jim, assuming that all you say is true, what would you do if NIPCO were large enough to rank with the Majors?'

Northcutt's eyebrow angled upward.

'I'd be right in there, battling to get my share,' he replied. 'You can either be an idealist or an oilman. You can't be both.'

Trevor Crewe's predictions proved accurate. Friction escalated until it resulted in a remarkable exchange of acrimonious messages between Winston Churchill and Franklin D. Roosevelt.

'There is apprehension in some quarters here that the United States intends to deprive us of our oil assets in the Middle East,' the British Prime Minister cabled Roosevelt.

The President replied: 'On the other hand, I am disturbed about the rumour that the British wish to horn in on Saudi Arabian oil reserves.'

Churchill made a placating move, cabling Roosevelt:

'Thank you for your assurances about no sheep's eyes at our oil fields in Iran and Iraq. Let me reciprocate by giving you fullest assurance that we have no thought of trying to horn in upon your interests or property in Saudi Arabia.'

Two factors averted the break. First, the American Government threatened to place severe restrictions on lend–lease supplies being sent to Britain. Second, the December 1944, counteroffensive launched by the Nazis in the Ardennes united the two countries again, at least for a brief period. When the Nazi thrust was contained and then turned back, and the Allied drive into Germany resumed, Britain found it had lost the oil war.

Germany, then Japan, surrendered.

Jim and Sam Schlechter flew to Europe. For the most part, the properties Jim had bought there had come through the war in fair to good condition. Still, arrangements had to be made for the repair of war-damaged or worn-out facilities. Local attorneys had to be retained and claims and documents filed, and new employees hired. Jim and Schlechter were gone for several weeks.

Shortly before leaving Europe, Northcutt heard of a tract of land that was for sale on the French Riviera outside Cap d'Antibes. The owner was a Nazi collaborator who had fled to Argentina and was desperate for money. The property was choice and ideally situated. Northcutt bought it.

'I'll build a villa there some day,' he told Sam. 'May even wind up living there permanently.' The attorney thought it was idle fantasy, but agreed that Jim had obtained another great bargain.

The pace did not let up when Northcutt returned to the United States. There were negotiations only he could conduct, deals only he could close, and he insisted on making personal inspections of all NIPCO operations. Even when in Los Angeles, he worked incessantly, meeting with executives, formulating plans, making NIPCO grow.

Pamela announced that she was pregnant.

Jim was overjoyed, bought her more jewellery – but a new thermofor process cracking unit was scheduled to go on stream at the NIPCO refinery in San Mateo. Two days later, he went to San Mateo, where he stayed a week.

Pam consoled herself with the thought that once the baby

was born he would change and pay more attention to his family and less to business.

NIPpy Gasoline and motor oil were still marketed only along the West Coast, but sales boomed. Crude in excess of NIPCO's own refinery requirements was sold to other companies or shipped overseas aboard Northcutt Seven Seas Transport Company tankers. The fleet had been enlarged by the purchase of nine war-surplus tankers. Four larger vessels were being constructed.

Pamela was in her ninth month. She experienced the first pangs of labour and went immediately to Hollywood Hospital, resentful and anxiety-ridden because Jim was in Venezuela. He was notified and chartered a plane for the return flight to California. When he arrived at the hospital, his child had been born.

'When can I see him?' he demanded.

'You mean when can you see her.' Pam's obstetrician smiled. 'Your wife gave birth to a girl.'

Jim overcame his initial disappointment within a few weeks. His daughter was, as everyone who saw her said, a lovely child. He called her Kathy or Kath and she had Pamela's fine features and red hair and his grey eyes.

Northcutt doted on Kathy, and she adored her father.

'Maybe a boy next time,' he told Pamela.

Pam was greatly pleased. Jim was home much more now. Their relationship seemed to return to its original level of intensity. Then Pam detected a fundamental contradiction. Jim made love to her with no less physical ardour than before, but his emotional involvement had diminished.

Another child, hopefully a boy, would make the difference, she told herself. Katherine was only six months old when Pam missed a period. Tests confirmed her pregnancy. When she was in her second month, she miscarried.

Examinations indicated that Pam had a cyst on her uterus, and an operation was recommended. The cyst proved non-malignant, but a hysterectomy was necessary.

With apparent equanimity, Jim Northcutt accepted the fact that his wife could bear no more children. He was tender and loving towards her while she recovered. Although Pam had been warned about having sexual intercourse for at least a full month, she understood her husband's physical needs.

'Let me make love to you,' she pleaded.

He smiled. 'No, honey. I'll wait.'

He moved into another bedroom. Suddenly, there was again need for him to make frequent, albeit fairly short, trips. Pamela was deeply hurt.

When she could resume her sex life, their first attempt was a dismal failure. Neither she nor Jim achieved orgasm. He left the next day – for Washington, where he remained two weeks.

Did she still want her marriage, Pam wondered. Yes, she decided after endless soul searching. She did. Because of Kathy – and because she still wanted to be Mrs James L. Northcutt.

'Jim. Sleep with me tonight,' Pam pleaded one evening.

She had made a special effort to be beautiful for him. Yes, he thought, she was as lovely as ever. She responded fully when he pulled her to him. There was desire in his kiss, but when they went to bed Pamela sensed that he had been with another woman earlier.

While Jim slept serenely beside her, Pam lay awake – unfulfilled and infinitely sad.

Jim returned to his old habits, and he saw much of Steve Kostis and Lloyd Birdwell. Birdwell was beginning to show evidence of his horror of germs.

'Nobody here with a cold?' he would demand as he joined his companions.

The three went on sprees much as they had during the years before the war. Soon Pamela could not avoid seeing occasional newspaper items. There were gossip-column reports of James Northcutt dining with this or that actress or cruising aboard Birdwell's yacht with some woman ambiguously identified as a 'starlet' or 'model'.

For a long time, Pam forced herself to ignore the evidences of Jim's infidelity. Then a series of events made it impossible for her to pretend any further.

Lloyd Birdwell persuaded Jim to spend a weekend at his Topanga Canyon house.

'You need a vacation,' Birdwell said. 'I have the women lined up. All choice merchandise.'

Northcutt reflected that he could use an old-fashioned sex wallow. He was at Birdwell's home on Friday evening. Lloyd had invited three of his close business associates, and there were several attractive girls, including a pair of chestnut-haired identical twins.

'Jeanne and Jan,' Lloyd introduced them. 'A great sister act. They're for you, Jim. Have fun trying to figure which is which.'

The girls were young, eighteen or nineteen, Northcutt guessed. Later, when he took them to the bedroom that had been assigned to him for the weekend, he discovered that whatever their age, they were virtuosos.

'Lloyd said you were good, and we should give you the full treatment,' Jeanne murmured when they were in the bedroom.

They did, changing places often. Northcutt's pleasure was immeasurably increased because he could no longer tell the identical twins apart. It was a bizarre experience, as if one woman had somehow managed to duplicate herself and perform different acts simultaneously, and the night swiftly built into a draining erotic marathon.

It was late when Jim fell asleep, but the twins woke him early. They resumed their ministrations.

'Like?' Jan asked.

'You're both terrific,' he said, sandwiched between the two girls. He was mildly curious. 'What else do you do?'

'Sing and dance,' Jeanne – he thought it was Jeanne, and not Jan – told him. 'That's why we're here. Lloyd owns that movie studio. He said he'd give us a break if we came out for the weekend.'

Jeanne and Jan Duschau.

James Northcutt and Lloyd Birdwell would have reason to remember the twins and their names.

For some reason, Lloyd forgot his promise to them. He even refused to speak to them when they telephoned him during the next two weeks. Jim, of course, had put them completely out of his mind after the weekend party at Birdwell's ended. To him, the twins were like Kleenex: they had been handy, readily available – and disposable after use. Then, one morning, two police officers were ushered into his NIPCO office. They were polite, deferential, but they said they had a warrant for his arrest. On a charge of statutory rape.

'A Mr and Mrs Merle Duschau swore complaints against

275

you and Mr Birdwell. They say you had sexual relations with their daughters.'

'The twins!' Jim groaned. 'But they're over the legal age!'

'They're not. They won't be sixteen until next month.'

'Holy Christ! Give me a minute to call my lawyer!'

Northcutt and Birdwell were immediately released on bail, but the story of their arrests was splashed across the newspapers.

TYCOONS CHARGED WITH SEX-OFFENCES AGAINST FIFTEEN-YEAR-OLD GIRLS

'Our babies were virgins before they were ruined by those two men,' Mr Merle Duschau told reporters, reading from a prepared statement. 'They were two innocent little girls . . .'

Mrs Duschau was photographed weeping and comforting her twin daughters who, according to the captions, also wept.

'They looked at least eighteen,' Jim told Sam Schlechter.

'They always do,' Schlechter retorted drily. 'Otherwise men wouldn't get hit with phoney statutory rape charges.'

The Duschaus, parents and daughters, revelled in the publicity. Then Jim and Lloyd each paid them $100,000, and the charges were dropped.

Pamela Northcutt could hardly pretend she was unaware of the scandal. Deeply hurt, Pamela's pride none the less prevented her from saying anything to Jim, and she kept up a brave front when with others.

'How do you put up with it?' a woman friend – herself twice divorced – asked Pam.

'Most wealthy men do the same things,' Pam replied coolly. 'Except that some sneak around the corners – like your ex-husbands.' She still wanted to preserve her marriage and she could not leave Jim without breaking Kathy's heart.

When home, Jim devoted most of his time to Kathy. The entrepreneur and empire builder had turned into a father who delighted in spoiling his little daughter.

Pam sought to caution him.

'You shouldn't make such a fuss over Kathy. When you're gone, she finds herself in a partial vacuum.'

'Best thing in the world for her,' was Jim's reply. 'It'll help her understand she can't have everything she wants all the time.'

His attitude towards Pam was friendly, but platonic. She tried to adapt herself and succeeded for what seemed a very long time to her. Then, at last, she began a discreet affair with one of the 'British Colony' members. It bolstered her ego to be wanted by a man who had shared the beds of several Hollywood beauties, but the affair fell far short of filling the void.

Northcutt quickly guessed that Pamela had a lover but he could not feel any jealousy. The idea of divorcing Pam never entered his mind. There were many advantages to having a lovely and charming wife, and he did not want to be separated from his daughter.

Jim's lack of reaction to her having an affair was the final blow to Pamela's ego and pride. Now she was certain that whatever love he had once had for her was dead.

8

In 1951 Abraham Schlechter suffered a stroke. His son, Sam, flew immediately to Tulsa. Abe lived for only two days. Before he died, he asked Sam to call Verna Fletcher and Jim Northcutt; he wanted to see them for the last time. Flying separately, they arrived in Tulsa hours too late. They stayed for the funeral services, and afterwards Jim took Verna to dinner at his hotel.

They had seen each other often in Los Angeles since 1944, but they hadn't been alone together for more than a few minutes since the night on the *Twentieth Century Limited*. Now Jim studied Verna carefully across the hotel restaurant table. Her blonde hair, while not as fine and soft as it had been, still showed no grey. Her blue eyes were as clear and long-lashed as he remembered them from long ago; the faint lines at their corners only seemed to make her face more expressive. Her figure had matured but remained lovely, and she moved with the easy grace of a young girl.

Verna read his thoughts. Her smile was wry, yet pensive.

'I'm a miracle product,' she said. 'A tribute to overpriced masseuses, cosmeticians and dressmakers.'

They drank their first martinis. Northcutt signalled for another round and lapsed into nostalgic melancholy.

277

'Abe left me the old supply-store bathtub in his will – Sam told me after the funeral,' he said and shook his head. 'I saw less and less of Abe over the years, but knowing that he's gone is like a kick in the stomach.' He gazed at her. 'Remember what he called us? The three *oysvorfs* – outcasts.' He took a deep breath. 'Anyway, we all did pretty well for outcasts, didn't we?'

Depends on how you look at it, Verna mused, observing him from under her lashes. Damn it, the attraction was still there, as strong as ever. Purely physical? What the psychiatrists call sensory fixation.

'We ought to form an *oysvorfs* survivor's club,' she said, sipping her fresh martini. 'One down. Two to go. Us.'

Verna had been recognized by diners in the hotel restaurant. They stared at her and wondered who the big, rugged man with her could be. A woman came timidly to their table and asked for Verna's autograph.

'... and I saw your last picture...'

'You're very kind,' Verna replied automatically, signing her name. 'Thank you very much.'

The woman took the autographed menu and moved off.

'See, you're famous,' Jim said.

'Yeah,' Verna nodded. 'Famous.'

When their sirloins arrived, both found they had lost their appetite for food. Jim brooded, then glanced at Verna.

'Verna, let's do something.'

'What? Take in a movie?' She tried to make her tone flippant.

'Let's drive down to Logan tonight.'

Verna gazed at her plate. 'We don't have to go to Logan, Jim.' She reached for her handbag and stood up from the table. 'You have a suite here, don't you?'

Their lovemaking began with an almost furious passion. Then it became increasingly tender and, after several hours, they slept.

Jim was the first to awaken. For a moment he was not in a hotel bedroom. He was with Verna in her bed in Logan. They would make love again. He would bathe, dress and eat some food prepared by Celia. He would drive his Model T roadster out to the fields and go on night tour ...

His sense of place and time reoriented, bringing him back to the here and now. Their night together was the reality. Verna lay sleeping beside him. He gazed at her in the dim light of the curtained room and once more, for a brief instant, three decades were obliterated. She was as she had been. Then.

'Verna.'

'Mmm.' She stirred, fitting her body more closely against his. Her lips were against his shoulder and moved, kissing it. She was awake yet not awake, but she responded hungrily.

Jim had made plans for an early return to Los Angeles, but these were forgotten.

He looked at his watch. It was almost noon.

'It would be nice to spend the day together,' he said.

'All day – and another night,' Verna smiled. She had noticed he still carried the geyser charm she had given him in Logan, and she was moved.

'A lot of other nights,' he said.

'I don't know about that, Jim. It probably wouldn't work.'

'It might. We could try.'

We could, Verna reflected. God knows, I want to.

'We'll see,' she told him.

'Care for brunch?' Northcutt was famished.

'Love some.'

'Shall we have it sent up?'

'Uh-huh. Along with champagne – and a dinner menu. I don't want to get out of bed at all today.'

'Neither do I.' Before he picked up the telephone to call room service, he held her in his arms and kissed her.

Jim stopped travelling. He stayed in Los Angeles, preferring to spend his nights with Verna in her Beverly Hills home. They did not go out together in public. None the less, they could hardly expect to keep their affair a secret. First there were whispers. Then, thinly veiled items appeared in the gossip columns.

Pamela was stunned.

If it had been anyone but Verna Fletcher!

Now she was forced to face the final, dismal realization. From the very beginning, her life with James Northcutt had been based on nothing but fantasy. I love him, and he thought he loved me, she told herself. But I was only a surrogate. A substitute for Verna Fletcher, the woman he once loved and never stopped loving.

Suddenly, being Mrs James L. Northcutt had lost all importance. Pam was amazed how little emotion she felt when she made her decision and confronted Jim.

'I'm going to sue for divorce,' she announced.

'What about Kathy?' was his first question.

'I'll want custody. You can have unlimited visiting privileges.'

Northcutt felt a twinge of conscience because his only reaction was one of relief.

'Pam, I want you to know that Verna and —'

'Verna isn't the only reason,' Pamela broke in. 'You – and NIPCO – are moving to New York. There isn't anything for me there. My friends are here. I'm only thirty-six, and I *do* have my own life.'

'I see.' He had no arguments to offer.

Jim moved to the Beverly Hills Hotel the next morning. In the afternoon, he consulted Sam Schlechter.

'I don't lecture you often,' Schlechter told him. 'I have to now. Pam is right. All of us who know you can't understand why she hasn't divorced you long before this.'

Northcutt remained silent.

'I'll follow your instructions, of course,' Sam went on. 'However, if you're asking my advice, don't fight the suit and don't quibble about property rights or alimony.'

'Set it up with Pam,' Jim said. 'I'll sign whatever you stick under my nose. Just make sure I'll be able to see Kathy.'

That night, Jim told Verna. She made no comment.

'I – I thought you'd be glad,' he said.

'Why should I be?' Verna shrugged, walking across her living room to pour herself a Scotch. 'I've had three divorces.'

'I meant that when I'm divorced, you and I —'

'Oh, Christ!' Verna exclaimed. 'Don't tell me you're proposing?'

'We could —'

'No, we couldn't.' Her tone was firm, yet tinged with sadness. 'Maybe we could have – once. It's much too late now. We can't go back.'

'We have.'

'Sure. In bed. Where we create the illusion that we're thirty years younger.' She downed her drink. 'Beyond that? Absurd!'

'Absurd?'

'Certainly. You have – you *are* – NIPCO. That's first and foremost in your life, Jim. A wife doesn't even have a walk-on part in your script. She's a dress extra. Period. Now wait. I'm no better in my way. I have my career – and I love it. Any man I'd marry would have to be Mr Verna Fletcher, and he'd have to love *that*. You couldn't tolerate it. Not for one second.'

She shook her head and lit a cigarette.

'I told you a long time ago that you're not husband material, Jim.' She sighed. 'Besides, what could *any* wife give you that Pam hasn't – except more children? And I'm past the age for that.'

There was tenderness and understanding in her tone, but also finality. Shaken and confused, Jim said he would see Verna later and left.

He returned to his hotel. Two hours later, halfway through a bottle of Jack Daniel's, he found himself trying to sort out threads and fragments he had never really thought about before. To his dismay, he realized that he had always taken his personal life for granted. Events and people in it merely happened. And where the hell am I now, he thought, pouring another glass of whisky. I'm alone. In a hotel suite. Alone.

'Shit!'

He drank down the Jack Daniel's and hurled the empty glass at the opposite wall. It shattered, leaving a splatter of whisky stains on the wallpaper.

Verna, he thought. Then Pam. Then Verna again. Who the hell knows how many women in between? I'd have trouble even remembering most of their names. Only two ever counted for anything – and now they've both counted themselves out. I want money, power and sex, Abe Schlechter once told me. I do. And I have them. Only where does it all leave me?

The telephone rang. Scowling Jim let it ring five times before answering.

It was Sam Schlechter.

'Bill Manning phoned me from New York about an hour ago,' Schlechter said. 'He's an old friend and he quit Texaco today —'

'Jesus Christ, Sam. Tell him to get in touch with Luke or with the personnel department.' Northcutt's tone was dull, listless.

'He's not looking for a job. He gave me a tip. Texaco has been dickering for a fifty-station independent chain in New

England. The deal fell through, but the owners still want to sell. They're talking to Jersey Crest day after tomorrow. The chain would fit right in with our eastern marketing plans.'

Northcutt snapped alert.

'We'd probably have to move fast,' he said.

'Right away,' Sam agreed.

'You have the details?'

'Manning gave me most of them.'

'Great. Come right over. We'll talk – and then we can take a plane east first thing in the morning.'

Jim replaced the receiver. All thoughts of Pam and Verna had vanished. He prowled the floor impatiently, waiting for Schlechter to arrive.

9

Pamela was not vindictive and had no wish to create scandal. She obtained her divorce on grounds of mental cruelty.

Since 1950, Jim had been planning to transfer NIPCO's main offices to New York City. The company was ready to begin marketing operations along the eastern seaboard and had started a refinery in New Jersey. Now, in late 1952, Northcutt International Petroleum moved into its New York City head-quarters. Buying a townhouse on Manhattan's exclusive Sutton Place, Jim resumed his old patterns of serially monogam-ous affairs with women he installed in his home as resident mistresses.

His personal life was only incidental. He was more pre-occupied with business than ever before. The petroleum in-dustry was going through another era of drastic change.

The United States had become a net importer of oil. Foreign crude was cheaper to produce. The problem was further ag-gravated in 1950 when the United States Government entered into a secret agreement with American Majors, granting special benefits and tax advantages that made their overseas opera-tions even more profitable.

Domestic oil producers were pressing the Eisenhower Ad-ministration to restrict the importation of foreign crude. But for the time being, the President refused to take any action.

The United States continued to import low-cost foreign crude at the rate of 300,000,000 barrels a year.

Northcutt knew that he could not compete under these circumstances unless he had his own source of cheap foreign crude.

Jim urgently wanted a Middle Eastern exploration and drilling concession. But he and NIPCO were latecomers. Virtually all crude reserves and production in Asia Minor were monopolized by eight multi-national Majors. Six were American: Standard of New Jersey, Standard of California, Gulf, Texaco, Mobil and Jersey Crest. The two others were British Petroleum and Royal Dutch Shell. There were only two exceptions. American Independent Oil Company – Aminoil – and Pacific Western Oil.

Pacific Western Oil – PacWest – had acquired the Saudi Arabian half of the concession. PacWest belonged to independent oilman J. Paul Getty, and this greatly encouraged Northcutt.

'By God, if Paul can do it, so can we,' he told Sam Schlechter.

'Maybe,' Sam said. 'But do you really want to get involved in the Middle Eastern mess? It's mayhem. Always has been.'

'We have no choice. Unless we get low-cost Middle Eastern oil, sooner or later NIPCO won't be able to stay in the running.'

Northcutt asked the NIPCO research department to prepare a short history of Middle Eastern oil concessions for him. Copies of this résumé were on Jim's desk when he spoke with Sam Schlechter a few days later.

'Here's the bare-bones outline,' he said, handing Sam a copy. 'Let's start with this, then decide what more information we'll want.' He picked up another copy and his grey eyes were intent as they scanned the top sheet. The items on it were datelined and gave only key highlights.

1901–9:
Britain, through intrigue and the bribery of Middle Eastern rulers, obtains pre-eminent position throughout region.

1910:
America's Standard seeks foothold in Middle East. Its principal representative/agent is Rear Admiral Colby M. Chester,

USN (retired), former US Ambassador to Turkey. Chester, employing bribes – and, according to various versions, blackmail and similar tactics – obtains the concession for all oil rights in entire Turkish Empire. But Standard loses concession as the result of British diplomatic and other pressures against Turkish Government.

' "Diplomatic and other pressures," ' Schlechter said. 'That's a prize understatement.'

'It is,' Jim agreed. 'If I remember my oil history, British Intelligence assassinated two Turkish officials and framed several others in one way or another to force their resignation. Cost the British plenty in the long run, though. That operation was one of the reasons why Turkey hated Britain and threw in with the Germans in the First World War.'

'I just composed an adage,' Schlechter said. 'Wars run on oil and oil runs wars. How's that?'

'Not good – but far too right for comfort.'

They resumed their reading.

1914:
British Navy has begun converting from coal to oil. War in Europe seems imminent. British Government buys large interest in Anglo-Persian Oil Company, finances huge expansion in Persian fields. Winston Churchill states that Middle Eastern oil is identified with British national interests, thereby formally committing Britain to employ all diplomatic and military resources in support of further expansion of private British oil companies in Asia Minor. Conversely, these oil companies now have important voice in shaping British Government policy. It may be argued convincingly that from this time forward, oil becomes the major factor in all international relations.

1920:
Great Britain, France, Italy, Greece and Belgium sign treaty in San Remo, Italy, apportioning all Middle Eastern oil rights between Britain and France. San Remo Treaty gives League of Nations mandates over Iraq and Palestine to Great Britain, over Syria and Lebanon to France. Secret agreement between signatories gives all oil rights in former Turkish Empire to the Turkish Petroleum Company, controlled by the two royal

families and governments of England and Holland and the French Government.

San Remo Treaty also effectively nullifies the 1917 Balfour Declaration which guaranteed the establishment of a national homeland for Jewish people in Palestine. The British Prime Minister argued that implementation of the Balfour Declaration could anger Palestinian Arabs and hinder development of Mid-east oil resources. United States is completely shut out of Middle Eastern oil fields and, not having joined League of Nations, is unable to have San Remo Treaty amended or prevent its ratification.

'Britain and France sold everybody out at San Remo,' Jim commented. 'The Turks, Jews and Uncle Sam got the shortest end of the stick, though.'

'After five thousand years, a minor setback,' Sam grinned. 'We Jews are persistent as hell. The Zionists kept plugging away.' He glanced at the papers in his hand. 'We're up to 1921. That's when you started wildcatting, isn't it, Jim?'

'Yep, and I wasn't thinking about any international treaties. My horizons didn't extend beyond the boundaries of a six-hundred-and-forty-acre lease in Oklahoma.'

1921:
US begins making diplomatic protests over San Remo Treaty to Britain and France, the principal signatories. The protests are rejected or ignored.

1922–6:
US continues and increases fruitless diplomatic pressures against Britain and France over San Remo Treaty. Secretary of Commerce Herbert Hoover, as champion of US oil companies, formulates radical plan to break impasse. He prevails on President Coolidge to threaten to send US marines to Middle East if American companies are not allowed to participate in oil concessions.

'I remember hearing about that,' Jim said. 'Hoover, Coolidge and the Majors were even willing to risk a shooting war with Britain and France – at a time when we were producing more than seventy per cent of the world's oil.'

'They got swindled,' Schlechter said.

'Royally screwed, Sam. But what the hell, outsmarting Silent Cal and Herbert Hoover was no great trick. And the Majors were so greedy, they walked right into the trap.'

1928:
Britain and France make show of yielding to US demands by forming the Iraq Petroleum Company but give a consortium of five American oil firms less than a quarter interest. They are: Standard of New Jersey, Standard of New York, Gulf, Atlantic and Pan-American.

However, in return for their share in the Iraq concession, all five companies are required to sign the 'Red Line Agreement'. None may explore for oil anywhere in Asia Minor save for two exceptions: Bahrain and Kuwait. According to stories still current in the industry, these were omitted from the Red Line Agreement because British and French legal experts were referring to out-dated maps when drawing up the agreement. These maps did not show Bahrain and Kuwait as separate entities and thus they were not included.

By binding US oil companies to an agreement which greatly restricts their operations, the Iraq Petroleum Company is acting as an instrumentality of the British and French Governments, safeguarding their national interests. This, in turn, makes the British and French Governments instrumentalities of Iraq Petroleum in that they will enforce the provisions of the Red Line Agreement.

'Nobody could tell where Iraq Petroleum stopped and Whitehall and the Quai d'Orsay began – or vice versa,' Northcutt said.

'*Imperium in imperico*,' Schlechter grunted.

'That's about it.'

1933:
The Red Line Agreement is abrogated. The era of US Majors' domination of Mid-east exploration and production may be said to start in this year, when Standard of California obtains a Saudi Arabian concession that covers 400,000 square miles of land. Standard of California pays King Ibn Saud an initial cash consideration of $170,000. Saudi Arabia is to receive royalties on all oil produced under a complicated formula. In actual practice, at the beginning these royalty payments prove

to be less than 15 per cent of the concessionaire company's net profits.

'Those were the days,' Jim mused aloud. 'The Arabs were glad to take pennies for their concessions and willing to settle for almost any royalty payments. They ran between twelve and eighteen cents a barrel.'

'You won't find bargains like that any more,' Schlechter said. 'The Arabs have got a lot smarter.'

'The Majors haven't, though. They still have taxi-meter mentalities, thinking in nickels and dimes. No wonder the Arabs keep asking for more, and they'll keep on doing it. In the long run, the big companies are going to wish they'd given those countries a fairer slice of the profits.'

Cash payments for concessions had spiralled higher and higher over the years. Initial considerations were figured in the millions. Royalty payments had also gone up – to 25 per cent of the net profit, plus many fringe considerations. Northcutt felt certain all would go even higher.

He had resolved that if he obtained a concession in the Middle East, he would start off on a much more liberal basis. He planned to share profits fifty-fifty with the host country. He believed this would insure the future of the concession.

1936:
Standard Oil of California, holding Saudi Arabian concession, forms the Arabian American Oil Company (ARAMCO). A year later, Texaco buys a half-interest in ARAMCO. Eventually, this vastly rich company will be owned by four US Majors: Standard of California, Standard of New Jersey, Texaco and Mobil. ARAMCO itself is strictly an oil-producing company. The shipping, refining and marketing of all crude produced by ARAMCO in Saudi Arabia are handled by separate partner-companies within ARAMCO.

1939:
Outbreak of World War Two halts Middle Eastern expansion programmes.

1941–3:
Saudi Arabia, becoming aware of its commercial and strategic importance, demands that US Government make cash com-

pensation for loss of oil revenue due to wartime suspension of production. When Washington hesitates, British Government provides King Ibn Saud with funds on tacit understanding that ARAMCO concession will be given to British companies after the war.

While Britain tries to steal US concessions in Saudi Arabia, we try to take over British oil in Iran. United States sends troops and military, police and civilian advisors to Iran. Officially, they are there to expedite and protect American Lend–Lease shipments to Russia. Actually, this is all-out attempt to influence the Iranian Government and persuade it to switch oil concessions from British-owned Anglo-Iranian Oil to consortium of American Majors.

US Government is made aware of Britain's growing influence in Saudi Arabia. ARAMCO representatives demand that Administration intervene. President Roosevelt agrees and orders that Saudi Arabia be made a recipient of Lend–Lease aid. US eventually pours more than $100 million into Saudi Arabia for only effective purpose of protecting ARAMCO concession.

1944:
Harold B. Hoskins, President Roosevelt's representative to an Anglo-American conference on petroleum concessions, recommends to Roosevelt that US actively oppose all Zionist claims to Palestine. This, Hoskins says, will engender friendship of Arab countries. Secretary of State Cordell Hull concurs.

Roosevelt instructs the State Department to inform all Arab diplomats that the United States will not support Zionist aspirations. America will work to maintain the status quo in Palestine as an inducement for Arab countries to permit increased exploration and drilling by US oil companies after war ends.

Roosevelt personally tells Ibn Saud: 'I am essentially a businessman, and as a businessman I am very much interested in Saudi Arabia.' Reportedly, he also gives Saud assurances on the Zionist question.

'Ibn Saud sent Roosevelt a pair of white Arabian horses – and FDR was ready to sell the Jews of Europe down the river for them,' Jim said. 'How many people know that – or would believe it if you told them, Sam?'

'Not many Jews, I'm afraid.' Schlechter shook his head. 'They believed in Roosevelt.'

1948–9:
AMINOIL, a consortium of ten US oil companies, obtains Kuwait's undivided half of Neutral Zone concession. Pacific Western Oil Company (owned by Getty interests) obtains Saudi Arabia's undivided half of Neutral Zone concession.

1953:
Discovery-well completed in Neutral Zone. Crude oil reserves in place are conservatively estimated at 11 billion barrels as Neutral Zone is proven to have five pay zones.

'What's left in the Middle East?' Sam asked, studying a map of the region open on Jim's desk.

'Not much,' Northcutt conceded. 'The Majors have got an almost total monopoly on two-thirds of the oil reserves known to exist outside the Communist bloc. On the other hand, if Paul Getty and PacWest were able to open up an eleven-billion-barrel field two years ago, there may still be something left. I'll have to take a close look out there for myself.'

'Don't get your hopes up too high.'

'God damn it, Sam, I have to keep up my hopes,' Northcutt said. 'ARAMCO is lifting oil for ten, twelve cents a barrel in Saudi Arabia. It's got wells with twelve, fifteen thousand barrels a day *settled* production. They're making fifty cents a barrel profit. On a fifteen-thousand-barrel well, that is almost three million dollars a year. From a single well, Sam!'

'What can I say? If you want to go out to the Middle East and start hunting for concessions, take off. I'll stay here and mind the store.'

The emirate of Qantara is a two-thousand-square-mile island located in the Persian Gulf. In 1955, it had an illiterate and ill-fed population of 175,000 that was largely nomadic and eked out a bare existence from arid land.

Qantara had been surveyed by several large oil companies. Their verdict was unanimous. There was no oil.

Arriving in Ayat, Qantara's capital, Jim made his own survey. He had his pilot fly him over various parts of the island at low altitudes during the next few days.

He studied the terrain. His old instincts were awakened. Creekology told him the geologists and geophysicists were wrong. The topography of Qantara fitted no textbook description of oil-bearing land, but then neither had the Peavey property or many others on which he'd drilled by hunch and struck oil. More overflights convinced him. The island was a freak, but the terrain contours somehow reminded him of the Red Beds area of Oklahoma. For years, oilmen had avoided the Red Beds area because of unanimous opinion that it could not possibly be oil-bearing. Then someone had drilled – and opened up a rich new field. Now Jim's responses were strong – and familiar.

He returned to Kuwait and cabled Sam Schlechter.

'CROTCH TWITCHED AT 500 FEET OPEN NEGOTIATIONS SOONEST'

Schlechter could not conduct the negotiations personally. The Emir of Qantara – like almost all Arab rulers – refused to have dealings with businessmen of the Jewish faith. Sam designated one of his senior partners to open conversations with the Emir. A seasoned attorney, he was impeccably Gentile.

Two months later, NIPCO had the concession for all of Qantara.

Late in 1955, Jim Northcutt called Sam Schlechter into his office.

'Sam,' he said, when Schlechter had seated himself, 'do you remember that property I was planning to build on, the one near Cap d'Antibes? Well, I'm ready to start now. I'll have a house, and it'll be my personal headquarters.'

'You'll live abroad?'

'It's the ideal answer. I'll be midway between the States and Qantara. We'll find a good man to be president of NIPCO and run things from New York. But I'll still be giving the final orders. I own the majority of NIPCO stock. What I say goes, whether I say it in the boardroom or over a transatlantic telephone.'

Northcutt grinned.

'Besides, you'll be here, Sam. It's as you said when I went to Qantara. You'll be minding the store.'

11

Jim and his ex-wife Pamela communicated regularly, but almost exclusively in regard to their daughter Kathy. Pam had remarried in 1960 and was happy with her new husband. She had legal custody of Kathy, who lived with her most of the year in California. But Pamela placed no restrictions on Kathy's visits to her father and usually complied with any wishes or suggestions Jim made concerning the girl. She agreed in 1962 when he asked that Kathy be allowed to spend a year in an exclusive French finishing school.

Kathy was delighted, not only because she liked the idea of going to school in France but because she was able to spend much of her free time with her father.

'You get a kick out of being here at Bonheur,' Jim observed to Kathy one weekend.

'I get a kick out of watching you operate,' she said. 'You're not afraid to take on anybody – but in your own way, you're just as ruthless as any of them.'

Her father laughed.

'Have to be, Kath,' he said. 'Money and the milk of human kindness don't mix very well.'

'I know,' Kathy said. 'The meek don't inherit much, do they, Dad?'

He changed the subject to one that had been on his mind for several months. He wanted Kathy to attend Vassar after leaving the French school.

'No,' she shook her head. 'I've already decided on Bryn Mawr.'

'Why?'

'Suppose I said it's just because I like the name?'

Northcutt frowned but said nothing. Kathy had served notice that she had a mind of her own, and, when she wished, would make her own decisions. Even if – as he suspected – she had only chosen Bryn Mawr on the spur of the moment to prove her independence.

The first warnings of approaching oil shortages could be detected in 1970. Latin American and Middle Eastern oil-producing countries were voicing demands for larger shares of the profits earned by concessionaire companies, who resisted stubbornly. Privately, their executives argued that the host countries were already enjoying enormous revenues, and so it seemed at first glance. In 1971, Venezuela received $1·76 billion. Saudi Arabia's oil revenues topped $2·2 billion, with the total for all Persian Gulf countries and Libya topping $10 billion.

On the other hand, the Majors were eager to raise their refined-products prices in the United States. This, despite gasoline surpluses so great that many retailers were offering gift premiums and trading stamps to motorists. Some even temporarily ignored the one-cent differential agreement and lowered their retail prices.

There was widespread agitation in all industrial and manufacturing sectors to eliminate or drastically revise environmental control laws. Factory owners and utilities companies balked at being ordered to burn low-sulphur – and thus higher-priced – oil. Coal mining companies rebelled at laws requiring them to restore lands made useless by strip-mining operations. The Majors demanded the relaxation of laws and regulations governing oil and gas exploration and development, the building of pipelines and the construction of refineries and deep-water terminals.

'There is no real shortage, but the various factors at work are on a collision course,' James Northcutt predicted.

By early 1973, the shortage was beginning to take form. Sensing America's economic uncertainty, the Middle Eastern oil-producing nations seized the initiative.

The United States obtained 4·2 per cent of its oil from Libya. The price of Libyan oil had already jumped from $2.90 to $4.90 a barrel, but now Libyan strongman Muammar Qaddafii nationalized all foreign oil companies operating in his country. Saudi Arabia, having bought a 25 per cent share of ARAMCO, thereby becoming a senior partner in the company, indicated it would soon want no less than 51 per cent. The other Arab countries were following suit.

All, that is, but the emirate of Qantara.

James Northcutt had given the Qantara Government a 50 per cent share of profits from the concession from the very start. Qantara made only minor demands.

'They want us to build a new hospital in Ayat and give our Qantara employees a ten per cent wage boost,' Mark Radford, the resident manager in Qantara, reported to Northcutt. 'The Emir is merely saving face, showing that he can crack the whip, too.'

'It's a hell of a lot more reasonable than the wholesale black-mail other companies have to put up with these days,' Jim said. 'Build the hospital and put through the raise – across the board and retroactive for six months.'

The entire Middle Eastern situation exploded in October 1973, when Egypt and Syria attacked Israel. During the Suez Crisis conflict of 1956, Jim had seen Israel as a low-cost police force, whose victory would benefit oil interests. As long as the Arabs had Israel to worry about, they would not be thinking about nationalizing oil-company properties. His observations during the Six-Day War of 1967 had confirmed this feeling.

Now, the United States sent Israel arms and supplies. Russia furnished the Arabs with weapons that were superior in quality and quantity. Neither side won a clear-cut victory, but for the first time the Arab forces had not suffered defeat at the hands of the Israelis and had retaken much territory they had lost previously.

To the Arab world, this was victory, and the Arab oil-producing countries embargoed oil sales to nations they felt were giving material or moral support to Israel. The embargo against the United States was total – with a single exception. The Emir of Qantara refused to join in the boycott. NIPCO continued to produce and ship Qantara crude.

James Northcutt saw beyond the immediate effects of the Arab action. He called Sam Schlechter, Peter Keeley and Mark

Radford to Bonheur for a strategy meeting.

'The Majors are going to use the embargo as a pretext to claim there is an oil famine,' he predicted. 'The United States obtains eleven per cent of its crude from the Middle East and Libya. The gap could be closed by increased domestic production and larger imports of oil from Canada and Latin America, but it won't be.'

'No, it won't,' Peter Keeley agreed. 'The public will be made to swallow the doomsday shortage-stories fed out to it. The Majors are going to blow the eleven per cent shortfall into a full-scale crisis. They want higher prices, bigger tax breaks and an end to environmental control laws – among other things. They'll keep the shortage real enough until they get what they want.'

'Where does it leave us?' Mark Radford asked.

'In fine shape,' Northcutt grinned. 'You push Qantara production to the limit, Mark. We'll have a terrific competitive advantage. NIPCO sales and profits will shoot sky-high.'

Events after the fall of 1973 proved Northcutt right and Peter Keeley's estimates of major-company motives and intentions accurate. One after another, the governments of countries crippled by fuel shortages acceded to the demands of the petroleum industry's giant corporations.

Verna Fletcher paid an unannounced visit to Bonheur in March 1966. Jim was highly pleased. He was astounded to find that she looked like a woman in her mid-fifties instead of sixties. He complimented her and she credited the phenomenon to the Niehans cellular therapy clinic in Switzerland.

'I've been taking the Niehans treatments for years.'

'Something else we have in common,' Jim told her. 'So have I.'

'Obviously,' Verna grinned. She had been introduced to Northcutt's current mistress, an attractive dark-haired young woman who appeared sleek and content.

After dinner, Jim and Verna went to his study, where they drank Jack Daniel's, reminisced and grew mellow.

'Not at all like the kitchen of my place in Logan,' Verna said, raising her glass. 'Funny how easy it is to look back at it now that I'm rich, retired and don't give a damn.'

They drank.

'You know, we're still partners in a sense,' Verna said. 'I

bought ten thousand shares of NIPCO stock once. I've hung on to it.'

'I've still got this.' Jim took the gusher charm from his watch pocket and held it up. 'It brought me a lot of luck.'

Verna finished her whisky and shook her head.

'Not in your marriage.'

Northcutt replaced the charm and filled their glasses.

'Hell you say. I got Kathy out of my marriage. She's quite a girl – and I'll drink to that.'

'I've never met your daughter,' Verna said. 'I've seen photographs of her, though. She's lovely, but there's a lot of you in her.'

'Hope so.'

'A female James Northcutt,' Verna mused aloud, sipping whisky. 'Now there's something to challenge the imagination.'

'Sure is,' Northcutt chuckled.

'I pity the men on the receiving end,' Verna smiled.

'Including me?'

'Nope. She's probably the only women who's ever been able to handle you, my friend – and you love it.'

Jim cocked his head to one side. His expression was quizzical.

'Y'know, there's a question I've wanted to ask you since God knows when. You were married three times. How is it you never had any kids?'

Verna emptied her glass, stared into it.

'I couldn't. Ever.'

Northcutt blinked.

'Is that why . . .'

'Why I wouldn't marry you, even way back when?'

She held out her glass. He filled it and his own.

'Uh-huh,' Verna said. 'That was the main reason, Jim.'

They were silent for a long minute. Then Jim spoke.

'Why don't we get drunk?' he asked.

'Why the hell don't we do just that, partner,' Verna said and felt very old.

12

When the First Energy Crisis tapered off, James Northcutt saw a chance to achieve the greatest success of his career. In China.

The limitless potential of China as an oil producer had been long known. During World War Two, the US State Department acknowledged the country's importance in a petroleum-policy paper, stating: 'In China there are great possibilities for the postwar period.'

President Roosevelt sent Patrick Hurley to China as his political representative. Hurley was a leading corporation lawyer who represented American multi-national oil companies. He sought to obtain Chinese oil concessions for American Majors from Chiang Kai-shek. Reportedly, he acquired them, but Chiang was driven from the Chinese mainland by Mao Tse-tung's Communist armies.

During 1973, the Chinese People's Republic demonstrated it had begun to develop its petroleum reserves by selling 8 million barrels of crude to Japan. Thereafter, the Peking Government realized oil could be a most lucrative source of foreign exchange and decided to drill more wells, build modern refineries and construct petrochemical plants. China put out feelers indicating it would welcome co-operation from Western free enterprise in developing its reserves.

American and British Majors ignored Peking's overtures. They were steeped in the belief that 'Red China could not be trusted' and feared adverse public reaction if they dealt with Maoist China.

James L. Northcutt had neither prejudices nor fears. He went to Peking, as he said, 'Like any good salesman chasing a hot prospect.' A bluff entrepreneurial realist who talked facts and figures, Northcutt won the confidence of Chinese officials. Accompanied by NIPCO engineers and other specialists, he shuttled back and forth between Bonheur and Peking. An agreement began to take shape.

NIPCO would explore, drill, open up new fields and produce oil and also build and initially operate refineries and petrochemical plants. The company would receive fees plus a share of the crude oil and natural gas produced during the first ten years. The arrangement would be worth some $8 billion to NIPCO over a decade.

Because NIPCO was an American company, agreements required US Government approval. This approval was pending when the Arab oil-producing countries imposed a new oil embargo on the West and the Second World Energy Crisis developed. It was then that petroleum industry Majors finally awakened to the realization that China was the richest oil prize left in the world. And, they were in danger of having it taken from them by an upstart independent.

Powell Pierce of Jersey Crest Oil took the initiative. He prevailed on two other large companies to join forces with Jersey Crest and wage an all-out war against James Northcutt and NIPCO.

The other Majors were content to have the three companies obtain the Chinese agreements. All would be satisfied by what they viewed as their consolation prize. The renegade wildcatter Jim Northcutt and his company had defied them all for more than fifty years. Now, at last, both would be annihilated.

BOOK FOUR

1

13 July

It was past 3 A.M. when a green Ford Torino drove into the Kenwood Parking Garage and Service Station on Forty-eighth Street between First and Second Avenues. It pulled up in front of the twin pumps emblazoned with 'NIPpy, The Power-Packed Wildcat' trademarks.

Two men got out of the Torino. The driver was thickset, his companion more slender and somewhat taller.

'Morning gents,' John Laskowski, the night attendant, said as he came out of the cubicle office to wait on them.

'Got gas to sell?' the thickset man asked.

'Sure.'

'Great. Fill the tank and park this heap for a few hours. My friend and I are going to see a couple of broads who live around the corner.'

'I'll have to give you a claim slip,' John Laskowski said and started back towards the office.

'We got no time,' the taller man said.

'Mister, I have to give you a claim check.'

'Hold it, you!' The order was harsh, menacing.

Stick-up, Laskowski thought, halting in his tracks. He started to raise his hands. 'Dough's in the register,' he said over his shoulder. 'Help yourself. It ain't locked —'

Both men hit him at once. The first drove a brass-knuckled fist against the side of his head. The other rabbit-punched him. Laskowski tried to shout for help, but his voice was choked off. He slumped to the concrete floor of the garage. The men stood over him and kicked his head until certain he was unconscious. Then they turned and left.

The block was deserted at that hour. The men walked rapidly to Second Avenue and stood on the corner for a few seconds. A black Buick materialized and drew over to the kerb. They got into it, and the car drove off.

Five minutes later, the incendiary device in the back seat of the green Torino ignited. The Ford's gasoline tank blew up, and the fuel tanks of the thirty or so other cars parked in the

Kenwood Garage began exploding one after another. Mercifully, John Laskowski did not regain consciousness as flaming gasoline enveloped his body and burned him to death.

Mark Radford was told of the Kenwood Garage fire when he arrived at his office in the NIPCO Building. By then, police and fire department officials were being quoted as saying that 'arson was suspected'. No authorities had yet sought to look behind the 'strange coincidences' of NIPCO-brand service stations in various eastern states. Evidently, law-enforcement agencies preferred to believe the fires were unconnected.

Mark telephoned Robert di Lorenzi.

'Come up here as soon as possible, Bob.'

di Lorenzi arrived with his bodyguards, who waited in the anteroom. Mark and his visitor then closeted themselves in Mark's private office.

'Another one, practically on our doorstep,' Radford said.

'I laid it all out for you day before yesterday,' di Lorenzi shrugged. 'We know Jersey Crest is paying Charles Farrier and his mob to torch your dealers' stations. Let my outfit give some Jersey Crest dealers the same treatment. Then maybe this Powell Pierce character will call Farrier off.'

'No go.' Mark shook his head. 'Pierce won't quit and Jersey Crest's too big. All we'd have is leapfrog escalation. We don't want that if there's another alternative, and I think there is.'

'I'm listening.'

'Suppose a key man is removed?'

'Who?'

'Charles Farrier.'

There was a moment's silence. Robert di Lorenzi's face was impassive, but he was thinking.

'It can be done,' he said at last. 'Only it'll be expensive. Hit men won't move against a *capo* like Farrier unless they get twenty, twenty-five thousand apiece. We'd probably need four, five guys.'

'All right,' Mark said without hesitation. James Northcutt had given him full authority and set no limits on costs.

'One other thing, Mark. I got my word from Steve Kostis: You people are to have anything you want as long as you pay the going rates. All the same, you're civilians outside the – hell, why crap around? – outside the rackets. My men get nervous doing big jobs for civilians. They'd want some extra insurance – like having you come along for the hit.'

'I expected that,' Radford said, taking a deep breath. 'If I'm there, I'm an accomplice. No danger of my blowing any whistles. Okay, Bob. Tell me where and when.'

'Stay near a telephone for the next few days,' di Lorenzi said. 'Call my office and leave numbers where I can reach you in a hurry.'

Powell Pierce's manner was distant when he told Guy Bannister to sit down.

'You said you wished to see me urgently, Bannister.'

'My sub-contractors stepped up their operations, Mr Pierce. They're asking for the higher fees they were promised.'

Pierce compressed his lips.

'Your firm, Federpol, is deep in debt to this company,' he said.

Guy Bannister swallowed. He had sent Russell Peterson, an employee he believed completely reliable, to Zurich. Peterson had drawn a million dollars from a secret Jersey Crest account and vanished.

'We'll find Peterson and the money soon,' Bannister said. Charles Farrier's European associates were tracking Peterson down.

'Then you'll have no problems,' Powell Pierce said. 'But until the money is returned, you'll simply have to pay the sub-contractors from your own funds. Don't forget, Bannister, I've been forced to send one of my own men to Zurich for another million dollars. I'm not especially pleased with your performance. Now, if you'll excuse me.'

When a worried and shaken Guy Bannister departed, Pierce told a secretary to call Arthur Gerlach in Washington. Russell Peterson's disappearance had left Pierce no option but to establish direct contact with the chief presidential advisor. He had done that the previous day. Another call would provide additional mutual reassurance. Pierce needed full co-operation from the Administration if his campaign against Northcutt International Petroleum was to succeed. Gerlach, on the other hand, wanted to be certain of receiving his promised bribe.

'My personal representative will be in Washington to see you tomorrow,' he told Gerlach. 'I trust your plans remain unchanged.'

'They're the same as they have been,' Arthur Gerlach said. 'Secretary Engelhardt will be on television tomorrow night. He'll talk about the fuel shortage in general – and about certain independent operators in particular.'

'Excellent,' Jersey Crest's Board Chairman said.

James Northcutt was in his office suite before 9 A.M. His mood was remarkably energetic and enthusiastic. It had to be, he told himself. He had played a colossal bluff by ordering a 10 per cent increase in fuel allocations to dealers and distributors. With Qantara knocked out by industrial sabotage, NIPCO's flow of crude was 25 per cent below refinery requirements. Unless the shortfall was made up – and then some – NIPCO's above-ground crude reserves would be soon depleted. Northcutt believed he might have found ways to obtain what his company needed. At 9.05 A.M., he began summoning executives to his office.

'Get me a report before noon on all tankers available for charter in the Persian Gulf,' he told one astounded vice-president.

'But, J.L., our Qantara installations aren't operating —'

'God damn it, just do as you're told!'

Robert Binnig, the regimental-moustached vice-president in charge of advertising, was next.

'Start a saturation campaign – today, if you can work the necessary miracles,' Northcutt said. 'Buy newspaper space and radio and TV spots. Beat the drums about how NIPCO has increased its gasoline and fuel allocations. Now tell Harold Elbert to come in.'

Harold Elbert, administrative assistant to the president of NIPCO, had stayed on after Peter Keeley's forced resignation.

'Take down a shopping list,' Northcutt instructed. 'I want every item bought or contracted for by five this afternoon.'

Elbert produced a memo pad and pen.

'Twelve Cadillac limousines,' Northcutt began. 'The most expensive models loaded with every extra in the manufacturer's catalogue. They're to be identical in everything but colour. Get the widest possible range there. No two colours alike. It should be easy. Caddy dealers are overstocked on limousines because of the fuel shortage.'

'We're buying them retail?' Elbert asked, his eyes widening.

'Hell, yes. We want instant delivery. The cars have to be

ready for air shipment abroad in forty-eight hours.'

Elbert blinked and nodded uncertainly.

'Then call Lionel or whatever company it is that had the world's biggest and fanciest model-train layout at the last Frankfurt and Milan trade fairs,' the oilman went on. 'Buy it.'

'The electric train set?' Elbert asked in dismay.

'I imagine it'll cost around a hundred thousand bucks, but don't argue over price. We'll need their schematics and one of their people who can travel at our expense to set the thing up.'

Northcutt's eyes were gleaming.

'Get in touch with the guy in charge of foreign franchises for Coca-Cola. We want the franchise for Qantara. We'll pay any price. We'll also want a commitment for construction of a complete bottling plant there. A letter of agreement should be drawn up right away. Sam Schlechter will check with you later today about the details.'

That was the last item. Once outside Northcutt's office, Harold Elbert stared at his notes. A round dozen Cadillac limousines. A $100,000 toy train set. A Coca-Cola franchise and bottling plant.

James L. Northcutt had gone stark, raving mad.

Samuel Schlechter was grim when he came to see Northcutt before noon.

'Barbara Wallace's lawyer, Dwight Farquhar, didn't wait out the week he promised to give me,' Schlechter announced. 'He delivered Barbara's ultimatum. She wants a third of your NIPCO stock —'

'What?' Northcutt roared, half-rising from his chair.

'For God's sake, calm down and listen. I said she wants a third of your stock. Otherwise, she goes to the Inland Revenue Service and gets you indicted for tax fraud.'

Jim Northcutt's face was livid.

'The bitch is insane!'

'Easy, Jim. You paid her personal bills and those of other women out of corporate funds. I warned you about doing that over the years, but we won't go into it at this late date. The fact remains, it *is* fraud. There's no question but that the government would bring criminal charges against you and make them stick. After that, you'd have a flood of minority stockholder suits. Take my word, with all our other problems, Barbara Wallace could prove to be a fatal blow to you and NIPCO.'

'It's not Barbara who's insane!' Northcutt shouted. 'It's you, Sam! Jesus Christ, a third of my holdings!'

'Damn it,' Schlechter snapped. 'That's her demand. I asked Farquhar if it was negotiable. Naturally, he said no – but of course it is. Everything in the world is negotiable.'

'I won't give Barbara a share of stock or another dime!'

'I doubt if her demands are *that* negotiable,' Sam said drily. 'You'll probably wind up having to pay her a fortune.'

'The hell I will.' Northcutt chewed his lower lip. 'What did you tell this Farquhar?'

'That I'd confer with you and talk to him again in a few days.'

'Can he be bought off?'

'For what purpose? Barbara would only retain another attorney or march straight over to the I.R.S. No, Jim. We have to make her an initial counteroffer and start bargaining.'

'There must be another out.'

'Not any I can see short of murder,' Schlechter said glumly. To his astonishment, Northcutt suddenly seemed to shift into an almost ebullient mood.

'We'll discuss it later. I want you to see Harold Elbert.' Jim had thrust Barbara Wallace from his mind for the moment. No matter what Schlechter thought, he would find some means of silencing her – without a payoff.

'Why Elbert of all people?' Schlechter asked.

'Let him tell you – if he's not in a state of complete shock. I've been pissing away more of the company's money, Sam.'

Once leaked, corporate secrets spread rapidly.

Powell Pierce had told three of his executives that Federpol's Russell Peterson was missing, along with a million dollars in Jersey Crest funds. Perhaps one of them talked. Possibly it was a Federpol secretary who talked out of turn. Whatever the transmission routes, the tale reached Mark Radford via Ned Winters, a friend who worked for Mobiloil.

'You heard the latest making the rounds about how Jersey Crest was taken for a bundle?' Ned asked during a phone conversation.

'No, but I'd like to,' Mark said, sharply alert. Any gossip concerning Jersey Crest was of interest.

'Seems they hired some agency to send a guy to Switzerland on one of those draw-out-cash-and-launder-it errands. Two million, as I hear it. The guy got the money and took a walk.'

'That is funny,' Radford said, with an artificially casual chuckle. 'They got the posses out after him?'

'Nope. That's the biggest laugh. Nobody ever can in deals like this. Jersey Crest would have too much explaining to do about how the money got to Switzerland in the first place and what they were going to do with it.'

Mark sensed that the morsel of gossip was worth very thorough investigation. He spent almost two hours calling men he knew in the oil business and other fields. When he was finished he had most of the picture pieced together. It was sufficiently startling for him to arrange a conference with Northcutt, Schlechter and Robert di Lorenzi for the following morning.

2

14 July

It was the first time James Northcutt or Samuel Schlechter had met Robert di Lorenzi.

'Let me start by thanking you for your help,' Northcutt said.'

'It's cash and carry, Mr Northcutt,' di Lorenzi smiled. 'If you owe any thanks, they're to Steve Kostis.' His smile turned to a look of surprise as he saw Northcutt take a sack of Bull Durham from his desk drawer and start rolling a cigarette.

'A lost art,' Jim grinned. 'You do the talking, Mark.'

Radford leaned forward and recounted what he'd learned from Ned Winters the day before.

'I checked further,' he went on. 'From what I was able to gather, Federpol – that's Bannister's so-called industrial public relations agency – sent a man named Peterson to Zurich on the tenth or eleventh of this month. He was to pick up some Jersey Crest money. There's disagreement about how much. Versions vary from one to three million.'

He drew hard on his Salem.

'Supposedly, Peterson picked up the money —'

'And kept on going with it?' di Lorenzi interjected.

Radford nodded. 'He and his wife have both vanished.'

'Bannister has Charles Farrier's European buddies hunting for Peterson,' Robert di Lorenzi said.

'You know this?' Northcutt asked, his eyebrow slanting high.

'It's an educated guess,' di Lorenzi replied. 'This bird Peterson doesn't have much to worry about if he's careful. The connections Farrier has in Europe aren't very good.'

'How about yours?' Sam Schlechter inquired.

'Mine are,' di Lorenzi said, 'and Steve Kostis's are even better.'

'Do you think they could find Peterson and his wife?' Mark asked.

'If they're in Europe and still alive, I'll guarantee they can. I take it you want them found.'

'They're to be treated with kid gloves,' Jim Northcutt said. 'I'd like to have them convinced that Bannister and Pierce want them killed.'

'They probably do,' di Lorenzi declared. 'Farrier's contacts must have orders to recover the money and get rid of the Petersons.'

'We're prepared to offer Peterson all the protection and support he might need,' Schlechter said.

'In return for what?' di Lorenzi asked, his eyes shrewd.

'Everything he can tell us about Bannister, Jersey Crest, Powell Pierce and their operations,' Sam replied.

'What about the money?'

'Peterson can keep it all,' Northcutt said. 'I'm not in business to hire skip-tracers for Powell Pierce or collect Jersey Crest's accounts receivable.'

As the meeting ended, di Lorenzi gave Mark a hard look. 'Where will you be around ten-thirty, eleven tonight?'

'At my hotel. Why?'

'There's a one-in-three chance we may get moving on Charles Farrier tonight. The odds are we'll draw a blank, but be ready to jump if I call you.'

Mark ran his tongue over his lips and nodded. di Lorenzi stood up, ready to leave.

'You told Northcutt you'll be going along when we hit Farrier?' he asked.

'Hell, no,' Radford replied. 'I haven't even told him it might happen.'

'Jesus Christ! Why not?'

'Should be obvious. The fewer people who know, the happier we'll all be. And that includes James L. Northcutt.'

Kathy Northcutt and Mark Radford had an early dinner and then went to his suite at the Drake. They had an hour in which to make love before Energy Resources Secretary Rowan Engelhardt's 8.30 television address to the nation, which they both wanted to see and hear.

Kathy and Mark sat propped up in bed watching the television screen. Rowan Engelhardt, dressed in a dark suit and an aura of sincerity, epitomized the high-ranking bureaucrat. He opened his talk with a candid admission that the latest energy crisis was worsening and went on to outline the immediate measures being taken by the Administration.

'... as before when we faced a serious energy crunch, certain restrictions will be enforced by the federal government. These will insure a more equitable distribution of the energy resources at the nation's disposal...'

Mark ruffled Kathy's copper-coloured hair with one hand. 'You'd almost think he believed what he was saying,' he muttered. Kathy laughed and moved closer to him.

'This Administration's long-range programme will make the United States entirely self-sufficient in the production of energy sources within a decade,' Rowan Engelhardt's precisely modulated voice declared.

'First, it will remove all restrictions on the price of fuels of every kind. Fuel producers must receive a fair return on their investments in order that they may expand and increase their production.

'Second environmental control laws must be further relaxed. True, this may cause minor inconveniences such as slightly increased air pollution in some scattered areas. However, intelligent Americans will realize that when industry is allowed to use lower grade fuels, there will be that much more higher grade fuel for running automobiles and heating homes.

'Third, there should be liberalized depreciation allowances and other federal tax incentives that will encourage energy-source producers to risk more of their capital...'

Kathy made a face at the screen. 'What a bore!'

'Be more reverent,' Mark scowled at her. 'That jerk is a shaper of our national destiny, young lady.'

309

He turned away from the television set and kissed Kathy's breasts.

'The speech, you sex maniac,' Kathy said, grasping his head with both hands and twisting it back towards the screen.

Rowan Engelhardt was clearing his throat discreetly.

'Many of you are confused about the energy situation. Your confusion is not lessened by the actions of opportunists and speculators who seek to take advantage of the crisis for their own profit. There are, for example, oil companies that promise solutions to shortages through enormously costly exploration projects in foreign countries that have long shown their hostility to the United States ...'

Mark Radford sat bolt upright. 'That son of a bitch!' he exclaimed. 'He's zeroing in on NIPCO!'

'You can't be sure,' Kathy said.

'God damn it, he doesn't have to mention names. Everybody in the industry and on Wall Street is going to realize he's talking about NIPCO and China – and declaring that the Administration is against the deal. Against us!'

He fell silent, listening.

'... we must solve our long-term fuel problems at home, and not look for solutions in dangerous adventures. Nor can we raise our hopes merely because irresponsible companies seeking competitive advantage suddenly throw hoarded reserves on the market ...'

Mark groaned.

'That does it,' he told Kathy when the speech had ended. 'He couldn't have made it any clearer that the Administration is declaring war on NIPCO if he'd spelled out your father's name and his social security number!'

'Where do you think that's going to leave NIPCO?' Kathy asked.

'In worse trouble than before,' he said, switching off the set. 'NIPCO stock will nose-dive on the market Monday. The Honourable – my ass! – Secretary Rowan Engelhardt has announced to the country that Northcutt International Petroleum hasn't a chance of getting government approval for its Chinese trade agreements. He's also telegraphed to one and all that the Administration is going to start a planned campaign of harassment against NIPCO – and we'll be hurting.'

'Beginning to feel defeatist, Mark?'

He was pacing up and down the floor of the bedroom. 'I

can't afford to be! Kathy, I'm an avowed Northcutt supporter,' he said, turning to face her. 'That puts me on the blacklist of every Major. If NIPCO goes under, I'll be lucky to find a job as a roustabout.'

'Come back to bed.' Kathy's lips were moist, and the request was soft-spoken. He joined her, and she held him.

'Are you always like that when you're mad?' she asked.

Mark was amazed at the speed with which his anger receded when Kathy held him in her arms.

'Depends who I'm with.' He kissed her lips. Her tongue stabbed deep into his mouth. Then she tipped her head back and away from his.

'We haven't made love like this in days,' she said. 'I mean lying on our sides, face to face.'

'Then let's,' Mark said, his blue eyes dark.

Their mouths locked again and Kathy's slender leg slid up along his deeply tanned thigh and gripped his hips.

Mark had told Kathy he might receive a telephone call and have to leave. She accepted his explanation that it was urgent and asked no further questions, but when the phone rang shortly before eleven, she sensed an immediate change in him.

Radford felt himself spooling up inside. It could only be Robert di Lorenzi.

'You alone, Mark?' di Lorenzi's voice asked.

'No.' The inner-tension springs coiled tighter.

'Then don't say much, just listen. Be on the south-east corner of Eighty-first and Madison at twelve-fifteen.' He repeated the place and time. 'Got it?'

Mark said he did and di Lorenzi hung up.

Kathy eyed Radford closely as he cradled the handset and got out of bed.

'Are you in trouble, Mark?'

'No, I'm not. What makes you think I am?'

'Negative vibes. You're sending them out all over the place.'

He moved towards the bathroom. 'The only thing I'm sending is you – back to the Pierre after you've taken a quick shower and dressed.'

She remained in bed while he showered. When he came out of the bathroom rubbing his straw-coloured hair with a towel, she smiled at him.

'I've decided to stay here and wait for you,' Kathy said.

311

Mark stopped drying his hair and let the towel hang loose in his hand.

'Sorry, honey,' he said. 'No way.' A great many things could go wrong. If anything did, police – or Charles Farrier's thugs – would come to search the suite. He couldn't allow Kathy Northcutt to take the risk of being there. Nor could he tell her the truth. 'I may have to bring some men up later for a conference.'

Kathy recognized that he was lying.

'Oh, I see.' Her tone was flat, cold.

She showered and dressed very quickly.

'I'll take you to the Pierre in a taxi,' Mark said. 'I have time.'

'Don't bother. I'll get there by myself.'

'Okay, honey.' His preoccupation was obvious and when he moved towards Kathy to kiss her, she evaded him and stalked out of the suite, slamming the door behind her.

3

15 July

At exactly fifteen minutes past midnight, a dark blue Chrysler sedan drew up at the traffic light on the south-east corner of Eighty-first Street and Madison Avenue. Robert di Lorenzi sat next to the driver. Mark got into the rear of the car. He recognized the two men with di Lorenzi as the Mafia chieftain's bodyguards. Mark knew them only by their first names. The driver was Joe. The man in the rear seat was Eddie.

'Nervous?' di Lorenzi asked as they headed uptown.

'Scared shitless,' Radford admitted.

'Don't be.' di Lorenzi lit a cigarillo. 'We got to a guy who works for Charles Farrier but hates his guts. He set Farrier up for us. It's going to be a cinch. Farrier does everything on schedule. That's a big mistake in his business – or mine.'

'I see,' Mark said in a tone indicating that he didn't.

'It's like this,' di Lorenzi explained. 'Earlier tonight, Farrier went out to Brooklyn to get laid, like he does every Friday night. Same time, same dame. He always leaves her at midnight, sharp. His driver takes him home. It being summer, that's to a fancy layout he has on Greenwood Lake, in Jersey.'

He gestured with the cigarillo.

'Farrier's in a real rut. Always takes the same route from Brooklyn. Tunnel to Manhattan. West Side Highway to George Washington Bridge. The bridge to Jersey. We have him taped – plus we had a bleeper hung on his car. It broadcasts continuous radio signals.'

He held up a small but elaborate transistor radio receiver.

'When Farrier gets within a mile and a half of us we start hearing bleeps. The closer he gets, the louder they get. Since we know his car, it's easy to pick him up. The rest is fool-proof.'

Mark nodded as though convinced, but when he lit a Salem, his hands were shaking.

They drove in silence. Joe finally turned into a dismal West Side street in the mid-One Hundred Sixties and pulled up behind a large tractor–semi-trailer rig parked on the left. The words *Clinton Hi-Speed Movers* were painted across the doors of the Fruehauf trailer.

Eddie got out first, then di Lorenzi, carrying the radio receiver, and finally Mark. They walked to the cab of the truck–tractor. The two men inside looked like ordinary truckers. Despite the muggy July heat, they wore faded windbreakers, driving gloves and billed caps with Teamsters Union buttons pinned to them. The man behind the wheel leaned out of his window and stared at Mark.

'He the civilian, Boss?' he asked di Lorenzi, who nodded.

di Lorenzi switched on the receiver. Several minutes went by. To Radford, they were endless. At last, they heard faint bleeping sounds.

'Start rolling,' di Lorenzi told the driver. He, Radford and Eddie returned to the Chrysler. Eddie now sat next to the right-hand rear door. He took two suit jackets from the rear window ledge and laid them on the seat beside him.

The truck pulled ponderously away from the kerb, moved down the street, the Chrysler following. Soon, the truck reached the bridge approach and stopped. di Lorenzi listened intently as the bleeping noises grew louder. After a few seconds, he said something to Joe, who gave three short blasts on the horn. The truck rolled forward onto the bridge-entry ramp. Joe waited a bit longer. The bleeps became shrill. di

Lorenzi switched off the set.

'Fifth car ahead,' Joe grunted, easing the Chrysler into the traffic stream on the ramp.

Mark counted cars. The fifth was a shiny white Lincoln Continental. Charles Farrier, he thought. The man on a schedule.

Once on the upper-deck roadway of the George Washington Bridge, Radford saw the Clinton Hi-Speed Movers truck. It was lumbering along the inside lane about fifty yards in front of them. The white Lincoln, doing a steady fifty miles per hour, passed the truck and swung over to the inside lane.

'Get ready,' di Lorenzi warned.

The big truck accelerated, pulled even with the Lincoln and held there until both vehicles were almost halfway across the bridge. Then the truck swerved and began fish-tailing wildly.

The driver of the Lincoln braked. Desperately – and in vain. The yawing trailer slammed against the Lincoln, and there was a rending crash as metal ripped and crushed metal and the Lincoln was crushed against the giant horizontal bridge-support girders. The truck rocked dangerously, then jolted to a halt.

West-bound traffic suddenly turned into a chaos of skidding vehicles. Joe guided the Chrysler to a stop immediately in front of the truck. Eddie, suit jackets in hand, leaped out of the car. di Lorenzi followed, with Mark on his heels.

Someone inside the mangled wreckage of the Lincoln was still alive and screaming in pain. The driver of the truck was the first to reach the wreck. Mark sprinted around the tractor and joined him. The man behind the wheel of the Lincoln had been crushed to a ghastly pulp. The man who cried out was Farrier.

The trucker thrust an object the size of a baseball into the wreckage. 'Let's get the hell out of here!' he rasped to Mark.

Occupants of other cars were running towards the mangled Lincoln, some sincerely hoping to be of some help, others merely morbidly curious. All had their attention focused on the wreck and none noticed Radford and the truck driver as they returned to di Lorenzi and the others.

The two truckers stripped off their windbreakers, gloves and caps and flung them over the guard rail into the Hudson River, more than two hundred feet below. They put on the suit jackets Eddie gave them, and they now appeared to be clerks

314

or salesmen rather than teamsters.

There was a muffled explosion inside the wrecked Lincoln. Instantly sheets of flame boiled up and out as gasoline from the torn fuel tank ignited. There was a terrible – and final – scream from amidst the flames. Those who had been crowding around the wreck scattered, running for safety.

'That does it,' di Lorenzi said. He led the way to the Chrysler. He and Mark got into the front seat with Joe. Eddie and the two truckers sat in the back.

Sirens were shrieking. Port Authority police and emergency vehicles were speeding to the scene from the New Jersey side. The first police car stopped. Two uniformed officers sprang out. One carried a hand fire extinguisher. The other stood in the roadway.

'Clear the area!' he bellowed. 'We gotta get equipment in!'

The Lincoln blazed furiously and the truck had caught fire.

A car started up and headed for the Jersey side. Joe followed.

'Neat,' di Lorenzi said when they were past the toll gates. He turned to look at Radford. 'We weren't noticed. The truck belongs to a friend. By now, he's reported it stolen. Another couple of hours, and this Chrysler won't even exist. No loose ends.'

Mark swallowed. 'Farrier's driver was killed, too,' he said.

'Sure,' di Lorenzi nodded. 'The bastard was Farrier's bodyguard. He thought we were just going to gun Farrier down and he set him up for us. A bastard who'll sell out his boss can't be trusted by anybody.'

Radford was forced to concede the elemental justice. Minutes later – and to his dismay – he realized that he had absolutely no feelings of guilt over being an accessory to double murder.

Joe drove south. Outside Hoboken, he turned off US 1-9 and went to a large auto-wrecking and scrap-metal yard where several men waited. Mark overheard one of them speak to di Lorenzi.

'We'll burn your Chrysler first, then run it through the shredder. There won't be a trace of it left.'

A Pontiac and a Chevrolet were parked inside the yard entrance. di Lorenzi, his body guards and Radford got into the Pontiac, leaving the Chevy for the two men who had been in the truck. By 2.45 A.M., they were back in Manhattan. di Lorenzi offered to drop Mark at his hotel, but Radford got out at Forty-second Street and Sixth Avenue.

'I'll talk to you later in the day, Bob,' he said.

Mark wanted to see Kathy Northcutt. He hailed a taxi and told the driver to take him to the Pierre Hotel. Then he remembered how Kathy had stormed out of his suite a few hours earlier.

'I've changed my mind,' he told the hackie. 'Go to the Drake instead.'

Even though it was Saturday morning, several NIPCO executives and a large number of other home-office personnel were at their desks. James Northcutt's order increasing product allocations to distributors and dealers and the host of problems that beset the company had created an enormous backlog of administrative work.

Northcutt himself was in his office early. He had set a 9 A.M. meeting with Samuel Schlechter and Mark Radford. They arrived to find the oilman rancorous, his seamed face grim. He limited his greeting to a nod indicating they should sit in the chairs that had been placed close to his desk.

'Hear Engelhardt's speech last night?' Northcutt asked and went on without waiting for replies. 'It's going to do us serious damage. Next Monday NIPCO stock will slide – five points at least. Probably more.'

He scowled.

'That bureaucratic son of a bitch even made it plain the government will try to block our deal with China. Jesus! I hate to think what the reaction is in Peking!' Northcutt took a deep breath. 'I suppose I should get in touch with the Chinese diplomatic reps in Washington —'

'Why not make a quick trip to Peking, Jim?' Schlechter interrupted. 'Have a talk with the men at the top.'

'What more could I say there than here? We negotiated in good faith. They're ready to carry out their end, same as I'm ready to carry out ours. But the Administration's bushwhacking us.

'I'm going to save that deal.' His expression changed, becoming stubborn rather than angry. 'It's the biggest of my life. I won't lose it.'

Northcutt suddenly looked away. It was almost as if he was

316

abashed at having revealed too much of his inner self.

'Anything further on Barbara Wallace?' Jim asked.

'I talked with her lawyer, Dwight Farquhar, late yesterday afternoon. I hinted we might consider some sort of arrangement —'

'For God's sake, Sam! I told you I won't —'

'Easy, Jim. I said I *hinted*. It's all I did. To gain time and keep Barbara from losing her patience and going to the tax authorities. All the same, I still think you'll have to bargain with her sooner or later.'

Northcutt turned to Mark Radford.

'And your glad tidings?'

Mark saw that neither Northcutt nor Schlechter had heard the television and radio newscast items about Charles Farrier. Nothing had appeared in *The New York Times* because the paper's Saturday-morning edition went to press earlier than on other days. However, the *Daily News* carried the story, and Mark had a copy with him. He decided against mentioning Farrier until he could speak with Northcutt alone.

'Only one small bright spot,' Mark said. 'Reliable sources say Jersey Crest has already started to complain because Birdwell Equipment isn't meeting delivery dates on orders.'

'How about that man, Russell Peterson, who took Jersey Crest's money?' Northcutt asked. 'Any word on him?'

'It's too soon, J.L. We only put di Lorenzi to work on that day before yesterday.'

The three men discussed NIPCO affairs for an hour. Then Sam Schlechter excused himself. When he had gone, Mark took a copy of that morning's *Daily News* from his attaché case. He opened it to the centrefold photo section and laid it on Northcutt's desk. A photograph of a wrecked and fire-gutted automobile covered half the left-hand page. Radford pointed to the picture caption.

'GEORGE WASHINGTON BRIDGE HORROR: The charred remains of Charles Farrier, a successful New York City realtor, and his chauffeur were found in this mangled and burned-out wreckage early today. The car, which belonged to Farrier, exploded and burned after being struck by a heavy truck. The truck was stolen and police are searching for two men who were in it but somehow managed to flee the scene of the crash without being observed. (For details, see story on Page 3.)'

Northcutt didn't bother to turn to the Page Three story. He

raised his right eyebrow high and gave Mark a sharp look.

Northcutt thrust the newspaper aside. 'Thanks, Mark,' he said quietly – and his mood underwent an abrupt change. 'Brace yourself,' he said with a trace of a smile. 'I'm sending you back to Qantara. Tomorrow.'

Radford's blue eyes widened. 'What?' he blurted. 'That is – I always figured I should be there. Still, with everything else —'

'Listen for a second. Have you heard the whispers making the NIPCO rounds that I've lost my mind?'

'They weren't quite that strong,' Radford said. 'But there has been talk about you giving Harold Elbert and some other people weird instructions.'

'Charter tankers, buy Cadillacs and so on. Is that it?'

'More or less.'

Northcutt's grey eyes gleamed. 'Mark, let's talk about His Royal Highness, Sheikh Maktoum ben Khalifah, the Emir of Qantara. From all I've been able to observe over the years, he's one-third moneylender, one-third playboy and one-third perpetually starved ego. Now, then. How do you suppose I intend sending His Nibs into raptures of delight?'

Radford burst into laughter. Everything clicked into place.

'With a rainbow assortment of Cadillacs air-freighted to Kuwait and trans-shipped to Qantara by freighter,' he replied. 'Plus the world's fanciest set of toy trains. Plus a Coca-Cola bottling plant for Qantara, practically the only Arab country that doesn't have one.'

'Right. His own, personal plant. NIPCO gives him the franchise and plant as a present. Gratis. NIPCO pays all the operating expenses. As a result, the Emir will be able to give his loyal subjects oceans of free Coke. He'll be the only Arab potentate able to make *that* statement.'

Mark nodded enthusiastically. The Emir was a devout Muslim. No alcoholic beverages were permitted in Qantara. But most Arabs loved Coca-Cola. If the Emir could give the soft drink free to his people, he would gain more *sharaf* – honour – than if he killed a thousand infidels barehanded at the gates of Mecca. Most important, Arab rulers placed incredibly high values on gestures and symbols.

'His Highness will be overwhelmed,' Mark said. 'But what do we want from him?'

Northcutt grinned. 'Crude,' he said.

'Qantara won't be back to normal for some weeks, J.L.'

'We can't wait. We have to make up what we're drawing from our above-ground reserves. The Emir can make it possible for us to start crude shipments on their way from the Mid-east in days.'

'How?'

'In two ways. We have millions of barrels of crude backed up in field and storage tanks on Qantara. We can't ship because our port facilities at Batir aren't operative. But if we rigged emergency hose lines —'

'We can't, J.L. Not according to our concession agreement.'

'The Emir can permit an exception. Sure, improvised hose lines will leak. We'll have to spend a fortune cleaning up oil spills in the harbour. But we'll ship crude oil.'

'*If* Maktoum ben Khalifah gives permission.'

'It's going to be your if, Mark. You'll be my official gift-bearer. Use your charm' – Northcutt cocked his eyebrow – 'if it can do what it's done to my daughter, you shouldn't have any problems.'

Mark blinked. It was Northcutt's first direct reference to his relationship with Kathy.

'I said the Emir can help us two ways,' the oilman went on. 'I've just told you the first. The other is tricky, but from our standpoint the more important. We need much more crude than we can get out of Qantara with improvised loading methods.'

'We can't buy from other companies,' Mark said.

'No, there's a shortage, and the Majors have shut us out. They wouldn't let us have crude even if they had it to spare. On the other hand, the Arab oil-producing countries are awash with crude.'

'They won't sell to us, either. They're sticking to their boycott. We were lucky the Emir was the one holdout.'

'You've just hit on the secret, Mark. NIPCO can't buy crude, but the Emir stands in with the other Arab countries, even if he didn't join in either of their oil embargoes.'

'Qantara doesn't have to buy crude.'

'Ah, but the Emir can go to other Arab rulers in the Persian Gulf and say, "Come, my blood brothers. Sell *me* a few hundred thousand barrels of oil." '

'The others would know immediately he's fronting for us.'

'They wouldn't admit it openly, not even to themselves,' Jim smiled. 'They have revenue problems because of the embargo.

They can use those extra dollars. Besides, there's professional courtesy among potentates – or there should be.'

Radford had been thinking while he listened and had formed an idea.

'There's one other present you should send the Emir, J.L.'

'My God, what?' Northcutt groaned.

'A gift so loaded with symbolism it'll blow his mind. A lordly gesture that only one great man can make to another. One that says you are his equal in rank and power, even if you're not of royal blood.'

'Go on,' Northcutt urged, his interest aroused.

'You personally have some oil wells on properties you hold in fee – that you own and not simply lease.'

'Sure I have.'

'Then put the icing on His Highness's cake with a deed to a producing well here in the United States. Play it as the magnanimous act of one great and powerful landowner demonstrating his willingness to share his holdings with another.'

Northcutt frowned, then beamed.

'Now why the hell didn't I think of that?'

'Because you're like most old-time wildcatters. You'd rather give away your house, lot and back teeth than an oil well.'

Mark was right, Northcutt reflected. So much so that the billionaire was already having second thoughts, but he forced these from his mind. Deeding a producing well on US soil to the Emir would be a master stroke that went straight to the most vulnerable area of Arab – and the Emir Maktoum ben Khalifah's – psychology.

'You'll have the deed and photographs of the well by tomorrow,' he assured Radford. 'I'll give him a fair producer —'

'You're hedging, J.L.,' Mark said, much amused. 'Another few minutes and you'll shave the lordly gesture down to a three-barrel-a-day stripper.'

'Okay, a *good* producer,' Northcutt muttered grudgingly.

'Have someone load a barrel of crude aboard the plane. I'll deliver it and tell the Emir it's from *his* well.'

'That's impossible. How're we going to get a barrel of crude from a particular well to New York in time —'

'Any barrel of crude will do,' Mark chuckled. 'He'll never know the difference. Only make sure it's a higher grade than what we're taking out of Qantara.'

Northcutt looked at Mark with new respect.

320

'Take the rest of the day off – you'll need it to pack,' he said. 'Then be over to my house on Sutton Place at eight tomorrow morning. We'll go over everything again. You can count on taking off in my plane around one in the afternoon.'

Radford stood up. Since Northcutt had made open reference to his relationship with Kathy, he felt no reluctance to say that he'd be calling her later at the Pierre for a dinner date.

Northcutt looked at him oddly.

'Didn't she tell you?' he asked.

'Tell me? What?'

'Why, hell, Mark. Kathy phoned me at home at seven this morning. She was going away for the weekend – up to the Cape with some friends of hers. She won't be back until Monday afternoon.'

Mark studied his employer's face to see if he was hiding something. But Northcutt's expression was frank, open – and, indeed, a bit puzzled.

'No, she didn't say a word to me,' Radford said. 'Do you know who she's staying with or where she can be reached by telephone?'

'God damn it, son. I'm sorry, but I don't.'

Sic transit, Mark thought.

'I'll be at your house in the morning, J.L.,' he said. 'At eight o'clock. On the dot.'

4

16 July

The decor of James Northcutt's Sutton Place townhouse contrasted sharply with the interior setting of Bonheur, his mansion on the French Riviera. Northcutt had bought the townhouse in 1952, when he transferred NIPCO's headquarters from Los Angeles to New York City and Pamela had divorced him. Wanting a showplace bachelor residence but being wholly occupied with business affairs, he had given fashionably overpriced interior decorators and art consultants a free hand and a blank cheque. The results were predictable.

Furniture in the Sutton Place house was eighteenth century and florid. Paintings were largely of French Academy genre and displayed in ornately carved gilt frames. He had not lived overly long in the house. By 1955, the construction of Bonheur was underway, and he made it his permanent residence less than two years later when the discovery well on Qantara blew in. Since then, his visits to the United States had been few and of short duration, but he kept the Sutton Place house fully staffed and maintained.

On the rare occasions when Northcutt was in New York, the dark-panelled second-floor library of the house served as his study and work area. The shelves were laden with books in matched hand-tooled leather bindings. Two Chardins – one of dubious authenticity – a Claude Lorrain, a Fragonard and a Delacroix hung on the walls. A purported Charles Cressent desk was placed near one of the tall windows overlooking Sutton place.

'Welcome to the Parke-Bernet Rom,' Jim Northcutt said with cheerful sarcasm when Mark Radford was ushered into the library. He waved a hand. 'Take any chair. They're all equally uncomfortable for anyone your size or mine.' He made a wry face. 'I wish to Christ that Norton Simon or Tom Hoving or somebody would drop by and make me an offer for every damned thing in the place.'

Mark glanced around him. Uncomfortable or not the furniture was of museum quality. As for the paintings, he guessed that the Fragonard alone was worth upwards of $100,000.

Mark was pleasantly surprised by the oilman's early-Sunday-morning appearance and manner. Northcutt looked rested and filled with energy. He was casually dressed in slacks and an open-throated sports shirt. The garb somehow accentuated a virility and rugged musculature remarkable for a man his age.

'Had breakfast?' Northcutt asked.

Radford said he had, but would enjoy having coffee.

'So would I,' Northcutt nodded. He rang for a servant, and a Georgian silver coffee service and Sèvres cups and saucers were brought within minutes.

'Sam should be here soon,' Northcutt declared. 'He's bringing all the documents. He's had whole herds of his junior partners galloping all over the country to tie things up ever since I had my first brainstorms last Thursday.'

Mark finished a cup of coffee and shot his employer a suspicious look. 'The well you're giving the Emir . . .'

'Don't worry, he won't be short-changed. I'm deeding over a thousand-barrel-a-day producer I own in New Mexico – and Jesus, how I hate doing it!'

Radford helped himself to more coffee.

'Did anyone scour up that symbolic barrel of crude?'

'It's already aboard my plane,' Northcutt said. 'I even had the barrel painted purple, yellow and green' – these were Qantara's national colours – 'with a star and crescent and a royal emblem to boot.'

'Nice touch,' Mark applauded.

'I thought you'd appreciate it.' Northcutt studied some memoranda that lay on his desk. 'Oh, yes. All twelve Cadillacs were air-freighted out in chartered planes yesterday. They'll be in Kuwait late today.'

He picked up another sheet of paper.

'Harold Elbert was on the line at seven-thirty this morning. He spent the night out at Newark Airport making certain the electric-train set was snug in the cargo hold. A manufacturer's engineer by the name of Weaver will fly over with you. The layout is knocked down, in sections, of course. He'll supervise assembly. Assign NIPCO electricians to work under him when you reach Qantara.'

A few minutes later, Samuel Schlechter arrived, carrying a briefcase that bulged with papers. They included letters of agreement between NIPCO and Coca-Cola, the plans of a bottling plant similar to the one NIPCO would buy for the Emir and, it seemed to Radford, whole bales of other documents.

'We'll give all these a quick once-over now,' Schlechter said. 'Then you can study them more carefully on your flight across, Mark.' He began passing papers to Northcutt and Radford.

The double doors of the library opened.

'Oh, I'm sorry, Jim!' a woman's voice said. 'I didn't know you were busy.'

She was thirtyish, dark-haired, sultry and wearing a red silk-jersey jumpsuit.

Mark Radford smiled inwardly. Now he understood why James Northcutt was in such good spirits.

'I am busy, Arlene, and will be for quite a while,' Northcutt said. 'But don't go until you've met these gentlemen.'

He introduced her as Arlene Barnes. Obviously, she was Jim Northcutt's latest mistress. A very recent acquisition, Schlechter and Radford guessed – correctly, for Arlene Barnes had moved in only two days before.

Arlene smiled at them, blew Jim a kiss and went out, closing the doors behind her. The three men returned to their work.

The Jersey Crest Oil Company maintained a suite at the Hotel Plaza for use when top executives had to hold extraordinary and highly confidential conferences. The suite was sound-proofed and swept daily by electronics technicians to insure that no listening devices had been installed.

Although he loathed coming into New York City on Sunday, Powell Pierce did so on this particular Sunday. His chauffeur brought him from his Duchess County estate to the Plaza. At 10 A.M., he was in the Jersey Crest suite, meeting with Guy Bannister.

'We can talk freely here,' Pierce informed the one-time CIA agent. 'There's no need to beat around the bush or avoid mentioning names. I want you to give me direct answers to my questions.'

'Yes, sir,' Bannister said nervously.

'Do you know who killed Charles Farrier?' Pierce asked.

'I know – but it doesn't do us any good. Farrier was killed by the mob Northcutt hired to stop the station fires. It's run by Robert di Lorenzi. Nothing can be proved, though.'

'Will Farrier's death have any effect on the work his organization has been doing?' Pierce asked.

'I'm afraid it will, Mr Pierce. One of his men tipped me off that – well, that Farrier's bunch is backing out.'

Powell Pierce's lips tightened.

'And what if we offer the man who steps into Farrier's shoes more money?'

Bannister needlessly adjusted his necktie with one hand.

'That might get results,' he said. 'Only it wouldn't be soon. It'll take weeks before Farrier's people get themselves reorganized – that's how things go with these outfits. When the *capo* is knocked off suddenly, there's always a shake-up and usually considerable jockeying for power.'

Pierce's expression revealed nothing. 'This rival group, Bannister. Can we outbid Northcutt for its services?'

Bannister shook his head. 'No. As I understand it, di Lorenzi got his orders to help Northcutt straight from the most powerful syndicate bosses. He couldn't cross them.'

Pierce frowned and was silent for several seconds.

'A side issue, but important,' he said finally. 'Farrier undertook to have some of his European – associates, I suppose one would call them – track down Russell Peterson. Is that part of the arrangement being cancelled also?'

Guy Bannister brightened.

'I asked about that specifically,' he replied. 'Farrier's people are going ahead with it.'

'A very minor consolation, but a consolation none the less,' Pierce murmured, then his tone hardened. 'How do you propose to fill the gap left by the loss of Farrier's organization?'

'I'm not sure yet, Mr Pierce. I'll find some answer, though.'

'I expect you to do precisely that, Bannister – and as quickly as possible.' Pierce smiled. 'When you do, let me know, and I'll see to it that you are advanced funds again.'

It was a few minutes before noon when Jim Northcutt stood up.

'We seem to have covered everything,' he said to Schlechter and Radford. 'Unless, of course, you have any questions, Mark.'

Radford tapped his two attaché cases, both filled to capacity with papers. 'I've got dozens of them, J.L.,' he said. 'Only I'm not about to ask them.'

He and Schlechter got to their feet.

'Stay for lunch, Mark,' Northcutt urged. 'Sam is.'

'We were aiming for a one o'clock take-off from Newark,' Mark said. 'I can just about make it.'

The oilman gave him a long look that was almost fatherly.

'Would it boost your morale if Sam and I went out to the airport with you?'

Mark was deeply touched by the offer.

'It'd make me feel silly as hell,' he said quickly. He hesitated a second, then added, 'You can do me a big favour, though. When you see Kathy, tell her I'm sorry I – uh – missed her, didn't get a chance to say good-bye.'

Northcutt put out his hand.

'I'll do that, son,' he said. He and Schlechter accompanied Mark to Northcutt's limousine and both wished him luck. They knew only too well that much of their own future and

NIPCO's depended on what Radford would be able to accomplish in Qantara.

Mark could sense the anxiety of the flight crew and cabin attendants when he boarded the NIPCO Boeing at Newark Airport.

Nothing spreads faster than gloom, he thought, as he checked details with flight captain, co-pilot and steward. Rumours of NIPCO's troubles had no doubt reached them, and it was safe to assume even they understood the implications of the speech that had been made by Energy Resources Secretary Rowan Engelhardt. They're sweating, Mark mused, wondering how long it'll be before they receive pink slips with their paycheques.

'All cargo has been loaded,' the captain told him, holding out the manifests. They had been double- and triple-checked. 'Your luggage is also aboard, Mr Radford.'

'And our passenger?'

'Mr Alonzo Weaver. He's in the lounge compartment.'

'Then we can take off whenever you're ready.'

Mark walked back into the cabin and received a surprise. For some reason, he had expected that Alonzo Weaver, the engineering representative of the model-train manufacturing company, would be fusty and middle-aged. But Weaver was in his late twenties, a strapping six-footer and black.

'The Alonzo is too much,' Weaver said when Mark introduced himself. 'Call me Lon. Everybody does.'

Weaver had been aboard for nearly an hour. He had found himself a seat in front of a table on which he had spread out circuit diagrams and schematics.

'I take it those are the plans for the Qantara and NIPCO Central,' Mark said, taking a seat opposite Weaver and belting himself in.

'Complete with tunnels, drawbridges, semaphors, automatic freight-handling gadgets – everything but federal loans to keep the trains running,' Weaver nodded, grinning.

'Must be something when it's assembled and operating.'

'The wildest ever.'

'This your first trip abroad?' Mark asked.

'Not abroad – you'd be amazed at how many model-train freaks there are in Europe and Japan. It's my first jaunt to the Middle East, though.' Lon Weaver's ebony face showed curiosity. 'This Emir character. Is he hooked on model trains?'

'Nope. He never had one before. But gadgets fascinate him.'

'They fascinate me, too,' Weaver said. 'Much bigger gadgets, though.'

'How come you're into model trains, then?'

'Man, when I got my degree in electrical engineering from N.Y.U. I had to grab the best Equal Opportunity offer I could get.' It was a statement made without any trace of resentment.

'If you're interested, try us when you get back,' Mark said. 'I'll give you a note to our personnel department.'

Weaver's mobile features formed themselves into a sceptical expression.

'Thanks – but since when have oil companies started hiring blacks on the white-collar side of the business?'

'Not long, and they haven't hired many,' Radford admitted. 'Most companies, especially the big ones, held to the pure white-only line. That's all changing. And we've always got openings for qualified engineers.' He grinned. 'Of all types, sizes, shapes and colours.'

Alonzo Weaver stared down at his circuit diagrams.

'Thanks again – and I mean it,' he said. 'But I'll stay where I am. I have a wife and two kids. The company I work for is solid.'

Mark peered closely at Weaver.

'You're not so sure about NIPCO being solid?'

'I didn't mean – oh, hell, I might as well be honest. There's talk that your company might be in a tight bind.'

My God, Mark Radford thought. The rumours had travelled far. They'd even reached the ears of men employed by model-train manufacturers. He was grateful when the Boeing's engines started to whine. The noise was an excuse for making no further comment, and he leaned back in his seat, trying to fight off his own feelings of depression.

5

17 July

The airport runways in Qantara were too short for landing by
large jet planes. The NIPCO Boeing 727 landed at the Kuwait
International Airport. Radford and Weaver disembarked to
wait while cargo and luggage were transferred from the Boeing
to a NIPCO Otter which would take them the rest of the
way.

Radford and Weaver sat in the VIP lounge. The air-conditioning system in the ultramodern terminal was out of order.

'As usual,' Mark told the electrical engineer. Having spent
years in the Middle East, he withstood the oppressive heat
much better than Weaver, who sweltered. 'I couldn't begin to
count how many times I've been through here – coming or
going – and I'll be damned if I can remember any time when
the air-conditioning did work.'

'It's murder!' Weaver panted. He was in shirt sleeves and
wearing lightweight cotton trousers, but perspiration poured
down his face. He mopped at it incessantly with a handkerchief.

'I hate to tell you, Lon,' Radford laughed. 'This is fresh and
invigorating compared to Qantara.'

Weaver's attention had shifted elsewhere.

'The looks we're getting from some of the Arabs sitting in
this sweatbox drop the temperature fifty degrees,' he said.

Mark purposely ignored the remark.

'I read 'em loud and clear,' Weaver persisted. 'They're not
for you, Mark. They're for me. The old White Massah looks.
Get the hell off the sidewalk, nigger. Clue me in. Some of their
mothers are as black as I am.'

Radford's reply was evasive.

'You're an American black sitting with an American white.
They have no great love for either of us.'

'Bullshit. They may not love you, white buddy, but it goes a
lot deeper where my black hide's concerned. I can psych that
easy.'

Maybe it was better that Weaver learn the uglier facts o

Middle Eastern life, Mark thought. 'These are rich Arabs – flying first class or in their private planes,' he said. 'They're used to having blacks as servants – or even slaves. It might be different if you were a Moslem black, but it's obvious that you're not.'

'No suh, *effendi*, I shoah ain't,' Weaver said acidly. 'Same deal down in Qantara?'

'I'm happy to say it isn't.'

'Why the difference?'

'Simple. The Qantarans never went slave raiding in Africa like most other Arabs, and until NIPCO struck oil on their island, they were so poor they couldn't buy slaves from the traders.'

An airport official appeared.

'Your aircraft is ready, Mr Radford.'

Mark grinned at Weaver. 'Come on, trusty toy-train bearer.'

'Yassuh, white *bwana*.' Alonzo Weaver laughed.

The flight to Qantara took barely an hour. George Needham and several NIPCO staff members were at the airport outside Ayat.

Needham pumped Mark's hand. 'Hard to believe you've only been gone three weeks. Seems more like months, what with all that's been happening here.'

'I guess you've really had it rough, George.'

'At first. But we've accomplished a lot, thanks to you and the Old Man. We got everything we asked for without any questions or home-office static. That helped, believe me.'

Radford glanced up at the fierce morning sun. In another hour and a half, the heat would be at its daily peak.

'We'll go have a confab in your office, George,' he said and turned to Alonzo Weaver. 'Want to supervise the unloading of your railroad, Lon?' Weaver nodded. A large NIPCO truck was parked near the Otter. 'That's for the cargo. We'll leave a company car, too. When you've finished, the driver will bring you over to the NIPCO administration building. I'll be there.'

Mark asked George Needham nothing about the actual sabotage that had crippled NIPCO's facilities or about Chuck Ungar, his wife and the others who had been killed. He had learned all there was to know from the reports Needham sent to James Northcutt and the company headquarters in New York. Nothing could be gained by rehashing past history, and there was little time for anything but immediate problems.

George Needham was a veteran field man. He had taken over as acting resident manager after Ungar's death and done a superb job. He was entitled to know the facts as they were, and Radford summed up the situation for him as they sat in Needham's office.

'... and either we start shipping crude to the States, or NIPCO is just about finished,' Mark concluded.

Needham chewed on an unlit black cigar. 'That bad, huh?'

'Couldn't be much worse.'

'Okay, Mark. The Old Man cabled me personally. He said you had the same authority as he does. That's all I need to know. Start giving orders, and I'll rawhide the ass off everybody we got working for us over here.'

'It's not that simple, George,' he said. 'We've got plenty of crude in storage tanks here, but our offshore loading facilities are out of commission —'

'Sure as hell are – and will be for weeks.'

'We have to improvise hose lines —'

'Can't. It's prohibited.'

'Not if I can talk the Emir into giving us special permission. I have to see him. That's my first hurdle.' Mark ground the Salem he had been smoking into an ashtray. 'Now let me go find out when His Nibs will allow me into the throne room.'

'Stay where you are,' Needham said, getting up from behind his hopelessly overloaded desk. 'The Emir assigned a different liaison officer to us two weeks ago. The new guy and I get along fine – long as I lay heavy *bakhshish* on him. Which I do. He's in his office downstairs. I'd best go buttonhole him right now.'

'Be free with the *bakhshish*. I have to see the Emir. Tomorrow, if at all possible.'

Needham frowned. 'Christ, Mark. You know His Royal Highness usually farts around for a week before granting an audience.'

'Tell him I have something very special for him,' Mark said. 'We can't afford delays, George.'

The danger to NIPCO became greater when the Monday workday began eight hours later in New York.

Jim Northcutt had predicted the speech by Rowan Engelhardt, the Energy Resources Secretary, would have an adverse effect on NIPCO stock values. But even he had not dreamed shares would plunge five points during the first half hour of trading. As the morning wore on, the price continued to decline.

It was only the prelude.

At around 10.30 A.M., Senator John Bosworth called Schlechter from Washington.

'Brace yourself, Sam,' Bosworth warned. He went on to relate that a Treasury Department source had told him the Internal Revenue Service intended making a special – and searching – audit of NIPCO tax returns for the past several years. Obviously, it was a harassing tactic, for the news would be 'leaked' to the press later in the day.

'It's all being orchestrated by someone pretty high up in the Administration,' the Senator said. 'Arthur Gerlach's my favourite candidate for the son of a bitch in charge.'

Normally, the prospect of an I.R.S. audit of NIPCO's tax returns would have caused Schlechter little concern. The company's tax accounting was no less honest than that of any large corporation. Now, however, it represented a dangerous threat, and Schlechter rushed to see James Northcutt.

'The announcement of the audits will play hell with public confidence in NIPCO,' Sam declared. 'People want to suspect the worst about any corporation – and especially any oil company.'

He took a deep breath before continuing.

'If Barbara Wallace talks, you and the company are in deep trouble, Jim.'

Northcutt had allowed Barbara and his other mistresses to charge their personal bills to company accounts. Large as the total amount involved was, it represented no more than a petty-cash item to the billionaire. But if Barbara revealed now what she knew to federal tax investigators, her information could destroy the company.

'We don't dare stall her any longer,' Schlechter said.

'But she wants a third of my NIPCO stock!'

'I have an idea, Jim. Maybe we can use one disaster to stop another. NIPCO stock nose-dived this morning and is still going down. Maybe Barbara is afraid it may hit bottom. She might be willing to settle for less – perhaps much less – in cash.'

Northcutt realized that his inner rage was futile.

'All right, Sam,' he muttered in resignation. 'Start dickering with her lawyer.'

The I.R.S. leaked the story of its plans to audit NIPCO tax returns at one o'clock. The item was on the financial wires within minutes. NIPCO stock fell another $4\frac{1}{2}$ points.

Powell Pierce immediately began exploiting NIPCO's weakening situation. At Pierce's instigation, a former colleague who was currently the president of the National Petroleum Council issued a public statement. Although he spoke as an individual, it was made to sound as though he was expressing the views of the Council itself.

'The Northcutt International Petroleum Company recently announced an increase in product allocations to its wholesale and retail outlets. A study of NIPCO's crude oil reserves and present production indicates the company cannot possibly continue such accelerated deliveries for more than a few weeks. The appropriate authorities should seek to determine if the step taken by NIPCO's management was not merely one intended to avert the decline in the company's stock prices which none the less began today.'

The statement was tantamount to an accusation of fraud. In Washington, a Chinese commercial attaché conferred with a US Assistant Undersecretary of State. The attaché indicated that his superiors in Peking were growing concerned over the future of the projected trade agreements with NIPCO.

'I have been instructed to make inquiries,' he said.

Couched in diplomatic euphemisms, these inquiries sought to determine the government's position in regard to the agreements. Was there any truth to the rumours that US agencies were attempting to block the agreements? Should there be confidential discussions at higher diplomatic levels to expedite approval?

The Assistant Undersecretary said he would have to consult with his own superiors.

Word of the Chinese attaché's visit and conversation flashed up the State Department organization chart and across Pennsylvania Avenue to Arthur Gerlach in the White House.

'Our policy is not yet completely defined,' he said. 'Naturally, we are as concerned with performance as the People's Republic of China. The Chinese should consider with utmost care the possible danger of making such a huge deal with a comparatively small independent oil company. It could even be suggested that they would be more certain of the contractor's performance if they worked with a consortium of multi-national Majors. There would be no question about the consortium's reliability.'

That, Gerlach thought, should finish NIPCO's chance of ever getting the Chinese deal. Powell Pierce could have no complaints. He and Rowan Engelhardt were giving full value for the half million dollars each of them had received from Pierce's representative the week before.

Samuel Schlechter returned to James Northcutt's office at five o'clock in the afternoon. The two men dismally surveyed the havoc wrought by a day filled with disasters.

NIPCO stock had closed at 42½, down 16¾ points from its level of the previous Friday.

Battered from all sides by bad news, employee morale had plummeted. Two vice-presidents had submitted letters of resignation. A score of lower echelon home-office employees had given their notice. The manager of the NIPCO refinery in San Mateo had Telexed his resignation – 'formal letter to follow, airmail, registered'. The marketing division had received frantic telephone calls from distributors and dealers in a dozen states.

Northcutt rubbed his jaw wearily and closed his eyes for a moment.

'Barbara's lawyer,' he said. 'Did you reach him, Sam?'

Sam nodded. 'For all the good it does, my hunch was right. She – or at least her attorney – is worried about what's happening to NIPCO. He set a cash price.'

'How much?' Northcutt rasped.

'I'd rather not tell you until I've bargained further,' Schlechter muttered.

Northcutt's face was drawn with fatigue.

'Looks like the roof is falling in, Sam.'

'Sagging, but not falling. Not yet.'

'How do you propose we hold it up?' the oilman said. 'With press releases?'

'By letting Mark Radford play out our hand. By the way, have you heard from him?'

'Only a Telex saying he had arrived and hoped to see the Emir tomorrow,' Northcutt replied. 'In any case, even if he gets everything, we solve just one problem.'

'It could be the key, Jim. Put the day's catastrophes in

333

proper perspective. The worst blow of the day was the state-ment issued by that bastard from the National Petroleum Council, accusing us of lying, perpetrating a fraud. Once we demonstrate that NIPCO can deliver as promised, we've shored that sagging roof.'

'True, our dealers —'

'Not only our dealers. We'll have established NIPCO's credi-bility and integrity to everyone – investors, consumers, the press and public. NIPCO stock will start climbing rapidly.'

'That process could take weeks. In the meantime, the stock will go lower. I wouldn't be surprised if it nose-dived to twenty, possibly even ten.'

Schlechter smiled.

'Get down to basics, Jim. What do you really care about the price of NIPCO stock? You own most of it and you know the actual underlying value. You can wait for it to rebound.'

Jim's eyebrow flickered upward and he nodded.

'You're right there,' he said. 'I really don't give a shit what I'm worth on paper.'

Crude – and credibility, Jim mused. If we have supplies of the former from the Middle East, we'll re-establish the latter in the States. That in itself would at least blunt many of the other threats.

'I guess it all does depend on how Radford makes out in Qantara,' he murmured. He unconsciously reached for the luck charm Verna Fletcher had given him. He rubbed it lightly between his thumb and forefinger. He needed luck now more than ever.

6

18 July

Oil royalties have built countless architectural eyesores in Middle Eastern Countries. None surpasses the ugliness of the Emir Maktoum ben Khalifah's palace on the western, closer-to-Mecca outskirts of Ayat. Part Miami Beach hotel, part Cecil B. De Mille fantasy, it was a disaster punctuated by towering minarets made of stainless steel and coloured glass.

Always avid to receive costly gifts, Emir Maktoum ben Khalifah had agreed to receive Mark Radford, George Needham and Alonzo Weaver in mid-morning. The three men arrived in a NIPCO company car followed by a pick-up truck carrying a gaudily painted barrel of crude oil and some native labourers. The two vehicles were waved past the concrete blockhouses that served as the palace gates. The car was met at the main entrance to the five-storey palace by an escort of the Emir's armed retainers. The truck was ordered to a remote side entrance.

The ruler of Qantara had elected to receive Radford and his companions in private chambers rather than an official reception room. They were escorted through a maze of corridors and up a winding staircase protected by polished bronze railings set with semi-precious stones. Finally, they were ushered into the Emir's presence.

The Americans bowed their heads. Mark carried an attaché case in his right hand. Weaver held another in his left.

'Your Royal Highness,' Radford said.

A plump and frog-faced man, the Emir Maktoum ben Khalifah sat on an ornate sofa strewn with cushions. His skin was walnut-hued and wattled. He fondled his Moslem prayer beads and recited the ritual invocations of Allah, concluding with the traditional secular greeting, 'mit ahlan wasah'lan – a hundred times welcome.'

Having observed the conventions in Arabic, he switched to English, which he spoke remarkably well. Qantara had once been a British Protectorate. Although it did nothing else for the Gulf emirate, Britain had provided English teachers for Qantara's royal family.

'You nearest my person,' the Emir said. A chubby hand waved the three men to couches. 'I am pleased to see you again.'

'Your Highness does me great honour,' Mark answered.

Tea was served with sweet cakes and sticky date-confections. The Emir made inquiries about the health of James Northcutt. Through it all, a half-dozen of his heavily armed aides stood motionless and watchful. At last, the Emir leaned back against his cushions.

'You request an audience, Mr Radford.'

'On behalf of Mr Northcutt, Your Royal Highness.'

'Then I am doubly honoured.'

'Mr Northcutt extends his respects and warmest good wishes to Your Royal Highness,' Mark intoned. 'He realizes that the destruction of our facilities has caused Qantara the loss of much revenue and suffering. He is confident that what has been lost shall be recovered many times over.'

'By the will of Allah,' the Emir murmured piously.

'By the will of God,' Mark said 'Mr Northcutt desires to demonstrate his gratitude for the solidarity Your Royal Highness has shown.'

The Emir's eyes brightened. Northcutt had sent gifts – but where were they?

Radford opened his attaché case and took out a dozen eight by ten colour photographs. He presented them to Sheikh Maktoum. 'These automobiles will arrive in Qantara by ship this week. It is Mr Northcutt's most earnest hope that they bring pleasure to Your Royal Highness.'

Now the Emir beamed and shuffled through the photographs. He already had two or three Cadillac limousines; he could not remember exactly how many. There were so many other cars in his garages. But a dozen Cadillacs, exactly alike save for colour! He tried to think if any other Arab ruler had such a fleet. No, he gloated, not even Faisal could boast of such an array of identical models, all for his personal use.

'If Your Royal Highness will permit.' Mark nodded to Weaver.

The slender black opened his own attaché case, took out more photographs and some diagrams and moved to the Emir's couch.

'There is no other set like this in the world, Your Royal Highness,' Alonzo Weaver said, displaying pictures of an elaborate model-train layout. 'It can be installed in whatever part of the palace Your Royal Highness prefers.'

'All these things move?' The Emir was beside himself, poking a chubby forefinger at the photographs. 'This – and this – and this?'

'Yes,' Weaver nodded. 'It is a miniature railroad that is unique.'

Sheikh Maktoum rubbed his hands delightedly. Weaver returned to the couch he shared with George Needham.

Mark cleared his throat and began to speak. He told of the Coca-Cola franchise and bottling plant, lowering his voice for dramatic effect when he described how NIPCO would build the

336

plant and operate it without expense to the Emir.

'And here are the documents.' Radford presented them with a flourish.

Maktoum ben Khalifah was ecstatic. He would be able to make a truly royal gesture to his own people by providing them with free Coca-Cola. At absolutely no cost to himself. The Emir would be the envy of all the other rulers in the Persian Gulf states.

'Indeed, Mr Northcutt has sent a princely gift,' he said.

'Ah, but there is yet another, Your Royal Highness.' Mark turned to George Needham. 'Have the package brought in, George.'

The Emir leaned forward. A few moments later, three men pushed a heavy-duty hand truck into the room. There was a steel oil barrel painted with Qantara's national colours on it. The Emir's face fell.

'Oil from Your Royal Highness's own well in America – in the state of New Mexico.' Mark said. 'Mr Northcutt gives you one of his wells as a gesture of personal friendship.' Radford placed a thick sheaf of documents before the Emir. 'The deeds. And I am pleased to inform Your Royal Highness the well produces a thousand barrels of sulphur-free, high-gravity oil daily.'

Sheikh Maktoum was enraptured as he fingered the documents. Had Gulf ever given one of its American wells to the Emir of Kuwait? Or ARAMCO to King Faisal? Not that he could remember – and he certainly would have heard about it. The Sheikh understood the symbolism: one potentate granting a piece of his lands and holdings to another. He signalled an aide.

'Make all this known,' he said in Arabic. He indicated the barrel. 'Display it where all who come to the palace may see!'

The aide bowed and hastened to obey.

Sheikh Maktoum grew thoughtful. The presents – especially the bottling plant and American oil well – would bring him much honour. However, Northcutt no doubt wanted something in return.

'The black man is not with your company?' he asked Mark.

'No,' Radford replied.

'Then he may leave,' the Emir said.

Alonzo Weaver allowed himself to be escorted from the room.

'How may I show Mr Northcutt my gratitude?' the Emir asked.

Mark's belly tightened. Everything depended on what was said in the next few minutes. He had rehearsed what he would say – and how – a dozen times in his mind. Yet, suddenly, he felt unsure, even afraid.

'Mr Northcutt is, as I have said, aware of the effect loss of oil revenue has had on Qantara,' Radford began. He outlined the plan to jury-rig hose lines and pump oil from storage tanks aboard tankers anchored off Batir until the regular, permanent offshore loading facilities were back in operation. NIPCO would clean up all oil spills and pay liberal compensation if any beach-front properties were polluted by crude.

Mark observed the Emir retreat into himself. I'm not getting through, he thought. I'll have to shift the approach. His mind searched frantically for the way.

'But these are trivial matters,' he declared with an elaborate shrug. 'As ruler of Qantara, Your Royal Highness can dispose of them with a wave of a hand. Far more important is Mr Northcutt's plan' – there, not request or proposal, but plan – 'to establish a working partnership that will make Qantara a commercial force in the Middle East.'

That brought a glimmer of response from the Emir.

'Other Arab countries have large surpluses of oil they cannot sell because of their embargo,' Mark continued. 'As a result, their revenues are also down. Some would sell their share of crude produced under concessions if it could be done without violating the embargo.'

Flickers of rising interest from the Emir.

'Qantara hasn't embargoed oil,' Mark said. 'Nor is Qantara on the list of countries boycotted by other oil-producing Arab states. If Qantara were to buy crude and then resell it, there would be no violations of agreements. Qantara would profit, for the usual high commissions would be paid to Your Royal Highness.'

Now, what I hope to Allah is the clincher, Radford thought.

'The world hunger for oil will continue long after the embargo is lifted. By then, Qantara will have established itself as a country that not only produces oil, but is also one of the world's important brokers of Middle Eastern petroleum.'

Sheikh Maktoum's face bore the faint trace of a smile. He was aware that NIPCO desperately needed crude oil. Northcutt was a fox.

Mark held his breath. George Needham remained immobile, his hands buried in his lap so that no one could see that he had his fingers crossed. Now it remained for the Emir to decide.

'No, Mr Radford,' the Emir said and for a moment Mark's heart stopped beating. 'No, the question of using temporary hose lines at Batir is not important . . .'

He's playing with me, Radford thought.

'. . . I will give permission, but there must be an increase in the tax your company pays on the oil it ships from Batir.'

There goes our whole marketing price structure, Mark reflected.

'If it is in reason, Your Royal Highness . . .'

'One American dollar per barrel.'

Mark knew that the Emir, like all Arabs, enjoyed bazaar haggling. 'There have been many increases in the posted price of Middle Eastern oil, Your Royal Highness,' he said. 'A dollar a barrel is very high.'

'Are you empowered to accept a seventy-five-cent-a-barrel increase,' Mr Radford?'

'I, personally, have authority only to agree to a fifty-cent-a-barrel rise without consulting Mr Northcutt,' Mark lied. He had no authority to agree to any increase. The subject had not even been discussed in New York, but he willingly accepted the responsibility.

'Then let it be so. Fifty cents.' The Emir chortled inwardly. He had made his original demand on sudden impulse. The victory was a bonus, and it made him feel expansive. 'My ministers will communicate with the other Arab states today,' he said. 'Perhaps we shall be able to buy their surplus oil as Mr Northcutt suggests.'

Mark remembered almost nothing of the rest of the meeting. Later, when he, George Needham and Alonzo Weaver were outside the palace gates, his pent-up tensions exploded in an ear-splitting whoop. Needham and Weaver laughed, but the Arab driver jumped in his seat and almost ran the car off the road.

There is an eight-hour time difference between Qantara and New York City. The Telex addressed to James Northcutt and sent from Ayat at 12.54 P.M. came over the wire at the NIPCO Building on Park Avenue at 5.54 A.M. The night Telex operator had strict orders. Any such message was to be delivered to Northcutt at his home, regardless of the hour. Another night-shift employee took it to the oilman's Sutton Place house.

Jim Northcutt slept alone. His new mistress, Arlene Barnes, had her own bedroom – and, in any event, he had been too dispirited to take much interest in her the night before.

Shortly after 5.30 A.M., a servant knocked on Jim's bedroom door.

'A company man just brought a cable, Mr Northcutt,' he said.

Jim hurried to the door, and tore open the envelope and read the Telex.

EMIR AUTHORIZED EMERGENCY HOSE LINES SUBJECT FIFTY CENT BARREL ADDED TAX WHICH I OKAYED. WE START RIGGING LINES TODAY. ONE TANKER YOU ORDERED TO BATIR ARRIVED YESTERDAY. WILL LOAD SOONEST. EMIR ALSO AGREES BROKERAGE PROPOSAL AND IS QUERYING OTHER RULERS. REGARDS, RADFORD.

A step forward, Northcutt thought exultantly, reading the Telex again. Crude oil shipments from the Persian Gulf could still right the balance.

Even this degree of encouragement was sufficient to activate inner mechanisms, and Northcutt experienced a sudden surge of physical response. He thrust the Telex into a pocket of his dressing gown, hurried to the bedroom where Arlene Barnes slept. He entered without knocking, moved directly to her bed. He reached for the bedside lamp and turned it on. Arlene stirred, murmured something in half-sleep and finally blinked open her eyes.

'Jim. What's the matter?'

'Nothing.'

He was already stripping off his dressing gown and pyjamas. She edged over to make room for him in the bed. He joined her, his need imperative.

Hurt and bewildered by Mark Radford's behaviour on Friday night, Kathy Northcutt impulsively left the next morning to spend a long weekend with friends on Cape Cod. While there, she read that Charles Farrier had died in an auto accident, but had no reason to connect his death with Mark's mysterious

340

'business appointment'. She returned to New York late Monday afternoon expecting to find flowers and messages from a contrite Mark Radford. Instead, she learned he was in Qantara – and that Monday was a day of unrelieved reverses for her father and NIPCO.

Kathy slept badly Monday night in her Hotel Pierre suite. She arose at eight feeling exhausted and depressed. She was lonely for Mark and regretted having succumbed to a childish feeling of revenge. But above all, she felt helpless. The battle to save NIPCO was going against Jim Northcutt – and being fought on levels at which she could do nothing.

A bath failed to raise her spirits. The breakfast she ordered from room service went uneaten. She thought of a hundred things she could do that day, rejected them all. Kathy was still in her suite when the telephone rang a few minutes before noon.

'Miss Verna Fletcher calling from California, Miss Northcutt,' the hotel operator said.

Kathy's grey eyes widened in astonishment. She knew all about her father's relationship with Verna, but had never met her. The connection was made.

'Hello, Kathy. This may be a bit awkward, but Lloyd Birdwell told me where you were staying. I'm calling because of your father.'

'Oh?'

'I hear Jim's in a real mess. Lloyd gave me some details.' There was a brief pause. 'Kathy, my accountants claim I'm worth eighteen million dollars. Not so much, considering what's involved, but it's ready money. I want *you* to tell me straight. Would it help Jim?'

My God, Kathy thought. Verna Fletcher must still be in love with Dad.

'Verna – you're wonderful. I don't know what to say. Except that Dad's problem isn't money. He has all the capital he needs —'

'Lloyd said the same. I didn't know whether to believe him. Want to tell me your version, Kathy?'

Like Birdwell and Kostis, Verna Fletcher was one of her father's true friends. She began to relate the story.

'... and then there's Barbara Wallace —'

'Who?'

Kathy explained.

'... she really has Sam Schlechter worried,' Kathy concluded.

'That's not surprising. Men are intimidated by women like that. Only other women can beat them.'

'I agree.'

'Kathy, did Jim ever tell you I was a parlourhouse madam when I met him?'

'Yes.'

'I learned plenty about how to handle vicious bitches when I was a madam' – a throaty chuckle – 'and a lot more while I was in the movie business.'

'If you have any ideas, Verna —'

'I sure have. You and I should be able to make mincemeat out of that conniving bitch.'

'You're probably right,' Kathy Northcutt exclaimed.

'Then it's settled. I'll fly out tomorrow,' Verna said. 'Book me a suite at the Pierre. But don't say a word to Jim.'

7

19 July

'God-damnedest Rube Goldberg layout I've ever seen,' George Needham growled from around his ever-present unlit cigar.

'What counts is that it works,' Mark Radford said.

They stood at the edge of a dock at Batir. Both were red-eyed and haggard from lack of sleep, and their workclothes were stained with sweat and dirt. But their own efforts plus round-the-clock labour by hundreds of men had produced results.

Although NIPCO's regular port and deep-water terminal facilities were still inoperative, the 140,000-ton tanker lying a mile offshore was taking on a cargo of crude oil. Dozens of squat, ugly barges and scows anchored in a row from shore to ship served as pontoon-like supports for jury-rigged hose lines. Crude from intact NIPCO storage tanks was being pumped through the lines to the tanker's manifolds and into its holds. The improvised system was costly, slow and wasteful. However, as Mark pointed out, it worked.

George Needham scowled disapproval at the huge dark patches that had formed on the water. Crude oil was leaking from hose joints and couplings. Nothing could be done to prevent it.

'Hate to think of the clean-up job,' he said.

'Can't be helped.' Mark rubbed at the stubble on his face. 'We'll worry about it later. Come on, George.' He turned and they started towards the shore end of the dock, where a company car waited.

'The Old Man should breathe easier now,' Needham remarked.

'Too early to start celebrating,' Radford said. 'We don't even have the first tanker loaded. We need a lot more loads and in a hurry.'

'Hell, we're making progress.'

'And we're both ready to drop.' Mark yawned wearily.

'Quit bitching,' Needham grinned. 'Think of poor Weaver.'

Mark nodded. Agog at the idea of having the world's most elaborate model railroad, Emir Maktoum ben Khalifah had insisted that it be installed in his palace without delay. Alonzo Weaver, recognizing the need for keeping the Emir happy, agreed to work non-stop to rush assembly. He and several NIPCO electricians were, indeed, slaving away.

'It's damned ironic,' Needham continued as he and Radford were driving towards the office. 'We're dealing in terms of oil by the tens of thousands of tons. Lon Weaver is up at the palace working with two-ounce toys. If he flubs, the Emir may get pissed off. Tankers could go empty because a model train runs off the track.'

'Nails, shoes, horses and kingdoms,' Mark said. His eyes burned. He closed them for a moment. 'To say nothing of riders.'

His weariness disappeared when they arrived at the NIPCO administration building in Ayat. The Emir's liaison officer and a covey of self-important, burnoused palace aides were waiting for them. Evidently some of the Arab oil-producing countries had been looking for face-saving loopholes to circumvent their own oil embargoes. The Emir's inquiries had brought astonishingly quick affirmative replies from Saudi Arabia and Abu Dhabi. Both owned a percentage of the oil produced by concessionaire companies. They would sell this crude to Qantara with no questions about what the Emir of Qantara wanted with it.

'Your Excellencies, Mr James Northcutt will be deeply grateful to His Royal Highness and to each of you when he hears of this,' Mark told the palace delegation. He made a mental note to send each member *bakhshish*.

A Qantari official produced several cables which specified quantities, prices and terms of payment. The cables indicated too that tankers could begin loading whenever they arrived. The sheikhs must be feeling the money pinch, Radford thought. They hadn't wasted a minute in leaping at the proposal – but stipulated payment on delivery.

'I shall inform Mr Northcutt,' he said. 'The necessary arrangements will be made.'

The delegation finally departed.

Mark first thought to place a transatlantic call to James Northcutt at his home. But it was 11 A.M. in Qantara, only 3 A.M. in New York. Besides, it could be an endlessly frustrating task. If Qantari operators didn't spend the entire day calling the wrong number in the wrong country, they were likely to disconnect in the middle of a conversation and take another day to re-establish the connection.

Radford settled for a long, detailed Telex. After he finished dictating it to a secretary, he debated sending a regular cable to Kathy Northcutt. He decided against it. Personal considerations would have to wait until he had finished the business assignment her father had given him.

'Things are swinging in our favour for sure,' George Needham grinned. 'Even you have to admit it now.'

'Maybe – just maybe,' Radford hedged. 'Who can tell what's going on behind the scenes between here and the States?'

He would have been considerably more optimistic if he had known what was to transpire that day in the city of the Doges.

Having planned carefully, Russell Peterson felt reasonably secure. He correctly reasoned that Guy Bannister and Powell Pierce would not dare to report his disappearance with Jersey Crest's million. That would reveal the existence of a secret Jersey Crest account. Such a revelation could expose the fact that the money had been intended as bribes for Arthur Gerlach and Rowan Engelhardt.

Nevertheless, Peterson had taken precautions for he was aware that private investigators might be sent to find him. In

344

Zurich, he and his wife Mae had had their hair dyed. They bought expertly forged passports for $5,000 apiece – in the names of Martin and Ruth Henderson. With the year-round tourist flow washing over the European Continent, two Americans could lose themselves very easily, especially if they were travelling under assumed names with perfectly counterfeited passports.

'Where do we go from here?' Mae asked her husband in Zurich.

'Venice,' he told her. 'By train.'

The decision was a shrewd one. Italian border guards barely glanced at American passports. Tourists were not required to fill in any forms when entering the country. Their luggage was never examined. If Martin and Ruth Henderson kept the suitcase containing sheafs of $100 bills with them at all times, it – and they – would be safe.

Italy's banking rules were another consideration. Italian banks opened chequing and savings accounts without demanding more than a quickly flashed passport, a signature – and money. As for Venice, the choice was inspired. The city had only a small resident foreign population and no foreign colonies. Non-Italians living there did not clot into national groups – and there was no US consulate.

Arriving in Venice on 13 July, the 'Martin Hendersons' checked into the Hotel Luna, and on the next day went to the main branch of the Credito Italiano near the Rialto. The bank manager was accustomed to dealing with American tourists who decided to stay in Venice.

'We'll be here a few months,' Peterson/Henderson said. He asked to open $5,000 chequing and $3,000 savings accounts. The amounts were entirely in keeping with ordinary patterns, and there was nothing unusual about an American counting out eighty $100 bills.

'And a safety deposit box.'

'*Certo*, Signor Henderson.' The bank manager smiled.

That afternoon, the 'Martin Hendersons' went apartment hunting. They found a furnished flat on the third floor of a building facing the Campo Santa Maria Formosa. The rent was inordinately high – the equivalent of $650 a month – which was why it was available, an apartment for American tourists who didn't know any better. The couple moved in on 16 July, determined to live there quietly until – as Peterson

345

assured his wife – 'everybody gives up trying to locate us'. Then they could go elsewhere and live on the scale justified by the nine-hundred-thousand-plus dollars now lodged in their safe deposit box.

Mae Peterson was not entirely convinced.

'You've always said Guy Bannister is a vindictive bastard,' she reminded him. 'He's bound to have people looking for us.'

'Now Mae. You're always worrying,' he replied.

Early on Wednesday morning, 19 July, the doorbell rang. Russell Peterson pushed the button releasing the downstairs entry lock and stood on the landing in front of his apartment.

'Signor Henderson?' a man's voice called from below.

'*Si.*' Russell Peterson's Italian was almost non-existent. He shouted over his shoulder to his wife, who was in the *salotto*, the drawing room. 'Mae, how do you say, "What is it?"'

'We speak English, Mr. Henderson,' the voice said. Then, as the two men ascended the stairs, Peterson experienced a cold clutch of fear. Men who spoke English coming to see him?

The men were of medium height and neatly dressed. One was about forty, the other under thirty.

'Rinaldi – and this is Lucca,' the fortyish man said. 'We are not from the police and we have nothing to do with your former employer. Let us go inside and talk.'

Peterson was too shaken to prevent them from entering and led the way to the *salotto*.

Mae Peterson turned pale.

'How – how did you find us?'

'You disappeared from Zurich,' Lucca shrugged. 'That meant you bought forged passports. There are three dealers in such merchandise. When paid, they tell about the passports they have sold. Once we learned you were now Ruth and Martin Henderson, inquiries to hotels and banks ...' His voice trailed off.

'Sooner or later, the others will also find you,' Rinaldi spoke up.

'Others?' Mae whispered fearfully.

Rinaldi nodded and told them that Guy Bannister had hired thugs to hunt them down and very probably kill them.

'We are on behalf of Mr James Northcutt,' Rinaldi continued. 'He will guarantee your safety – if you help him. If you don't ...' Rinaldi spread his hands.

'The money,' Russell Peterson inquired in an uneven voice. 'Does Northcutt want that?'

'What money?' Lucca smiled, showing white teeth. 'Our instructions are to tell you Mr Northcutt knows of no money. He wants only a statement from you. An affidavit signed before the American consul in Milano.'

Peterson understood. By co-operating with Northcutt he would remain free and rich. If he failed to help him, Guy Bannister would have another fate in store for him and Mae. 'I'll give the statement,' he said.

'I will go now and telephone my contacts in New York,' Rinaldi said. 'Lucca will stay here with you.'

'To make sure we don't run out?' Russell Peterson asked.

'*And* to protect you,' Rinaldi said.

James Northcutt started the day with a meeting of all NIPCO home-office executives. He read aloud the Telex he had received from Mark Radford and then passed out copies. Clearly, NIPCO had won a new lease on life, but Northcutt cautioned against over-optimism.

'While we're off one hook – or will be – we're still hanging from others,' he said. 'Now get cracking. I want tankers on the way from the nearest ports, credits transferred and all other preliminaries taken care of today.'

The executives filed out of the office. Minutes later, Northcutt received a telephone call from Robert di Lorenzi.

'Some friends checked in with me – from Venice,' di Lorenzi said. 'They found Russell Peterson.'

'Good work,' Jim Northcutt said. 'Did Peterson make a deal?'

'My people say he'll swear an affidavit. They can have him and his wife at the Francia-Europa Hotel in Milan tomorrow morning. Someone you trust completely should be there to meet them.'

'I have just the man,' Northcutt said. 'He'll be there.'

Verna Fletcher arrived at Kathy Northcutt's suite shortly before four in the afternoon.

'You should have let me meet your plane,' Kathy said. 'Or at least called me when you got to the hotel.'

'Easier this way,' Verna said. 'I'm checked in, unpacked – and ready for action.'

347

'Would you like a drink first?'

'I'd love one. Do you have any bourbon?'

Verna Fletcher was in her seventies. Kathy not yet thirty. But despite the age difference, there was an instant rapport between the two women.

Verna studied Kathy while she poured two drinks. The girl has her mother's hair and facial structure, Verna thought, but otherwise she's all Jim Northcutt. Same expressive grey eyes, same screw-the-world independence, same fearlessness.

She took the drink that Kathy handed her.

'Here's to your father,' Verna said, raising her glass. She downed the bourbon and smiled. 'I'm really sorry you and I didn't get to know each other long before this.'

'So am I.' Verna Fletcher is the woman Dad should have married, Kathy mused, sipping her own drink. She must have been gorgeous. But more than that, she's the same breed as James L. Northcutt. 'I'd love to hear about what he was like and what he did in Oklahoma.'

'He wasn't much different than he is now,' Verna said softly. 'Jim had two big hang-ups. Oil and beating the world. He always knew what he wanted. He never changed.'

'He never did,' Kathy said.

'You're afraid for him, aren't you, Kathy?'

'Very much so. Dad was sure that what he accomplished in China would put NIPCO on top of the world he's always been out to beat. Then, all of a sudden, the whole picture flipped over. He's in deeper trouble than he's ever been.'

'Then let's get down to business,' Verna said, her blue eyes keenly alert. 'You start. By telling me everything, and I mean *everything*, you know about Barbara Wallace.'

8

20 July

The co-pilot of the chartered Lear jet had to go back into the cabin and shake Mark Radford's shoulder to wake him.

'We're at Malpensa,' he announced.

'Jesus!' Mark exclaimed. He tried to rub some life into his

face. 'Mind if I shave before I offload myself?' he asked.

'Go right ahead.'

Radford hoisted his big frame out of the seat, took his toilet kit and a clean shirt from an overnight bag and headed aft. Every step was an effort. He had never been so tired in his life.

At three-thirty the previous afternoon, he and George Needham had gone to Needham's residence in the NIPCO housing compound. They had eaten, bathed and then tried to catch a few hours of desperately needed sleep. At six-thirty, the Telex from James Northcutt was brought to Needham's quarters.

There could be no more sleep after that. Northcutt's instructions were unequivocal. Mark Radford was to be in Milan in the morning. George Needham would take over Mark's special assignments in addition to his own duties as acting resident manager.

The two men had stayed up the remainder of the night, swallowing Dexamyl spansules while they meticulously went over all that Needham would have to do. Then Mark composed a flowery letter to Emir Maktoum ben Khalifah. He apologized for his abrupt departure and assured the Emir that George Needham now had full authority to speak and act for James Northcutt. It was all drudgery that sapped what little remained of the men's energies, offset only by the light note Alonzo Weaver provided when he appeared a little before midnight. Although he, too, was on the verge of total exhaustion, Weaver was greatly amused and he opened a flat leather box to display a glittering decoration.

'Dig this,' he said. 'Order of the Qantarise Lion and Scimitar. First Class. The Emir freaked. He and his whole court are having a ball running his model railroad.'

'You didn't manage to get the whole thing set up already?' Mark asked in astonishment.

'Less than a third, but we spliced it together so that section would operate independently until the rest was done.' Weaver closed the box and slipped it into a pocket. 'I figured the top priority was to keep His Nibs happy.'

'How the hell can I say thanks, Lon?'

'For what, Mark?'

'For busting your ass.'

'Your goal orientation is catching. Anyway, busting my ass to help a four-billion-dollar corporation feeds my ego.' The tall black man became serious. 'Think you've turned your situation around?'

'Partly,' Radford nodded. He eyed Weaver squarely. 'If we win, there's a big-gadget engineering job wide open for you, Lon.'

'I might just take it. Right now, I'm taking my ass to bed. I got the other two-thirds of a railroad to start building again in the morning.'

Mark left Qantara before dawn aboard a NIPCO Pilatus. The Lear jet, chartered for him by the home-office, was waiting at the Kuwait airport, but there were delays in obtaining flight clearance. When, at last, the plane took off, Mark fell asleep. He slept during the entire flight to Milan.

Three people met Radford at Malpensa Airport. One was an attorney from the firm that represented NIPCO's Italian subsidiary. The other two were women, bilingual stenographers. Mark dismissed the attorney; no matter what the home-office thought, he wanted no Italian lawyers present when he confronted Russell Peterson Then he chose one of the stenographers, a plump brunette who gave the impression of being both efficient and trustworthy. He and the stenographer then took a taxi. Following Northcutt's instructions, he told the driver to take them to the Hotel Francia-Europa.

Rinaldi was waiting for Mark in the hotel lobby. He identified himself and said Russell and Mae Peterson were in a suite upstairs.

'My colleague is with them.'

'Has Peterson said anything to you?' Mark asked.

'Yes, a great deal,' Rinaldi smiled. 'He is a very frightened man.' His smile deepened. 'I think you will be amazed at what Peterson has to tell you, Mr Radford – and very pleased.'

The downward spiral of Northcutt International Petroleum Company stock had continued. On Wednesday, it closed at 31, for a total loss of 28½ points in three days. There was talk of suspending the stock as well as rumours of an S.E.C. investigation.

Jim Northcutt anticipated further drops, and he spoke to the head of the large brokerage house with which he had dealt for years.

'When NIPCO touches twenty, start buying for my account.'

Northcutt sought personal profits. Crude shipments from

the Middle East would enable NIPCO to fulfil all its promises of increased product allocations. Once that was demonstrated, the stock would begin to rise. His profits would be in the millions. And, if other problems facing NIPCO were resolved, the shares were certain to rebound and reach new highs, and his profits would be in the tens of millions.

Jersey Crest's Board Chairman, Powell Pierce, was stunned and infuriated. James Northcutt had managed to outsmart him – and the Majors forming the Middle Eastern monopoly – by breaking the boycott.

'We look like fools!' he told his executives in New York, making no effort to hide his outrage. 'Jersey Crest stays on the Arab embargo while an independent manipulates a tin-pot Emir, makes an oil broker out of him and starts buying all the oil it wants!'

Northcutt's manoeuvre was a serious setback to his plans for forcing NIPCO out of business.

Pierce held phone consultations with the heads of American Protyle, Richland Consolidated and other major oil companies. He received scant encouragement. His conversation with the president of Western Impex was notable for its candour.

'NIPCO is sliding out of the trap,' Pierce said.

'We don't like it any more than you do, Powell,' the Western Impex president declared. 'Look at the big picture. The Arab boycott keeps the oil shortage going over here, and that's good for all of us. We're getting everything we wanted from price increases to new legislation. We can't stop Arab rulers from buying and selling among themselves, even if one of them is fronting for NIPCO. And we certainly can't agree to the Arabs' demands – or there won't be any shortage.'

'Granted,' Pierce said. 'On the other hand, NIPCO is going to gain a competitive edge.'

'For a short period. We can all live with it. After all, the first energy crisis cleared out around thirty per cent of the independents. This one will eliminate even more, and then we won't have any competition worth mentioning.'

Frustrated by the stand taken by his petroleum-industry peers, Pierce summoned Guy Bannister to his office.

Bannister had nothing to offer, either.

'Farrier's outfit refuses to do any more work on NIPCO

service stations,' he said. 'I've approached other organizations like it. They won't even listen. What happened to Farrier scared them all, and as I've told you, some top syndicate people are backing Northcutt.'

Bannister tried to provide some encouragement.

'Frankly, Mr Pierce, I don't think you need to put any more pressure on NIPCO. You have Gerlach and Engelhardt working for you down in Washington.'

Powell Pierce smiled a barely perceptible smile. Yes, he mused. He did have Chief Presidential Advisor Arthur Gerlach and Energy Resources Secretary Rowan Engelhardt working for him – and against NIPCO. He would simply have to be patient. James Northcutt had won nothing more than a brief reprieve.

There had been a note of extreme urgency in Kathy Northcutt's voice when she called Samuel Schlechter and insisted on seeing him. Schlechter juggled his jammed appointments calendar and created a free hour beginning at 11 A.M. He expected Kathy to come alone. He did not dream that she would arrive at his offices with Verna Fletcher.

'It's been years, Sam!' Verna kissed his cheek. He was Abe Schlechter's son and seeing him brought back more memories. 'How many? Ten?'

Schlechter's surprise increased when he remembered that to his knowledge, Kathy and Verna had never met.

'More like twelve,' he said. 'During one of my business trips out to the Coast. At a party somebody gave.' If Kathy and Verna were merely making a social call, he wished they had made it at some other time. His work load was enormous.

'We're not here to make small talk,' Kathy said, reading his thoughts. She quickly recounted the telephone conversation she had had with Verna two days before. 'I mentioned Barbara Wallace, and Verna flew out from California yesterday,' she concluded.

Schlechter looked perplexed.

'Why?' he asked Verna. 'Do you know Barbara Wallace?'

'Personally? No. I've known a thousand poisonous little bitches exactly like her.' Verna's tone, at first sour, now became wry. 'I learned how to take care of them when I was a madam – and got a post-graduate course in Hollywood. How do you think I survived, Sam?'

'Well —'

'Don't try to answer,' Verna laughed. 'Being a man, you can't. Infighting with Barbara Wallace is a purely female combat art.'

'You've had private detectives watching Barbara, haven't you, Sam?' Kathy asked.

'Yes.'

'And her lawyer?'

'I did get a background investigation on him.'

'Verna and I would like to see all the reports.'

Sam blinked. 'Maybe I'm dense, but what for?'

Kathy countered with her own question. 'How much luck have you had with Barbara?'

'Very little,' Schlechter admitted.

Kathy cocked her right eyebrow. Exactly like Jim, Verna Fletcher thought.

'You've been going by the book, Sam,' Kathy said. 'Trying to negotiate a settlement —'

'Naturally.'

'Barbara started out by demanding a third of Dad's stock. Have you got anywhere?'

Schlechter scowled. 'Farquhar is now talking twenty-five million. My instinct is he won't go much lower. I haven't dared tell Jim yet.'

'Twenty-five million!' Verna exclaimed. 'No wonder you haven't dared tell Jim.'

'Farquhar knows how much damage Barbara can do,' Schlechter said morosely. 'If she volunteers her testimony to the I.R.S., Jim will be indicted. With the climate in Washington and public attitude towards oilmen and oil companies, he would certainly be convicted on several counts of tax fraud.' He sighed. 'Sure, we could keep him out of prison by appealing – but his and NIPCO's reputations would be finished.'

Verna leaned forward in her chair.

'Sam, Farquhar is sleeping with Barbara, isn't he?'

'Good guess. According to the surveillance reports —'

'I wasn't guessing,' Verna interrupted. 'Females like Barbara Wallace always leap into bed with the shysters who help them shake down their ex-lovers. It never fails.'

'What if they are sleeping together?' Sam said. 'Barbara isn't going to be frightened off by any fears of scandal.'

Verna grinned. 'You're thinking like a man.'

'Sam.' Kathy's voice was impatient. 'Give us those reports.'

Schlechter gazed at the two women.

'If you'd only tell me what you intend doing.'

'Nothing that will make things any worse than they already are,' Kathy assured him.

'Marilyn,' Sam said, depressing a key on his desk-top intercom. 'Bring me the investigation reports on Wallace and Farquhar.'

At 11.55 A.M., James Northcutt had two NIPCO vice-presidents in his office.

'Mr Radford is calling you from Milan, Mr Northcutt,' his secretary informed him.

Northcutt asked the two vice-presidents to leave and took the call.

'I have the affidavit,' Mark said. 'Duly executed before an American consular official. Beautifully decorated with stamps and seals and bright red ribbons.'

'And you're drunk.'

'Groggy only. From lack of sleep, J.L.'

'How much is Peterson's statement worth to us?'

'You wouldn't believe all that Peterson spilled even if I told you, and I can't. Not over a telephone. I'd estimate its assay value to NIPCO at a billion dollars a page. Minimum. As you'll see when I bring it in tomorrow.'

'When are you flying back?'

'First plane in the morning.'

'Why not tonight?' Northcutt demanded. 'There should be several flights out of Milan.'

'I have to make arrangements for Peterson and his wife so they'll be safe. That was part of the deal.'

'Then Telex your flight number,' the oilman said. 'I'll send someone to meet you at the airport.'

'Make it Sam Schlechter. He might want to grab a copy and fly right down to Washington.'

Northcutt's eyebrow shot up high. 'The statement is that hot?'

'J.L., it's so hot it may just melt the roof off the White House!'

354

9

21 July

Northcutt and Schlechter were both at Kennedy Airport when Mark Radford arrived aboard a morning Alitalia flight.

'I decided I'd better be here too,' Northcutt growled to Mark. 'I couldn't stand the damned suspense.'

His limousine stood outside the International Arrivals Building in casual disregard of parking regulations. The three men got into the passenger compartment. Northcutt told his chauffeur to remain parked where he was. Sam flicked the switch that rolled up a glass partition and sealed them off from the chauffeur in soundproofed isolation.

'How is Kathy?' Mark asked as he opened his attaché case.

'Don't know,' Northcutt replied. 'Haven't seen her in the last couple of days.'

Schlechter remained silent. He had said nothing to Northcutt about the visit Kathy and Verna had made to his office.

'Here they are.' Mark gave copies of Russell Peterson's affidavit to the oilman and the attorney, holding one himself. The three men began reading. Mark followed along, ready to answer any questions.

'My God, man!' Jim Northcutt exclaimed after scanning only the first two pages. 'You weren't joking!'

It was all there. Russell Peterson had witheld nothing. Guy Bannister's relationships with Powell Pierce, Charles Farrier and Gerhard Hohenberg were spelled out in detail.

'... Federpol, the firm by which I was employed, retained an underworld organization to carry out numerous fire-bombing attacks against service stations selling Northcutt International Petroleum Company products. This was done on behalf of Mr Powell Pierce and the Jersey Crest Oil Company, clients of Federpol. My employer, Mr Guy Bannister, also hired a sabotage organization, headed by a Gerhard Hohenberg in Istanbul...'

Mark Radford grinned. 'It gets better as it goes along,' he said.

Jim Northcutt turned a page, his grey eyes widening.

'. . . I personally made the initial approaches to Mr Arthur Gerlach, the Chief Presidential Advisor, on 25 June. It was understood that Mr Gerlach and Energy Resources Secretary Rowan Engelhardt were to receive cash payment of one million dollars. They were to use their official positions to discredit the Northcutt International Petroleum Company and Mr James L. Northcutt. Mr Powell Pierce, who would supply the money, wished to have approval of Northcutt International Petroleum's agreements with the People's Republic of China blocked. Mr Gerlach agreed to prevail upon the Chinese Government to deal instead with a consortium formed by the Jersey Crest Oil Company . . .'

'You could almost call this overskill,' Northcutt chuckled.

'Useful, but hardly conclusive,' Schlechter said in a cautionary tone. 'All we have here is the unsupported testimony of a single individual. Who, we should remember, is not very likely to return to the United States and elaborate on this affidavit in person.'

'We know that – but who else does?' Jim said. 'Peterson's statement is enough to justify an investigation – and if no one's interested in making one, Jack Anderson would jump at the chance to publish it.'

He gave his copy back to Mark.

'I've gambled my hide on a lot less,' he said. 'We're all going to Washington – right now.' He touched a switch, rolling down the partition. 'Take us to La Guardia, fast,' he told his chauffeur.

They made the next scheduled American Airlines flight for Washington with only minutes to spare. At 10.55, they landed at the National Airport.

'You two see Bosworth,' Northcutt told his companions. 'I'm going to pay an undiplomatic call on the Chinese diplomatic mission.'

Senator John Bosworth's jaw dropped as he read the Peterson affidavit.

'Do you realize what you've got here?' he said to Schlechter and Radford. 'This will blow the new Administration apart!'

'Which is something we'd much prefer to avoid,' Schlechter said. 'My experience has been that when there are explosions, everybody gets hurt.'

356

'For Christ's sake, Sam!' Bosworth protested. 'Unless you use this —'

'Oh, we want to use it, John. Only we're liable to get much further if we do it quietly.' Schlechter smiled. 'How soon can you arrange a meeting with the President?'

The question startled John Bosworth.

'Uh – in a week, maybe,' he said.

'What if you and Senator Hurley say you want to discuss a matter of great political importance?'

'Probably much faster, provided we're not shortstopped by Gerlach.'

'Do your best, John. An Oval Office klatsch – for you, Hurley, Jim, Radford and me. Tomorrow or the next day.'

'That's going to be damned rough.'

'Do it,' Sam said, and got to his feet. Mark followed suit. 'We're going back to New York. Call Jim or me the minute you have things set.'

James Northcutt's visit to the Chinese diplomatic mission was brief. He asked to see the chief of the mission and, when he had identified himself, was received without further delay. The preliminary courtesies exchanged, Jim came to the point.

'You have doubtless been hearing many negative things about my company,' he said with the blunt frankness he had found that the Chinese understood and appreciated from Western businessmen. 'I am here without previous notification or appointment to make a request. Please notify Peking that I came to guarantee that our trade agreements will be approved by the United States within two weeks.'

'Mr Northcutt, I shall of course transmit what you have told me. However, you are a private citizen. May I inquire how you propose to guarantee what your government will do?'

'With my own money,' Northcutt replied. 'In the event the agreements are not approved within two weeks from today, I shall indemnify the Chinese People's Republic. With a payment of fifty million dollars. You will have a formal commitment to that effect by tomorrow morning.'

That, James Northcutt reasoned, would prevent the Chinese from opening negotiations with the Jersey Crest consortium until the deadline had passed. By then, the Peterson affidavit should have had its sandbagging effect on the Administration.

*　　*　　*

357

Northcutt appeared to be bemused on the flight to New York. He listened with only half an ear to what Schlechter and Mark told him about their conversation with Senator John Bosworth. He volunteered no information regarding his talk with head of the Chinese diplomatic mission.

Fifteen minutes after they were aloft, Northcutt ordered drinks. A double bourbon for himself. He swallowed it in one gulp, and there was a sudden gleam in his eye.

'Shale oil,' he said. 'Do you realize there are two thousand billion barrels of oil waiting to be extracted from shale formations in Colorado, Wyoming and Utah alone?'

Sam and Mark stared at him, then at each other.

'The British were producing oil from shale as far back as 1915 or so,' Northcutt went on as though delivering a history lecture. 'Only the British oil cartel bought up the leases on shale-bearing land and all the processing patents.'

He rubbed his jaw.

'Pretty much the same thing happened over here. The Majors have been stalling for decades on developing shale oil reserves. Afraid it would knock the bottom out of crude prices.' He smiled. 'We have a hundred thousand acres of shale-bearing land under lease out west. With regular crude prices up to eleven dollars a barrel and higher – Christ! We should be able to extract oil from shale and sell it around six-fifty, seven a barrel.'

He busied himself rolling a cigarette. When he had it lit, Jim blew smoke towards the cabin ceiling.

'Mark, make a mental note. I want cost estimates on a pilot plant. Shale-oil production is going to be NIPCO's next project.'

Radford felt something akin to awe. The old man had barely begun to glimpse the first signs of hope – and even these were still without real substance. Yet, he was already thinking far ahead, planning a great new venture.

Sam Schlechter was beaming inwardly. He was neither awed nor greatly surprised. Jim Northcutt was only being himself, the eternal wildcatter impatient to make his next big strike.

Northcutt had taken pen and notebook from his pocket. He was making notes and calculations and did not speak again until the plane touched down at La Guardia.

Then the oilman's mind was abruptly refocused on matters of immediate concern. The entire situation would have to be reviewed in light of the latest developments. Existing plans had to be revised, new orders and instructions issued.

'Not quite four o'clock,' he noted as they prepared to disembark. 'We'll work late tonight, and you might as well figure on putting in a full day tomorrow, too.'

When they were in the NIPCO office suite, Radford excused himself and telephoned Kathy at the Pierre.

'Miss Northcutt is not in,' the hotel switchboard operator told him. Mark left a message and went into Northcutt's private office.

Jim waved him to a chair near an elaborate Uher tape recorder.

'Turn that thing on,' he said, 'and give Sam and me a complete rundown on Qantara and your dealings with the Emir. After that, fill us in on any details regarding Russell Peterson that aren't in his affidavit. A secretary will type your report.'

Mark opened his attaché case and took out a folder filled with papers and notes he had brought back with him. He switched on the recorder and began speaking. Northcutt and Schlechter listened attentively.

Kathy Northcutt had instructed the switchboard and front desk to tell all callers she was away from the hotel, but she was in her suite with Verna Fletcher. They had spent most of the previous day studying the investigators' reports they had obtained from Sam Schlechter. The outlines of a scheme they instinctively felt would demolish Barbara Wallace had begun to take form.

On Friday morning, they went to Kathy's bank. Next, they visited a law firm Verna Fletcher had frequently used in the past. She and the senior partner were old friends. She could ask him for advice that Sam would never give for fear of embroiling Kathy in trouble. After that, Kathy and Verna lunched at Le Perigord, returned to the Pierre and went over their plans step by step.

'It's really a simple scenario,' Verna said. 'Let's look at our main characters. Barbara Wallace – small-time hooker with big ideas. Give her a bad shock, and she'll fall apart. Then we have Dwight Farquhar, a terror as a shyster lawyer, but at heart, one hundred per cent pure john.'

She held up the voluminous background report on the attorney.

'Farquhar is a square. He belongs to all kinds of clubs and associations. His wife is even worse. Then, there's his daughter. She's going to have a coming-out party in the fall.'

'He does seem to be vulnerable,' Kathy said. 'But with so much money involved, he might show some courage.'

'We have to convince him he won't get any money. But let's stay with what we know about him. He's obviously worried about keeping up appearances.'

'The scared-rabbit husband grabbing quickies,' Kathy added.

'The world's full of them.' Verna flipped through the report. 'Farquhar slips up to Barbara's hotel room after office hours, twice, three times a week. Doesn't even take her out to dinner – and by eleven, he's on his way home. With the story that he's been busy with a client.'

'Which he has, truthful man.'

'The Saturday thing is the most helpful,' Verna said. 'Each Saturday since she's been in New York, Farquhar has gone to Barbara's hotel at one in the afternoon and stayed until three-thirty.'

'We'll have to give letter-perfect performances,' Verna continued, 'right down to the last word and gesture. It's going to take a lot of rehearsing.'

Mark did not leave Jim Northcutt's office until after 10 P.M. He took a taxi to the Drake. There were no messages in his box. It was, he reflected gloomily, a good thing that he was so tired. At least he could go to sleep quickly, without thinking too much about Kathy or what she was doing.

10

22 July

Mark did not telephone Kathy in the morning. Since she failed to call him back, he assumed she was away overnight. He had to accept the possibility that she was with a man, and the thought made his mood dismal. After breakfast, he went to the NIPCO building. Jim was already there. Sam arrived soon afterwards. The three men resumed their work where they had left off the night before.

They were about to take a break for lunch when a secretary informed Northcutt that he had a call from Senator John Bosworth.

'Dick Hurley and I used up a year's supply of favours owed us,' Bosworth told the oilman. 'We got us all invited to a White House prayer breakfast tomorrow morning.'

'A prayer breakfast?' Northcutt snorted. 'Jesus Christ!'

'He won't be there personally,' Bosworth laughed. 'The Reverend Steven Howell Stone is standing in for him. You know, the man who puts God on the front page. Anyway, we all have to be at the West Gate at seven-thirty. Sharp. The President is giving us thirty minutes in the Oval Office after the last amen.'

'Sounds okay, John.'

'There's one hitch. Arthur Gerlach will be at the meeting.'

After a moment's reflection, Northcutt said, 'Could be a big advantage. We'll fly down this afternoon, stay at the Hilton. I'd like to talk with you and Hurley this evening.'

'About six-thirty, Jim.'

Northcutt turned to Mark and Schlechter. 'Go pack and meet me at Newark in two hours.'

Mark returned to the Drake. There was still no word from Kathy. He was at the Newark Airport long before either Northcutt or Schlechter.

Barbara Wallace was staying at the St Mortiz Hotel on Central Park South, where she had a double room on the sixth floor.

On Saturday morning, Kathy Northcutt registered at the St Mortiz and obtained a sixth-floor room. At 12.15 P.M., she met Verna Fletcher in the hotel lobby. There had been several photographs of Dwight Farquhar included with the investigators' reports, and they would have no difficulty recognizing him. Farquhar, conservatively dressed and purposeful in expression, came into the hotel minutes before one o'clock and went directly to an elevator.

'Give him thirty minutes,' Verna said. 'With that type, it's hello – and into bed. Which is where we want to find him.'

At one-thirty, they took an elevator up to the sixth floor.

Barbara Wallace made a convincing show of climaxing at the same time as Dwight Farquhar.

361

'There, baby – hey, what the hell?' He released her suddenly, and she straightened up. Someone was knocking on the door.

'Probably a chambermaid,' Barbara whispered. Raising her voice, she called out, 'Who is it?'

'Kathy Northcutt.'

'My God!' Barbara Wallace gasped. Dwight Farquhar leaped from the bed and grabbed for his clothes.

'What the hell is she doing here?' Barbara demanded. Farquhar shook his head – he had been about to ask the same question.

'We want to talk to you and Dwight Farquhar,' Kathy said. 'We know he's there.'

Farquhar, in shorts and undershirt, fumbled with his trousers and stared at Barbara. Kathy had said *we*.

'Put on a nightgown and stay in bed,' he rasped. 'You're ill.'

'The hell with her. I won't open the door.'

'Do what I tell you!' Dwight Farquhar ordered.

Barbara ignored him. 'I'll call the desk and have you thrown out, Kathy.'

'You can't. I'm a registered guest.'

'God damn it, a nightgown!' Farquhar said. Barbara cursed and went to the bathroom. She returned moments later in an ice-blue nightgown and climbed back into bed. By then, Farquhar was dressed. He checked himself in a mirror, squared his shoulders and opened the door.

'Now, then!' he barked. He recognized the lovely young redhead as James Northcutt's daughter. The other woman was older – in her late fifties, he thought at first glance, then on closer look revised the estimate upward. She looked vaguely familiar.

'How do you do, Mr Farquhar,' Kathy said, her voice cool, polite. 'You don't mind if we come in, do you?' The attorney with whom Verna had spoken emphasized they should enter Barbara's room only with permission, even if it was just implied. Farquhar had reflexively edged aside. Kathy and Verna stepped past him.

'Hello, Barbara,' Kathy said. The woman in the blue nightgown merely glowered.

'Who are you?' Farquhar demanded of Verna as he banged the door closed.

'Verna Harkness. An old friend of the Northcutt family.'

The actress, Farquhar thought. No wonder she looked familiar.

'Miss Wallace hasn't been feeling well,' he said.

'Nice of you to stop by and look after her so regularly.' Verna smiled and made herself comfortable in an armchair. She opened her large Hermes handbag and pulled out copies of the private detectives' report.

'Barbara has been under surveillance,' Verna went on. 'Mrs Farquhar may be interested to find out how often you visit her.'

Farquhar glared at her.

'Throw them out, Dwight!' Barbara said.

'Calm down, Barbara.' Kathy took a chair near the bed. 'We're not here to make trouble for either of you. We want to help Dad.'

'Your father has an attorney!' Farquhar snapped.

'Yes, and Sam and I have been begging him to change his mind.' She turned to face Barbara. 'Dad has decided he won't pay you anything. He doesn't care if he is indicted. You'll hear about it formally from Sam Schlechter Monday morning.'

Dwight Farquhar and Barbara Wallace glanced at each other. Neither of them had ever seriously considered the possibility that Northcutt would be willing to face tax-fraud charges.

'He'll be convicted!' Barbara said.

'Maybe,' Kathy replied. 'But he says he'd rather spend the money fighting the case – that he can stay out of prison by filing appeals for years.'

Farquhar wet his lips. NIPCO was in difficulties. Its stock was still sinking. Northcutt probably no longer cared about his or his company's reputation. And if he were indicted, there would be nothing for Barbara but vengeful satisfaction – and there would be absolutely nothing for him.

Kathy met Farquhar's eyes. 'Call Schlechter,' she said. 'I'll give you his home telephone number. I don't want Dad indicted. Maybe Sam —'

'Don't,' Barbara commanded. Kathy had always been deeply attached to her father. Maybe there was another way. 'What else do you have to say, Kathy?'

'Barbara, if you go to the I.R.S., you'll be even with Dad, but what else will you have? Only whatever is left of the fifty thousand he gave you in France.' Kathy paused, stared at the carpet. 'You might even have to give back the car and jewellery that Dad bought for you.'

Barbara's eyes flicked to Farquhar. 'Is that true?'

He hesitated.

'If he won't tell you, I will,' Verna spoke up. 'Minority stockholders are bound to file lawsuits. The courts could order that you return whatever Jim gave you.'

'Only a remote possibility,' Farquhar said at last.

But it *is* a possibility, Barbara thought miserably.

'And, of course, you'll be dead socially,' Verna said.

'What the hell do you mean?'

'You'll be marked as an informer for the I.R.S.' Verna shrugged. 'Do you think anyone with money would ever speak to you again?'

'Jim dumped me!' she shouted. 'He gave me a lousy hand-out. I'm not going to sit still for it!'

'That's why I'm here,' Kathy said. 'I have my trust fund. I can't touch the principal, but the income is mine. I want to save Dad. I can't pay what you've been asking, but I can make it worth your while – and yours, Mr Farquhar.'

Farquhar's expression indicated he was already calculating how much the traffic might bear.

'I took Barbara as a client without a retainer,' he said. 'I presume you recognize that I'm entitled to —'

'You son of a bitch!' Barbara flared.

'That's how it always is,' Verna said softly. 'Lawyers want theirs off the top.'

Kathy opened her white linen handbag and produced a cheque.

'I'm offering you a hundred thousand dollars, Mr Farquhar. The cheque is certified.' She held it up.

'What about me?' Barbara screeched, leaping from the bed and going to Farquhar. 'If I ever opened up with what I know about you —'

He spun around. For a moment, it appeared that he would hit her.

'Barbara,' Kathy said. 'I'm going to pay you, too.'

'How much?'

'The same. Plus two thousand a month for a year.'

'No!' Barbara said. 'That's just another hand-out!'

Kathy stood up. 'We'd better go, Verna.' The two women started for the door.

'Wait a moment.' It was Farquhar who spoke. Verna and Kathy stared at him silently. 'Sit down – please.'

'We'll stand,' Kathy said. 'There's no use carrying this any further. You've made up your minds. I've done all I can for Dad.'

'I'll take the cheque, Miss Northcutt.'

'You rotten bastard!' Barbara howled. 'I'll get another lawyer and fix you *and* Northcutt!'

Farquhar sneered. 'The next lawyer you retain will want cash in advance. What could he do for you – except to keep you out of jail? There won't be any more money from Northcutt, no matter who represents you.'

Kathy had the cheque in her hand.

'Just sign a short statement saying that you're withdrawing as Barbara's attorney,' she said. 'I imagine there's stationery in that desk.'

'Dwight!' Barbara protested.

Farquhar paid no attention to her. He went to the desk, took stationery from the drawer and a pen from his pocket and wrote hurriedly.

'I'll report you to the Bar Association!' Barbara shouted.

'Go ahead.' Farquhar shrugged. 'You wanted to blackmail Northcutt. I refused to help you. That's my story.'

Kathy and Verna watched the byplay in silence.

Farquhar gave Kathy the sheet of St Mortiz stationery on which he had been writing. She glanced at it, handed him the cheque. Neither of them said a word. He put the cheque in his pocket and left, still without speaking.

Barbara Wallace's face was livid with rage. Farquhar had built up her hopes that she would get millions. And now in less than an hour those hopes had all fallen apart. She had perhaps $45,000 remaining in a French bank. The $1,500 monthly allowance from Northcutt would be stopped. Her threat to report him to the Internal Revenue Service no longer had meaning. She could still harm him, but she would be harming herself, too.

Barbara sat on the edge of the bed, her defeat all too apparent.

'My offer still stands,' Kathy said softly.

Barbara nodded numbly.

Kathy held out a piece of paper. 'You'll have to sign this.'

'What is it?'

It was a one-paragraph statement. Simply worded, it declared that a $100,000 bribe was being given and taken in order to suppress information concerning a possible federal criminal offence. 'We both sign it,' Kathy added. 'You take one copy. I take another. It should be enough to make both of us keep our promises.'

The expression on Barbara's face became crafty. 'I'll have to pay tax on the money you give me.'

Kathy sighed. 'No, you won't. It's a gift. I'll pay the tax.'

Without another word, Barbara arose, took the pen and signed.

'Your performance was magnificent,' Verna told Kathy as they left the St Mortiz. 'You should have been an actress.'

'With you directing me, I couldn't miss,' Kathy grinned. 'Wait until Dad and Schlechter hear!'

'I'm not sure that Barbara won't have second thoughts,' Verna mused aloud. 'She may still try to double-cross you and Jim.'

'She probably will. But not for the year that my cheques keep coming in. That'll give Dad's accountants time to go back over the books and do whatever accountants do to cover up past sins.'

When they returned to the Pierre, Kathy stopped by the front desk and picked up her mail for the first time in more than two days. She shuffled through the telephone messages as they rode up in the elevator.

'Mark's back!' she exclaimed.

'Who?' Verna asked.

The car had reached Kathy's floor.

'Mark Radford,' Kathy replied. 'He works for Dad, and he's been in the Middle East. We – that is I got into a huff and didn't have a chance to see Mark before he left.'

'You are – as they say these days – badly hung up,' Verna observed with a smile as Kathy opened the door to her suite. 'What's he like?'

What is Mark like? Kathy pondered for a moment and found the answer. 'In many ways, very much like James L. Northcutt – and I don't give a damn if my Electra complex is showing.'

Kathy telephoned her father's Sutton Place house. A servant told her he had gone to Washington and would not return until some time the next day. She tried Sam Schlechter's residence next and learned that Sam was with her father. Then she called the Drake.

'Mr Radford left word to tell all callers he will be out of town until tomorrow,' she was informed.

Kathy knew her father and Schlechter had always stayed at the Mayflower whenever they went to Washington. She placed a call to that hotel.

'Neither Mr Northcutt nor Mr Schlechter are registered, and we have no reservations for them.'

Kathy frowned as she replaced the receiver. She wondered what her father, Sam and very probably Mark Radford were doing in Washington on a Saturday. She feared that some new crisis had arisen. She wished that she could tell them about what Verna and she had accomplished with Barbara.

'I'll order some champagne,' she said to Verna.

Verna grinned. 'While you were busy at the front desk, I told the concierge to have a magnum of Taittinger sent up. We'll get drunk, and I'll tell you all the stories you want to hear about Jim.'

11

23 July

The White House prayer breakfast ran its seemingly interminable course. Aides finally ushered James Northcutt and his party to the Oval Office in the West Wing. Northcutt, Sam and Mark were apprehensive. Senators Hurley and Bosworth could afford to be relaxed; they were simply performing a political chore and stood to gain, no matter what the outcome.

Senator Hurley made the introductions. The President appraised his visitors. The old oilman, tall, grizzled and still tough. A considerably younger man of much the same breed, even taller, with keen blue eyes and sun-seared features. The attorney, somewhere near sixty, compactly built and clearly shrewd and able. He suspected they made a formidable trio.

The President seated himself behind the Buchanan desk flanked by flags and surrounded by symbols of power. His manner was coolly urbane, that of his Chief Advisor Arthur Gerlach, alert and wary.

'I dislike Sunday conferences,' the President said to Senator Hurley. 'However, you emphasized urgency and national interest.'

'As chairman of the Senate Energy Resources Committee, I think any matter concerned with fuel shortages deserves top priority,' Hurley said. He gave Xerox copies of the Russell Peterson affidavit to the President and Arthur Gerlach. 'I urge you to read this, Mr President.'

James Northcutt watched the Chief Executive and held his breath.

The President began reading, and his broad face paled. He had taken office in January fiercely determined that there would be no scandals like those which rocked previous administrations. An honest man, he appointed Executive branch officials he believed were equally honest. His initial reaction to the Peterson affidavit was one of shock. Then loyalty to his subordinates and confidence in his own judgement reasserted themselves. Grave accusations were being levelled by some obscure individual with unknown motives. Unless substantiated, they meant nothing. Yet, Senators Hurley and Bosworth evidently put stock in the allegations, and they were neither fools nor political innocents. Common sense advised a cautious approach.

'A potentially explosive document.' The President looked grim.

'Another conspiracy theory,' Arthur Gerlach said with a show of bravado. 'Great fiction, but what backs it up?'

Jim Northcutt's grey eyes turned almost black. 'Facts!' he snapped. 'NIPCO stations fire-bombed. Our Qantara installations sabotaged. A Cabinet Secretary has made public speeches discrediting my company. Federal agencies have blocked approval of NIPCO's trade agreements and contracts with China. Shall I go on?'

'I'm not personally aware that all these things happened,' the President said. 'Even if they did, they are not in themselves evidence supporting the charges made by the man who swore the affidavit.'

'Obviously, there is no evidence.' Arthur Gerlach shrugged.

'Oh, there's enough to justify inquiries by my committee,' Senator Hurley said. '*If* that proves necessary.' It was an unmistakable ultimatum. Either the Administration took corrective action, or there would be a raucous Senate investigation.

'The FBI could get to the truth fast,' John Bosworth suggested casually as he lit a Montecruz panatella.

'Call in the FBI because a billionaire oilman is paranoid?' Gerlach snorted. 'Senator, the media would slaughter us for catering to private interests in a time of national energy crisis.'

'You didn't worry about media reaction when you got the I.R.S. to start special audits of NIPCO's tax returns,' Bosworth said.

A blunder. Jim Northcutt winced inwardly. The President's angry frown showed that he resented Bosworth injecting this new charge.

'Mr President,' Jim said in an effort to redress the balance. 'My associates and I can corroborate much of what Peterson says. We're ready to speak with FBI agents immediately – even today.'

'Gerlach leaned forward. 'If anyone talks to the FBI, it should be Peterson.' He knew Russell Peterson had absconded with Jersey Crest's money and probably would not dare return to the United States. Gerlach turned to Sam Schlechter. 'You're Mr Northcutt's attorney. I assume Peterson is your client, too.' The innuendo suggesting collusion was obvious.

'No,' Sam shot back. 'Unlike you, Mr Gerlach, I have never met Russell Peterson.'

'Of course I met him.' Gerlach radiated candour. He could not deny what was recorded on the White House visitors' register and his own appointments calendar. 'He had excellent recommendations.'

'From Mr Powell Pierce?' Schlechter asked quietly.

'He was employed by a public relations firm Mr Pierce had retained. They were planning a programme that would explain the reasons behind the fuel shortage to the public.'

The President experienced a sinking sensation. There were too many coincidences. Gerlach's responses and explanations were too quick and glib. There had to be some substance to the charges.

Richard Hurley spoke. 'Naturally, if my committee investigates, Peterson and everyone mentioned in his affidavit will be subpoenaed. I'm sure you won't mind appearing, Mr Gerlach.'

'Of course not!' Gerlach snapped.

There was silence. The President closed his eyes for a moment. He realized that Hurley and Bosworth were adamant. Senate hearings would smear his Administration. A major scandal so early in his term could be ruinous.

John Bosworth studied the famous Oval Office carpet with the presidential seal woven into it. 'I've known Jim Northcutt a long time,' he said, as though musing aloud. 'Last thing he wants to do is embarrass you or your Administration, Mr President.'

He looked up, waved his panatella in a conciliatory gesture.

'Must be a compromise solution,' he said. 'There usually is.'

Northcutt glanced at Schlechter and Radford. Bosworth was signalling to the President that a deal could be made.

Richard Hurley followed Bosworth's lead. 'Everybody in Washington knows how misunderstandings can cause bureaucratic foul-ups,' he smiled. 'If the snarls that are creating difficulties for Mr Northcutt and his company can be untangled – well, I really wouldn't see much purpose in making any investigation.'

'Wait a moment, Senator,' Arthur Gerlach said. He recognized the danger to himself in the trade-off proposal. 'You expect —'

'Never mind, Art,' the President stopped him and nodded slowly to Hurley. 'I understand you, Senator. You have my assurance that federal agencies will be ordered to expedite appropriate action.'

Northcutt looked at Sam Schlechter and Mark Radford. Their faces were impassive, but their eyes gleamed.

Senator Richard Hurley produced a pocket diary and ballpoint. He opened the little book, made a note. 'One less item for Wednesday.' He grinned amiably. 'That was the day I had set for bringing the Peterson affidavit to the committee's attention.'

'Yes,' the President said. 'You can cross the item off, Senator.'

When the others departed, Arthur Gerlach remained behind with the President in the Oval Office. The President sat silently, staring at Gerlach with a look that eloquently expressed stunned disillusionment and contempt. Finally he spoke.

'I suggest you get in touch with Rowan Engelhardt,' he said. 'I want his resignation on my desk today. Along with yours.'

* * *

James Northcutt restrained his optimism.

'The world looks brighter and I feel better, but I'm not ready to celebrate,' he said on the flight back to New York. 'The President could have a change of heart.'

'I'm inclined to doubt that,' Sam countered. 'Hurley and Bosworth earned their money. They made their position clear, and the President was impressed, to say the least.'

'He damned near had a cardiac arrest,' Mark said.

'Never count chickens – or politicians' promises,' Northcutt muttered. 'Not even when the politician is a President. Just remember he has an Arthur Gerlach for a right-hand man and that Powell Pierce is hiding in the bushes. Now let's all have a drink – and start to sweat over what will happen next week.'

Sam Schlechter had arranged to have his own car and chauffeur waiting at Newark Airport and said he would drop Mark at the Drake. Jim's limousine took him to his Sutton Place house.

'Miss Northcutt would like you to call her immediately, sir,' the butler told Jim.

'I will. Oh, where is Miss Barnes?'

'She went out early. Didn't say when she'd be back.'

Déjà vu, Northcutt thought. He remembered how he had arrived at Bonheur from Peking to find Barbara Wallace absent, away in Paris. Suddenly, he decided that Arlene Barnes was eminently expendable. Schlechter could draw up the necessary documents Monday, he mused, and I'll send Arlene on her way – even if that does set some kind of record for short-lived relations. At least Arlene Barnes would not be another Barbara, he consoled himself. She knew nothing, and all her bills had been paid from his personal funds.

Northcutt went into the library and called his daughter.

'I'm coming right over,' Kathy said. 'With surprises.'

Kathy arrived twenty minutes later. With Verna Fletcher. Jim was open-mouthed.

'You look idiotic, Jim,' Verna said and embraced him.

'What are you doing in New York?' he stammered.

'That's part of a long story Kathy and I have to tell you.'

They went into the drawing room, and Kathy related the confrontation she and Verna had had with Barbara Wallace and Dwight Farquhar. Northcutt roared with laughter.

'My daughter, the con artist,' he spluttered.

'Thank Verna,' Kathy said. 'I only followed her script and played my part the way she coached me. It worked.'

'Sam Schlechter's professional pride will be crushed,' Jim chuckled.

'He's in the wrong profession to handle people like Barbara and Farquhar,' Verna laughed. 'What's the old saying? Set a thief to catch a thief?'

'Huh?' Northcutt's eyebrow rose. 'I'm confused.'

'To catch a hustler and her pimp, set an old madam.'

Kathy broke into their exchange. 'Was Mark with you, Dad?'

'He was,' Jim replied.

'Where is he now?'

'At his hotel, I think.'

Kathy dialled the Drake.

'Stay where you are,' she said when she had Mark Radford on the line. 'I'll be there in half an hour.' She hung up. 'I'm going to raid your kitchen and wine cellar,' she told her father. 'To fill a picnic basket. If I can find one.'

Twenty minutes later, Kathy paused at the drawing room doorway. The butler was with her, carrying a heavy basket.

'I'm borrowing your car and chauffeur, Dad.' She smiled at Verna. 'The two of you can talk your heads off – and you will.' She waved a hand and hurried from the house.

'So you and Kathy finally met,' Northcutt said when she had gone. 'What do you think of her, Verna?'

'Like father, like daughter – stubborn and smart. And I envy you, friend. So ring for somebody to bring out the Jack Daniel's.'

'I'll get it myself,' Jim grinned.

Mark Radford fumed in his hotel suite. He had been overjoyed to hear Kathy's voice. But she'd said nothing except to rap out what he heard as a curt order. He wasn't to leave – because she was on her way over. She was being Katherine the Great again, he reflected angrily. He was dressed in slacks and sports shirt and had mixed himself a large Scotch and water. He watched the clock. Kathy had said half an hour. Forty minutes passed. Mark made himself another drink. He was halfway through it when he heard the knock on his door. He stalked to the entrance foyer, flung the door open – and gaped.

Kathy was wearing a cerulean-blue silk rain cape zipped up

to her throat. There was a bellboy with her. He carried a huge basket. She flashed Mark a smile and went into the sitting room.

'Put the basket right there,' Kathy said, pointing to the middle of the carpeted sitting room floor. The bellboy did as he was instructed. 'Would you tip him, please, Mark?'

Radford pulled bills from his pocket, thrust one at the bell-hop.

'What's in that?' Mark asked, nodding towards the basket and feeling foolish as he did.

Kathy spread the fingers of her left hand and began tallying with her right forefinger. 'Umm. Pâté, caviar, prosciutto, roast chicken, asparagus tips, French bread, fruit, three kinds of cheese, two bottles of chilled champagne, plus odds and ends. We're going on a picnic.'

'A picnic?' His voice was incredulous.

'Yes. And, we're going to have it right here.'

'In the suite?'

'It's pouring rain outside.'

Mark stared at her, then at the windows. The afternoon sky was clear, the sun bright.

'Well, we can pretend it's pouring rain, can't we?' Kathy shrugged, went to the window and dropped the venetian blinds.

She returned to the basket, knelt down, the rain cape forming a bright blue circle around her. She took a linen tablecloth from the basket and spread it.

'Oh, I forgot,' she said. 'There's Sacher torte, too.'

Mark was completely baffled. 'I can't stand Sacher torte,' he said.

'Neither can I.' Kathy was taking out napkins, plates and silver. 'We'll give it to the people down the hall.'

'What people down the hall?'

'If we knock on enough doors and ask, we're bound to find somebody who likes Sacher torte.'

'Kathy, I think you've flipped.'

She ignored him. 'Oh, damn. I forgot glasses. Do you have any?'

'Only the usual tumblers.'

'They'll have to do,' she sighed. 'Get three.'

'Three?' Then he saw she had set three places. 'Who else is going to be here?'

'Oh, I thought you might like to invite whoever you were

373

out with the Friday night before you left for Qantara.'

Well, I'll be damned, Mark thought. The dawn. She was sore because she thought I was going out with some other girl on the night I met Bob di Lorenzi. I can't tell her about Farrier – but I might as well get some mileage out of her suspicions.

'Sure, the cute little brunette,' he said. 'I'll call her. She may be available – she usually is —'

Something large and black flew through the air and splattered against the wall inches from his head. He saw that it was the Sacher torte – and began to laugh.

'You bastard!' Kathy was reaching for something else to throw.

'Hey, not the pâté!' Mark protested. 'I like pâté!'

She stopped and glared at him.

'You ought to take off that stupid cape,' he said.

'Then help me with it!' Kathy stood up, still glaring.

Mark was grinning broadly. He walked across the room and stood behind her. She waited until he was in back of her and pulled down the zip. Mark reached his hands forward. His fingers closed on silk and he started to ease the cape off her shoulders.

'Jesus Christ!' he exclaimed. Kathy was wearing nothing beneath the rain cape.

She whirled, the cape dropping to the floor.

'You God-damned jerk!' she said, and she was in his arms, her naked body pressing against his. One of her hands went to the back of his head, pulled it down until her moist and open lips could reach his mouth and cover it hungrily. Her other hand fumbled at the buttons of his shirt.

'You have too many clothes on,' she murmured against his lips. 'Take them off – please, Mark.'

His hands were caressing her shoulders and back. He was reluctant to let her go to undress himself, but he did.

'Here,' she said, lowering herself to the carpet and pulling him down beside her. 'Ever go on a picnic and make love?'

'Never on a picnic like this.' He reached for a sofa cushion, pulled it free and gently eased it under Kathy's head.

'Have you?' Mark asked.

'Have I what?'

'Made love on a picnic?'

'Not one like this.' Kathy's arms went around him. He was lying on the floor at an angle, his chest against her firm breasts,

374

and they kissed.

Kathy moaned and moved her body, urging him to cover it with his own. Mark shifted position. There was a clatter as one of his feet struck plates and silver set on the tablecloth.

'I hope that's not the pâté.' Kathy laughed softly.

'Felt more like the roast chicken.' He kissed her breasts.

'How can you tell?'

'I have very sensitive toes.' He strained against her.

'So have I,' Kathy murmured. She was suddenly frenzied, demanding.

'Oh, my God, Mark – make love to me!'

There was a tempestuous fury to their movements as their bodies joined.

Kathy clung to Mark.

'I've told you before,' she whispered. 'It was never like this with anyone else. Never. God, I can't count how many times —'

'Don't try.' He kissed her cheek.

She turned him on his back, propped herself on one elbow and leaned over him, her long red hair brushing against his chest, her grey eyes soft and lustrous.

'Mark.' Her smile was tender, adoring.

'Uh-huh.'

'Our picnic. I'd love to feed you. Are you hungry?'

'Not for food.'

'Thirsty? We have champagne. It won't stay cold long.'

'How long before it gets warm?' Mark grinned.

'Another hour or two.'

'We'll drink it then.' He drew her down to him.

12

28 July

The first four days of the week had produced one punishing setback after another for Powell Pierce.

On Monday morning, a terse White House announcement revealed the resignations of Arthur Gerlach and Rowan Engelhardt. News commentators talked of 'the Sunday Slaughter' and 'the new Administration's first purge'. They speculated wildly over the reasons why the two key men had resigned. Fortunately for Pierce, none of them was able to learn the truth.

Tuesday, the Northcutt International Petroleum Company issued a press release listing the names of its own and chartered tankers en route from the Persian Gulf with crude for its refineries. Although weeks would pass before the tankers arrived, oilmen realized NIPCO would now be able to meet all its refinery requirements before above-ground crude reserves were exhausted. Wall Street responded predictably. NIPCO stock spurted up six points in the day's trading session.

On Wednesday morning, the Secretary of State lauded Northcutt International Petroleum's 'foresight and enterprise' in having conducted negotiations 'of unprecedented significance' with the Chinese Government. He declared that the agreements between NIPCO and Peking would receive US Government approval within the week. NIPCO stock soared eleven points.

The next evening, the head of the Chinese diplomatic mission had been James Northcutt's dinner guest.

It was against this background that Guy Bannister arrived at the Jersey Crest Tower on Friday morning. Powell Pierce's secretary had instructed him to be there at 9 A.M., and Bannister was prompt. He tried to quiet the fears that gnawed at him as he went into the Jersey Crest Board Chairman's office. Pierce's carefully laid plans were in a shambles, and it was by no means unlikely he would seek to make Bannister the scapegoat.

To Bannister's initial astonishment, Pierce was friendly and ingratiating. Then the former CIA agent smiled to himself. Pierce wants – no, he needs something, and badly, Bannister mused.

'Are you aware what was behind the resignations of Gerlach and Engelhardt?' Pierce asked.

'Word got to me, yes.'

'Gerlach has been in touch with me,' Pierce continued in a hard tone. 'He has copies of an affidavit Russell Peterson signed.'

Bannister nodded knowingly. It was inevitable that Arthur Gerlach, enraged at his dismissal, would seek to extort money from Pierce.

'He's hinting that he'll leak the affidavit unless he's paid off. Is that it, Mr Pierce?'

'Yes.'

'You'd like me to – ah – persuade him to keep quiet without being paid?'

'That's what I had in mind.'

Bannister examined his fingernails. Pierce held him and his firm, Federpol, liable for the million dollars Peterson had taken.

'Mr Pierce, the million —'

'Of course,' Pierce said. 'Dissuade Arthur Gerlach, and I will consider the account settled.'

If Powell Pierce is willing to write off a million dollars, the sum Gerlach is demanding must be astronomical, Bannister thought.

'I can take care of Gerlach,' he declared confidently. There were dossiers of information that could put Arthur Gerlach behind bars for years. And there were other methods of insuring his silence – or of silencing him.

Bannister stood up. 'What about Northcutt, Mr Pierce? Is there anything more —'

'No!' Powell Pierce grated, tasting his own bile. 'There is nothing further to be done.'

At 9.20 A.M., James Northcutt lolled back in his Eames chair. His long legs were stretched out and his feet were planted on top of the desk in his library. Sam Schlechter sat opposite, in the wing chair that Northcutt deemed to be the only one in the room besides his own that was comfortable, and drank coffee.

'I didn't expect you to call me over here today, Jim,' Sam said. 'I thought you'd be in your office bright and early.'

Northcutt cocked his right eyebrow and shifted his feet a little.

'The head of the Chinese diplomatic mission gave me a T'ang Dynasty vase last night, Sam. It's over a thousand years old. Which is about five hunded years younger than I feel.'

'Crap. I can't remember how long it's been since you looked as good as you do right now.'

'Looks deceive, counsellor.'

'Not me. The last four days have done more for you than those Niehans shots you take. So stop pleading senility.' A sudden thought struck Schlechter, and he groaned audibly. 'Is this a build-up to let me know you've already found a replacement for Arlene? My God, we only got rid of her day before yesterday!'

'Nope, not yet.' Jim laughed. 'I don't have to worry, though. Before she left for California on Tuesday, Verna promised that if worse came to worst, she'd scout around and find me one.'

Sam tipped his head to one side. 'Didn't Kathy go with Verna?' he asked.

'They took my plane. Kath wanted to pay her mother a visit.' He scratched his jaw. 'That's peculiar,' he mused aloud. 'I was married to Pam for years. But when I think of her, it's not by name – but as Kathy's mother.'

'Jim, I have nine thousand and two headaches waiting for me at my office. Do me a favour and stop farting around. Talk sense!'

Northcutt grinned, swept his feet off the desk and leaned forward.

'I figure I can finally celebrate,' he said. 'The last battle has been fought and won. NIPCO isn't only out of the pot, it never smelled sweeter. All the world's biggest independent oil company can do from now on is grow bigger.'

He yanked open a desk drawer, took out a Bull Durham sack and started to roll a cigarette.

Schlechter's exasperation mounted.

'Jim.'

'Yeah?' The tip of Northcutt's tongue slid slowly along the edge of the cigarette paper.

'Will you for God's sake get to the point?'

The oilman lit his cigarette and exhaled smoke through his nostrils.

'The Chinese delegation left early last night,' he said. 'That gave me plenty of time to admire my T'ang vase and hold one of my private stockholders' meetings.' He chuckled and went off on another tangent. 'Incidentally, buying NIPCO when it was low, I picked up another four per cent interest, bringing me up around sixty-five per cent. And I've already doubled what I paid. I hope you did yourself some good, Sam.'

'I bought,' Schlechter nodded.

'Had faith in the company, huh?'

Not the company, you old bastard, Sam thought, but said nothing.

Jim flicked cigarette ash into a ceramic tray on his desk.

'Anyway, back to last night. I had time to think, make decisions and wake up a lot of people and give them orders. Like to hear my Number One personal decision?'

'Not unless you get around to telling me in the next eight or nine hours.'

'I'm going back to Bonheur, Sam. I'm going to lie in the sun, swim – and who knows? – raise rabbits or roses.'

Jim stuck the cigarette between his lips and let it dangle there.

'I figure I've done my part for NIPCO – as I said, the last battle.'

'You're retiring?' Schlechter asked in disbelief.

'God damn it, I didn't say that. I'll be keeping my eyes on what's being done. But I did quit as president of NIPCO. A little before midnight last night.'

'Who are you hiring in your place?'

'I'll tell you, Sam. But I want Kathy to find out by herself.'

'When is Kathy due back?' Schlechter asked.

'At eleven. I sent my car out to meet her.'

Northcutt remained in his library when Schlechter left. He grew pensive and took from his pocket the charm Verna had given him in Oklahoma. He stared at the tiny gold oil derrick with the black onyx plume set above the crown block.

There it was, Jim mused, the symbol that gave the answers to the questions of what he had always wanted. A long-ago conversation with Abe Schlechter came back to him. He had remarked that oil represented wealth, power – and sex, that somehow, they all seemed to go together.

'And you want them all, don't you, Jim?' Abe had said.

I did. And I still do, Northcutt thought. After more than half a century, my wants – and needs – haven't changed. He grinned inwardly. At least I'm consistent.

He toyed with the derrick charm. What had Abe Schlechter called the three of them? *Oysvorfs*. Verna Fletcher, parlour-house madam, Abraham Schlechter, Town Jew, Jim Northcutt, $14-a-day driller. The three outcasts.

Memories. Remote names and events.

Judge Henry Kendall. Will Dubbs. Luke Rayburn. The roustabout who had got drunk and fallen down the hold of the Peavey Lease – oh, yes. Peewee Carter. Everett Cade – that bastard. Ed Doheny, who had helped Jim out in California.

The memory of countless battles flashed through Jim Northcutt's mind. I've managed to win them, he reflected – even this last one, and it will be the last. NIPCO was safe, secure – and younger men could guide it to bigger successes in the years ahead.

Not bad for an *oysvorf*, Jim smiled openly – and he fingered the derrick charm once more before putting it back into his pocket.

Kathy did not think it unusual that her father's limousine was waiting when the NIPCO Boeing landed at Newark. But she was surprised when the chauffeur said she was to be taken directly to the NIPCO Building.

'Those were Mr Northcutt's orders,' the chauffer said. 'He'd like you to go straight up to his office, Miss Northcutt.'

'Is anything wrong?' Kathy asked, frowning.

'Not a thing. Guess it's just one of Mr Northcutt's whims.'

Kathy used the express elevator and got off on the top floor of the NIPCO Building. She went directly to the presidential office suite. Aides and secretaries recognized her and merely murmured polite greetings as she hurried through the anterooms and on to the private office where she expected to find her father.

She opened the door without knocking. 'Dad —'

Kathy stopped, her eyes snapping wide.

Mark Radford was behind her father's desk, speaking to someone on the telephone. He looked up at her and smiled. Kathy blinked and lowered herself into a chair. Mark cut his conversation short, and stood up.

'Where's Dad?' Kathy asked.

'At his house. He's trying to get things organized for his move —'

'Move? Where?'

'He's going back to France.'

Kathy leaped from her chair.

'Hey!' Mark said, coming from around the desk. 'Don't rush off. He won't be leaving for a few days.'

She stared, her mind seeking to interpret registered impressions.

'What are you doing in here – and behind that desk?'

Radford's grin was almost boyish.

'James Northcutt got tired of being the president of his own company,' he said. 'He likes it better at Bonheur, where he can relax and run the operation by remote control, as he put it.'

'But you – at his desk?'

'The facts of corporate life being what they are, it's not really *his* desk, Kathy. It's the one the company president uses.'

'Don't tell me Dad made you —'

'Uh-huh,' Mark nodded.

Kathy looked stunned.

'What, no congratulations?' Mark said, smiling.

Kathy said nothing in reply. She took a step and was in his arms, kissing him deeply, lovingly.

'I – I'll have to do some assimilating and adjust to all this,' she said finally, moving out of his embrace. She was suddenly aware that her eyes were misting and not quite sure why.

'It's almost noon,' Radford said. 'Let's do the quiet-place-for-lunch bit. We'll have a drink, talk, and you can start adjusting.'

Kathy nodded. He took her hand, and they started towards the door.

'Mr Radford.' It was a secretary's voice coming over the intercom. 'Mr Schlechter is calling. He says it's important.'

Mark halted, releasing Kathy's hand. 'I'll talk to Sam before we go,' he said – over his shoulder, for he was already walking towards the desk. He leaned across it. 'Put Mr Schlechter through,' he said into the intercom and picked up the telephone.

'Hello, Sam,' he said.

'Are you sitting down, Mark?' he heard Schlechter ask.

'No.'

'Then plant your feet so you'll be braced.'

Mark cupped a hand over the mouthpiece.

'Shouldn't be more than a couple of minutes,' he said reassuringly to Kathy. He removed his hand from the transmitter. 'Go on, Sam.'

'Okay.' Schlechter sighed. 'You're aware of the oil-shale land NIPCO has under lease in Colorado.'

'Sure,' Mark said. 'J.L. is eager to start developing it. I've been gathering preliminary estimates on a pilot project for him all week. Looks pretty encouraging.'

'Not as of this morning. We're about to be buried in lawsuits.'

'Who's suing and why?' Mark demanded.

'On the record, the plaintiffs are twenty-seven upright justice-seeking citizens contesting the legality of NIPCO's leases on

381

the shale lands. Actually, they're dummies for two Majors. They want to keep us from developing the leases – and, need I tell you? – they have high hopes of taking the leases over themselves.'

'Do they have a case?'

'Hell, no. But we're liable to have a long struggle in the courts.'

Mark Radford's first impulse was to tell Schlechter that he would call Jim Northcutt immediately. But then he remembered. He was now the president of NIPCO. He was in charge. The responsibility was his.

'Do you want to come up here, Sam?' he asked.

'Yes. We should start talking right away. I can be on my way uptown in two minutes. Will you be in your office?'

'I'll be here, Sam.'

Mark Radford replaced the receiver slowly. James Northcutt believed he had fought the last battle, but he hadn't. NIPCO was still an independent – and the oil industry remained what it had always been. The struggle for survival would never end.

'Mark.'

Radford looked up.

'God, honey, I'm sorry,' he said. 'There's a problem. Sam's rushing over. I can't even guess when we'll be through.'

There was an extension telephone on an end table near Kathy. She picked it up.

'Please get me Mr Babbington,' she said to the secretary who came on the line.

'Babbington?' Mark asked. 'Who is he, honey?'

'The best caterer in town.'

'Oh, no!' Mark protested. 'Kathy, not here!'

'Why not? After Sam leaves, we can lock the doors . . .'

She turned away from him and spoke into the telephone.

'Do you have any Sacher torte?' she asked as an opener. 'You don't?' She flicked Mark a glance and a smile. 'Good. Then suppose we start with pâté, caviar and a magnum of Dom Perignon . . .'